Praise for the submarine novels of
MICHAEL DiMERCURIO

Terminal Run

"Compelling and visionary. DiMercurio's characters run as deep as his submarines themselves!"
—Joe Buff, author of *Crush Depth*
and *Thunder in the Deep*

Threat Vector

"Michael DiMercurio plunges you into the world of undersea warfare with stunning technical accuracy, the best and brightest heroes, and a deadly look at the future."
—C. A. Mobley, author of *Code of Conflict*

Piranha Firing Point

"If dueling with torpedoes is your idea of a good time, you'll love it." —*The Sunday Star-Times* (Auckland)

Barracuda Final Bearing

"Terrific. . . . The fighting really goes into high gear."
—*San Francisco Examiner*

"A stunningly effective technopolitical thriller . . . a dandy hell-and-high-water yarn." —*Kirkus Reviews*

"Impressive. . . . Those who thrill to the blip of sonar and the thud of torpedoes will relish this deepwater dive." —*Publishers Weekly*

continued . . .

VERTICAL DIVE

Michael DiMercurio

AN ONYX BOOK

ONYX
Published by New American Library, a division of
Penguin Group (USA) Inc., 375 Hudson Street,
New York, New York 10014, USA
Penguin Group (Canada), 90 Eglinton Avenue East, Suite 700, Toronto,
Ontario M4P 2Y3, Canada (a division of Pearson Penguin Canada Inc.)
Penguin Books Ltd., 80 Strand, London WC2R 0RL, England
Penguin Ireland, 25 St. Stephen's Green, Dublin 2,
Ireland (a division of Penguin Books Ltd.)
Penguin Group (Australia), 250 Camberwell Road, Camberwell, Victoria 3124,
Australia (a division of Pearson Australia Group Pty. Ltd.)
Penguin Books India Pvt. Ltd., 11 Community Centre, Panchsheel Park,
New Delhi - 110 017, India
Penguin Group (NZ), cnr Airborne and Rosedale Roads, Albany,
Auckland 1310, New Zealand (a division of Pearson New Zealand Ltd.)
Penguin Books (South Africa) (Pty.) Ltd., 24 Sturdee Avenue,
Rosebank, Johannesburg 2196, South Africa

Penguin Books Ltd., Registered Offices:
80 Strand, London WC2R 0RL, England

First published by Onyx, an imprint of New American Library,
a division of Penguin Group (USA) Inc.

First Printing, December 2005
10 9 8 7 6 5 4 3 2 1

To Loss

I dream of the one
Who healed not with time
But with love
And caught me when I fell.

Touch me any time you want
Any way you want
She said,
My body and my soul belong to you.

Memory flows around our moment
Rapids swirling over a rock
My life altered in a long ecstatic held breath
I let go and I was alone again.

Was it a dream? I wonder
Was I in a catastrophic crash
That took me to a heavenly hour
And only now I realize I'm gone?

Give me more time, I pleaded.
Let me fill her hours,
Her days, her heart
Give me more of her.

The answer came
In a life-wrenching crisis
The reply was *no*
Spoken in a tender regretful whisper.

I remain lost.
The silence mocks me.
My heart once beat only for her
Were that it would now beat for me.

My one, my dearest, my hope—
I watched you while you slept
Without you now, my soul sleeps
The dreams always of you.

"*Jihad*, in the form adopted by the GIA, accords with the teaching of true Islam. . . . There will be no salvation . . . unless we bear the slogan: 'Hang the last infidel from the intestines of the last Christian priest.' The only weapon we Muslims have to face the modern machinery of the enemy is *jihad*, the continuation of *jihad* and 'love of death.' The rulers [of Algeria] are apostates, and killing them is the only solution."
—Sheikh Abu Qatadeh ("the Palestinian") Al Falastini, unofficial propaganda minister and "theorist" for the Algerian terrorist organization known as the GIA (Groupe Islamique Armé or Armed Islamic Group)

"Seeing naval forces on the horizon is intimidating. *So is not seeing them* . . . Today, our nation's submarines complete more stealthy missions than ever before. They're putting cruise missiles on target without warning, gathering and sharing intel with the battle group and joint forces, deploying special warfare personnel and launching and recovering UUVs and UAVs. At Electric Boat we're not only changing the way the world thinks about submarines, *we're changing the way it looks at an empty ocean* . . . General Dynamics / Electric Boat / Stealth Starts Here."
—General Dynamics ad, July 2004 *Submarine Review*

"You will serve in the most advanced technical submersible platforms known to man. Craft that serve as the farthest extended invisible bulwark of American defense. You will go from here to earn your dolphins, representing your qualification and acceptance as a United States Submariner. I have previously mentioned how I envy you. I have had my opportunity to dance the saltwater fandango with the Goddess of the Main Induction. I have experienced the camaraderie that you will soon experience. I have heard the creak and groan of steel at depth, but nowhere near the depths of the modern marvels you will ride."

—Bob "Dex" Armstrong

"O God, smash the teeth in their mouths;
break the jaw-teeth of these lions, Lord!
Make them vanish like water flowing away;
trodden down, let them wither like grass.
Let them dissolve like a snail that oozes away,
like an untimely birth that never sees the sun.
Suddenly, like brambles or thistles,
have the whirlwind snatch them away.
Then the just shall rejoice to see the vengeance
and bathe their feet in the blood of the wicked.
Then it will be said:
'Truly there is a reward for the just;
there is a God who is judge on earth!' "

—Psalm 58, Part III

Vertical Dive—U.S. Submarine Force term describing an infrequently used arctic operations maneuver that allows a submarine to submerge from a stationary position on the surface. The tactic may be used to resubmerge after surfacing through ice. It may also be used during certain diver operations or to depart an anchorage in stealth.

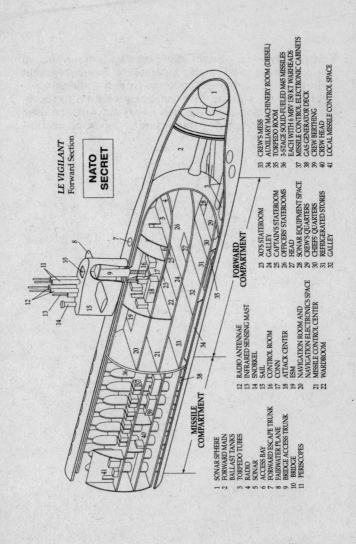

LE VIGILANT
Forward Section

NATO
SECRET

MISSILE COMPARTMENT

FORWARD COMPARTMENT

1 SONAR SPHERE
2 FORWARD MAIN BALLAST TANKS
3 TORPEDO TUBES
4 RADIO
5 SONAR
6 ACCESS BAY
7 FORWARD ESCAPE TRUNK
8 FAIRWATER PLANE
9 BRIDGE ACCESS TRUNK
10 BRIDGE
11 PERISCOPES

12 RADIO ANTENNAE
13 INFRARED SENSING MAST
14 SNORKEL
15 SAIL
16 CONTROL ROOM
17 CONN
18 ATTACK CENTER
19 ESM
20 NAVIGATION ROOM AND NAVIGATION ELECTRONICS SPACE
21 MISSILE CONTROL CENTER
22 WARDROOM

23 XO'S STATEROOM
24 GALLEY
25 CAPTAIN'S STATEROOM
26 OFFICERS' STATEROOMS
27 HEAD
28 SONAR EQUIPMENT SPACE
29 CREW'S QUARTERS
30 CHIEFS' QUARTERS
31 REFRIGERATED STORES
32 GALLEY

33 CREW'S MESS
34 AUXILIARY MACHINERY ROOM (DIESEL)
35 TORPEDO ROOM
36 3-STAGE SOLID-FUELED M45 MISSILES EACH WITH 6 MRV 150 KT WARHEADS
37 MISSILE CONTROL ELECTRONIC CABINETS
38 GAS GENERATOR DECK
39 CREW BERTHING
40 CREW HEAD
41 LOCAL MISSILE CONTROL SPACE

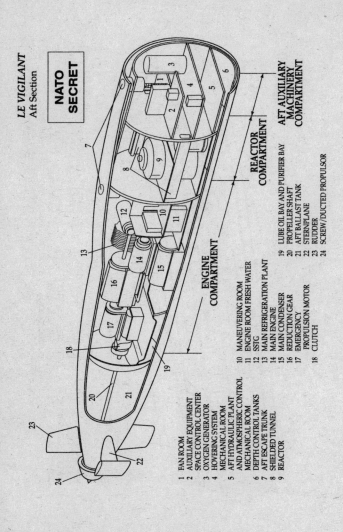

LE VIGILANT
Aft Section

NATO
SECRET

AFT AUXILIARY
MACHINERY
COMPARTMENT

REACTOR
COMPARTMENT

ENGINE
COMPARTMENT

1 FAN ROOM
2 AUXILIARY EQUIPMENT
   SPACE CONTROL CENTER
3 OXYGEN GENERATOR
4 HOVERING SYSTEM
   MECHANICAL ROOM
5 AFT HYDRAULIC PLANT
   AND ATMOSPHERIC CONTROL
   MECHANICAL ROOM
6 DEPTH CONTROL TANKS
7 AFT ESCAPE TRUNK
8 SHIELDED TUNNEL
9 REACTOR

10 MANEUVERING ROOM
11 ENGINE ROOM FRESH WATER
12 SSTG
13 MAIN REFRIGERATION PLANT
14 MAIN ENGINE
15 MAIN CONDENSER
16 REDUCTION GEAR
17 EMERGENCY
    PROPULSION MOTOR
18 CLUTCH

19 LUBE OIL BAY AND PURIFIER BAY
20 PROPELLER SHAFT
21 AFT BALLAST TANK
22 STERNPLANE
23 RUDDER
24 SCREW/DUCTED PROPULSOR

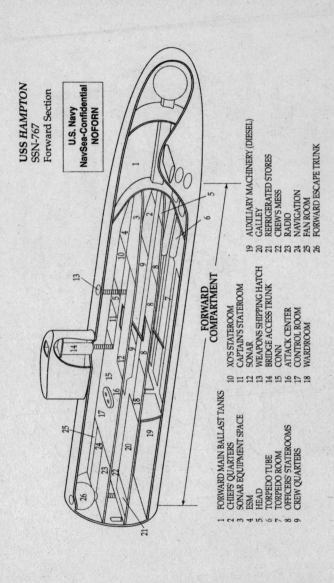

USS HAMPTON
SSN-767
Forward Section

U.S. Navy
NavSea-Confidential
NOFORN

FORWARD COMPARTMENT

1 FORWARD MAIN BALLAST TANKS
2 CHIEFS' QUARTERS
3 SONAR EQUIPMENT SPACE
4 ESM
5 HEAD
6 TORPEDO TUBE
7 TORPEDO ROOM
8 OFFICERS' STATEROOMS
9 CREW QUARTERS
10 XO'S STATEROOM
11 CAPTAIN'S STATEROOM
12 SONAR
13 WEAPONS SHIPPING HATCH
14 BRIDGE ACCESS TRUNK
15 CONN
16 ATTACK CENTER
17 CONTROL ROOM
18 WARDROOM
19 AUXILIARY MACHINERY (DIESEL)
20 GALLEY
21 REFRIGERATED STORES
22 CREW'S MESS
23 RADIO
24 NAVIGATION
25 FAN ROOM
26 FORWARD ESCAPE TRUNK

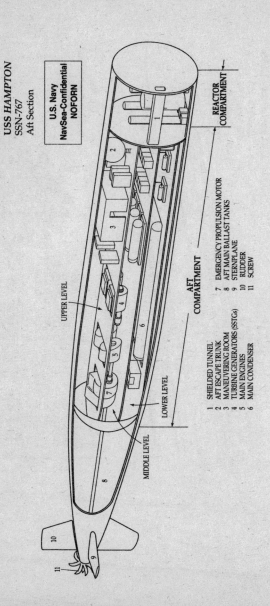

USS HAMPTON
SSN-767
Aft Section

U.S. Navy
NavSea-Confidential
NOFORN

UPPER LEVEL

LOWER LEVEL

MIDDLE LEVEL

REACTOR
COMPARTMENT

AFT
COMPARTMENT

1   SHIELDED TUNNEL
2   AFT ESCAPE TRUNK
3   MANEUVERING ROOM
4   TURBINE GENERATORS (SSTGs)
5   MAIN ENGINES
6   MAIN CONDENSER
7   EMERGENCY PROPULSION MOTOR
8   AFT MAIN BALLAST TANKS
9   STERNPLANE
10 RUDDER
11 SCREW

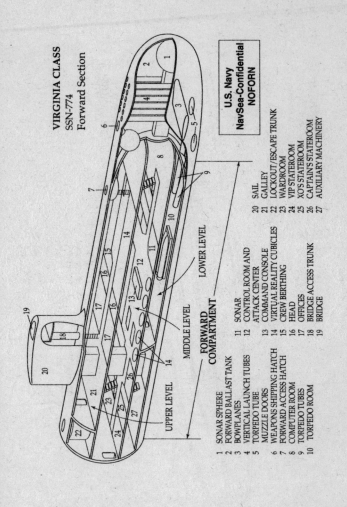

VIRGINIA CLASS
SSN-774
Forward Section

U.S. Navy
NavSea-Confidential
NOFORN

1 SONAR SPHERE
2 FORWARD BALLAST TANK
3 BOWPLANES
4 VERTICAL LAUNCH TUBES
5 TORPEDO TUBE
   MUZZLE DOORS
6 WEAPONS SHIPPING HATCH
7 FORWARD ACCESS HATCH
8 COMPUTER ROOM
9 TORPEDO TUBES
10 TORPEDO ROOM

11 SONAR
12 CONTROL ROOM AND
   ATTACK CENTER
13 COMMAND CONSOLE
14 VIRTUAL REALITY CUBICLES
15 CREW BERTHING
16 HEAD
17 OFFICES
18 BRIDGE ACCESS TRUNK
19 BRIDGE

20 SAIL
21 GALLEY
22 LOCKOUT/ESCAPE TRUNK
23 WARDROOM
24 VIP STATEROOM
25 XOS STATEROOM
26 CAPTAINS STATEROOM
27 AUXILIARY MACHINERY

UPPER LEVEL

MIDDLE LEVEL

LOWER LEVEL

**FORWARD
COMPARTMENT**

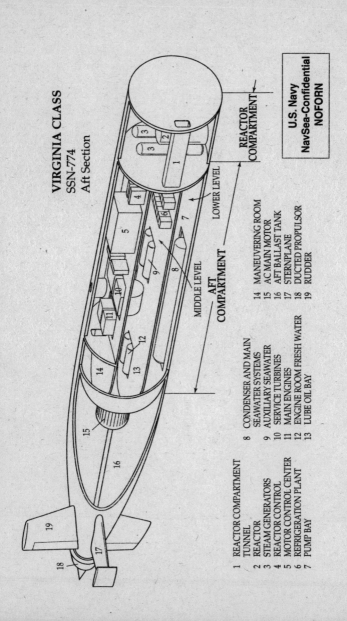

VIRGINIA CLASS
SSN-774
Aft Section

REACTOR COMPARTMENT

AFT COMPARTMENT

LOWER LEVEL

MIDDLE LEVEL

U.S. Navy
NavSea-Confidential
NOFORN

1 REACTOR COMPARTMENT TUNNEL
2 REACTOR
3 STEAM GENERATORS
4 REACTOR CONTROL
5 MOTOR CONTROL CENTER
6 REFRIGERATION PLANT
7 PUMP BAY

8 CONDENSER AND MAIN SEAWATER SYSTEMS
9 AUXILIARY SEAWATER
10 SERVICE TURBINES
11 MAIN ENGINES
12 ENGINE ROOM FRESH WATER
13 LUBE OIL BAY

14 MANEUVERING ROOM
15 AC MAIN MOTOR
16 AFT BALLAST TANK
17 STERNPLANE
18 DUCTED PROPULSOR
19 RUDDER

BOOK 1:

▼

Storm Surge

1

He turned away from the dark window to look into her eyes, her face dim in the light of the three candles on the bedroom's marble fireplace mantel. Her hair was long and as gleaming black as a raven's wing, but it had been weeks since she had let it fall naturally to her shoulders. She had twisted it into a loose bun, her hair swooping low over her ears and rising in the back. She'd lost her figure, at least in the middle, but her legs were as long and slim and toned as they had been the winter before. Her chest had become bigger, but she had always been generously endowed. She had a thousand complaints about her body but, in his mind, there was nothing about her he would change.

She sank deeper under the covers and shivered as a sudden gust pelted the window with rain and the century-old house creaked in protest. "We have to check the weather report," she said softly. The oak tree outside the house shook, its branches scraping the eaves. The candles dimmed from a cold draft as lightning lit the room for an instant, the rumble of thunder following. He tried to look out the window, but though it was early in the afternoon of an August Sunday, it was dark as midnight. Lightning struck again, the strobe light of it flashing in the room. He opened his mouth to speak but the sudden crash of thunder interrupted. He waited for the relative quiet of the wind before answering.

"Power's out," he said finally, his smoothly rich tenor voice deliberately soothing. "We'll check the weather report when it comes back on." He sat at the end of the bed, one hand on her leg. He wore only boxer shorts and an old gray T-shirt that spelled in blue block letters the word NAVY. The wind-burned skin at the corners of his eyes crinkled as he smiled, the crow's-feet arriving earlier than they did for most men. The gray in his hair had also come early, but at age forty, little else gave away his age. His body was still lean and muscled, though nothing like it had been when he'd had a shot at being the boxing champion of his class. His face seemed carved by a haphazard sculptor, his individual features far from perfect; among them a severely broken nose from a fifteen-round fight he'd lost by decision, a slightly cauliflowered ear, a deep scar on his protruding chin, cold and harsh gray-blue eyes, the prematurely silvery gray hair, and white but uneven teeth, but when regarded together, they gave him a uniquely rugged, tough look. His appearance was so distinctive that not long ago a local newscaster who'd seen him in a grocery store had been inspired to feature him in a long news segment about his job, which had made him temporarily famous and had been responsible for some of his midcareer success.

"There's more to think about now than just us," she said quietly. "You should turn on your laptop. Maybe you can get a wireless connection and see what's going on with this storm."

Her voice had always had a strange effect on him. There was a mysterious music to it that went beyond the mere melody of the sound of her vocal cords. There was an indefinable, barely noticeable accent that he hadn't heard before he fell in love with her, but it was there in every sentence. She had grown up outside Philadelphia in Haddonfield, a colonial town on the New Jersey side of the Delaware River, but the lilt and cadence of her voice didn't sound mid-Atlantic. Sometimes when she spoke he would listen to her as if straining to try to identify a nearly forgotten but hauntingly familiar song playing on the radio, and soon he would lose the meaning of her words in the richness of the sounds of her voice. Over the past eight months he had studied her, more intensely than any woman he had ever known. Despite his attention, he still could not predict what she would say or do or feel next. It was one of a thousand of the quirks that he loved about her.

"Laptop's in the truck," he said. "I can stay here with you or get soaked going out to get it."

They had met under the strangest of circumstances, and many would condemn him for choosing her. His career had survived because the people closest to him found no fault in his choice, but it didn't alter the fact that he had become involved with a woman who worked for him. He and she had suffered through a terrifying maritime disaster that had silenced the critics. Their beginnings had brought them to the hour of their deaths, and if not for the man who had plucked them from the hellish flames, they would now be buried with the wreckage at the rocky bottom of a two-mile-deep sea. In the days that followed, there were a dozen times he wondered if he had actually died or if the reality he was living now had just been imagined in that last half second of life.

In this new life, nothing was like it had been before. It was fortunate for him that he had her, because without her the guilt of losing over a hundred souls in his charge would have ruined him. Before the disaster, he had been more a man of action than reflection. The world had been simple, painted in black and white. There had been good and there had been evil. He had been on the side of good. Until the day that those good men had sent him on a suicide mission.

After the hydrogen bomb detonated, a hundred and seven of his crew lay quiet at the bottom of the cold Barents Sea. When he regained consciousness, there was no longer the pure good against unholy evil. Black and white had yielded to infinite shades of gray. There was a new quality to him, one of thoughtfulness, a quality he had never held in high esteem before. In this new reality, there was plentiful guilt about the horror of that

day, but not the despair he would have felt if not for
her. He looked across the bed at her. With her alive
next to him, he felt an incredible, undeserved joy. That
he had lived was a miracle, but the fact that she had
lived was far more. It was a godsend, the granting of a
feverish, desperate deathbed prayer.

They had both dreaded the results of the medical tests
they had undergone in the next month while he waited
for his new assignment. The nuclear explosion had given
them doses of gamma, alpha and neutron radiation significant enough to kill them had they been in poorer
health. But there were more results. There were the
smallest diamonds of tears in her eyes as she told him
he was to be a father. He was stunned. The thought of
having a child together oddly seemed far stranger to him
than their surviving last winter's ordeal.

The coming child had changed him as much as his loss
at sea had, forcing him to examine every aspect of his
personality, to review every event of his life to see if he
were worthy. He concluded that he would never have
considered himself ready to be a father, but life had
made the decision for him. In the month that followed,
he had concentrated on his new job, the actions of performing it as natural as breathing. It was a surprise to
him when he realized that his altered self was better at
his life's work than he had been before.

But he knew the changes in him came from more than
the disaster at sea or his impending fatherhood. *She* had
changed him. There was something about her that
calmed him and gave him peace. She answered a vital
question posed by his life. The moments he spent with
her were the most important of his day. As he had
learned from his father's flawed example, he had always
presumed in his previous life that what he did for a
living defined him, that his work was the sum total of
his identity. Now he realized that what he did had only
an incidental relationship to who he really was. When
he thought of himself now, in those first few seconds of
waking in the morning or falling asleep in her arms at

night, he saw himself as her husband first, a father second and a seaman a distant last.

In the second month of his new assignment, there were more medical test results. She had smiled as she told him that the size of the baby proved that they had conceived the child during their first time together, in the early morning hours of what should have been their last day on earth. Later that night she had watched his eyes for his reaction as she spoke, her voice dead serious. "You know we should have died out there."

"I know," he had said, staring back at her. She'd never spoken of it since, and had practically forbidden him to bring it up.

Her voice trembled just slightly, as if she were confessing a deep secret. "Do you think our baby is the reason we were spared that day?"

In the darkness he smiled at her, pulled her close to him and told her the rational truth, or at least the truth he thought he should believe. "Sweetheart, we lived that day because our target had the heart to risk his own life to rescue us, even though doing that damn near killed him. I don't think it had anything to do with the baby."

She shook her head slowly. "He may be a saint," she said, "but Peter Vornado wasn't the one who decided we'd survive the radiation."

To that he had no answer.

Lightning lit the room suddenly as the house creaked again in a gust. The peal of thunder rattled the windows. She reached for him and pulled him closer to her. In the first months of her pregnancy she had always wanted to be naked with him in their big bed when they were together on weekends, but now she was always too cold. She dressed in heavy pajamas despite the warmth of summer on the Virginia coast, burying herself in the bedclothes.

He had wondered why she wasn't like other pregnant women in the summertime, sweating and complaining. She had an uncommon serenity about carrying a baby. Being pregnant had given her a glow, making her even more beautiful than she had been the first moment he had set eyes on her.

The lamp at the bedside suddenly flickered, then came on steadily. The power had returned.

She quickly found the remote control and the plasma flat-panel television came to life. She switched to the weather station. The forecaster seemed to stand high above the East Coast of the United States as he pointed to the dense clouds over Virginia.

". . . ever since Tropical Storm George came ashore late last night in North Carolina and Virginia, bringing with it several inches of rain and coastal flooding. But as you can see from the developing satellite image, George is nothing compared to the strength of Hurricane Helen, which formed off Bermuda four days ago. Helen is already a category three storm and is expected to become a category five hurricane within the next hours. The storm track of Helen is predicted to follow on the heels of George and make landfall here, on North Carolina's Outer Banks. If Helen's course doesn't turn, the East Coast should get a pounding not seen since the category five 'Great Labor Day Hurricane' that hit the Florida Keys in 1935—"

He blinked at the screen. When he'd left work on Friday there was nothing on the news about this hurricane, and now it was about to pound Virginia. Which meant he should already have been directed to get the ship to the safety of the calm waters hundreds of miles at sea. The phone should have rung a dozen times by now. He chanced a glance at her, knowing that she had to be thinking the same thing. There was a frown forming on her brow. She looked over, understanding in her eyes.

"—emergency hurricane preparations are being made by federal and coastal state authorities as residents are being advised to evacuate—"

The television and the nightstand lamp went suddenly black, the room again lit only by the candles. A violent banging sound came from below, startling her. He listened as the banging came again. It was too regular to be another clap of thunder and it wasn't the tree's branches smashing against the house.

"What was that?" she said. Her eyes darkened. An expression of fear came to her face. In all the time he'd known her, he had only seen that look a few times.

"Someone's out there knocking on the door. I'll get it."

She sank further under the covers and nodded as he stepped into his jeans. He carefully lifted one of the candles from the mantel and carried it down the stairs. When he opened the door the storm blew into the foyer and extinguished the candle flame. He had a momentary vision of a utility truck in the driveway, illuminated by a flash of lightning, and a short stranger in drenched yellow raingear standing on the porch.

The visitor shouted over the noise of the storm, "Commander Dillinger?"

He grabbed the figure by the collar and pulled him into the house and slammed the door behind him.

"Good God, get in here out of the rain, man," he said.

The soaked guest pushed off his hood. It wasn't a man at all, but a woman who, in the dimness of the foyer, looked like she was in her early twenties.

"Thank you, sir," she said, wiping the rain out of her face.

He recognized her. She worked for Smokin' Joe Kraft, the boss. "Petty Officer Leonah, right?" She nodded. "Let me get you a towel," he said, turning.

"No thank you, sir," she said. "There's no time. Hurricane Helen's coming. CinCLant's ordered the entire Atlantic fleet to sea immediately. I've got to get to the other captains."

He turned to look at her. "Why didn't you guys just call?"

"Phones are out," she said, glancing out at the storm.

"We've all got cell phones."

"The cell and wireless networks became overloaded and crashed after a dozen cell towers got knocked out by lightning, so Admiral Jones invoked the emergency wartime sortie procedure, which means we should be landing helicopters in people's front yards to collect them, but the choppers are all grounded in this weather. So they sent me out to notify the commanding officers, who are responsible for getting the rest of their people to their ships."

"If you ask me, Paully Jones should have waited till the storm blew through." He gestured out the window. "Going out in this is insane. It's goddamned unsafe. And it'll take hours to get my men aboard with all the phones out." He didn't mention that the engineroom had been torn down the week before for some unusually invasive maintenance, and that would add more time until they could leave. And running out to sea in a storm like this was begging for a major accident.

"Sir, Helen's coming faster than they thought. The fleet needs to get to safety before the sea state rises too high. That's just my guess, Commander. I didn't dream up the orders, sir, I just follow them."

"I know. I'm sorry. Who's next on your list?"

"Only two left. Captain McDonovan of the *Virginia* and Captain Vornado of the *Texas*."

"Vornado's on my way in. I'll take care of notifying him." It was ideal, because both his and Peter Vornado's chief engineers lived in Vornado's neighborhood, and the engineers were the first ones required aboard, to wake the nuclear reactors and start the steam plants. This way he could spend a few minutes with his old Annapolis roommate before they went to sea.

"Thank you, Commander, but if you can't find him, don't waste time. Just get to your ship and radio squadron staff when you get in. We'll track him down." She pulled her hood back up, stiffened to attention and threw him a quick salute. "Good luck out there, sir." She turned, opened the door and vaulted back out into the darkness of the roaring storm.

Commander Burke Dillinger stared at the puddle of water on the marble floor of the foyer as the lightning flashed in through the windows, his mind far away. When he looked up she stood halfway up the curving staircase. His eyes drifted to her swollen stomach and he thought for the hundredth time that from a few yards away the only sign that she was eight months pregnant was the circle of her belly. Above and below, she seemed no different than she had been before.

"Natalie," he said, regret in his voice, "we've been ordered to sea. I have to go."

"I know," she said slowly. "I heard. I'm worried about you. Going out in this storm—it doesn't make sense."

"Did you see the size of the hurricane on the global weather image? I'm not the one you should be worried about. You need to evacuate. And I don't want you driving to your mother's by yourself. I'll arrange a car service. Or maybe you and Rachel Vornado could get out of town together."

"Burke." She smiled as if indulging a wrong-headed but beloved child. "I'm a big girl. Too big," she laughed. "I can take care of myself. Come on, I'll help you pack."

Her expression and laughter were the first upbeat gestures he'd seen from her all day. She'd been preoccupied and sad since the storm began, but when he asked her why, she'd said that she was always disturbed by severe thunderstorms. She wasn't much of a liar, but she wouldn't budge from her story. He had wondered if he had done something wrong to bring on her melancholy, but she had smiled and kissed him. "Storms like this make me feel like I'm in a scary movie that I can't walk out of, that's all."

He frowned at her. Natalie Dillinger, formerly Lieutenant Commander Natalie D'Assault, U.S. Navy, retired, was one of the toughest and most resilient women Dillinger had ever encountered, yet she claimed to be afraid of a little rain.

She turned and hurried back up the stairs. When he got to the bedroom she was a flurry of motion. His sea bag lay on the bed. She folded clothes and placed them carefully but quickly into the bag. She rushed past him into the bathroom and packed his shaving kit, and when she emerged her eyes were swollen and the wet streak of a tear had come down one side of her face.

"Natalie, what's wrong?"

"Burke, you're exasperating me," she said, her voice breaking on the words. He had only seen her cry once, the day she'd told him that she was pregnant. "I'm pregnant, hormonal and my husband is leaving in a storm for parts unknown. What do you expect me to do?" She turned to him and he hugged her, the baby in her stretched abdomen between them. She liked it when he held her tightly, but he was worried he would squish the baby. He looked down at the bulge, wondering again if it were a boy or a girl. Natalie didn't know and didn't want him to know, insisting that a child's gender should be a surprise. He looked back up to her face and wiped his hands across her cheeks to dry her tears.

"I'm sorry to leave like this," he said gently, kissing her lips. She sniffed, kissing him back perfunctorily.

"Come on, Commander. Let's get you to sea."

"We should talk about what you're going to do," he protested.

"You just worry about you and your people. I'll take care of the house."

"To hell with the house," he said emphatically. "It's been here a hundred years. If it's the house's time, it'll go. If not, it'll be here standing. I want you out of town."

"I know," she said, looking down. "But you're out of uniform and you need to mobilize."

The impulse seized him to make love to her before he left. It was odd, because the last thing on his mind was sex, but this sortie to sea could keep him away for a week, and when he got back, the house might not be here anymore. Four days from now this very spot might be a pile of hurricane-flattened rubble. It occurred to him that this could be the last time they might have sex in this bed. Natalie's romantic thermostat had always run hot, and pregnancy had increased her appetite even more, but the last month had been difficult for her. She had been nauseated with an odd late-term morning sickness, and for the first time in their relationship she hadn't wanted sex. It had been weeks since they had been together, and that and the nausea had worried Dillinger, but this was his first time as a father. It was probably to be expected. Dillinger had stoically withstood the sexual drought, but the idea of disappearing for a week made him suddenly crave her. He missed her already. He pulled her into a deep kiss, but she circled her tongue once around his and pushed him away.

"There'll be plenty of time for *that* when you get safely home, young man," she said, smiling bravely. But the tears had returned and her nose began to run. "Go on, get out of here. You're holding up the whole Navy." She turned away from him and pulled a fully rigged working khaki uniform out of the closet and handed it to him. "Get dressed while I use the bathroom, and I'll meet you at the front door."

That was his Natalie, he thought. Vulnerable and hiding under the covers from a thunderstorm one minute, the next pragmatically rushing him out the door and ready to stare down a category five hurricane by herself. There were times he wondered if somewhere deep inside her, she made conscious decisions about which emotions to feel next, because while she certainly had emotions, they didn't have her.

He sighed in disappointment, but realized she was right. He ditched his jeans and stepped into the creased khakis and his at-sea boots. He checked himself in the mirror as he tucked in his shirt, then grabbed his bag and hurried to the foyer. He found his raincoat and shrugged into it, pulled on his garrison cap, then turned to the foyer table to take the keys to the truck. He tossed the keys back, thinking Natalie needed the truck to leave town. He got her car keys and as he looked up, she came down the stairs. Her expression seemed stern and forced.

"Take care of yourself," he said. "I left you the truck. It'll be better in the weather."

She nodded, as if she didn't trust her voice. She sniffed once and pulled him into a hug. He felt the baby digging into his midsection and he kissed her throat.

"I love you," he said. He couldn't seem to make himself move. Something seemed wrong about this. It felt as if he were leaving for a year instead of a week.

She bit her lip. This time her voice was gentler. "I love you, too, honey. You'll be back week after next. We'll take a few days off and do something."

He smirked. "Yeah, like replace the windows in this old place."

"You didn't say you'd be careful."

"I'll be careful, but—"

She suddenly reached behind him and opened the door, and the rain blasted into the house. He felt her hand in the small of his back pushing him out into the storm. She slammed the door shut behind him. He turned and shouted through it.

"Bye, sweetheart!"

"Be careful!" she shouted back at him.

He knocked his platinum Academy ring twice on the wood of the door, an ancient gesture of farewell.

His uniform was soaked by the time he retrieved his laptop from the truck and loaded it and his sea bag into the trunk of Natalie's car. He climbed into the driver's seat and backed out of the driveway, the house invisible in the blur of the rain on the windshield. He looked up to try to see the window of the master bedroom, but the dimness of the candlelight couldn't be made out from the street.

Dillinger pressed his palm against the foggy side window. "Bye, Natalie," he whispered. After a moment he hit the gas and the big Mercedes accelerated down the soaked street.

2

It took almost an hour to make what was normally a fifteen-minute drive to Peter Vornado's house. Three times Dillinger had to backtrack when the roads were choked with floodwater, the trip made even worse by the geography of the Tidewater area of Virginia, where there were so many inlets and bays that the road map resembled a maze. Finally Dillinger pulled into Vornado's driveway. The lights were on, so at least they had power. Vornado's beloved antique Corvette—the one Dillinger had given him years before—was parked out front, but it would be useless on the flooded roadways. Dillinger was soaked to the skin from the sprint from Natalie's car to the front door. Before he could raise his hand to knock, Rachel Vornado opened the door and motioned him into the house.

"Here's a towel," she said, a frown darkening her pretty features. "Give me your raincoat and dry off."

"Hi, Sugarplum." Dillinger grinned at her. "You don't seem surprised to see me." Dillinger had been calling her endearing nicknames since the beginning, in honor of their shared joke that he had wanted to compete for her affection the night that Vornado met her. But instead of her usual bright reply with her own endearment, she just frowned.

"The girl from squadron said you'd be by." There was an alarming lifelessness to her voice.

"She came over?" That was odd, Dillinger thought, after he'd volunteered to notify Vornado.

"Our landline's off and on. She was able to get through."

Dillinger frowned at Rachel's air of sadness and anger. It was more than that, he thought. There was something almost despairing about her. Obviously it was the hurricane that had frightened her. Rachel was tall and slim, with a dark, exotic and extraordinary beauty. She had shining, long hair with an indefinable shade between auburn and chestnut. Her eyes were deep and wide, almond-shaped turning upward at the corners, of a sandy color flecked with both deep brown and green streaks. Her eyelashes were naturally long and curving. Her looks could stop traffic, yet she had always been completely blind to her effect on men. And she had certainly aged gracefully, Dillinger thought. She was as slim and beautiful as she had ever been, and if anything, the years had made her even more appealing. She had grown her hair back out after having cut it drastically last summer, when all the troubles had begun that culminated in November's final disaster.

Two decades ago she had stood in a flowing black gown sipping a drink at the balustrade of the Naval Academy's Memorial Hall, overlooking the courtyard below. Vornado had seen her two seconds before Dillinger and claimed the honor of being the first one to talk to her, with the understanding that had he failed, Dillinger could make the second run on her. But two minutes after Vornado introduced himself, Rachel and he were a couple. In the years afterward, Dillinger would joke with Rachel that he had always waited for the two of them to fight and split up so he could have his chance. Rachel would smile sweetly and tell him it would have done him no good. What in God's name, Dillinger wondered aloud, had Vornado said to her that night that had allowed him to claim this prize of a woman so quickly and so completely? Vornado would smile mysteriously and say that Rachel simply had a deep and unfailingly accurate intuition about a man's true character, jokingly implying that Dillinger had fallen short. Dillinger always laughed but warned Vornado not to neglect her, lest a real man swoop in and rescue her.

Dillinger had been Vornado's best man at their wedding shortly after Annapolis graduation. In the entryway a large framed photograph showed Rachel and Vornado together under the crossed swords of Vornado's friends, with Dillinger the lead swordbearer, grinning at the two of them on that lighthearted day. Dillinger glanced at it for a second, wondering what had happened to them all—somehow when they were in their early twenties life had had such bright promise and potential. Now that he had turned forty, the world's currents seemed to have brought them to a darker place, where life felt heavier, more serious, where every one of their decisions seemed to have dire consequences. He tried to shake off the sudden ill wind that had blown into his mood—surely he was just as worried about the hurricane as Rachel was, his mind preoccupied with having to leave Natalie behind.

He looked back at Rachel, thinking that under normal circumstances her high spirits would pull him out of this odd dread he felt. He smiled at her, hoping it would improve her mood, but she just frowned back. Perhaps there was more to her mood than the storm, he thought. There were a thousand things that might be upsetting her, such as the struggles of being a mother to two older children and one preschooler, or the hassles of having a heavy full-time job while her husband disappeared to sea for weeks or months at a time. Dillinger hoped it wasn't the third possible reason.

Vornado had almost died twice last year, his second encounter with death happening on the same day that had threatened to kill Dillinger and Natalie, but that probably wasn't the issue. During last year's operation, something had happened to Vornado that Rachel would never understand, that no wife would. And either that thing remained a secret between them, a barrier to intimacy, or the revealed truth could shatter their marriage. If it were to come up, Dillinger had once thought, he would be able to tell which it was just by the expressions on their faces. A doubt bit at him, because in some ways Rachel reminded him of Natalie, with the same calm, determined, forthright approach to life's problems. A year ago Rachel wouldn't have been acting this way.

He gave her a serious look. "You ready to hightail it to the hills?"

"We're packing now," she said. "But we're not leaving until the rain stops and some of this floodwater drains. The roads are terrible and so's the traffic." She bit her lip. "As I'm sure you're aware." Her voice became bitter. "Evacuating in the face of a natural disaster, the one time a woman needs a man, and where is *he*?" She said the last word as if unwilling to say Peter's name. "Playing with his billion-dollar toy." She tried to smile, but it didn't reach her eyes. "Sometimes I think you men will never grow up."

Dillinger nodded, not knowing how to respond to her, his doubts about Vornado's marriage rising again.

"Where is Peter, hon?" he asked quietly.

"In the shower. Can I get you coffee while you wait?"

"No thanks. Don't let me hold you up. I know you're busy." He called up the stairs, forcing his voice to sound more carefree than he felt. "Where's my first lieutenant? Peter Junior!"

Vornado's son came clomping down the stairs, a grin on his nine-year-old face. "Uncle B.K.!" He grabbed Dillinger's hand in a tight handshake. Dillinger feigned pain, sinking to his knees.

"You got the grip, son," he said, mussing the boy's hair. "Can you go back up and ask your dad to get his butt out of the shower?" Peter Junior took the stairs two at a time. Dillinger glanced at his watch, a huge, heavy, absurdly expensive black-faced Breitling aviator's watch that Vornado had given him for Christmas last year. It was half past five, which meant they wouldn't be in the channel until well after dark. All he could hope for was a break in the rain. He stepped into the kitchen and glanced at the television, where the local news was devoted to the two storms, the one hitting them now and the much worse one on its way in. The picture switched to show Interstate 64, which was clogged with traffic as the city's residents began the evacuation. Great, Dillinger thought. It could take hours to get to the pier.

"Hey B.K.," an expressionless baritone voice said from behind him. Dillinger turned to greet his old friend.

"Peter," he said, smiling and holding out both of his fists as if ready to start a boxing match, which had been the way they met, in the ring on Induction Day at the Naval Academy, completely bloodying each other. Vornado smashed his fists into Dillinger's, then reached out to shake his hand, his grip as tight as his son's moments before, but there was something troubling in Vornado's expression, making Dillinger wonder what was going on in this house.

Vornado was a head taller than Dillinger and as slim as the day he'd graduated from Annapolis. A week didn't go by that he didn't get in thirty or forty miles of running, even if it meant running in place between his broiling-hot main engines. His hair was blond, his eyes denim blue, his skin pale. He had a strong chin and stark cheekbones, allowing him to pull off a convincing war face when he needed it. Years ago Dillinger had teased Vornado that he had been born forty. Vornado had always possessed an air of unquestioned authority, perhaps something that came from being the oldest brother in a household struggling through the loss of Vornado's mother, or perhaps something he had been born with. From the day they had met in the boxing ring, Vornado had reminded Dillinger of his own older brother, his innate confidence something Dillinger had envied, studied and emulated. But unlike hot-tempered Dillinger, the inscrutable Peter Vornado had always kept his emotions closely guarded. Dillinger wondered if that would be true today.

"Nice weather we're having," Vornado commented.

"Beautiful, but it's time to pack both pairs of your underwear into your briefcase and come with me. Smokin' Joe wants us all out in the op area by midnight."

"At least we won't have to go far," Vornado said, buttoning his khaki uniform shirt. "The surface sailors will have to haul ass all the way to the North Atlantic to get away from this thing. We can linger just beyond the continental shelf, one day's transit from the pier. A thousand feet beneath a category five hurricane, the ride's as smooth as being in the basement of an office building."

"I hope to hell it doesn't become a category five, or we'll have a lot of cleaning up to do." Dillinger glanced around, wondering if this house might also be a pile of rubble by the time Helen roared through.

The doorbell rang, startling Dillinger. Rachel opened the door and a Virginia state trooper stood on the porch. She invited him in and he stood in the foyer, dripping.

"Afternoon, ma'am," he said. "Sir," he addressed Vornado, "are you ready?"

Dillinger lifted an eyebrow.

"Two minutes," Vornado said to the trooper.

Dillinger pulled Vornado aside. "What's this all about?" he asked quietly.

"Kraft called for a police escort. Without flashing lights and sirens we won't make it to the pier in time. And Kraft's ordered all ships to depart the minute they have steam in their enginerooms, no matter who's missing from the crews. So he thought it would be good to get the senior officers of each ship aboard."

"We're sailing short-handed?"

Vornado nodded. "Anyone we're missing we can meet at sea. Once this storm dies down the choppers can fly. We'll pop up, take on the stragglers and pull the plug again."

"We need to pick up our engineers at least," Dillinger said.

Vornado shook his head. "I called mine, and he and his state trooper picked up yours. They should both be at the pier by now. And squadron ordered all duty officers to start the reactors."

"Except mine," Dillinger said. "I'm down hard. I've got to put the engineroom back together first."

Vornado smiled slightly. "Hey, someone's got to be last to drag their lame asses out of port. May as well be you, B.K."

"Screw you," Dillinger said.

Rachel stood in the hall as Peter Junior lugged Vornado's sea bag down the stairs. Vornado and Dillinger got into their raingear. Before saying good-bye to Vornado, Rachel looked at Dillinger.

"What's Natalie doing?"

Dillinger shrugged, embarrassed. "All I could do was leave her the truck. You know how independent she is."

Vornado nodded. "Hard to remember that *she* used to work for *you*. It always seems the other way around."

"Tell me about it." Dillinger smirked.

Rachel spoke, her voice uncharacteristically harsh. "You left a woman eight months pregnant alone with a hurricane coming and just handed her the keys to the truck? What kind of husband *are* you?" Rachel frowned. "Jesus, Burke. You could have at least asked if I could help take care of her."

Dillinger stared at Rachel, stunned. He'd never seen her like this.

"Why don't you two just get out of here?" Rachel continued, her voice bitter. "Go play sailor while we women take care of the world, as usual."

Vornado frowned, shaking his head. He put his hand on her shoulder and whispered something in her ear. She frowned in anger and turned to hurry up the stairs. Vornado's children appeared in the foyer. Marla, the oldest, was a younger copy of her mother, reminding Dillinger of that night in Memorial Hall. Vornado kissed her, then hugged his son. Little Erin, the blond three-year-old, hugged his leg, upset that he was leaving. Dillinger waited while Vornado sank to one knee and kissed Erin, and stroked her platinum blonde hair while looking up at the older children and telling them to co-operate with their mother. Vornado pulled on a blue baseball cap with gold embroidery forming laurel leaves on the brim, with a U.S. Submarine Force dolphin emblem on its face, the gold thread spelling USS *TEXAS* SSN-775. Vornado nodded at the state trooper. The door opened and the three of them stepped out into the howling spray of the storm.

For the next twenty minutes Dillinger drove quietly, the only sounds the blast of the defroster fan and the slapping of the wiper blades set on high speed as he followed the state trooper through a dozen back roads to skirt the flooded streets. Finally they took an on-ramp to the interstate, but it was bumper-to-bumper, nothing but red brake lights extending as far as visibility allowed in the weather. The trooper's beacons suddenly lit up and his siren blared. Dillinger followed him in the shoulder as they sped past the stalled traffic. When the trooper turned off the siren, his lights still flashing, Dillinger spoke without looking over at Vornado.

"What the hell was that all about?"

Vornado didn't answer immediately, but stared out the rain-streaked window. When he spoke, his baritone voice was level and expressionless.

"Rachel had a bad night."

Dillinger considered the statement. He had wondered privately if this would happen, but had placed his bet on his friend's ability to build a mental wall between himself and the memories. It occurred to him that Vornado must have been talking in his sleep, and had said something Rachel had not been meant to hear.

They slowed suddenly as the trooper turned onto the northbound ramp for Interstate 65, his siren blaring again as traffic partially blocked the shoulder. When they sped up in the northbound shoulder, Dillinger asked the next question.

"You say something while you were asleep?"

Vornado looked at the floor of the car. "I've been

tired lately. We've been doing a lot of weekly ops in the VaCapes."

VaCapes was short for Virginia Capes Submarine Operation Area, an Ohio-sized square of ocean off the East Coast continental shelf where they did most of their tactical practice. Weekly operations were the worst, Dillinger thought, requiring frequent startups and shutdowns, preunderway checklists, all-nighters to get the ship ready to go on Sunday night, the concentrated vigilance required to pilot the ship out of the harbor, the week's operational demands themselves meaning little sleep at sea, followed by another risky shallow-water transit to bring the ship back into port, with the usual extreme overtime Friday night to shut down the reactor and take aboard stores. And then, after Saturday at the house, spent going through mail, paying bills, attending to errands, laundry and an annoyed wife, he would pack and go in Sunday night and do it all over again. A month of weekly ops could age a man five years.

"I know. You and your dogs have been conspicuously missing at happy hour for some time now." Dillinger's inner circle and Vornado's intersected at a waterfront dive established by one of Vornado's old mentors, a chief petty officer who had trained Vornado in the secret ways of the Silent Service decades before, when he was a neophyte submarine officer. "So you were tired, you were saying."

"Yeah. I fell asleep last night during—well, during a moment when you don't normally sleep. And those moments have become damned infrequent since I took Smokin' Joe's job offer."

Dillinger raised an eyebrow as he glanced at Vornado. Rachel had always been the understanding type, one of the few women who wouldn't normally take offense to her overworked husband falling asleep during a "tactical situation," but then, perhaps these weren't normal times.

"Is that all you did?"

Vornado shook his head. "Apparently I said another woman's name when I was out."

"Shit, Peter. Did you say anything else?" Here it came, Dillinger thought. Vornado might not have built that mental wall after all.

"Yeah, but I'm not sure what. Rachel won't say. But if I'm any judge of her, it was enough."

"Jesus. That's not good, in a hundred ways."

Vornado said nothing.

"Do you want me to talk to her?" Dillinger asked, trying to frame a conversation with Rachel that might make her see what that goddamned operation had done to Vornado.

"Thanks, but that would make it worse."

They rode on in silence, Dillinger following the trooper to the ramp to Interstate 564, the spur that led to the Norfolk Operating Base. This section of roadway was mostly deserted, and their escort sped up. Dillinger glanced at the dashboard clock, which showed it to be half past six. Within the hour Vornado would be in the channel, but it would be hours later before Dillinger would be able to follow him.

"So. You think she knows." It was a statement rather than a question. "What now?"

"I don't know. This is uncharted territory, but somehow I know she'll take it the wrong way. That's the damned thing about it. I didn't cheat on her, not really." Vornado paused.

"And yet," Dillinger said gently after a moment, "you did."

"I know." Vornado's voice had become hoarse and choked.

Dillinger glanced over in alarm, realizing he'd never seen Vornado this upset. Vornado's face was red and his eyes seemed swollen. He rubbed his eyes, then covered them, his face turned downward.

"But I can't explain it, not any of it."

Vornado was a devout Catholic, a devoted family man, one of the first from their class to have a child. Of all their classmates, he'd always had the best marriage. And now last fall's operation was taking more hostages.

Dillinger had always thought he himself had had the more difficult burden in the aftermath of the disaster, since he had lost so many men, but then, Dillinger had found Natalie in the ashes, and since they had lived through it together, the experience had strengthened their bond. Meanwhile, Vornado had been required to feed Rachel a cover story that accounted for four missing months of his life. Against Rachel's suspicions Vornado couldn't defend himself, because the evidence that would exonerate him was classified three levels higher than top secret.

Dillinger tried to find some words of comfort. "Listen, if we weren't heading out, I'd buy us a bottle of scotch and we'd see if we could find the answer at the bottom of the bottle." God knows they had done that before, but in the past it had always been Vornado counseling Dillinger. How could he help a man who had always known all the answers?

Vornado laughed. "Maybe we should ask the trooper to pull over at the Dolphin so we can get that bottle of scotch to go."

"We'll be back soon," Dillinger said. "Maybe by then Rachel will cool down. And you can get your head together during this hurricane op to think about how to tell her the truth."

"I can't tell her the truth," Vornado said.

"She wouldn't understand?"

"That's one damned good reason. The other is that it's special compartmented information. It won't help Rachel or the kids if I spend my twilight years behind the bars of a military prison."

"If you get tired again, you're going to be sleep-talking the truth anyway," Dillinger said. "Who knows, maybe you already did."

"I never thought of myself as a security risk," Vornado said, looking out the side window.

"It's not your fault they sent you on the thing. You didn't ask for it. You just did your duty."

"Yeah," Vornado said, deep in thought.

"It'll be okay, Peter," Dillinger said. "A week and Rachel will calm down."

"It won't be a week," Vornado said.

"What do you mean?"

"Something's up," Vornado said. "It was starting to come out in all those weekly ops."

"What were you doing out there?"

"Sucking eggs," Vornado said.

Dillinger passed a nearly stopped truck with its blinkers on, barely noticing it as he focused on Vornado's words. *Sucking eggs.* There were times when an SSN, a fast attack submarine such as Vornado's or Dillinger's, trailed a friendly SSBN—a strategic ballistic missile submarine, the kind loaded with city-killer intercontinental ballistic missiles, those submarines known in the force as a "boomer." The idea of the attack sub trailing the boomer was to make sure there were no hostile attack subs lurking or in trail that would sink the boomer before she could execute her mission. Such an operation was called a "Security Exercise." Inevitably the name was shortened to "SecEx" but was pronounced by cynical attack sub crews as "suck eggs," which described the unpopularity of such operations among the SSN crews, who would rather be plying their trade spying in an enemy port, dropping off commandos, shooting torpedoes or tangling with enemy attack subs than playing security guard to a damned boomer.

SecExes were frustrating because of the rivalry between the two parts of the U.S. Submarine Force. Fast attack submarines, SSNs, had the top secret missions, regularly sailed into danger, and led a challenging, difficult life of excitement, spying on enemies in shallow harbors, dropping off CIA spies, tapping underwater data cables and covertly sinking terrorist ships. Meanwhile, ballistic missile submarines, SSBNs, simply went to the remote reaches of the deep sea and tried to stay away from other shipping while remaining ready to launch their ICBMs on orders from Washington. If there were an aviation equivalent, fast attack submarines were the fighters while ballistic missile subs were the bombers. During peacetime, the SSNs would fight the secret wars while the SSBNs would merely "hide with pride." But, in fact, the missions weren't the entire story. The boomers carried enough firepower to level the cities of an adversary, able to strike out from the secret depths of the ocean with a war-winning fury. While they were at sea, in locations unknown, they were a powerful deterrent to any country foolish enough to think they could win a surprise nuclear attack against the United States and live to tell the tale. Fast attack subs were able to do things no other element of the military could, but they were insignificant next to the value of the boomer fleet in strategic force and deterrent value.

"The usual shit?" Dillinger asked. "Try to trail the boomer and then lose him, to the delight of the boomer girls?"

"Some of that," Vornado said. "But this time it was different. The whole thrust of the exercises was to get a snap-shot off at the boomer the moment we detected him."

Dillinger looked over at his friend as he wheeled the Mercedes to the base entrance. The trooper waved at them as Dillinger tossed him a salute and opened the window at the guard shack. The rain hit him in the face and soaked his lap as he and Vornado showed their identification. The first security gate slowly rolled aside, admitting them between the inner and outer fence. When the outer gate shut behind them, the inner one rolled open, and Dillinger drove slowly toward the perimeter road to the piers. He looked back at Vornado, encouraging him to go on.

"There was more. We were to assume the boomer would not detect us or shoot back, even if we made a mistake. It wasn't a sub-versus-sub exercise, it was a 'find-'em-and-fuck-'em.' "

"That's odd."

"I know. We got the impression that something's going on with a boomer somewhere. That the admirals want us to be ready to take one out. I'm not talking about ready as in 'maybe someday.' Ready as in 'probably tomorrow.' "

Dillinger rolled to a stop at the pier three security building, his thoughts spinning about what Vornado had just said. Even the hurricane was forgotten.

"Keep going," Vornado said. "I'll walk in with you from the parking lot. We're both going to get drenched on the walk down the pier anyway."

Dillinger wheeled the Mercedes to the senior officer parking lot, finding his space with the blue sign, its gold lettering spelling C.O. USS *HAMPTON*. They climbed out, the rain soaking them as efficiently as if they'd stepped under a showerhead. Dillinger grabbed his bags from the trunk as Vornado shouldered his sea bag. They walked in silence in the rain, the wind picking up and driving the big drops nearly horizontally.

Dillinger shivered in the wind. "So," he said, nearly shouting to be heard. "They think one of *our* boomers could go bad?"

"No," Vornado said, leaning in close to Dillinger, one hand on his cap to keep it from flying off in the gale. "That's the disturbing part. They're not worried about us. They're worried about the other guys."

The other countries that operated ballistic missile nuclear submarines were Russia, China, England and France. Dillinger assumed Vornado meant the Russians. Probably political upheaval in Moscow had the Pentagon worried.

"The Russians again," Dillinger said

"No," Vornado said, glancing over. "There were three officers of the French submarine force on board for the last two weekly ops, with a French civilian. I think he was a spook. A high-ranking one."

Dillinger was going to respond, but they had reached the security building at the piers. They opened the doors and lugged their gear in for inspection, then submitted to an identification check and retinal scan. There were a dozen other officers and enlisted sailors in the building, checking in, all of them as drenched as Dillinger and Vornado. When they collected their bags at the other side of the building and emerged on the pier side, Dillinger walked close to Vornado.

"So you think there's something going on with the French ballistic missile fleet? Why aren't they training with their own attack submarines?"

"They did," Vornado said. "But their boomers are too quiet. Their own attack subs can't hear them."

"So something's up with a French ballistic missile sub. Did the French guys speculate?"

"No. But they were very interested in our acoustic advantage over our own boomers."

"Virginia class is whisper quiet, that's for sure," Dillinger admitted.

Vornado shook his head. "It's the FY-zero-eight sonar upgrade. The machine is good. With the FY-oh-eight, your ship will have the same acoustic advantage over the boomers that we have. Did they finish your upgrade yet?"

Dillinger nodded. "Just finished pierside test-out on Saturday. I'm armed and dangerous now." But Dillinger wasn't thinking about the new sonar, but about the French sub force. "So, you said it would be more than a week. You think after we clear the stormy waters, you're being sent to the east Atlantic to try out your skills on the French?"

They walked to the beginning of pier three, the home of Submarine Squadron Eight. The sign showed a mean-looking shark pushing an eight ball. To the right, the tender ship *Olympus* lay tied up, the hulking vessel a gray-painted ocean liner, the interior filled with parts storage holds, machine shops, offices, welding bays and weapon bins. It was the headquarters of the squadron, the upper decks taken up by squadron staff's offices and staterooms. On the highest deck their boss, Commodore Smokin' Joe Kraft, presided over the squadron, an enlightened and benevolent dictator who had been a force in both their lives.

"Maybe. But it won't just be me. It'll be you, too. Now that you've got the sonar upgrade, our ships are going to head east and keep going."

"That doesn't make sense, Peter. Did the French lose a boomer or not? Are we just going to play with them in an exercise? Or is it . . ." Dillinger stopped on the pier and pulled Vornado closer. "Is it war?"

Vornado's face was flushed, perhaps from the chill of the rain, or from the argument with Rachel. He blinked at Dillinger. "They'll call it an exercise, B.K. But they might do that so that we don't lose our cool. I don't know. All I know is that the brass have loose stool over the whole thing. There is definitely something up with the French submarine force."

"Shit," Dillinger said, looking up at the darkening clouds, the rain falling into his eyes. "Natalie needs me here. Bad time for an op."

"Yeah," Vornado said. "I know what you mean. Rachel picked a hell of a time to have a major issue with our marriage."

Dillinger nodded, but he was thinking that she hadn't asked for it either. It had never been easy for either one of them to try to imagine what went on in their wives' heads, but Dillinger could well imagine that Vornado vanishing for four months in that odd emergency last summer, then coming back with no explanation and muttering another woman's name in his sleep would make any woman furious. Probably the only way she wouldn't be angry would be if she didn't love him. The question was, would Vornado tell her the truth or keep quiet? Either way, it might not satisfy Rachel.

What was it Vornado had said in his sleep other than the woman's name? That might have been even worse. Other than Vornado, Dillinger was the only person not wearing a CIA identification badge who knew the whole ugly truth, and that was only because he had been there. Dillinger wondered what he could say to Rachel that would help his friend, but he came up with nothing.

"It'll be better when we get back," Dillinger said, not

really believing it, as they walked past the submarines tied up on the sea end of the tender. McDonovan's boat lay tied up on the left, then Willey's on the right. They passed another berthing space with two more subs on either side, then reached the end of the quarter-mile-long jetty of concrete, where the last berths were located.

To some sailors, these would be the cheap seats, fifteen hundred feet from the land side and that much farther from the parking lot. But to Dillinger, this was the only place a self-respecting submarine captain would want his ship tied up. Here, with the ship pointed seaward, all they had to do was toss off the lines and throttle up, and they were gone. Further inland, those ships in the tight slip between the piers of the naval station would require two tugboats each to pull the hulls gently away from the concrete pier. Submarines were famously unmaneuverable in restricted waters, and their nose-cones were made of delicate fiberglass, unable to be indiscriminately banged into piers. But out here at the end, they could go to sea as easily as one of the flashy and maneuverable surface warships, with their fancy thrusters and multiple screws. The destroyer and cruiser skippers would back out in a flourish, their radars spinning in unison, their flags flying, their horns blasting, as if making fun of their humiliated cousins in the submarine force who were helplessly pulled out with double tugboats. On his previous submarine, the venerable USS *Tucson*, Dillinger had always requested to be the boat tied up at the very end of the pier. Vornado had never cared. To him, getting underway with tugboats was just another fact of life. It was mere coincidence that his ship was tied up way out here with Dillinger's. Since he was at sea so much the past month doing his weekly ops, the only space left on the pier was out here.

They paused at the point on the pier even with the sterns of the submarines. On the left lay the USS *Hampton*, of the Los Angeles class, Dillinger's ship. The old girl had formerly been commanded by Vornado before

last summer's operation. Now that *Tucson* was gone,
Smokin' Joe had offered Dillinger Vornado's old boat.
On the right was the USS *Texas* of the Virginia class, the
newest fast attack submarine in the fleet, Peter's fiefdom.
Vornado and Dillinger had always been the two top submarine commanders in the squadron, paired off against
each other by the commodore, each one competing for
the squadron's one "battle E" emblem for combat excel-
lence. In the old days before last summer, they had both
taken the competition seriously, pushing their crews to
perform and win the trophy, but perhaps now they
knew better.

Vornado turned to Dillinger. "I guess this is it for a
while, B.K."

"Good luck out there, pal," Dillinger said, thinking
more about French ballistic missile submarines than
the hurricane.

Vornado punched Dillinger's fists, then reached out to
shake his hand. Dillinger pulled him into a bear hug,
suddenly missing his friend as if they were to be gone
for years. For the second time that day, a simple good-
bye made Dillinger irrationally emotional. What the hell
was wrong with him, he wondered. Vornado slapped his
back, then stepped away.

"Good hunting," Vornado said. He turned and walked
to his gangway. His topside watchstander came to rigid
attention and saluted. Vornado saluted back, turned to
the flag flying aft and saluted it. Vornado's ship's loudspeaker crackled over the noise of the rain. "*Texas*, arriving!" Vornado looked over after tossing his bag down
the hatch. He nodded once, then vanished into the
submarine.

Dillinger stood there in the rain, his mind numb. It
took a conscious effort to turn away from the *Texas* to
look at his own submarine.

3

Ever since being appointed a sea captain, Dillinger understood something the others did not. On the day of an underway, a captain should never do what Vornado had and simply walk aboard, not even in weather like this. To simply walk aboard without acknowledging the spirit and majesty of the ship would violate her. A ship was not just a collection of welded hull plates, rotating steel machinery and electrical cables. It had a soul and a personality, and only a fool would believe otherwise, particularly since the sea was always so eager to swallow those arrogant enough to challenge it without being in tune with the rhythms of the ship beneath their boots. The true seaman knew his vessel like he knew his wife. He knew how she would behave under stress, how she would handle the next gigantic wave, how her deck would tremble and tilt on a flank run snap roll. A true sea captain didn't just cross the gangplank and grab the wheel, he walked slowly around her from the pier, examining every sign, every nuance, attuned to every whisper from the vessel. The captains of the air knew all this. For a long hour they would walk slowly around their winged, jet-engined behemoths and inspect every seam, every rivet, every tire tread. They called it a safety inspection, but it was really their way of paying homage to the being that would be the only thing between them and a plunge to their deaths. Yet, where this ship would go tonight there would be as many hazards as any sky flown by the aviators, so he would pay her the respect she deserved.

The dark, low, dangerous streamlined shape tied up
to the pier was christened the USS *Hampton*. Her name
had been carried with honor by four previous American
warships. She was born a fierce Confederate gunship
that patrolled the James River and valiantly fought the
battles of Dutch Gap and Chaffin's Bluff, but was set
afire and destroyed by her own navy as the enemy Union
forces closed in on Richmond, the war and her sacred
cause lost. Her soul had returned in a humble oceangoing tug that patrolled Hampton Roads, the hard labor
and dreary duties of that incarnation absolving her of
her wartime sins. She returned from that life as a more
aggressive World War II submarine chaser and training
vessel, then progressed to a third lifetime as a post-war
amphibious transport. But her destiny and her potential
remained unfulfilled until she was reincarnated in 1993
by the Newport News Shipbuilding and Drydock Company. Since she had taken on this magnificent flesh of
high yield–high tensile steel, with a beating heart of
bomb-grade uranium, she had been a lucky ship, always
at the center of the action, always successful, inevitably
one of the first ships called on by squadron and the
admirals when there was trouble. She had won Presiden-
tial Unit Citations and Meritorious Unit Citations, one
after the other, from the cruise missiles she'd launched
in the Iraq war to the commandos she'd landed in the
tense Panama operation, from the top secret evacuation
of Rogachev in the Black Sea when she'd taken two
Ukrainian depth charges, one of which had blown off
her sail and threatened to flood her from where the periscopes had been, to the near disaster of an international
incident on that ultrasecret northern run to the Arctic
Ocean, concluding with Operation *Stolen Arrows* in the
South Atlantic. There was no doubt that *Hampton* had
lived nine lives and lived them well, but Dillinger prayed
she had nine more. On her decks walked the most inspired, dedicated and professional sailors and officers in
the United States Navy, and she had been commanded
by a succession of the Navy's most courageous and dar-

ing captains; the last one Peter Vornado himself. That Dillinger had been named to command this venerable ship was a deep honor, particularly given the fate of his last command.

Hampton was curvaceous, her rounded, perfectly sculpted flanks rolling gently to the water aft, her cylindrical hull disappearing into the choppy black water of the slip. Far aft of that, her rudder protruded vertically, as if disembodied, the shape of it reminding him of an airliner's vertical stabilizer. On top of the rudder the white navigation light was lit, its wattage normally bright as a police searchlight, but it appeared dim in the storm. Dillinger looked deliberately down at the black rolling waves of the slip where the rudder vanished. Here the business of propulsion happened. He had seen her lying helpless in the drydock and had stood far below her, staring upward at this very spot. Right there, under the chop of the waves a half-dozen feet further aft of the rudder, the hull came to a pointed cone where the ten-foot-diameter brass screw's seven scimitar-shaped swirling blades waited to spin and accelerate the ship. To either side were horizontal stabilizers with vertical winglets at their ends. Below the conical aft hull, the rudder's lower portion extended vertically downward toward the bottom.

Dillinger looked forward along the long hull, the blackness of it uninterrupted for nearly two hundred feet before the hardened steel of the sail rose abruptly from the deck, the tower an unadorned vertical wing. Barely visible in the fog and the rain were several masts raised from the sail. He walked slowly forward, taking in every detail—the shorepower cable gantry extending from the pier to the after hatch, where the black cables, each thicker than his arm, snaked into the opening where they were bolted into the ship's electrical buses. The doubled-up mooring lines curving from the pier to the deck, where they were lashed to cleats that rotated out of the smooth hull when the ship was in port. The ballast tank vent covers, bolted over the huge valves that would allow air to leave the ballast tanks so that they could intentionally sink below the waves. The sagging American flag on a small flagpole aft. The gangway placed just aft of the sail. The canvas tent placed over the forward escape trunk hatch, which was located near the gangway landing, also aft of the sail. Dillinger continued until he could see the bow. The bullet nose of the submarine curved down to the water, the shape of it meant to divide the water at speed. He could make out the twelve doors of the vertical launch tubes, from which Tomahawk missiles would fly in a moment of national anger.

He stopped at the end of the pier. He looked out at the water of the Elizabeth River, blown into three-foot whitecaps by the gale, then turned back to the *Hampton*. From this angle she was even more graceful, her streamlined hull ready to slice through the sea on any mission her Navy ordered her on. Dillinger glanced north, toward the berth of the USS *Texas*, Vornado's ship.

The *Texas* was longer than *Hampton* by seventeen feet, and her sail was placed further forward than *Hampton*'s. On top of *Texas*' sail, the radar mast made slow circles as it searched out into the harbor. On her hull, deckhands in foul-weather gear and kapok life jackets stood ready while the squadron's line handlers waited on the pier to disconnect her mooring lines and toss them to her deck. At the top of her sail, two officers stood, one talking into a radio and the other looking out at the river. The taller, thinner of them, Vornado, waved down at Dillinger. He returned the gesture with a salute, his thoughts returning to Vornado's words about the French. Whatever was going on, it would happen without Dillinger, he thought.

Dillinger listened as Vornado's officer of the deck, young Deke Flynn, shouted down to the pier with his bullhorn, ordering the lines to be taken in. The deckhands burst into motion, pulling the heavy lines off the bollards and tossing them to the crew of the *Texas*. A long, wailing blast roared out from Vornado's horn as his submarine announced herself to be fully underway.

Slowly she advanced beside the pier, her rudder moving abreast of Dillinger until it cleared the end of the jetty and Flynn put the rudder over to right full. The Virginia-class submarine gracefully turned and headed north into the river. Dillinger wasn't quite sure he saw Vornado's hand waving just as the sleek, low, black shape vanished into the fog and rain.

For a long moment he stared after it, his heart feeling suddenly heavier with Vornado's absence. He took a deep breath and turned back to the *Hampton*. He became aware of someone standing next to him. He couldn't make out much about the figure other than that he wore the same yellow raingear as the squadron line-handlers and was half a head taller than Dillinger. But by the way he stood next to Dillinger, without saying anything, Dillinger knew he was the duty officer. After the months of his command of the *Hampton*, his officers knew to leave him alone in the hours before an under-way unless he spoke to them. Dillinger would listen to his ship first, his men second.

Finally Dillinger broke the silence. "I'm ready for your report," he said.

"Evening, Captain," the rain-suited figure's voice half shouted over the roar of the wind and rain. The voice belonged to Lieutenant Commander Matt Mercury-Pryce, his old communications officer from the *Tucson* who, with a half dozen other officers, had joined him here on the *Hampton*. On this tour of duty, Merc was the navigator and one of Dillinger's principal aides, the ship's third-in-command after the executive officer. Just a year ago Mercury-Pryce had seemed so young, his wiry body toned from endless mountain bike rides, his dark hair streaked with blond, an able seaman who would never grow up, his spare time spent drag racing, skiing, surfing, sailing, drinking and womanizing, but like Dillinger, when he'd been pulled out of the sinking, burning hull of the *Tucson*, it had changed him. Merc was far more serious now. Gone were the blond streaks, re-placed with gray, and gone with them was his old adventurer's attitude. He was married now, one of the old men of the ship. Dillinger had asked Commodore Kraft for Merc by name, and had almost doubted that Mercury-Pryce would join the crew, but when he reported aboard, Dillinger felt like the ship had been completed somehow. There were times when Dillinger thought that if he'd ever had a son, this would be what he would be like, and like a stern but doting father he had nurtured the younger officer's career, praising his victories in public and reprimanding his mistakes in private, the advice pouring from his lips unbidden, all of it absorbed by his serious young navigator.

"Reactor plant is shut down to cold wet layup," Mercury-Pryce began, giving the same status report Dillinger had heard every morning for two long weeks. "Main coolant pumps are secured with the reactor on emergency cooling. Main seawater system remains tagged out for the work on the MSW-3 valve. Main steam system is tagged out and isolated for the work on the port main engine throttle. The executive officer and the department heads are aboard and preunderway checklists are substantially complete for all systems except engineering." Merc stopped and shook his head, as if the report disgusted him.

Behind them, a long blast of an air horn sounded over the water; another of the squadron's submarines now underway and ready to drive out into the Elizabeth River Channel. Dillinger turned to see, but visibility had closed to the point that the pier vanished in the fog not far from the *Hampton*'s rudder, making the jetty seem surreally disembodied from the rest of reality. The world had shrunk so that the only things that existed were their ship and a three-hundred-foot length of pier and the rain that fell on both. Maybe the gods would ease up and this weather would break by the time they were ready to go, Dillinger hoped.

"Status of the main seawater valve replacement?"

"The parts miraculously arrived this afternoon. Squadron's buttoning up the system now. Engineer's waiting with a SUBSAFE hydrostatic test package."

Dillinger shook his head. The weather had invoked a "tactical situation." There would be no leisurely in-port testing of the system that kept them safe from the pressure of the ocean. The test would have to be done at sea. If it failed and flooded the ship they'd isolate it and limp by with half of the engineroom shut down.

"We'll skip the test." The engineer would have a stroke over this, but there were more important things than his precious reactor plant.

"Yes, sir," Merc said, like a bored student in a high school play delivering a line he'd rehearsed a hundred times. Merc probably had known from the moment the hurricane deployment order came down from squadron that the seawater system would be used without being tested.

"Port main engine throttle?" Dillinger asked. The second annoying piece of maintenance that had been ongoing since they pulled in from the Gulf of Mexico run was taking forever.

"It's amazing, sir. Parts for that also managed to get found when Helen was forecast. The casing was being bolted on and torqued when I left the engineroom."

Interesting, Dillinger thought. He smirked, seeing the hand behind their lingering maintenance problems belonging to Smokin' Joe Kraft. It must have been the old man's benevolent way of giving them a short, well-deserved vacation. Maybe he should have shorted the *Texas* of parts, Dillinger mused, so that Vornado could get some rest.

"Patty's got a test package for the steam system as well, Captain."

"He may as well file it," Dillinger said. "We'll do an op-check as we come into the power range. Is the engineer aboard?"

"He's been waiting for you. He wants to make a report."

Dillinger nodded. "Crew?"

Merc shook his rain-hooded head. "It's not good, Captain, but it's a lot better now than two hours ago. We're missing about thirty. Executive officer and the yeoman are burning up phone lines, but every five minutes we lose a connection, so they sent a couple of the torpedomen out in the yeoman's van to find the men. Then Commander Willey came over and stole half a dozen people for the *Jacksonville*. I've seen equipment cannibalized, but never a crew. It sucks being the last ship ready to go, Captain."

Had it been anyone other than George Willey, Dillinger might have gotten his back up, but George was an ex-*Hampton* sailor and Vornado's old exec, and could be forgiven this one time. Even as Dillinger completed the thought the roar of tugboat engines drew his attention to the slip, where the USS *Jacksonville* slowly glided by the berth of the *Hampton*. He looked up to the rain-soaked flying bridge atop her sail, where a bearded man stood at attention and gave him a formal salute.

"Did he take anyone from the wardroom or goat locker?"

"Yessir," Merc said, sounding bitter. "He took the COB and Ensign Wang."

"Godammit," Dillinger cursed. They could get by without the torpedo officer, but the damned chief of the boat?

"I know. XO is furious. There's no way he would have given up the COB unless Commander Willey came over personally."

"Thank you, Nav," Dillinger said, using Merc's nickname as the ship's navigator. "Let's get below." He adjusted his sea bag on his shoulder and walked to the gangway. At the brow the topside watch came to attention and saluted. Dillinger recognized the youth as Sonarman First Class MacKenzie. He saluted back, turned and saluted the soaked American flag aft, then walked over the narrow gangway to the hull. When he stepped onto the slick black hull it was like stepping onto the back of a whale, as the antisonar sound-coating foam of the hull gave from his weight. He ducked under the tent over the after escape hatch, and as he did, a loud crackling came from the 1MC shipwide public address announcing system. Sonarman MacKenzie's voice boomed out over the pier and echoed upward from the maw of the hatch.

"*Hampton*, arriving!"

Dillinger smiled. Hearing that was always the best part of the day. The smell of the rain yielded suddenly to the vinyl scent of the tent, then to the beloved perfume of the ship—sharp electric-smelling ozone, lazy-Sunday-lunch-cooking grease, acrid diesel oil, sulfury diesel engine exhaust, hometown-auto-garage-machinery lube oil and promising musk of freshly brewed Columbian coffee. For a half second he breathed in that smell, the scent the same yet subtly different for every submarine. He remembered the first time he had smelled it, as a midshipman taking a tour of a visiting sub at anchor off Annapolis, back when he was a shaven-headed plebe.

The dimness of the tent and the hatch maw gave way to the institutional fluorescence of the interior lighting, the usual cavelike submarine interior seeming bright after the darkness of the storm. The sounds hit him next. There was a barely noticeable high-pitched whining sound in the background that played a duet with the bass roar of the air handlers blowing air through the fan room and distributing it throughout the ship. The chatter of conversation came from below, where the hatch emptied into the crew's mess.

"Down ladder!" Dillinger shouted, a prelude to him dropping his sea bag down to the lower hatch ring because it could slip and continue down the twenty feet to the middle level deck, and hit someone. The bag stayed inside the forward escape trunk. Dillinger glanced up for a moment, out the tent flap back to the rain-sheeted pier, his submariner's instinct making him take one last look and one last breath before he vanished into the hull, because in this dangerous business God alone knew if it would be his last taste of real air. He looked back down and stepped into the darkness of the forward escape trunk, a ten-foot-tall cylinder of steel big enough to hold ten men crowded together, lit only by two bright incandescent bulbs in wire cages. From this space an emergency escape could be conducted, the trunk acting as an airlock, but whenever Dillinger thought about it, he shivered, a part of him dreadfully fearful of a quarter mile of ocean overhead. If it ever came to it, he would rather go down with the ship than leave it through this terrifying mechanism. Imagine, he thought, a submarine commander who was afraid of deep water.

He shook his head and lowered himself quickly down the ladder to the hatchway at the bottom of the escape trunk. He shouted "down ladder" again and tossed his bag down the second hatch, then followed it, emerging from the darkness of the trunk into the brightly lit crew's mess.

Dillinger's boots landed on the middle level deckplates in the after starboard corner of the crew's mess. He turned and picked up his bag. As he straightened up a resounding cheer broke out among the crew. Dillinger looked up in surprise and watched as the men in the mess rose to their feet and applauded in genuine, raw enthusiasm. One of them shouted his nickname among the crew, *El Jefe*, as if he were a ruthless and powerful South American dictator.

"Spit in the eye of Hurricane Helen, Skipper," a young voice in the back shouted.

Dillinger stared at the crowd for a moment, the rainwater running down his soaked face, a smile coming to his lips, the crow's-feet at his eyes crinkling in pleasure. As he walked forward to leave the room, his only reply was to raise his fist in acknowledgment, his usual gesture to the crew that he would "fight the ship" just as he had once fought in the boxing ring.

At the forward end of the cramped efficiency of the cantina-style mess was a narrow laminate-paneled centerline passageway leading to the crew's quarters. Halfway down the passageway was a steep flight of stair steps leading to the upper level. Dillinger took the stairs two at time, turned the corner at the top and walked forward down the centerline upper level passageway toward the control room. He opened the door to his stateroom, dropped his bag and walked into the stainless-steel head between his and the executive officer's stateroom. He dumped his clothes to the troweled stone deck and stepped under the stinging shower spray.

He toweled off and donned a fresh working khaki uniform. As he tied the laces on his dry pair of at-sea combat boots a knock came at the door. He looked up to see the face of his second-in-command.

"XO," Dillinger said, using the centuries-old Navy nickname for the executive officer. "Come on in." Dillinger sank into his high-backed leather command chair and folded down his desk. His bunk, tucked into the outboard alcove of the tiny room, was folded up into the bulkhead like the bed of an old Pullman train cabin, a small café table taking the bunk's place with two small booth benches on either side. Dillinger waved his exec to a seat at the table.

Steve Flood was a tall, lanky, affable and bright lieutenant commander. He had perfect, sculpted, almost feminine facial features under a thick head of hair that he combed back over the top of his scalp. He was popular with the crew for his easygoing manner and genuine care for the welfare of the men. He had a way of whipping up enthusiasm among the crew for even the most tedious business, which had made him successful as the ship's king of administration and paperwork. Flood represented the *Hampton* to the outside world, particularly to squadron, and he represented the intentions and commands of the captain inward to the crew. A misstep in either task could prove disastrous not only to their careers but to the safety of the ship herself.

Dillinger had met Flood two years ago when he had first shown up to take command of the *Tucson*. Flood had been the chief engineer, there only a few weeks before Dillinger, and he and Dillinger had forged an instant alliance. During Operation *Stolen Arrows* Flood had stepped up to be Dillinger's acting exec, and had done such a tremendous job that Dillinger had resented the newly reporting XO. Natalie D'Assault would never do half the job Flood could, Dillinger had been ready to argue, but before he could make that case, they'd been ordered north. He'd been wrong about Natalie, but now that she'd left the Navy, Dillinger had immediately requested Flood as his second-in-command. Flood proved as good as his potential had promised, despite significant personal problems that surfaced after the disaster. Before *Stolen Arrows* he had been a newlywed, but six months after his return from the Barents run he was still waking up screaming. Finally Patricia Flood had given him an ultimatum—choose the submarine or her. Two months later, here he still was, and Patricia had moved on. He attended his wounds by surrounding himself with his machines. A talented mechanic, Flood had rebuilt motorcycles and vintage sports cars as a junior officer, and returned to the hobby to kill the time when he was away from the ship. There were times when Dillinger wondered whether Flood had made the right decision, but before he could urge the younger officer to try again with Patricia, she had announced her engagement to a civilian doctor. It had been a crushing blow to Flood, and since then he had doubled his hours on the ship, burying himself in his work.

"Evening, Skipper." Flood hadn't called him "Captain" since *Stolen Arrows*.

"What's the latest, XO?"

Flood withdrew a pack of gum with a raised eyebrow. Dillinger nodded. Flood had started smoking again after Patricia left, his habit restricted now that Navy Regulations made submarines nonsmoking areas.

"If not for engineering we'd be in the channel now. Schluss has been frothing at the mouth since the hurricane evacuation order came down."

"Bring him in."

Flood withdrew a small walkie-talkie from his belt. He summoned the engineer and a few seconds later there were two knocks on the door. The khaki-clad form of Lieutenant Commander Pat Schluss filled the small doorway.

"Cap'n, nice of you to show up," Schluss joshed with a bright, genuine smile.

Dillinger had recruited Schluss, the old damage control assistant from the *Tucson*, to take over as *Hampton*'s chief engineer. He was stocky, prematurely balding, while the remainder of his bearlike frame was absurdly hairy. He had a pockmarked, round, open face with dark, blunt eastern-European features. As if mocking his own lack of good looks, he wore thick, black, plastic-framed Coke-bottle glasses and refused to consider contact lenses or laser vision surgery. Oddly and mysteriously, Schluss—despite his looks—was completely irresistible to women and would have had the best social life aboard had it not been for the extreme hours he put in taking care of the nuclear beast. He was invariably optimistic and cheerful, finding humor in even the blackest situations. Back on the *Tucson*, Schluss was always the first officer to arrive at the liberty port bar. In Fort Lauderdale two years ago, Patty had commandeered the stage of a strip club and danced crazily in nothing but his boxers, his hairy chubbiness surrounded by cheering dancers, the officer's generously sized privates snaking out the slit in his shorts as he undulated, blind drunk, on the stage. The next morning Schluss had been sober as a judge as he professionally conned the *Tucson* out to sea for the Panamanian emergency.

Unlike Mercury-Pryce, Flood and the other ex-*Tucson* crew Dillinger had recruited for the *Hampton*, Schluss showed no signs of the trauma of the Barents Sea run, stubbornly remaining his old self. Patty's new and heavy responsibilities as the ship's chief engineer he accepted as if they were nothing more than an inconsequential errand. The incredible difficulty of the chief engineer billet had made young men old decades before their time, but Schluss acted as if he had dreamed· up the position for himself. He relished the job, from its piles of paperwork to the observation of the thousands of sacraments and rituals of the Navy's nuclear program. Schluss was the high priest of the nuclear temple, his flock composed of his nuclear-trained officers and enlisted men, and the machinery that took up nearly two-thirds of the ship's hull. Schluss regularly scolded and encouraged and talked to that machinery just as he did his men, as attuned to the living spirit of the ship as Dillinger was.

"Good to be here, Eng." Dillinger smirked. "Let me amend that. I'd rather be about two hundred miles east of here right now. Any chance your propulsion plant will allow me to get going anytime soon?"

Schluss became serious as he gave Dillinger a detailed report and requested to test the seawater and main steam systems, and Dillinger denied the requests and ordered Schluss to line both of them up for normal operation. Schluss swallowed, his normally open expression darkening.

"How long before propulsion's on the main engines?" Dillinger asked.

Schluss sighed. "Six hours. We should be ready to go by zero one thirty. Maybe two in the morning."

Dillinger glanced at Flood. This was a decision only Dillinger could make. Not even the squadron commander could weigh in on this—it was between him and God and NavSea's Naval Reactors Division. "Engineer, this is a 'tactical situation' as defined by the Reactor Plant Manual," he said formally. "Therefore, I'm ordering you to use an emergency heat-up rate to bring the reactor into the power range as fast as practicable and execute an emergency startup of the main steam system."

Schluss, still frowning, came to attention. "Sir, request permission to start the reactor, warm up with emergency heat-up rates and emergency start the engineroom."

"Granted," Dillinger said, glancing at his watch.

After the worried engineer left, Flood stood. "Skipper, if Patty's cooking the beast with emergency rates, we'll be ready to go within the hour, which means I'd better get what crew we have stationed."

"Let me know what gaps you're filling."

"Aye, sir. Request permission to station the maneuvering watch."

Dillinger nodded, returning to formality. "XO, station the maneuvering watch."

"Station the maneuvering watch, aye," Flood repeated back, then disappeared.

Dillinger was alone in the tiny sea cabin. He unpacked his laptop and plugged it in. The overhead speaker of the 1MC announcing system suddenly blared, "*Station . . . the maneuvering watch!*" Immediately a hundred footfalls and shouts came from outside the stateroom's door as the men hurried through the passageway, stationing the watch. For a long moment Dillinger sat back and listened to the noise, the sounds before an underway always an intoxicating music for him.

A knock came at the door. Mercury-Pryce stood by the doorjamb, his raingear dripping onto the rubber-coated deckplates outside the stateroom.

"Yes, Nav?"

"Captain, I've stationed the watch as officer of the deck." He paused, a flash of worry crossing his features. It hadn't occurred to him that Dillinger would invoke the dangerous emergency reactor procedure, and it had evidently rattled him. The old Merc of the *Tucson* days would have been indifferent, Dillinger thought. "Request permission to raise and lower masts as necessary, single up all lines, and rotate and radiate."

Dillinger granted the requests, then leaned back in the chair. "Who's relieving you for the underway?"

"Lieutenant Scottson, sir. He just arrived aboard."

"Very well. Once you're relieved, I want a marked-up watch-quarter-and-station bill."

"Aye, aye, sir. Also, Captain, topside reports the commodore's golf cart approaching from down the pier."

"Thank you, Nav," Dillinger said, dismissing the officer, and wondering what the commodore was doing making a personal visit when the tender ship *Olympus* was about to sail. As if in accompaniment to his thoughts, the 1MC speaker overhead clicked.

"*Commander, Submarine Squadron Eight, arriving!*"

Dillinger grabbed a fresh towel and hurried out of his stateroom, down the ladder to the middle level and aft to the crew's mess. While he waited he caught the supply chief's eye and ordered coffee. Two wet khaki legs came out of the hatchway set into the overhead as Captain Joseph Kraft emerged into the ship. He turned and saw Dillinger, and broke into a warm grin.

"Welcome aboard, Commodore," Dillinger said, handing his boss the towel. Kraft's wet hand grabbed his in a tight grip as he dried his soaked face. "Come on up to my stateroom."

Kraft hung his raingear in the passageway and draped the towel around his neck. In Dillinger's sea cabin, the supply chief had spread a linen tablecloth on the café table and set up coffee service for two, a crystal ash tray, a silver cigar cutter and a USS *Hampton* cigarette lighter off to the side. Kraft folded his tall frame into one of the bench seats, Dillinger sitting opposite, his eyebrow lifted as he poured coffee for them both. Kraft withdrew a leather case from his pocket, opened it and withdrew two Cuban torpedo Cohiba cigars, expertly cutting the ends off. He handed one to Dillinger and puffed his to life, then handed the lighter to Dillinger. Dillinger fired up the cigar, the mellow, smooth Cuban tobacco's aroma reminding him of the hours he and Vornado had spent at Kraft's poolside barbecues.

"How's the *Hampton*, B.K.?" Kraft asked, a serious expression in the faded blue eyes below the frown formed by his bushy eyebrows. Kraft was a head taller than Dillinger, with a full head of gray-blond hair cut into a tough-looking flattop. He carried twenty pounds he could afford to lose, but on his athletic frame it seemed to make him that much more imposing. Like

Dillinger, Kraft had also fought in the ring at the Academy, but he had graduated three years before Dillinger and Vornado arrived for plebe year.

Dillinger gave Kraft a short update on the ship, mentioning casually that he had ordered an emergency reactor startup, his eye on the commodore to see how he would react.

"That's why I came down," he said in his gravelly voice, "to suggest you declare this a tactical situation and emergency start, but I can see you're way ahead of me."

"We'll be underway within the hour, sir." Dillinger puffed the cigar and blew a smoke ring into the overhead. As if to punctuate his statement, the 1MC system suddenly clicked and Schluss' voice boomed throughout the ship, "*The reactor . . . is critical*!"

Kraft nodded, making no move to leave. "I've got something else for you," he said, his face expressionless. Kraft had always been a poker player, Dillinger thought. He waited patiently, trying to keep his own face inscrutable. "I won't know for certain for a few hours or a few days, but there's trouble brewing and I'm going to need to task the *Hampton*."

Dillinger blinked. "Are you talking about a mission, Commodore?"

Kraft nodded, his eyes unreadable.

"But sir, Natalie's almost at thirty-seven weeks. She's about to pop. I don't want to be on the other side of the globe, not now." Dillinger knew it was a weak argument. Natalie's condition wouldn't keep the submarine in port, and if Dillinger pushed the issue too hard he'd argue himself out of a job. He paused, looking into Kraft's unblinking eyes. "But then, if it weren't important, you wouldn't ask."

"B.K.," Kraft said slowly, "it's important."

"What can you tell me about this, sir?"

Kraft took a puff of the cigar and narrowed his eyes in the smoke. "The trouble's in EastLant. And I need your FY-zero-eight."

Dillinger stared back at the boss. Vornado had been right. EastLant—the eastern Atlantic—was suspiciously close to France. And the only reason Kraft would need *Hampton* instead of one of the other half dozen ships of the squadron was because of the Fiscal Year 2008 sonar upgrade recently performed to the BQQ-5E sonar system, which only *Seawolf, Connecticut, Jimmy Carter, Hampton, Texas* and *Virginia* had, and which made them all "next generation" sonar platforms, an order of magnitude more powerful than the previous sonar systems. And the three Seawolf-class ships were indisposed; the first in a drydock overhaul and the other two being refitted for special operations duty. A crisis that required their particular sonar platform had to involve catching a quiet submarine, Dillinger thought. He wanted to ask if the "trouble" were about the French ballistic missile submarine force, but knew that he couldn't divulge that Vornado had told him about the weekly ops. Vornado should have kept his mouth shut about that, but at least Dillinger could keep his secrets. It was possible that Rachel might not.

"*Virginia*?" Dillinger asked, knowing Kraft knew he meant, *why can't they go instead of us?*

"Problems," Kraft said, gesturing with his cigar. "Bugs in SES."

SES stood for sonar equipment space, which meant *Virginia*'s sonar was temporarily out of commission.

"What about the *Texas*?" Vornado's ship also had the FY-08 upgrade. "Vornado's armed and dangerous."

"*Texas* is going with you. You'll be assigned as a task group to a NATO task force commander."

"So, Commodore, this mission? Is it real? Or an exercise?"

Kraft's face settled into lines of fatigue, as if he had just taken on the weight of ten years. "It's just an exercise. But I can't begin to tell you how urgent it is. Your torpedo room loadout is all warshots except for four exercise ADCAP Mark 48s. There's a French nuclear ballistic missile submarine, *Le Vigilant*, that is departing from Port Brest in two days. It's manned by their submarine force's best crew, and commanded by a naval warfare genius, a guy who made his bones in their attack submarine force. You remember that scrape last year with the North Koreans, when they threatened the Japanese with that nuclear missile diesel submarine lurking off the Japanese coast? The sub that mysteriously sank with all hands even as we were on the way to take it down ourselves?"

Dillinger nodded. The Pacific submarine force had gotten the top secret orders to scramble a Los Angeles submarine out of Guam to sink the nearly whisper-quiet North Korean diesel, but before they were a day into the emergency op, the threat had ceased to exist but for an oil slick off the Japanese coast. The secret debriefing claimed that the diesel submarine's crew had made a grave submerged mistake, costing it the life of its crew, yet more testimony to the dangers of operating submarines.

"Well, they didn't go down from a short circuit in the trim system flood valve. They went down from a hole made by a torpedo. A French torpedo. Commander Jean-Paul Gardes' torpedo, to be more specific. The same man who is now in command of the SSBN *Le Vigilant*. Your exercise opponent."

It made sense, Dillinger thought. France and Japan had been involved in a military hardware sale when Japan finally made the commitment to employ nuclear power for its naval forces. It would have been the perfect opportunity for the French to demonstrate to the Japanese the abilities of their submarine firecontrol systems and weapons.

Dillinger turned his thoughts to the French sub commander. "So he's good."

Kraft rolled his eyes. "We should be so good, B.K. He was born to be a submarine captain, from what our intel says."

"So Vornado and I go out and find him, then pretend to sink him? Is that all?"

"That's the meat of it, B.K. The rest is in here." Kraft withdrew a compact disk from his raincoat. "I need you to sign the receipt accepting custody of that. The op order for what's officially called Exercise *Urgent Surge* is in there, but I'll need to bring you to periscope depth once you're out to give you last-minute instructions to vector you to the rendezvous point. Unfortunately, that may mean bringing you up in the middle of the hurricane."

"Aye, aye, sir," Dillinger said.

"There's also a full briefing package on the CD about the French boomer and its crew. Particularly about Commander Jean-Paul Gardes, captain of *Le Vigilant*. Find out who he is and how to beat him. Then get out there and put four exercise torpedoes into the son of a bitch before he puts any into you. And before he launches an exercise ICBM at the Atlantic test range."

Dillinger nodded. "Commodore, if I may ask, why now? Why is this exercise suddenly so urgent?"

Kraft sighed as he looked down at the desk. "Our intelligence people think that there is an imminent threat of a French boomer being taken by an Algerian terrorist group called the GIA. We've tried to convince the French that the security threats against their ballistic missile subs are severe and could have terrible consequences, but so far the French have remained stubbornly independent and have turned down NATO security assistance. They've gone so far as to suggest that even if a boomer gets taken, their own attack submarines can deal with it and sink a rogue boomer. The purpose of the exercise is to convince them that their ballistic sub is too quiet. It will easily evade their own attack subs."

Dillinger narrowed his eyes at Kraft. "So how is it that we got involved?"

"It's complicated. To dumb it down, it was the president's idea." The president was a former Navy officer, a SEAL commando who had made a splash in American party politics after his retirement when the Iraq war wound down. "He made a bet with the French president that they couldn't get by our submarines. But believe me, this is more than a good-natured wager between national leaders. If that boomer gets by us, while we all look like fools, it would be much worse. If we fail, the Senate Armed Services Committee may insist on some very radical measures to take care of foreign ballistic missile submarine threats."

"Radical measures? Like what?" Dillinger asked.

Kraft glanced at his watch, then seemed to debate with himself whether to tell Dillinger the truth. He took a deep breath. "Obviously this is so far elevated beyond top secret as to be something that was never said to you, B.K., but the answer is, we'd get orders to send out our attack submarines to sink every foreign boomer that exists. Out of self-defense. But an op like that would be a gigantic pooch-screwing cluster fuck. People would get killed. Our foreign neighbors would take it the wrong way. For God's sake, someone aboard one of the foreign boomers might even decide to launch an ICBM, thinking it the first indication of war."

Dillinger nodded. "But if we win and take down the French sub, doesn't that hurt our case that the French need to be careful of security? Wouldn't they return to complacency?"

"The French won't see it like that. They'll interpret it that we were right about all of it, that we would win the exercise and that French security is lacking. And if we humiliate the independent French just enough, they'll take action so that they will never be embarrassed by us again. A lot of our citizens believe the French are a bunch of sissies. Listen, they may love white wine and brie cheese, but they also came up with Napoleon, who came this close to taking over all of civilization, and they invented the French Foreign Legion. These guys absorbed tremendous losses in WWI. They can be very tough. Don't you or your crew doubt that for a single instant." Kraft frowned. "Besides which, Congress and the president are watching you, B.K." Kraft stubbed his cigar out in the ashtray, downed the last of his coffee and stood up. He looked into Dillinger's eyes. After the last few years together, Dillinger knew the old man could see into him, despite his best efforts to keep his face neutral. "So don't fuck up."

"Aye, aye, sir," Dillinger said, his expression appropriately serious.

"Something wrong, B.K.?"

Dillinger glanced at the deck, then back at the commodore. "Oh, it's just that I'm worried about Natalie, sir. I should be with her more."

"New-father nerves," Kraft said, his large hand reaching out and clapping Dillinger on his shoulder, his voice fatherly. "Mixed with a bit of natural parental guilt. Pregnancy is always a scary thing, B.K." Kraft glanced at his watch. "I'm going to miss *Olympus*' underway if I don't get moving now, though." He opened the stateroom door and donned his dripping raingear. Dillinger walked with him down the ladder to the middle level and through the pin-drop silent crew's mess to the lower hatch of the escape trunk. Kraft handed the towel back to Dillinger and narrowed his eyes as he shook Dillinger's hand.

"Don't worry, B.K.," he said quietly, trying to avoid their conversation being overheard. "You'll get back in time to witness the birth. Until then, good luck."

"Thanks, Commodore. See you at sea."

The commodore quickly took the ladder up into the darkness of the rainy night and vanished.

"*Commander, Submarine Squadron Eight . . . departing!*" the 1MC rang out.

For a moment Dillinger stood there in dismay. *Natalie*, he thought. He needed to call her, but what would he be able to say to her? *I won't be there until you're giving birth? I have to go play in an exercise? An exercise so political that the president is betting on it?* Jesus, this run was beginning badly, and that boded ill for the rest of it. Dillinger was as superstitious as any square-rigger captain had ever been. Right on cue, a stomachache bloomed below his ribs.

4

Dillinger woke before his 0630 wakeup call. He opened his eyes wide in the pitch-black room. Something was wrong. His heart raced as he threw off the covers and sat up in his rack, then realized what was different—it was the deck. The ship was once again rolling to port, freezing for a second, then rolling back to starboard, hanging up again before rolling back to port. Dammit, he thought, he'd ordered the ship rigged for deep submergence and taken down to a thousand feet to avoid the mountainous waves of the hurricane sea state topside. He'd never given the officer of the deck permission to take the boat back shallow. He glanced at the ship control readout panel at the head of his rack while reaching for the phone to the conn, the anger rising in his throat. He blinked at the panel and put the phone back. The depth readout was steady at a thousand feet. And he hadn't dreamed the roll of the deck. The ship was taking a ten degree roll here, almost a quarter mile beneath the surface. He dressed hastily, skipping his normal shower, and hurried out to the control room.

"Captain's in control!" the on-watch quartermaster, Petty Officer Second Class A. J. Anderson, announced.

The officer of the deck was Lieutenant Mikey Selles. "Morning, Captain," he said brightly.

Dillinger nodded, his attention on the inclinometer. The bubble inside tilted over as the deck rolled to starboard, the bubble reaching seven degrees. The deck stopped and began to roll to port, the bubble continuing past zero over to ten degrees. Dillinger stared down at the digital depth gauge, which was steady at one thousand feet. He turned and glanced at Selles.

"Helen's overhead," Selles said quietly. "It's a bad day for anyone topside."

Dillinger nodded, wondering how bad the damage would be to Virginia Beach and Norfolk. It was Wednesday, the day the worst of the storm was forecasted to make landfall.

"*Conn, Radio,*" an overhead speaker crackled.

"Radio, Conn, aye," Selles called to the overhead, not using a microphone. The radio room was patched in to the "conn open mike," a control room recorder that functioned like an airliner's cockpit conversation black box and, like the latter, was in a depth-hardened container. A second unit recorded the instruments of the ship control panel and the ballast control panel, the two instruments to be recovered and studied in the event of an unexplained sinking. The conn open mike was also piped into the sonar room forward and starboard of the control room, allowing the other operators to be plugged into any developing tactical situation.

Dillinger lifted an eyebrow. There was only one reason the radio room would be calling.

"Conn, Radio, we have a signal on the VLF loop antenna."

"Radio, Conn, aye," Selles said, reaching for a phone handset. He listened for a moment, looking at Dillinger. "You sure?" He nodded. "Very well." He hung up the phone.

"Captain, the first letter of our daily call sign is onboard from the VLF loop."

Dillinger tried to act as if it were completely routine. The VLF loop antenna received both VLF—very low frequency—radio waves and ELF waves. Extremely low frequency radio waves were the only ones strong enough to penetrate this deep into the ocean. Transmitting on ELF required a vast radio antennae farm with a dozen quarter-mile-tall radio towers requiring so much electricity that they were powered by their own power plant.

On the East Coast there were only two of them, one in Annapolis and the other in Cutler, Maine, both used for communicating with submarines far at sea. While it seemed handy to be able to talk to a deeply submerged submarine, even if it required bulky, expensive gear, it was a low-data-rate system, taking almost twenty minutes just to transmit one letter or number. As a result, ELF was only used for transmitting a submarine's call sign, a secret two-alphanumeric random sequence assigned in advance. The ELF system would transmit the call sign to order a submarine to periscope depth so that she could receive the high-data-rate transmissions from the satellite on the periscope or HDR antenna.

But coming to periscope depth in a category five hurricane—one severe enough that it tossed the ship this deep—was risky. The only reason ComSubLant would order them shallow would be if there were an emergency. Kraft's mysterious EastLant mission had become a reality, Dillinger thought.

"Conn, Radio, second letter of our callsign is onboard the VLF loop. Recommend coming to periscope depth."

"Radio, Conn, aye." Selles looked up. "Captain, we're ordered to PD in this." He gestured helplessly to the overhead. "We'll be like a cork in a blender."

Dillinger frowned. Commodore Kraft had really done it, he thought. Their tasking would take them to the surface in this sea state. "OOD, sound the collision alarm and rig ship for collision." That would alert the crew, get every man out of the bunk, get phonetalkers on the circuits in every space and prepare for a casualty. The waves topside were likely half a shiplength tall. Dillinger wasn't even sure he could get the radio antenna dry enough to receive a transmission from the satellite. But if it were urgent enough to call them to periscope depth, it must be urgent enough to risk the probable damage.

"Yes, sir," Selles acknowledged. "Chief of the Watch, sound the collision alarm and rig ship for collision."

The chief of the watch's voice came over the 1MC.

"*Rig ship for collision!*" A whooping, blaring alarm blasted out of the announcing speakers throughout the ship. The chief of the watch made his announcement a second time.

Dillinger pulled the 1MC microphone out of the overhead. "Attention all hands, this is the captain. We've just been ordered to periscope depth in the middle of the storm. Obviously, there is an urgent transmission that we need to receive, but proceeding shallow puts the ship at risk. All hands inspect their spaces for stowage for sea and prepare for high sea state. Casualty assistance team, lay to the crew's mess and stand by. Battlestations ship control party, report to control. Carry on." He put the microphone back in its cradle, noticing how serious young Selles looked.

He turned from the conn and saw Flood arrive in control, zipping up his coveralls. He looked at Dillinger with a knowing expression.

"Officer of the Deck, station the battlestations ship control party."

"Aye, sir," Selles said.

Eddie Scottson walked into control, rubbing his eyes. Scottson was the ship's damage control assistant, one of the engineer's principal lieutenants, responsible for the extensive engineering systems forward of the reactor compartment and, as his title indicated, the king of recovery from any ship-threatening casualty. He was older than most lieutenants, having entered an officer accession program after achieving success as an enlisted man in the surface Navy. "Cap'n," he said, nodding to Dillinger. Scottson and Selles conferred on the other side of the conn. Selles stepped off the conn platform.

"Captain, I've been relieved by Mr. Scottson as officer of the deck. Ship is at one thousand feet, course east, all ahead one-third with propulsion on the main engines, running main coolant pumps one through four in slow speed."

"Very well," Dillinger said.

"Helm, Quartermaster!" Scottson called. "This is Lieutenant Scottson; I have the deck and the conn!"

"Helm, aye," the battlestations helmsman said.

"Quartermaster, aye," Anderson replied from aft.

"Captain," Scottson said formally, "request to come shallow in preparation to coming to periscope depth."

Dillinger shook his head. "It won't do you any good to clear baffles at 150 feet. We won't hear anything upstairs but the roar of the waves. Clear baffles deep, then proceed immediately to periscope depth. Get up at eight knots, steep angle. I want you to use the Type Eighteen periscope, and be careful. It's altogether possible that the force of the waves could shear it off. If that happens, leave it up or you'll risk flooding us through the hull penetration. If you think the scope is in danger, retract it. And don't risk the HDR mast. We'll raise the BRA-34 and sacrifice it if necessary. Got it?"

"Yessir," Scottson said seriously. "Attention in control, radio and sonar," he barked. "My intention is to clear baffles deep and then proceed rapidly and immediately to periscope depth with no shallow baffle clear. Once up, we'll raise the BRA-34 and catch the broadcast, then proceed back deep."

"Conn, Sonar, aye," the sonar chief's voice came over the circuit.

"Conn, Radio, aye," the radio chief said.

"Sonar, Conn, report all contacts." Scottson stood on the conn and frowned at the sonar waterfall display. It was like staring at a television set with no signal, the screen covered with static and snow. The noise of the waves overhead was so loud that the other noises of the sea were drowned out.

"Conn, Sonar, hold no sonar contacts."

"Very well, Sonar, clearing baffles to the right. Helm, right full rudder, all ahead standard, steady course two seven zero."

"Right full rudder, all ahead standard, steady course

two seven zero, Helm aye. My rudder is right full and Maneuvering answers, all ahead standard, sir."

The ship slowly turned in the deep sea.

"Passing course south, sir," the helmsman reported.

"Very well," Scottson said, waiting. He was turning the ship to "clear baffles," to have the sonar sphere of the BQQ-5 look astern of them, in the area of the normal blind spot behind the screw. The towed array, a long hydrophone resembling a thick cable, pulled behind them by a mile-long steel cable, monitored higher frequencies and was able to hear behind them, but it could miss a lower frequency noise back there.

Dillinger's thoughts about the towed array reminded him—if they went to periscope depth with the towed array streamed, the force of the storm could shear it off.

"Off'sa'deck, after you're baffle clear and before you go shallow, retract the towed array."

Scottson glanced at him, frowning. He knew it was bad if the towed array had to be pulled in.

Dillinger glanced around the room, suddenly feeling the same way he'd felt in the bedroom of the house before he left, wondering if it would be damaged by the hurricane.

"Passing course two six zero to the right, ten degrees from ordered course, sir."

"Very well, Helm."

"Steady course two seven zero, sir."

"Very well. Sonar, Conn, steady course west, report all contacts."

"Conn, Sonar, aye."

There was a long pause. Dillinger glanced at the sonar repeater, but it was the same mass of jumbled static it had been before.

"Conn, Sonar, no contacts."

"Very well," Scottson said to the overhead. "Sonar, Conn, retracting the towed array. Chief of the Watch, retract the towed array."

The chief acknowledged and operated a lever on the upper back vertical section of the ballast control panel.

"Towed array coming in," he reported. A click sounded from his panel. He looked at the indication and swiveled in his chair toward Scottson. "Officer of the Deck, towed array is retracted."

Scottson took a deep breath, as if preparing himself for a footrace. "Attention in control, radio and sonar, proceeding to periscope depth. Helm, all ahead two-thirds. Diving Officer, make your depth six five feet, steep angle." Scottson grabbed the 7MC mike, the closed-circuit loudspeaker used between the control room and maneuvering. "Maneuvering, Conn, make turns for eight knots."

"Make turns for eight knots, Conn, Maneuvering, aye," the 7MC speaker blared.

"Ten degree rise on the bowplanes," Kenderson at the diving officer station ordered. "Sternplanes, twenty degree up angle on the ship."

The deck slowly inclined upward. Dillinger grabbed the handrail at the periscope stand, watching the digital depth gauge reel off the numerals.

"Nine hundred feet, sir," Kenderson announced.

The deck angled upward further. Scottson braced himself aft of the number two periscope.

"Seven hundred feet."

The roll of the deck grew worse. The inclinometer showed the tilt growing to ten degrees, with a larger roll to starboard. The seas were coming from the south. Already the motion of the ship was making Dillinger dizzy.

"Six hundred feet."

There was a tense silence in the room as the crew waited to arrive shallow.

"Five hundred feet," Kenderson announced. "Four hundred. Chief of the Watch, mark level, depth control two."

"Three zero percent."

"Very well. Three hundred feet. Sternplanes, ease your bubble to up fifteen degrees. Helm, bowplanes to five degrees rise. Two hundred feet, sir. Sternplanes, ease the bubble to up five. One five zero feet, sir."

The deck rolled to port beyond the ten degree mark, past fifteen degrees, finally holding at a twenty degree list, then suddenly rolling hard to starboard to twenty-two degrees. A bang sounded from behind the attack center—something had fallen out of a cabinet.

"Get us up, Dive," Scottson ordered. "Lookaround number two scope."

"One hundred feet, sir, speed eight knots. Nine zero feet. Helm, ten degrees rise on the bowplanes."

The digital depth gauge spun suddenly, going from ninety feet down to 110, then spinning up to eighty feet.

"Depth gauge becoming unstable, OOD, calling depth on the aux depth gauge. Eighty feet."

The deck had been rolling but had kept a constant up angle as they approached the surface, but suddenly it pitched downward. Dillinger gripped the periscope rail harder, his knuckles white. The ship plunged to a steep down angle.

"One six zero feet, loss of depth control," Kenderson called, announcing the obvious.

"Let's try again, Dive," Scottson ordered patiently, making rotations at the periscope.

Dillinger looked up at the periscope video camera, but it was too dark this far down to see anything. Kenderson pulled the ship out of its dive and began his second run on the surface.

"Twenty degrees rise on the bowplanes, ten degree up bubble," he ordered, leaning over again.

The ship rocked as it ascended the second time. Once again Kenderson called out the depth, the ship see-sawing on the way up. The deck rose to a steep up angle. This time Kenderson was losing it on the shallow end.

"Off'sa'deck, loss of depth control! Ship is broaching."

Dillinger watched the periscope video. One moment the screen was black, the next the view cleared with the

periscope view far above the trough of a wave. The deck
was angling down just as a huge wave rose in the crosshairs of the view. Dillinger's mouth opened in awe as
he stared at it. Even on the small video repeater he
could tell the wave was mountainous, perhaps sixty or
seventy feet tall as it towered over the scope view. It
quickly grew nearer as the deck inclined farther down.
The deck boomed beneath Dillinger's boots as the ship
took a violent lurch to port and plunged dramatically
downward.

"Two hundred feet, sir," Kenderson said, furious with
himself for his failure to keep the ship steady. It wasn't
his fault, and they'd be here all morning trying this. Dillinger's stomach sank and convulsed. He felt the contrac-
tion as he was about to vomit, but he'd skipped the
evening meal the night before and his stomach was
empty. He dry heaved for a few seconds, water leaking
from his eyes.

"Off'sa'deck," Dillinger said loudly. "I have the conn.
Attention in control. I intend to surface the ship with
the periscope retracted and the BRA-34 bumped out of
the sail. That will allow us more speed than eight knots."

"Quartermaster," Scottson called as he lowered the
periscope, "Captain has the conn, I retain the deck.
Lowering number two scope."

Dillinger stepped up to the periscope platform, hand-
over-handing the rails until he stood aft of and between
the two periscopes.

"Radio, Sonar, prepare to emergency surface. Radio,
as soon as the BRA-34 gets the broadcast, inform the
conn."

"Conn, Radio, aye."

Dillinger took a deep breath, just as Scottson had before the first attempt at coming shallow.

"Chief of the Watch," he said. "Bump the BRA-34
five feet out of the sail."

A thump of hydraulics sounded as the radio mast
raised slightly.

"BRA-34 bumped five feet, sir."

"Helm, all ahead full! Chief of the Watch, emergency blow the forward group!"

Martinez stared at him in astonishment, but stood up from his chair, gripping the handholds on the panel, and grabbed the forward gleaming stainless-steel lever above the port vertical section of his console.

"Emergency blow the forward group, aye, sir." He pulled down the plunger interlock at the end of the lever, then quickly rotated it into the overhead.

A loud clunking noise came from the chief's panel, immediately followed by a blast of sound roaring into the room, and instantly a rolling cloud of condensation spewed out from behind Martinez's panel into the space, the cold white fog appearing so fast that after two seconds Dillinger couldn't see Kenderson or the helmsman or planesman.

The emergency blow system put the large bottles of ultrahigh-pressure air into the forward ballast tanks through two eight-inch ball valves. Within seconds there would be enough high-pressure air roaring into the ballast tanks that the seawater inside them would flow out the bottom vents and the ship would become hundreds of tons lighter. The system was sized to be able to save the ship from a catastrophic flooding emergency at test depth, so in the lower pressure of shallow water it became that much more powerful. In three seconds the ballast tanks had gone dry.

"Chief, emergency blow the aft group!" Dillinger shouted over the roar.

The chief acknowledged from inside the fog bank. Dillinger couldn't see what he was doing, but suddenly the howl of the emergency blow system became an ear-piercing shriek as the aft system's rush of air commenced.

"Secure the forward blow," Dillinger ordered, counting ten heartbeats before making the second order. "Secure the aft blow!"

The diving klaxon rang out throughout the ship. Martinez's voice came over the 1MC, "*Surface, surface, surface!*"

"Ship is broached," Kenderson shouted from the clearing fog.

The deck's roll—severe before—was suddenly alarming. The deck rolled and kept going. For a frightening instant Dillinger was sure the ship was about to capsize. The deck rolled so far that he lost his footing and dangled from the periscope rail. What had been a floor had become a wall, and down beneath his feet was what had been the bulkhead. A heavy object flew past him, almost grazing his ear and then smashing into the fathometer console; a heavy technical manual that had come out of the bolted-shut bookcase. Dillinger heard two men scream, as he became dimly aware of a body flying past him just as the tech manual had. The second collision with the broken fathometer was a sickening crunch of bone and flesh.

The deck stopped its mad roll, but it hung up, making no move to right itself. Frozen in its sixty degree tilt, the ship began to pitch upward. Other men began to fall in the space as the deck—still rolled over nearly completely sideways—tilted upward into a forty degree angle. Everything that wasn't permanently bolted to the deck flew throughout the crazily sideways and half-upside-down world. A heavy steel valve handle tucked into brackets in the overhead fell out and came rocketing toward Dillinger. It hit the periscope pole with a tremendous crash and continued aft, a howl of pain arising from the aft part of the room.

"Oh, Jesus, Murphy's hurt bad!" a voice shouted.

The deck suddenly flew over to starboard, and all the men who'd fallen to the port side were rocketed to the starboard side. The up angle remained precipitously steep—if the diving officer's chair bolts gave, he'd fall right onto Dillinger.

The 7MC speaker suddenly squawked from what had been the overhead. "*Reactor scram!*"

"Oh, fuck!" a voice shouted, the cacophony of sound breaking out in the room as the air handlers wound down. The deck rolled back from the precipitous starboard roll and continued to port.

They had just lost the reactor. Without it, regaining control of the ship depended on getting back deep.

"All stop," Dillinger ordered.

"Ship is still broached," Kenderson said.

"*Radio, Conn, broadcast aboard, BRA-34 coming down!*" the overhead speaker rasped.

"Maneuvering, Conn, shift propulsion to the emergency propulsion motor," Dillinger barked into the 7MC microphone. "Advise when ready to answer bells."

The deck bucked under Dillinger, throwing him forward between the periscopes to the desk at the forward railing of the conn. He grabbed the sloping part of the desk before his head smashed into it. Out of his peripheral vision he sensed objects and bodies flying forward. For just an instant he shut his eyes, not wanting to see this horrible moment, but he forced them back open. The digital depth gauge came into focus, its inscrutable numerals reading 289. How in God's name had they gone that deep so fast?

Dillinger pushed himself up to a standing position, realizing that the deck had become more of a downward-pointing ramp than a horizontal surface.

"Dive, mark your bubble," Dillinger called, the ship control panel blocked by Kenderson's back.

"Down five zero degrees, Captain! Depth, three five zero feet!"

Dillinger tried to find the 7MC mike. "Maneuvering, Conn, status of propulsion!"

He let go of the microphone and it hung, disturbingly, almost parallel to the deck. The ship was plunging down.

"Maneuvering, Conn, propulsion shifted to the emergency propulsion motor, ready to answer all bells!"

"*All back full!*" Dillinger shouted.

"Four hundred feet," Kenderson called. "Still diving."

"Chief of the Watch, vent the aft group, emergency blow the forward group!"

"Venting aft, blowing forward!" Martinez shouted. The roar of the HP air system sounded again. The steep dive must have dumped most of the air out of the forward ballast tanks.

"Six hundred feet. Seven hundred feet! Down angle is six zero degrees!"

Jesus, Dillinger breathed. A sixty degree dive—they were headed for crush depth with the emergency blow system almost exhausted.

The down angle increased until Dillinger was sure he was staring straight down at the ship control console. The forward bulkhead had become a wall.

"Captain," Kenderson shouted, his voice strained and trembling, "down angle *seventy degrees*!"

Mother of God, a voice in Dillinger's mind screamed in panic, *we're in a vertical dive.*

"Twelve hundred feet, sir!" Kenderson said. "Thirteen hundred! Test depth, sir, and down bubble is seven one degrees!"

They could use the reactor, Dillinger thought. Fifty years ago the *Thresher* sank because, in an emergency flooding, the crew had followed procedures and shut down the steam system during a reactor scram, but while it may have saved the reactor, it had doomed the ship. If Dillinger pulled too much steam from the boilers with the reactor shut down, the pressurized water circulating in the reactor would become cold enough to restart the reactor, and when it restarted on its own, it would be so out of control the energy release in the reactor compartment would be certain to breach the hull from the force of the steam pressure. The engineers called it a cold water accident precipitating a prompt critical rapid disassembly, but the forward sailors—nuclear laymen—felt free to label it what it was: *an explosion.* But in the seconds before that happened, Dillinger would have the massive thermal power of the wounded reactor to save them rather than the diluted and weak emergency propulsion motor. But shifting propulsion back to the main engines would take vital minutes, and God knew, the engineroom crew would have to climb a vertical wall to get to the clutch to shift propulsion, and while he waited, what little astern power from the EPM he had would be lost.

This is it, that voice in his mind said again. *This is how you die. This is when you die. Today, Wednesday morning before breakfast, before coffee, before your morning shower, you'll be inside a steel coffin, imploded inside a helpless wreck that is sinking because you made a mistake following insane orders to come to periscope depth in a hurricane, and because of you, your wife will be a widow and your child will be an orphan. Any other husband would have let his exec take the ship out—*

"Dive!" Dillinger yelled. "Mark depth and bubble!"

"Fourteen hundred ten feet, ninety feet from crush depth, down angle is sixty-five degrees, sir!"

Wait, Dillinger thought, the angle was coming off. The dive was easing.

"Sixty degrees, sir."

Dillinger waited, praying every schoolboy prayer he'd ever learned.

"Thirteen fifty feet, down fifty-five degrees."

He watched the ship control readout, biting his lip so hard he could taste blood.

"Conn, Maneuvering," Schluss' voice rang out on the 7MC, "reactor is critical!"

Only a few more minutes, Dillinger thought, and Schluss could get the reactor back online.

"Thirteen hundred feet, ship's bubble, down four seven degrees. *We're pulling out of the dive, Skipper!*"

The sounds of the crew cheering floated through the thick air to Dillinger's ears, sounding as if they were coming in slow motion. A dim, distorted voice reached him as if it came from the bottom of a well—*El Jefe saved the ship*. It took Dillinger a long, stunned second to realize the voice was talking about him. *It was over*, he thought. *They'd live.* He wondered, in a back corner of his mind, if it had been the prayers that had saved him or just instinctive seamanship. With the angle coming off, in no time they'd be going upward again from the air in the forward ballast tanks.

"Chief of the Watch," he ordered, his voice deep and authoritative, "secure the emergency blow forward, vent the forward main ballast tanks!"

"Twelve fifty feet, down angle ten degrees," Kenderson reported.

"Conn, Maneuvering," Schluss called on the 7MC, a distinct note of pride mixed with relief in his voice, "reactor is in the power range, electric plant is in a normal full-power lineup, secure rig for reduced electrical and recommend shifting propulsion to the main engines!"

"Helm, all stop." Dillinger reached for the 7MC mike. "Maneuvering, Conn, shift propulsion to the main engines!"

"Twelve hundred feet, ship's bubble down five degrees, sir," Kenderson said.

"We have casualties in control, sir," Eddie Scottson said quietly. "We need the corpsman ASAP."

"Call him on the 1MC," Dillinger ordered.

"Eleven hundred feet, ship is angling up."

"Conn, Maneuvering, propulsion shifted to the main engines, ready to answer all bells!" the 7MC speakers squawked with Schluss' voice.

"Helm, all ahead standard," Dillinger ordered. "Diving Officer, regain depth control and make your depth one thousand feet!"

"Regain depth control, make my depth one thousand, Diving Officer aye." Kenderson sounded like he'd never been in danger. Dillinger shot a look over at him. Kenderson's hair was plastered on his scalp, completely wet from sweat.

"*Corpsman, report to control!*" Scottson said on the 1MC.

Dillinger took a deep breath, but as he let it out he saw the blood on the deck. There was so much of it; it seemed as if someone had emptied a gallon of red paint over the aft part of the room. He turned and saw Petty Officer Dick Murphy, the firecontrol technician of the watch, lying in the glistening red puddle, his face stained red, his forehead a mass of gore. Lying beside him was the valve handle of the inboard induction system, which had let go from the overhead brackets during the dive.

"Steady at one thousand feet, ship's angle zero, sir," Kenderson said.

The deck still rolled, just slightly, from the waves high overhead.

Dillinger rubbed his eyes. They'd lived to tell the tale, he thought, but what a hell of a way to start the run. His head spun as he watched the corpsman attend to Murphy and the other injured watchstanders. Whatever had been important enough to call them from deep in a hurricane had to be damned serious.

"Radio, Conn, did you get our message traffic?"

"*Conn, Radio, yes,*" the overhead speaker rattled. "*We have one message, marked 'flash,' personal for commanding officer.*"

"Radio, Conn, aye. Mr. Scottson, take the conn," Dillinger ordered. "Get reports of damage and casualties from all stations." He stepped down from the conn and aft to the navigation tables, where firecontrol technician Dick Murphy lay, his head now wrapped in bloody bandages.

"Doc, how bad is it?"

The corpsman, Chief Hospital Corpsman Phelps Navone, stood and led Dillinger a few steps forward, then murmured too low for anyone else to hear. "He needs to be in a hospital. He's got a skull fracture and a serious brain injury. He may never regain consciousness here. Truth of it, Captain, I can't treat this. He could die."

Dillinger narrowed his eyes at the older man. Doc Navone had come from the surface navy; a wiry, short, intense man with a severe crew cut. He had no friends aboard, regarded as being overly somber. He had taken qualifying in submarines as if it were a life or death situation, knocking on stateroom doors at three in the morning for qualification signatures. Quirks aside, Navone seemed a fine medic, but then Dillinger had yet to see him handle a difficult case.

"We can't come back up in this, Doc," he said. "We could hurt someone else."

"You could shoot one of those SLOT buoys," Navone urged. "Tell squadron we need a medical evacuation chopper."

The phone whooped at the chief of the watch's station. He listened for a moment, then spoke loudly to Chief Navone. "Corpsman, engineer reports two severe injuries in aft compartment upper level and requests you lay aft."

Navone turned and hurried out of the room just as the radioman of the watch came in with a clipboard. He handed it to Dillinger. Dillinger opened it and read the flash message. It was short and to the point, and was just as he thought—an operation order change revising their vector to the probable intercept point for their opponent. They were also to acknowledge receipt of the messages by ejecting a submarine-launched-one-way-transmitter SLOT buoy. A SLOT was the size of a baseball bat, preloaded by the radiomen with a message, then ejected from the signal ejector, which was a small torpedo tube fired from either the aft compartment or the forward compartment. It would rise to the surface, pop out a whip antenna and transmit their message to the communications satellite overhead, while allowing the submarine to avoid detection. Dillinger could include the status of the injured in the transmission and request the medevac chopper, but before he did that he wanted to make sure Navone wasn't overreacting.

"Officer of the Deck, get the navigator and XO to my stateroom. When the doc finishes aft, send him to my stateroom and tell him to be ready to give us a status report and a recommendation. And have the radiomen break out a SLOT buoy."

Dillinger left the room and shut his stateroom door

behind him. He collapsed into his command chair, shut his eyes and cradled his head in his hands. They had been seconds away from crush depth, he thought. Best not to think too much about this, he warned himself. He realized his upper coveralls were soaked with sweat.

Hell of way to start an operation, he thought. And it wasn't even real.

5

"Wake up, asshole," Emile Everard said, his caustic voice dripping with mock contempt. "The van gets here in nineteen minutes and you're driving us out, although God alone knows why; you can barely drive a fucking car, much less a fourteen-thousand-ton nuclear submarine." Everard opened the door, reached down for his roommate's partially packed sea bag and threw it across the room. It made a perfect bull's-eye on the head of the bed, where Jacques Legard lay fast asleep despite Everard's announcement. There was motion under the covers, and the duffel bag and bedclothes fell off the bed and a beautiful woman sat up.

"Oh, hi, Aurélie," Everard said, recovering quickly, his voice as charming as if he'd just unexpectedly met her at a fruit stand on the street. He even bowed slightly in the doorway of Legard's room.

The girl brushed her raven black hair out of her eyes and waved a hungover hello.

"Jacques in there by any chance?" Everard asked as the woman dropped her head back onto the pillow.

"*Mmm*," she moaned, pointing with her hand toward the bathroom. She never had been much use first thing in the morning after two bottles of wine. Which was the funny part, since Everard had used the wine to get her to consent to sex, but all it did was put her to sleep.

"*Jacques!*" Everard called at the door to the bathroom.

"What?" The weak voice came from the other side.

Everard listened, thinking he heard the sound of retching.

"Jesus, Jacques, we make ship's movement in seventeen fucking minutes! Let's *go!* You're going to make Rhino look bad, and no one makes a fool out of *le Rhino*. Or lives to tell the tale, anyway."

"Be right there." There was the definite sound of someone throwing up, the sound of the toilet flushing, then gargling. The door opened and Jacques Legard stepped out. He was dressed in perfectly starched and creased dress whites, his ribbons perfectly aligned, his submarine insignia gleaming. Lieutenant Jacques Legard was a twenty-six-year-old youth of medium height, a slightly built, nondescript, crew cut, brown-haired, beady-brown-eyed, pasty-complected Parisian, but a man who somehow had been given God's codebook to women and used it with vigor. Rare indeed was the woman he took to bed for the second time, and rarer still was the night in port that he slept alone.

Legard gave a mock salute, his eyes steely if red-rimmed. He passed by Everard on his way back to his room and shut the door.

"And dammit, Jacques," Everard shouted through the door, "do you think, with twenty-eight million beautiful, single French women, you might possibly keep your filthy, dripping cock *out* of my girlfriend?"

"Never was your girlfriend," Legard's muted voice replied.

"Bullshit!" Everard said, raising his voice. "I was going to ask her to marry me—" Just then the door flew open and Legard emerged, his jaw clenched in his tough-guy imitation, with Everard shouting about marriage to a naked—a spectacularly and gloriously naked—Aurélie. She looked up, her body as perfect as a goddess's, and smiled at him.

"Why, Emile," she said, pleasure in her voice. "I never knew. Is that a proposal?"

Everard shook his head and threw his hands in the

air. "Fucking sail-away day," he shouted to the ceiling, and to no one. "It always *sucks!*" He hurried to the front door of their flat, where Legard stood waiting.

Lieutenant de Vaisseau Emile Everard was the senior lieutenant on board *Le Vigilant*, having reported to the shipyard construction crew at Cherbourg Shipyard exactly one week before Legard. He was older than Legard by a year, graduated the year ahead of him at the *École Navale*, but had taken a year to get a graduate degree at Oxford before reporting to the nuclear training pipeline. And though he was older and more senior than Legard, he was constantly exasperated by the younger officer's calm confidence, that same cool certainty that talked every woman within shouting distance into his bed. Which was frankly ridiculous, Everard fumed, because Legard was frankly homely while Everard had the slim, well-muscled height, the square-jawed good looks, the startlingly blue eyes and blond hair. He'd even been approached to be a recruiting model for the *Marine Nationale*. He'd even once measured the dimensions of his sex organ and browbeat Legard to do the same, and even in that category he had Legard beat. But somehow Legard always got the girl, and Everard was perpetually single and climbing the walls over it.

"You've got no *panache*," Legard had tossed off one night when Everard complained. "No *joi de vivre*. Women aren't looking for pretty looks, or muscles, or even a horse cock. They want to be taken care of in every way. They want certainty. Confidence. *Balls*."

Apparently, Everard thought, it was not something that could be taught, though he kept hoping for some of Legard's castoffs, as Aurélie might have been. He took a deep breath and grabbed his sea bag, and shut the flat door behind them. Out front the van was already waiting. They clambered in for the short ride to the base. At least the navy provided transportation on sail-away day, Everard thought, so they wouldn't have to take public transportation or worse, park their car on the

basc lot for over two months. As the van rattled down
the narrow streets, Legard put his officer's cap low over
his eyes and began snoring.

At the outer security checkpoint, everyone got out
of the van to have their identification checked. Everard roused Legard, who yawned, stood and got out for
the ID check. The van passed into the security check
shed, where it parked over an undercarriage maintenance bay to be checked for bombs or strange pack-
ages while the interior was searched and sniffed by
dogs. The security forces were taking no chances, that
was certain. The van rolled out of the checkpoint and
when each of the sailors and officers had passed
through the eight-foot-tall, heavy-barred turnstile gate,
they got back in the van for the ride to the inner security perimeter.

It was a perfect day outside, Everard thought. Sunny
and crisp, not too hot, yet not cool. It would have been
the perfect beach day, and a Friday at that. He shook
his head. Sail-away day was the worst Monday of the
year no matter what day of the week it fell on. Not only
that, but he had blown his last night to grab some female
companionship, and sixty days was a damned long time
to be without a woman.

The van rolled to a halt at the inner base security
fence, this passage much more intense than the first. The
van was not allowed to drive in, so they all disembarked,
the walk all the longer with their heavy sea bags. They
filed out, lugging their belongings, and went into a building, where each man went to a table, put the contents
of his pockets on the surface and emptied his duffel bag.
Each search area had a curtained-off enclosure where
they each removed their uniforms. Their uniforms were
checked, then a security detachment of the DPSD, the
military security police, searched their bodies. The idea
was that it would be easy to conceal a plastic Glock
under one's crotch, or even transport individual components of a plastic weapon in a body cavity. Not that the
DPSD checked every cavity—it was enough that they

could if they became suspicious. Everard could hear Legard chuckle.

"Hey, Emile—I got the female inspector," he said in a singsong, taunting voice.

"Fuck your mother, Jacques," Everard said cheerfully.

Finally the inspection was over. Everard donned his uniform, collected his things in his sea bag and shouldered it for the long walk down the missile facility pier.

"Gorgeous day," Legard said.

"At least you'll be out in the weather with the wind in your hair," Everard grumbled. I'll be splitting atoms back aft. May as well be submerged ten minutes from now."

"Well, if I can get any pretty women on the yachts to show me their breasts, I'll be sure to call you in nuclear control."

"Asshole," Everard said. Legard just smiled.

At the end of the pier, a large high-bay metal building stood, the S616-Class Missile Loading Facility. The edifice was fully a quarter mile long. Somewhere deep inside, guarded by DPSD security forces wielding automatic rifles, machine guns and grenade launchers lay the most formidable weapon system on the face of the planet, the brand new, Triomphant-class ballistic missile submarine *Le Vigilant*, under the command of the most talented submarine captain to sail the seven seas since the navy of Napoleon. Who knew, Everard thought, had *Capitaine de Frégate* Jean-Paul Gardes been alive in 1805, all of Western civilization might right now be speaking French.

At the MLF Building there was one final security check. The two officers walked into the building, this check a random one. Everard apparently lost the roll of the dice, and was called back into an inspection room for his second strip search and submission of his baggage to an invasive check by the mirthless DPSD guards. When he finished, Legard had gone on inside the cavernous building. Everard shouldered his bag and walked into the interior.

The building was impressive on the inside. The lights were so bright the temperature was much warmer than outside. It was like being in a television studio, Everard thought. He checked his watch—it was 0645 hours, and officers' call was at 0700. Not much time to spare. After the obligatory ass chewing from their maniac executive officer, the Polar Bear, *Ours Blanc*, Everard would report back to the nuclear control room and take over from the unlucky son of a bitch who'd been on duty the night before sail-away—usually the most junior officer aboard, whether or not he were married, but on *Le Vigilant* the officer cadre was mostly single except for their stodgy senior officers. Amazing what marriage did to a man, Everard thought. The married officers never seemed to arrive hungover, never seemed frustrated or annoyed, but were consistently calm. They paid quite a price for it, if Everard were asked, as they were constantly calling their wives for permission—"Honey, may I stay late and work tonight?" "Honey, may I go to the officers' club for a drink with my division? Just one?" It would be a cold day in hell when Emile Everard begged a woman for permission to have a drink with his friends.

He arrived at the gangway. Beneath him, on the west side of the steel platform running lengthwise through the building, the ballistic missile submarine *Le Vigilant* was docked. For just a moment Everard stopped and looked at her. Not so much out of any seaman's superstition, but out of awe. No matter how many years he worked on the ship, it would never fail to take his breath away when he first looked down at her. The vessel was *gigantic*, an astonishing hundred thirty-eight meters long, a soccer field and then some, and twelve meters in diameter, which meant she had sufficient beam to be four decks tall in the interior. She drew 14,355 tons, the size of a respectable cruiser. She could do thirty-one knots submerged at a hundred percent reactor power, a few knots more if they overpowered the plant. Her pressurized-water K15 nuclear reactor pumped out 150 megawatts thermal, which allowed for 41,500 shaft horsepower at the seven-bladed scimitar-shaped screw that was housed inside a shroud, making it a ducted propulsor, one of the quietest inventions of the decade. She could dive to five hundred meters and had an endurance of eighty days, much longer if they rationed the food, perhaps up to five months. The only real limit to the vessel's submerged duration was not food, but crew psychology—eventually the men would start hallucinating, then fighting, and even mutiny started becoming likely, or at least that was the case according to the *Rubis* SSN endurance testing of the early 1990s.

Endurance was vital, Everard thought, because of the doomsday contingency. If France were preemptively struck by a nuclear assault, the mission of *Le Vigilant* was to do absolutely nothing. A sealed operation order governed the boat's actions in the event of such a disaster. It would tell the captain to wait two weeks or two months or longer. Then, on a randomly picked day after the incineration of the Republic, *Le Vigilant*'s missiles would fly from the sea, exacting their vengeance upon the country foolish enough to attempt to destroy France. That was why the endurance tests had been done, because it was important to know when the crew would crack, as eventually they were certain to do. The only troubling thing was, were they to need to execute the doomsday contingency plan, the crew would all know that their homes, their loved ones, everything they held dear, had been laid waste, flattened, burned beyond recognition, fused into glass, molecules of flesh and bone and blood made vapor and scattered in the shock waves, and if that happened, how would crew psychology fare then? How many days—no, hours—would it be before the men mutinied, not wanting to live the next months in the sterile can of the submarine, but wanting to be in the world; even the charred, destroyed world where their mothers and fathers and wives and children had passed?

There had been fleetwide rumors of testing the contingency plan. A crew would arrive, just as *Le Vigilant*'s crew was arriving this morning, and after submergence, the word would be passed that France had been wiped from the map. It would be an exercise, but a "blind exercise." Not even the captain would know it wasn't real. And the stopwatch would click, the ship wired for sound and video, the brass wondering how long it would take for them to go mad, or whether they would surprise everyone and do their duty, rising to missile-firing depth eight weeks or eleven weeks later and unleashing their missiles—unbeknownst to the crew, all the "warshots" replaced with dummy exercise weapons—upon the suspected "enemy"? Every sail-away day, Emile Everard wondered whether this might be the patrol that the admirals decided to test an SSBN crew, to see what its psychology was made of. And he wondered, did the mere rumor of being tested change the equation? If and when this actually happened, God forbid, would the crew perform its duty with the thought of the slim probability that it was all just an exercise, a bad dream?

How the admirals thought was not something a mere lieutenant like Everard could discern or even guess at. It never crossed his mind whether he himself would ever ascend to flag rank. He smiled, shaking his head. Everard was not the type who rose to command a fleet. That was reserved for superhumans like Jean-Paul Gardes, or Jacques Legard or Polar Bear Courcelle. Still, he thought, if he were to play his cards right, learn something along the way, he might rise to command a submarine. It seemed as if part of the equation was finding one of those superior beings and becoming indispensable to him. Just as he and Legard were to *le Rhino*. In that case, loyalty and strength of character might well pay off.

Everard let his glance caress the ship. She had a bullet-nosed bow on the right that rose gently, symmetrically out of the black water of the building's enclosure to become the cylinder of the hull for a third of the way aft along her long, slender, glorious length. There the sail smoothly rose to preside high over the deck, the vertical wing enclosing the masts and antennae and periscopes, their vital communications link to the government and military's command and control structures. The sail had fairwater planes—twin horizontal wing-shaped stabilizers, mounted up high, all the better to aid in depth control near the surface on the rare occasions the ship came to periscope depth. For most of her patrol, her extended floating wire antenna would keep her in receive-only communication with the SSBN Command Center in Brest, the contingency SSBN Lower Tier Command Center at the old facility at Houilles, and the SSBN Tertiary Command Center at Rosnay. And if all three of those command centers were knocked out by nuclear strikes, there were half a dozen C-160H Astarté communication relay aircraft, one of which would be airborne at all times during an alert status of "orange" or higher, capable of communicating with the submarine force to either instruct them to launch their ballistic missiles or to "check fire." And if all those measures failed, Commander Jean-Paul Gardes was the decision maker, empowered by the President of the Republic with the awesome power to retaliate on his own authority if he became convinced France had been attacked.

Aft of the sail, the turtleback of the missile compartment began, a flat, raised superstructure over the cylindrical pressure hull that contained the upper extension of the missile tubes, which were longer than the hull's diameter, and the missile tube doors. There were sixteen tubes, sixteen doors, sixteen three-stage solid-fuel-propelled M45 missiles, each with six multiple reentry vehicle thermonuclear warheads packing 150 kilotons of explosive power, and each with an astonishing range of 6,000 kilometers.

As the hump of the missile deck angled downward back to the cylinder of the hull, the engineering spaces began. The hull vanished under the water, with another fourth of the submarine's length submerged; the reactor compartment with the behemoth of the reactor and the turbine compartment, where the nuclear control room was tucked—Everard's watch station over the coming

hours. He checked in with the deck sentry, saluted the
flag of the Republic, and walked the gangway to the
hull. The gangway extended over the slip to the missile
compartment escape hatch, at the far aft end of the turtleback. He arrived at the wide-mouthed hatch, looked
around him at the interior of the Missile Loading Facility
building, and took his last breath of real air before
shouting a warning down the escape trunk.

"Down ladder!" He lowered his sea bag into the dark
maw of the hatch, let it fall to the bottom deck of the
escape hatch, then lowered himself down the stainless-
steel ladder into the hull of the ship. As always, it was
the smell of the submarine that reached his senses first.
The smell was at once indefinable and characteristic. Everard had once toured a World War II German U-boat,
and the smell was almost identical, which meant in some
ways not much had changed in half a century. The smell
was a witch's brew of sweat, sulfury diesel oil, even more
sulfuric diesel exhaust, cooking grease and the smoke
from burning it, amines used to purify the atmosphere,
ozone from the higher voltage equipment and—of
course—sewage, which was usually pumped overboard
by huge, positive-displacement pumps, but when the
equipment misbehaved would be air-loaded with high-
pressure air and blown overboard, but then the air that
had displaced the sewage would be brought back *into*
the submarine, for the atmospheric control equipment
to deal with. Everard would have liked to get his hands
around the throat of the designer who came up with that
brilliant concept, but they had thought it best not to
have a huge trail of air bubbles that would give away
the submarine's position. And the only other alternative
would be shitting in plastic bags, which had even less
appeal.

As Everard's head lowered past the smooth, cool polished metal of the hatch seating surface, the world above
vanished as if it had been a dream. Everard's surroundings were high-tensile steel, a cylinder of the escape
trunk, a huge airlock, which extended from the turtle-

back down to the upper overhead of the missile compartment upper level. Everard picked up his bag from the deck of the escape trunk, again announced his "down ladder" and tossed the bag far down to the deck below. He climbed the second ladder and emerged into the cramped auxiliary equipment space, which was a machinery room filled with atmospheric control equipment, components of the hovering system, and some of the missile tube support systems. To the uninitiated, it was a frightening mass of consoles and pipes and valves and motor starters and cables. To the submarine-qualified enlisted rating or officer, it was no more intimidating than the kitchen at the house, with each piece of equipment there for a particular function, each one in the service of the ship.

The next thing he noticed was the sound. The air handlers put out a low-pitched hum, a bass thrumming sound that would haunt his days and nights for the next sixty days. True, after some time a submariner barely noticed it, but the first nights home from a patrol, Everard could barely sleep from the chilling quiet of their flat—he grinned, knowing that the quiet was usually broken by one of Legard's women in her ascent to orgasm. Legard, he thought, that asshole, at least Everard would see him later, after watch. That at least made the voyage bearable, that the crew were his friends. Except perhaps their boss, the damned Rhino, who could be an evil taskmaster.

Everard picked up his bag for the third time and began his long walk forward, through the centerline passageway between the seemingly endless identical rows of missile tubes. Each one was huge, the size of an elevator shaft. They could have lowered his car into one of the tubes, he had once mused, they were so large. Finally he reached the frame 58 compartment bulkhead hatch to the forward compartment. He took several steps down, since the deck elevations did not align, so that he emerged into the forward compartment's second level, also called the 02 deck. Most of the 02 level was officers' country, with a narrow central passageway leading forward, the bulkheads covered in wood-grain laminate, the doors and edges trimmed in stainless steel, the door knobs also stainless. Had a visitor been brought here blindfolded and then released, he would have thought he'd been brought to a cross-country train passageway.

On the right, the starboard side, was the missile control center. This was where *le Officier d'Armes* De Lorme hung out with his missile technicians, when they weren't aft in the missile compartment fussing over their weapons. Farther forward, on the starboard side, was the officers' mess, then the officers' galley, where the cooks spent twenty-four hours a day conspiring to make the officers fat. It was a struggle trying to keep weight off at sea, but at least Captain Gardes allowed them to jog laps in the missile compartment upper level and lift weights in the missile compartment middle level. That and skipping two of the four scrumptious meals served a day could at least keep the weight gain to three kilos in a patrol, but the crew had to work extra hard on the off-patrol time to trim back down. A big part of the problem was the damned smell of the cooking—once a meal was in Everard's nostrils, he had to eat it. He had actually brought noseplugs on one patrol, but given them up after the kidding he had taken from the noncommissioned officers and enlisted ratings. Further forward were the officers' staterooms. Everard crashed into his, the one he shared with the Chief Engineer—*le Rhino*— and *Lieutenant de Vaisseau* Michel Gannt, the *Officier de Communications*. Everard was not thrilled about rooming with his boss, noticing that that bastard Legard had managed to get himself bunked in with *Navigateur* Molyneux and Tristan Cholmondeley, the electrical officer. He was of two minds—he felt, as the senior lieutenant on board, he should get to room away from his raging boss, the chief engineer, but then, he also thought that as the oldest lieutenant, he should be able to deal with the Rhino's mood swings, stand up to him.

"Godammit, Everard," Chief Engineer Teisseire bellowed a tenth of a second after Everard entered the cramped three-man stateroom, "you're fucking late again."

Lieutenant Commander *Rhinocéros* Teisseire was a hundred and ten kilograms, the sheer weight of him making him seem imposing, intimidating, even frightening. His bullish build and hot-blooded nature had led to his nickname, *Le Rhino*, given to him by his former commanding officer two sea tours before. He was a big man with big hands, a big face graced by a large nose, large blue eyes and a generous mouth. His hair was dark blond, somewhat thin, all of it curled tightly in small ringlets, making it seem as if he wore a toupee stolen from the scalp of Cupid himself, though no one ever had the boldness to tease him about it, not when those jackhammer fists seemed to swing about his body so readily. Teisseire, unlike many large men, did not have a heart of gold or a gentle nature. He was as raw as he looked, known for his eruptions into white-hot anger, but his saving grace was that his sense of humor was just as explosive. It had saved his career time after time, but he insisted that the *Marine Nationale* let him live because it was his very anger that kept the nuclear propulsion plant behaving; even the machinery, he claimed, afraid of his temper. He ran his junior officers, warrant officers and noncommissioned officers relentlessly, mercilessly, almost cruelly, but showed stark moments of pure generosity to them, and to a man they were all fiercely loyal to him, naming themselves *le brigade du Rhino*—"the Rhino's brigade."

There was some trouble in Teisseire's family. Michéle Teisseire was not a happy woman, and it had nothing to do with her husband's temper, but from an incident that happened in a liberty port over two years ago, when *le Rhino* had gone on a tear through an American party city, somewhere on the coast of their south—Fort Lauderdale, Everard remembered—where his fast attack submarine S605 *Amethyste* had docked for a diplomatic visit, there with a U.S. submarine. The two nuclear submarine crews, from two different cultures, but somehow, as sailors and submariners, quite the same, had gone drinking together. For the *Amethyste* the result was a minor disaster, and for Teisseire a larger one. He had held up the ship's departure and had to be found by the local *gendarmes* in a hotel room, bedded down with a black exotic dancer. He was brought back to the ship, where he was then serving as the *aide principal de propulsion*, the chief engineer's main propulsion assistant, completely drunk and threatening the police. He'd been confined to quarters, bellowing through the door that he was supposed to be on watch, starting the reactor. News in the navy traveled faster than the speed of light, and when *Amethyste* had returned to Brest, Michéle had packed and left. For two years Teisseire had attempted to win her back, pleading that a single drunken incident did not infidelity make, but Michéle had not agreed. Prior to the incident, she had worshipped him, giving him his two young daughters, five-year-old Claire and two-year-old Juliette. Teisseire had learned his lesson, and switched from the swashbuckling attack submarine corps to the calmer ranks of the ballistic missile submarines, then buried himself in his engineering department's work.

"What the hell, *Ingénieur*," Everard said, his jaw clenched. "I'm right on time. And I got the damned random search."

Teisseire clamped his lips in contempt, then left, slamming the stateroom door behind him. Everard stared after him, shaking his head. Fucking Engineer. Everard had almost been waiting for the reprimand, just to get it over with and have the rest of the day to himself. Why the man was so angry all the time was a mystery. For all Everard knew, that bitch of a wife of his was acting up again. Yet another reason to avoid marriage, he thought. That women thought they could keep children away from a father was a crime against nature, but that was the Rhino's problem. Who was he kidding, Everard thought. If the Rhino sneezed, all his officers and non-coms got a cold.

Everard checked the bulkhead chronometer as he tossed his bag onto his upper bunk, above Teisseire's, then left the stateroom and walked aft to the officers' mess. The mess was a fairly expansive room, which was rare in a submarine. At the aft end there was a seating area with a wraparound sofa, two large armchairs—both bolted to the deck—and coffee tables. The center of the room was taken up by a table large enough to seat the entire officers' compliment of the ship, all eighteen of them. At the end of the room opposite the seating area the captain's chair was located, the chair always vacant when the captain was absent, as he would be for officers' call. Officers' call was the *Cadre Dirigeant*'s show, in which *Ours Blanc*—Polar Bear—Courcelle would motivate them to get their duty done.

Since the day he had taken over from the building yard's executive officer, *Capitaine de Corvette* Vincent Courcelle had made an immediate impact as the highest-energy senior officer in the crew's collective memory. Courcelle was tall and bone-thin, with thinning, carrot red hair, an angular face with protruding cheekbones and a jutting jaw with a dimple square in the center of it, piercing bright blue eyes and a thick gray mustache. He had the sort of beard that showed a thick stubble the hour before the midday meal, and his hair seemed perpetually mussed no matter how much he tried to control it. It was not hard to imagine Courcelle habitually inserting his bony index finger into a wall socket, so frantic was his energy level, despite his nickname and reputation for keeping a cool head during an emergency—and, in fact, Captain Gardes had once kidded Courcelle that the only time he *was* calm was when the world was crashing around his ears.

Courcelle had won his nickname back on the fast attack submarine *Perle* during an under-ice run beneath the Arctic icecap when the inertial navigation system completely locked up, then failed, then burst into flames, the rolling, dense smoke first filling the control room and then the entire forward compartment, sending the on-watch crew into a near panic. Courcelle, then a lieutenant and *Perle*'s navigator, had been the deck officer at the time, and on instinct, purely from his memory of the contour of the ice overhead, had driven the ship back along her previous course to a polynya, a rare Arctic lake of thin ice. While breathing dry, canned air from the emergency air system, his narrow bug-eyed face shoved into a rubber gas mask, Courcelle had driven the ship blind with a ghostly calm certainty, while the ship's equipment either failed around him or was invisible in the thick, black, noxious smoke. On Courcelle's instinct, the ship returned to the thin ice where they could surface and ventilate. Ten days later, *Perle* emerged into the relatively open water of the marginal ice zone, to the uproarious applause of the crew, and since the day of the fire he had been known to the *Perle* crew as *le Ours Blanc*—Polar Bear—for his mysterious and instinctive Arctic navigation, and for his certainty and icy calm in the face of a disastrous emergency. The name not only stuck, but had been entered into his official service record. Courcelle had consequently been awarded the *Légion d'Honneur* and promoted on the spot from lieutenant to lieutenant commander, and given the second-in-command billet onboard the prestigious, brand-new ballistic missile submarine *Le Vigilant*.

Ours Blanc was as good a leader as was possible, but the job of executive officer was not an enjoyable one, as he was responsible for virtually everything. Every item of administration, the ship's relations with the brass, the logistics, the tactics—and even though each department head and division officer below him had the primary responsibility, so much could fall through the cracks in the rush to get the ship's business done that the Polar Bear had to use some extreme tactics at times to get that business done. Such tactics frequently involved verbal confrontation, sometimes public humiliation and, certainly, brow beatings during officers' call. And the worst officers' call was on sail-away day.

They would cast off the lines at eleven hundred hours, four hours from now. Between now and then, the ship would be buzzing with frantic activity, every officer and noncom furiously busy, the activity coming to a crescendo at the moment that they began their maneuver to leave the dock building. Fortunately, Everard would be aft as engineering officer of the watch in the relatively calm engineering spaces.

Everard took his seat at the end of the table opposite the captain's chair, though the very end was reserved for the supply officer. Next to him Jacques Legard plopped down. Everard was the *aide de commande de dommages*, the damage control assistant to the chief engineer, which meant he and his chief petty officer were responsible for all the engineering systems and auxiliary mechanical systems forward of frame 137, the reactor compartment bulkhead, in addition to the emergency diesel, the trim and drain system, the sewage systems, the vent systems, the hovering system, the atmospheric control gear, the hydraulic systems and a hundred more minor but vital muscles and organs of the ship. It was a difficult job, since it seemed something was always breaking, and the damned *Rouge* crew was far less attentive to its systems than Gardes' *Bleu* crew. Taking over the ship from *Rouge* always seemed to involve heartache. *Dear God*, Everard prayed silently, *please just get me through fucking sail-away day*. Legard opened a steno pad and put it on the table, his Mont Blanc pen on top of, ready to take notes. Everard felt a twinge of jealousy for the younger officer, who was so much more squared away in a hundred ways than he was. Legard was the engineer's main propulsion assistant, his main nuclear lieutenant. As the *aide principal de propulsion*, Legard was responsible for the nuclear and nonnuclear propulsion systems, which, frankly, was an easier job than Everard's. The nuclear mechanics were better trained and more motivated than the scurvy lot of Everard's division, and any part those prima donnas wanted, they immediately got, while some of Everard's requisitions languished unless he could make the case that they were required for ship safety. Plus, the nuclear machinery all resided in the reactor compartment and turbine compartment, and was in plain sight instead of snaking all through the secret parts of the vessel and bilges as Everard's machinery did. He smirked to himself, the thought crossing his mind that he would like to be reincarnated as Legard in the next life. This morning, hangover notwithstanding, Legard would be the deck officer for their departure, and would drive the submarine from the dock building to the dive point. Legard was to be admired, Everard grudgingly admitted to himself. After all, who else could drink and fuck all night, then calmly conn a gigantic weapon of war to the deep blue sea as if it were all in a day's work? As if hearing Everard's thought, Legard looked over the rim of his coffee cup at Everard, a wry smile crinkling his pasty features.

The other officers entered the room. The junior officers—the bachelors—seemed tired but purposeful, each of them having attempted to make the best of the eve-of-departure revelry. There had been a sail-away party at the huge three-story house of Victor Vasser, the sonar officer, which he shared with Rémy Sanxay, the missile officer, Michel Gannt, the communications officer, young Roland Beauvais, the more junior torpedo officer, Darman Rothsen, the supply officer, and Gerard Ramsden, the first lieutenant. The six nonnuclear officers—the "nose-coners," as Legard labeled them—were a relaxed lot compared to the engineering crew, and the party had gone late. They had invited two dozen local women, one of them fair Aurélie, whom Everard had hoped to bring home, but he stopped talking to her long enough to go to the bathroom, and when he returned she was nowhere to be found. He hadn't connected her absence to Legard's disappearance until this morning, the bastard. Everard grinned at the nose-coners, who nodded back from the opposite side of the table. The other junior officers filed in, then the department heads, and finally *Ours Blanc.*

"Good morning, gentlemen," Courcelle began cheerfully. "I have a special treat for you today. It's been too hushed to brief you on until now, but since we're sailing away, it can be released to you and your departments. We're not just going on strategic patrol this mission. This run, we get to play with NATO. Against our own SSN forces, those of the British Royal Navy and the best attack submarines of the American Navy." He paused, looking pleased with himself. "And not only that, we get to be the attacker instead of the hunted." A sly smile came to his lips. "As soon as we clear restricted waters, please bear in mind that you will no longer be French seamen. You'll be Algerian terrorists. If we can evade or sink the attacking submarine forces, slip away from any surface warfare task forces and launch an exercise ballistic missile down the Atlantic test range—better yet, two missiles—we win the engagement. And if we win"— Courcelle paused, his smile widening—"we get rewarded with a month of leave. We'll return to Brest for a fleet debriefing and turn the ship back over to the Red Crew for them to take a month of our strategic patrol while we relax."

"Oh, dear God," Legard said. "Can you imagine the faces of *le Équipage Rouge* when they hear they've got the boat back? While we live large on the beach?"

Everard couldn't help glancing at Torpedo Officer Roland Beauvais, who was seeing a woman who was the girlfriend of the communications officer of *Le Vigilant*'s Red Crew. There was a girl who had the best of both worlds, Everard thought. Two boyfriends, neither of which would ever interfere with the other, since they were rarely in port at the same time. Beauvais tried to keep his expression neutral, but his eyes had a shine to them, Everard thought.

The room's excited chatter continued for a moment

until the smiling *Ours Blanc* finally held up his hand for silence. "Gentlemen, to your stations, and let's have a successful patrol."

Everard clapped his friend Legard on the shoulder. "Don't run aground, Jacques," he cautioned. "We've got some attack boats to sink. Wouldn't do to have them watch us hung up on a sandbar."

Legard smirked. "You just concentrate on making your little teapot give me power when I need it," he said.

"Have a good watch."

Everard whistled as he headed aft, wondering what he would do with an unforeseen month of vacation.

6

Lieutenant de Vaisseau Jacques Legard paused to glance around the control room, which was buzzing with activity. The space occupied most of the upper level, perhaps the biggest room in the ship, and yet seemed cramped by consoles, the central periscope railed stand and the crowd of officers and enlisted men. On the forward port corner was the ship control station, where the helmsman and planesmen would stand their watches and control the ship's depth and attitude. The station resembled the cockpit of a small corporate jet, with control sticks, a central knee-level console, a forward control panel display and a back-slanted upper display. Behind it, on the port side, was the ballast control station, where the chief of the watch controlled over a hundred of the ship's systems, including the ballast tanks, the trim tanks, the trim and drain systems, the diesel, the masts and antennae, the hydraulic plant and the hovering system.

Along the port side aft of the ballast control station were the navigation electronic consoles, which showed the readouts of the ship's inertial navigation equipment and the global positioning satellite readouts. The secure fathometer was set into the consoles, reading out the depth beneath keel. Beside that was the under-ice sonar console, which was obviously dark during the entire patrol unless it was being checked out. The ship had the nominal capability to go under polar ice, but it was a remote contingency. On the starboard side of the room, in the forward corner, was the deck officer's sonar repeater station, which was a small console with two displays from the sonar system, one of them usually configured for "broadband" off the DMUX 80 sonar sphere in the bow or the flank arrays that were mounted on the hull; the second display used for narrowband reception from the DSUV 61 low-frequency linear-towed-array system.

Aft of the sonar repeater, taking up the rest of the starboard side, was the attack center, five operator consoles that allowed the ship to target and sink enemy submarines and ships. The forward four positions were tied into the ship's SAT—*systeme d'armes tactique*—firecontrol computer system, which took raw data from sonar and partially processed it for display and enhancement by the human operators of the system. The system was intelligent enough, if placed in an automatic mode, to come up with target parameters with the human operators, but so far it had been far outperformed by human ingenuity, which seemed to incorporate an element of either intuition or common sense, and so far no one had been able to program the SAT with either. The fifth console in the row, the furthest aft, was the weapon control console, tied into the DLA 4A weapon control system, which programmed both the torpedo tubes three decks below and the torpedoes themselves. Torpedoes were such smart weapons that programming them amounted to briefing them for an entirely independent mission.

On the starboard side of the aft bulkhead was the electronic warfare console, the Thomson-CSF ARUR13 and DR 3000U electronic countermeasures suite, where two operator positions observed the electronic intelligence from the surface, evaluating what radars were overhead, what radio signals flew through the airwaves, and from what direction. The ESM electronic surveillance measures function was more of an attack submarine issue than a ballistic missile submarine utility, which was why it was here in the control room rather than having its own separate, enclosed room. In addition, the radar display was located at the console, the radar used only during surface transits for aiding the navigator by showing the contours of the surrounding land, and for collision avoidance with other ships.

The center of the room was dominated aft by the rectangular, elevated, railed-in periscope stand with the dual Thomson Mod 5 periscopes, with all the same bells and whistles the attack submarines had, but again, such accoutrements were mostly unused, since it was rare on patrol that an SSBN would come to periscope depth, as her communications were all received while she was deep. The periscope stand's forward starboard corner featured a command console for the deck officer, with a sonar repeater display in the overhead, a periscope television display, all the internal communication speakers and telephones, and an array of alarms, with covered panels that controlled the evasion device launchers that would help them evade an incoming torpedo—as if *Le Vigilant* could ever be fired upon with Captain Gardes in command, Legard thought. The entire fleet knew he was the best captain in the force. The forward port corner had the command chair for the captain. It was prohibited for anyone to sit in it other than the commanding officer, but Legard had been known to commandeer the seat during his midnight watches.

Forward of the periscope stand was the deck officer's navigation chart table, which was immediately below the access trunk to the bridge at the top of the sail. The chart table was mounted on a rotating hinge so that it folded up while a vertical ladder folded down for access to the bridge. It was an innovative space-saving arrangement, since once the vessel was safely submerged, which it would be for a continuous sixty days, there was no use for the bridge access trunk, and the ladder would be stowed, the sanctity of the deck officer's chart table undisturbed.

Legard greeted the watchstanders in the space, accepting the weatherproof, waterproof orange coveralls from the chief of the watch. The chief was the leading noncom of the auxiliary division and reported to Legard, though it was often difficult to tell exactly who worked for whom. *Maître* Benoît Turnock was a barrel-chested, grizzled old man of thirty-five who had spent his years in the attack submarine force and, according to him, knew the auxiliary equipment better than he knew his own wife, although as Legard teased him, with the life of a submariner, that might not be saying much. They had a good working relationship and respected each other as officer and noncommissioned officer, but there was more than just the professional. Legard considered Turnock a personal friend, and the older man had provided useful advice on every subject from what car to buy to how to deal with *le Rhino*.

Legard carried his coveralls with him to the room aft of the control room, the navigation space. The navigation equipment was crammed into a room half the size of the control room, with the electronic cabinets of the ship's twin inertial navigation systems on the port side along with the satellite navigation receivers. The center of the room and starboard side had two large chart tables, where *Navigateur* Molyneux, his navigation electronics technicians and his quartermasters would perform the delicate and vital business of navigating the ship into and out of restricted waters.

Molyneux and his crew were already in the room, getting their charts ready for the voyage. Legard greeted him as he stepped into his coveralls, then emerged back into the control room. The executive officer was waiting for him on the periscope stand. Legard walked up on the starboard side, looking up at the tall, thin redhead.

"Lieutenant Legard," Lieutenant Commander Courcelle said, his voice still pleased from the morning briefing. "Station the maneuvering watch."

"Aye, *Cadre Dirigeant*," Legard said, coming to attention. "Station the maneuvering watch."

Courcelle hurried off the periscope stand and walked quickly forward to the access bay. Legard took the binoculars and VHF portable radio the chief of the watch held out to him.

"Chief of the Watch," Legard said to Turnock, "station the maneuvering watch."

Turnock acknowledged formally, then reached for a microphone on a coiled cord. The chief's voice boomed throughout the ship.

"Station . . . the maneuvering watch!"

Lieutenant Jacques Legard put the binoculars around his neck and climbed the ladder to the hatch set in the overhead of the control room that led to the bridge access tunnel. The tunnel was intentionally dimly lit, so that if the ship were transiting at night, little light would leak upward to ruin their night vision. The tunnel was a featureless, vertical, tight cylinder clad in stainless-steel sheet metal, with little more in it than the ladder, rotary light switches and a manifold station of valves. Legard climbed the seven meters to the top, where the upper hatch was covered with grating.

"Deck Officer to the bridge," he announced himself, and the grating was pulled aside so he could climb up. He emerged into the cockpit and the grating was placed back over the hatch. He looked over at the two men already on-station, *Enseigne de Vaisseau de 1re Classe* Roland Beauvais, the torpedo officer, and the lookout, *Quartier Maître de 1re Classe* Bruyere, one of Molyneux's enlisted men who was charged with keeping a watchful eye on surface ship traffic to help the deck officer avoid collision. Beauvais would be observing Legard drive the ship out of restricted waters, and depending on how the captain felt, he could take the watch-under-instruction when they reached deeper water with no surface shipping.

"Gentlemen," Legard said, returning the salutes of the junior deck officer and the lookout. "Mr. Beauvais, what have we got?" Legard asked, getting a briefing from the younger officer on the chart, the track leaving port, and the current and tides. It was good, Legard thought, to have the more junior officers onboard. They worked hard, rarely complained and were generally a well-educated lot, if inexperienced. Not that they should ever be complimented, as that would surely lead to swollen heads.

"The only thing we're missing is the captain," Beauvais concluded.

Legard checked his watch. It was ten minutes before eleven. "He'll be here."

The light changed suddenly. Legard looked up. The rollup door at the end of the building had begun to rise, the Missile Loading Facility Building preparing for their departure. On both sides, on the steel catwalks on the boat's flanks, linehandlers from the base began manning their stations. On the deck of the ship, the crew's linehandlers stood ready to manipulate the lines.

Legard's VHF radio rasped. "Marine Nationale sousmarin, *this is the MLF Docking Officer, radio check, over.*"

"Roger, Docking Officer," Legard spoke into his radio. "This is Navy Submarine, read you loud and clear, over." Identifying themselves as *Le Vigilant* on an open radio circuit was prohibited, so they just referred to the vessel as "navy submarine."

"*Dock is prepared for winch-out, over.*"

"Roger, Dock, status of tugboat?"

"*Submarine, Dock, tug is standing by at the exit.*"

"Roger, Dock, stand by."

The radio clicked twice, the docking officer's acknowledgment.

"*Bridge, Control,*" the communication box at the forward lip of the cockpit crackled, Turnock's voice sounding distorted and metallic over the circuit.

Legard pulled the box's microphone from its cradle. "Bridge, aye."

"*Bridge, Control, maneuvering watch is stationed,* capitaine *and* cadre dirigeant *are informed.*"

"Very well."

"*Bridge, Navigator,*" Molyneux's voice boomed over the box, his circuit much louder. Legard turned the volume down a notch.

"Navigator, Bridge, aye."

"Bridge, Navigator, dockside fix confirmed. Initial course out of the dock is two seven five. Speed of advance, ten knots."

"Navigator, Bridge aye," Legard answered, glancing at the chart to confirm his track showed an exit course out of Port Brest as 275, almost due west.

"Bridge, Control, captain is laying to the bridge," Turnock reported.

Capitaine de Frégate Jean-Paul Gardes took a last look around the control room, accepted the binoculars from the chief of the watch, then climbed the tunnel's ladder up to the bridge.

"Captain to the bridge," he said, announcing himself. The grating was pulled open by the bridge cockpit crew so that he could ascend.

"Good morning, Captain," Lieutenant Legard said as Gardes climbed up into the sail cockpit.

Gardes grinned at him in pleasure, his emerald green eyes crinkling into crow's-feet. His thick, dark blond hair was combed straight back, unusually short and plastered to his scalp with hair gel. His slim frame seemed bulkier in the orange foul-weather coveralls, his safety harness strapped around his torso. He was tanned and projected robust health, as if he were a yacht captain instead of a submarine commander. But what was most evident about Commander Gardes was that he seemed truly happy, his expression shining with satisfaction and pride the morning of this underway.

Gardes, though raised as the only child of an army general, was not a typical military officer. While he had a mind for strategy and tactics, and while he was a natural leader—and according to his seniors, a natural warrior— were he to join a party in civilian clothes, it would surprise those newly meeting him that he was a *Maritime Nationale* officer. He exuded a genuine warmth and interest, and was the sort of man who would be unable to pass a crying child on the street without dropping to one knee to cheer him up, smiling up at the mother and asking permission to wipe away the tears. It was the quality, according to his wife Danielle, that had magnetically attracted her to him, that bone-deep compassion and love of his fellow man. In the French Navy, his personality had rocketed him to success, his seniors becoming as drawn to him as Danielle had been. If Jean-Paul Gardes' character were his only recommendation, he would have fallen far short, but he had inherited other traits from his father, including a razor-sharp intellect that could operate unseen, invisible to those people who were threatened by intelligence. Gardes was, by education, a nuclear physicist, which had made the nuclear engineering of the submarine force easy by comparison, the jokes made by his peers during his youth that obscure subatomic particles were as well known to him as members of his own family.

Gardes had one other quality, one that had never been noted in his official performance evaluations, but as real as his political skills or his acumen, and that was a mild but solidly real clairvoyance. As with the rest of humanity, to Gardes, the future remained behind a dark veil, at least most of the time, but he could sometimes feel events before they happened. Three years ago, the morning the admiral had announced that Jean-Paul would take over the nuclear fast attack submarine *Emeraude*, Gardes had stood at his dresser and looked over at Danielle and tapped his left pocket, in the spot where submarine commanders wore their capital ship command pins. *By sunset I'll be in command*, he had said to his wife, uncertain himself why he had uttered such a thing. Six hours later he had sat in the admiral's lavish office and saw his mentor's smile as it was explained that he would take command of *Emeraude* for a vital mission for the security of the Republic, and the very next morning he was at sea with orders to sink the North Korean diesel submarine threatening Japan.

There was more to his spooky quality, which included an uncanny ability—some of the time—to peer inside people, to see them down to the bottoms of their personalities. It was not something Gardes consciously realized, at least not the majority of the time, but there were times someone came to him with a problem—or the problem he thought he had—only to have Gardes know exactly what was wrong and what the solution needed to be. Gardes had had his political enemies during his career, but each one he had neutralized or pacified by knowing what motivated the individual. Sometimes he felt he knew people better than their own mothers. Danielle had laughed when he had said something to that effect, early in their relationship, her eyes and her expression redolent of their early relationship lust, and she had said, *Jean-Paul, you found out things about me in your first hour with me that my mother will* never *know.* Gardes considered his sixth sense a gift, privately even believing that it was a temporary one, bestowed on him by divine providence for a short time for some unrevealed but important reason. He enjoyed the insight, respecting it and nurturing it as if it were a favorite but ailing child, but he never relied on it to get him out of a troublesome situation. If the second sight, as he had come to call it, helped him, he accepted and used it, but he never consciously counted on it coming to him. In the back corridors of his mind he had begun to believe that the moment he took the second sight for granted, it would evaporate like a pleasant dream.

"Morning, gentlemen." Gardes climbed out of the cockpit further up to the top of the sail, where there was a small standing space of a meter square railed in by temporary stainless-steel handrails, called the flying bridge. He latched the lanyard of his safety harness on the metal ring set into the handrails. Legard handed up the second VHF bridge-to-bridge radio to him, in case the commanding officer wanted to speak directly to one of the other ships or the docking officer.

"Your report, Deck Officer," Gardes asked.

"Yes, sir, the reactor is critical, electric plant is in a normal full-power lineup, main coolant is in natural circulation, propulsion is on the main engines, and I am intermittently spinning the shaft to keep the main engines warm. All mooring lines are singled up. Masts and periscopes are down until we exit the building. Our operation order is aboard and the track is laid. The docking officer reports manned and ready. The winch-out crew is ready. Our deck crew is ready. Request permission, sir, to retract the gangway."

Gardes nodded. "Yes. Take off the gangway."

"Remove the gangway, Deck Officer, aye," Legard replied formally, clicking his radio. "Docking Officer, this is *Navale Sous-marin*, over."

"Roger, Submarine, go ahead."

"Remove the gangway."

"Roger, Submarine, gangway coming off."

Legard looked aft to watch the overhead crane lift the aluminum ramp away from the hull.

"Navy Submarine, Dock, gangway removed."

"Captain, request permission to commence winch-out," Legard asked.

Gardes nodded. "Commence winch-out."

Legard acknowledged formally, then keyed his mike. "Navigator, Bridge, commencing winch-out."

"Bridge, Navigator, aye."

Legard put the VHF radio to his lips. "Dock, Navy Submarine, commence winch-out, over." Beauvais handed Legard his megaphone. Legard leaned over the sail. *"On deck! Slack lines as necessary to winch!"* The deck crew bent to their tasks, taking off turns of the mooring lines on the huge cleats, easing them just enough that lines one and two forward—attached to the port and starboard main winches—could pull the submarine out of the building and through the rollup doors where the tugboat awaited their emergence.

Slowly, almost imperceptibly, the ship began to move. It actually seemed as if the ship were rock steady and it was the building that was moving. Legard could see the huge winches forward, on either side of the building, slowly turning as they winched out the submarine. Legard leaned over the starboard side of the sail, making sure the ship wasn't about to hit the land side of the building, but the standoff was good. He pushed Beauvais out of the way and leaned over the port side. The distance was satisfactory to port.

Soon the rollup door of the building approached the bow of the gigantic submarine, the nosecone extending out into the blue water of the bay. Stark sunlight lit the bow, the line of light moving slowly over the flat black hull as *Le Vigilant* was hauled out of the building. Soon the sail moved under the rollup door.

"Submarine, Dock, winch stopped, standing by to switch lines."

"On deck!" Legard shouted into his megaphone. "Take in lines one and two! Stand by to winch lines three and four!"

The ship slowed slightly as the forward lines were taken in and the amidships mooring lines were wrapped around the winches by the building linehandling crew.

"Submarine, Dock, ready to winch."

"Dock, Submarine," Legard ordered on the VHF, "recommence winch."

The ship's motion, slowed slightly, began to accelerate. The sail passed completely into the sunlight. Legard reached into his coveralls pocket for his sunglasses. Beauvais did the same, the lookout likewise.

"Control, Bridge," Legard announced. "Sail is clear of the building. Permission granted to raise masts as necessary."

"Bridge, Control," Turnock answered. *"Sail clear, aye, raising number one and number two periscope, the radar mast and bumping up the radio mast."*

"Control, Bridge aye." Aft of them the bump of hydraulics sounded as the periscopes raised themselves far out of the sail, twin telephone poles reaching for the heavens. The radar mast came out as well, the radio mast far aft rising a meter above the top surface of the sail.

"Bridge, Navigator, request permission to rotate and radiate on the radar."

"Captain? Permission to rotate and radiate?"

"Rotate and radiate," Gardes ordered.

"Navigator, Bridge, rotate and radiate."

The radar mast began spinning slowly, the horizontal bar of it making a smooth revolution every second.

Legard scanned the bay at the mouth of the building. The tugboat idled, its length parallel to theirs, waiting for enough of the ship to emerge that it could be tied up. The ship continued to emerge until the turtleback was well out of the building. Again the lines were switched, with lines three and four taken in and lines five and six affixed to the winches. Finally all but the far stern of the ship was in the open bay water.

"Navy Submarine, tug Champney *Captain, over."*

"Roger *Champney* Captain, go ahead."

"Request to tie up, starboard-side-to to your port bow."

"Champney Captain, tie up, starboard-side-to on my port bow." He lifted the megaphone and shouted down to the deck crew to tie up the tug.

Legard pulled off his cap and wiped the sweat off his brow, then leaned over the port side to make sure the tug tie-up operation went smoothly, then looked aft to check the rudder emerging from the building. It was not quite out of the rollup door, but would be in thirty seconds.

"Navy Submarine, Dock, ready to release the winch. Good day and bon voyage, *sir."*

"Dock, Navy Submarine, roger and thank you. Navy Submarine, out." Legard leaned over the bridge coaming. *"On deck, take in lines five and six!"* he shouted. They were officially free of the building. "Lookout, hoist the flag of the Republic!" Aft, on the flying bridge, the lookout hoisted the national colors, the ship officially underway now that the last lines came onboard. Legard reached under the sail cockpit lip and found the air horn handle. He pulled it, an earsplitting blast coming from the ship's whistle. The entire city knew they were underway now, he thought. He let it blast for a full eight seconds, counting his own heartbeats. When he let the handle go, his ears rang from the noise. "Captain," he said over his shoulder, "*Le Vigilant* is underway."

"Very well," Gardes said, his voice pleased. The captain and his ship were back in their element.

"Navigator, Bridge, ship is underway," Legard said into his comm box microphone as he looked to port. The tugboat was fully tied up and the rudder had fully emerged from the building.

"Bridge, Navigator, aye."

"Nuclear Control, Bridge, stand by to answer all bells," Legard said into his mike.

Emile Everard's voice crackled from the comm box speaker, *"Bridge, Nuclear Control, standing by to answer all bells!"*

It was time to go. Legard took one last look at the bay, his seaman's eye feeling the current and the sea.

"Helm, Bridge, left full rudder, ahead one-third!"

"Left full rudder, ahead one-third, Bridge, Helm, aye!" a new voice, a much younger one, sounded on the circuit.

"Tug, Submarine, make your rudder left full, ahead one third."

The tug acknowledged, the tug's engine throttling up as it pulled the bow of the submarine through the turn. Legard checked aft, making sure the helmsman had the rudder in the right direction, left full. A confused helmsman could get them in trouble faster than the deck officer could get them out, which was why that watchstander was chosen so carefully. On the compass alidade, the ship's present heading displayed almost due north. The numerals slowly spun by the needle as the ship slowly rotated in the channel.

"Helm, Bridge," Legard ordered, "Steady course two seven eight."

"Steady two seven eight, Bridge, Helm, aye."

The ship responded, the world rotating around them. The seaway was empty but for a few sailboats on the Atlantic. It would have been a great day for pleasure boating, Legard thought.

"Bridge, Helm, passing course two eight eight, ten degrees from ordered course."

The MLF building was beginning to shrink behind them. They were almost all the way through the turn.

"Bridge, Helm, steady on course two seven eight."

"Helm, Bridge, aye," Legard acknowledged. "Helm, all stop. *On deck! Pass over all tug lines!* Tug *Champney* Captain, take in your lines, and shove off. Thank you and good day to you, sir."

"Navy Submarine, tug Champney *Captain, roger, sir, and* bon voyage.*"*

The tug's lines were disconnected and it sounded its horn twice, then throttled up and sped off to the south.

"On deck! Rig the deck for sea!" Legard watched as the deck crew scrambled, putting mooring lines into the line lockers and rotating the cleats so that the hull would be streamlined. When they finished, the ship would look as though it had never been tied up to a pier. Legard took a deep breath of the salty sea air. The gentle breeze of their passage in his face began to make him feel a bit better from the morning's hangover.

"Helm, Bridge, all ahead two-thirds," he ordered. The deck crew could handle the slight speed increase as they were finished on the bow, the bow crew laying to the aft turtleback to assist them.

"On the bridge," a chief from the deck crew called, "deck is rigged for sea with the exception of the missile compartment hatch! Deck crew laying below!"

"Very well," Legard shouted, putting his megaphone away. Finally, he thought, they were almost ready to put some turns on and get the patrol on its way.

"Bridge, Control," Turnock's voice squawked. *"Deck crew is aboard, last man down, hatch rigged for sea."*

"Control, Bridge, aye." Legard turned. "Captain, deck is rigged for sea. I'm speeding up in accordance with the op order."

"Very well," Gardes said.

"Helm, Bridge, all ahead standard."

The ship's acceleration created a tremendous bow

wave forward. The sea spilled over the top of the elliptical nosecone and rushed aft over the cylinder of the foredeck, on either side of the sail before washing down at the turtleback. The wind picked up, starting to rise until it made conversation difficult without shouting. The roar of the bow wave competed with it, the furious noise of the rushing sea musical. The radar rotated steadily up behind the captain, and the flag of the Republic whipped violently in the breeze.

7

Capitaine de Frégate Jean-Paul Gardes lit his cigar, the stogie clamped in his teeth as he nodded seriously at Executive Officer Courcelle to begin the operation briefing. The officers were gathered in the officers' mess, their eyes on the western Atlantic chart projected on the aft bulkhead. Courcelle sat on Gardes' immediate right at the head of the table. On Gardes' left sat *Capitaine de Corvette* Aymeric Teisseire, *le Ingénieur*. The seat next to Courcelle was empty, as it belonged to the navigator, who would give the briefing. Beside Teisseire sat Weapons Officer Bertrand De Lorme. The supply officer took the end seat, and between the department heads and the supply officer, the ship's junior officers sat alertly, their notebooks ready, their coffee cups filled. This was exactly what Gardes wanted, he thought, a crew taut as a coiled spring.

Courcelle brought the meeting to order. "Whenever you're ready, *Navigateur*."

Capitaine de Corvette Adrian Molyneux, the ship's navigator, stood at the chart with a laser pointer in his hand. Molyneux was of medium height, with a powerful build, the second sea tour officer a complete "gym rat," living in the missile compartment when he was off watch, running and lifting weights. He had a dark complexion, his lower face shadowed from the denseness of his beard, and nearly perfect feminine features. Were it not for the scar running diagonally across his right cheek and his stubble, he could easily have the face of a pretty woman, from his brown eyes with their long eyelashes below arched, curving eyebrows, to his sculpted cheekbones, his rounded nose, his full lips, his sparkling white teeth and his stark, square jaw. His hair was a diesel oil black, combed back straight on his scalp. His "beauty" had always been the subject of the crew's joshing, but it had never seemed to bother the navigator. He had recently pursued and wed a dark beauty, Anaïs, the honeymoon ending just the week before. Now that he had won the girl, the crew had been wondering aloud if Molyneux would continue with his rigid workout schedule, but he dismissed the speculation. Gardes suspected Molyneux's gym dedication to be the navigator's unconscious attempt to seem more masculine, the constant surprise his girl's face garnered wearing on him. All that mattered was that Molyneux was an excellent navigator, and navigation was critical to mission success for a ballistic missile submarine, since no target could be hit by an ICBM unless the launching point were known precisely, within feet. It was said that Molyneux could be blindfolded, spun around a dozen times and released in a dark, surging nightclub, and unfailingly navigate his way to the most beautiful woman in the room. Judging by Anaïs, Molyneux's reputation was based on fact. There was no doubt, with a wife with her beauty, the Molyneuxs would someday create gorgeous children. Molyneux was known for one thing other than his body building and womanizing—he was perpetually anxious. Since Gardes had known him, the young lieutenant commander had probably smiled only twice. He had a mannerism, when nervous, of holding his fist in front of his face, his forearm perpendicular to the deck, his fingers clenching slightly. It always appeared to Gardes as if Molyneux wanted to clasp his fist to his mouth and bite it, but knew that expression would brand him as being fearful, yet he didn't have the self-control to avoid lifting his fist part way. Perhaps, Gardes thought, Anaïs could calm him down and give him the confidence that so far had seemed to evade him.

Beside Molyneux, happily and quietly savoring a bite

of steak, was *Capitaine de Corvette* Bertrand De Lorme, the weapons officer, *le Officier d'Armes*. Lieutenant Commander De Lorme was taller than Molyneux but shorter than Courcelle and Gardes, with a slim build and a nearly bald head. He was older than Gardes by four years, having come up through the enlisted ranks as a missile technician. In his previous incarnation as an enlisted man, De Lorme had shown such calm maturity that he had achieved one accelerated promotion after another, rising to the rank of warrant officer, then, in a rare event, promoted into the regular officer ranks.

The week before, De Lorme had invited Gardes and Danielle to his home for dinner, where they had met De Lorme's wife Véronique, who was a few years older than De Lorme but had aged gracefully, the gray in her hair making her seem all the more attractive. De Lorme's children were teenagers; slim and sulky Mattheiu, fifteen, and his younger sister Marlene, a sassy thirteen-year-old. Gardes had tried to penetrate De Lorme's calm exterior, the one time he remembered consciously trying to employ his strange insight, but De Lorme remained unreadable and inscrutable.

De Lorme, as *Le Vigilant*'s weapons officer, was an integral part of the chain of command, and in certain circumstances had as much authority as the ship's captain. It would be his M45 missiles that would descend over the surface of the planet to destroy the cities of any power foolish enough to attempt France's destruction, and such awesome power was not trusted to just any officer, no matter how stable or loyal or patriotic or talented he might be. The *Force Océanique Stratégique*'s weapons officers were screened extremely carefully to ensure that they would have the judgment and nerve to launch such weapons, knowing that their pressing a button would kill untold millions of innocent women and children as well as France's enemies. It was a responsibility that few officers could shoulder but, as De Lorme was as old a soul as Gardes had ever met, it seemed entirely fitting that the awesome responsibilities of *le sous-marin de missile ballistique* were entrusted to such a man.

The junior officers at the table were each a young force of nature, Gardes thought, each man of them a raging bachelor. The oldest of them, the five lieutenants, the senior stable of officers who ran the ship, sat together, all of them having reported aboard when the submarine was still under construction. Teisseire's engineering officers Jacques Legard, the main propulsion assistant, and Emile Everard, the damage control assistant, sat beside Molyneux's senior assistant, Michel Gannt, the communications officer. Next to Gannt was Lieutenant Victor Vasser, the *officier du sonar*, and next to him was Rémy Sanxay, the missile officer, both of whom worked for *Officier de Armes* De Lorme. Grouped together between the lieutenants and the department heads were the younger officers, who had spent more or less a year aboard, and were still working on their submarine qualifications. Two of them belonged to the Rhino—*Enseigne de Vaisseau de 1re Classe* Tristan Cholmondeley, the *officier électrique* and Henri Rousseau, the reactor controls assistant. The other two were split between De Lorme and Molyneux—Roland Beauvais, the torpedo officer, and Gerard Ramsden, the navigator's first lieutenant. It was interesting to Gardes how the junior officers seemed unconsciously to take on some of the characteristics of their bosses. The Rhino's men were aggressive and almost overbearing. Molyneux's two officers seemed more subdued and intensely quiet, while De Lorme's boys projected a quiet confidence, perhaps even a cocky certainty, as between them they were responsible for the missiles and torpedoes of the greatest warship ever built.

"Good morning, gentlemen," Molyneux began. "Our departure vector from Brest brings us here, to the eastern Atlantic. We expect to encounter hostile NATO forces beginning here," he said, tapping the chart as an orange area appeared in the sea. "This is where we think the cordon of French fast attack SSNs will be lying in wait along our track. Assuming our tactics defeat the French SSNs, the next threat to us will be British Royal Navy submarines, which we'd expect would be in a zone meant to avoid them interfering with the search of the French. Beyond them, in more distant barrier search, we expect to encounter two U.S. Navy attack submarines, one an Improved Los Angeles-class ship with a modernized sonar, the other a Virginia-class."

"Question, *Navigateur*," Legard asked.

"Yes, Mr. Legard."

"If we're Algerian terrorists, didn't we sink right about here out of ignorance in operating a submarine?" Legard pointed to the dive point not far out of Brest.

Molyneux nodded. "Possibly. But the admirals think that if they attempt such a thing, they would have experts aboard. Not French experts, but foreign experts. Chinese ballistic missile submarine engineers or sailors."

"But if they had experts," Legard challenged, "and they are hell-bent on launching a missile at Paris, why wouldn't they launch right here?" Again Legard pointed to the submergence point off Brest. "That way they would get their missiles off before any of these antisubmarine forces get to them."

"Good question," Molyneux said. "The answer is called *T2K*, or 'time-to-knowledge.' Even with experts, it will take some time for an invading terrorist force to figure out how to operate the submarine and employ the ballistic missiles. The exercise script calls for a *T2K* of eight days. Which means we have to defeat the SSNs or else we would be on the bottom."

"The terrorists would have to be as good as we are," Legard said.

"Let's pretend, shall we?" Molyneux said, returning to his briefing and circling the laser spot on the American submarine barrier search point. "The American submarines. This will be the challenge, gentlemen. Our own attack submarines are no problem. Their machinery is older and louder, and we know their tactics. The British will be tough, but our multifrequency intelligence states that we have a six-decibel sonar advantage in the frequencies of long-range detection. That leaves the Americans, and the Yanks have parity with us in acoustic silencing. In some frequencies we are quieter, on some, they're more silent. That's why the captain has a way to get them." The navigator smiled. "*Capitaine*, do you want to brief the anti-American tactic?"

Gardes smiled. "It's simple, men. Mr. Cholmondeley, tell me something that will cause a submarine to increase its noise emissions."

Cholmondeley shrugged. "Steam generator blowdown is probably the loudest, Captain. Ultrahot, high-pressure boiler water blasting out into nearly freezing seawater. You can hear it a hundred miles away. Or snorkeling on the diesel generator. The diesel chugging away can be heard as far away as a blowdown, maybe even further."

"Not what I'm thinking of. Next. Mr. Legard?"

"If you want to increase the noise levels of an enemy submarine, Captain, get him to increase his speed."

"That's right, men. If the Americans can be made to increase their speed, they will be louder, and that applies for several key detection frequencies. So if the U.S. ships are sailing fast and we're crawling, we'll hear *them* long before they hear *us*. Everyone clear on this?"

The officers nodded.

"Good. Now, Weapons Officer," Gardes said, calling on De Lorme, "how would you get an enemy submarine to increase its speed?"

De Lorme smiled like a schoolboy who knew the correct answer. "Well, Captain, I'd probably shoot a torpedo at him."

Gardes smirked. "Good, but that is a bit aggressive—I'd expect that answer out of *le Rhino* here." Teisseire smiled. "But from you, Mr. De Lorme, please. A little submariner's subtlety is called for here. Perhaps the navigator can help us. Mr. Molyneux?"

"We use geography, gentlemen. The Americans will be coming across a distance, racing to get to us. They'll be trying to detect us along our most probable escape route from the restricted water of the far eastern Atlantic. They'll therefore be doing a barrier search that attempts to cover a lot of ground. Which means they'll be going ten knots. Maybe only eight knots, but perhaps as high as twelve. Or even fifteen. So, with the Americans rattling through the sea at ten knots, we will have a different speed. Two knots, just enough for bare steerageway, just enough to make the towed sonar array trail in a line behind us. Given two submarines equal in acoustic advantage, with one at ten knots and one at two, which one wins the battle?"

"*We* do," *le Rhino* said, punctuating his declaration with his meaty fist as it banged the table and made the coffee cups jump in their saucers.

Gardes grinned and puffed his cigar. It was going to be a good operation, he thought. The Americans had better take their vitamins, because *Le Vigilant* was about to humiliate them at their own game.

The phone from the control room buzzed. Dillinger picked up the handset and glanced at the chronometer, which showed it to be almost quarter to four in the morning, Zulu time.

"Captain," he answered.

"Captain, Off'sa'deck," Merc's voice said into Dillinger's ear. "We have a detect on a new sonar contact, Sierra five-seven, bearing east-northeast, possible submerged warship."

Dillinger smiled. Maybe this would be over sooner than he had thought. "Man silent battlestations," he ordered. He turned off his notebook computer, stretched and walked calmly out the door to the control room. As he walked in, he caught the wireless headset tossed him by Steve Flood and stepped up to the periscope platform, where he could see the consoles of the attack center and the sonar repeater. The room was a flurry of tense but hushed activity as watchstanders hurried to their stations. Dillinger put the headset on and adjusted the unit's boom microphone. The rig had only one earphone, so that Dillinger's other ear could listen to the watchstanders in the room, the 7MC speakers, the radar intercept speakers and the sonar hydrophone speakers.

"Sonar, Captain," Dillinger said, "Report all contacts."

"Captain, Sonar, aye," Chief Tom Albanese's deep, jocular voice said over the JA phone circuit. Albanese was a muscular thirty-four-year-old of medium height with a thick head of flaming red hair. He had a recruiting-poster face, with chiseled, nearly perfect features, wide blue eyes and a perpetually affable expression that easily broke out into a grin. Dillinger couldn't recall when Albanese didn't have a Gauloises French cigarette between his lips. His sonarmen joked that his emergency air breathing mask had a special cigarette hole cut into it.

Albanese was single and a bachelor of wide and ill repute, leading to a shipboard scandal when he was caught in bed with the former electrical officer's wife. The lieutenant had pulled the two apart and given each of them a black eye. A week later the officer left both the woman and the ship to go to shore duty, and it had been up to Dillinger whether to enter the matter in Albanese's service record. If he did, it would ruin the talented chief's career. If he didn't, he would enable further antics.

Dillinger knew how Natalie would have reacted— Albanese would have found himself being shot out a torpedo tube. And counseling would go nowhere. The ship's previous executive officer had warned Dillinger against trying to reform the sonarman, saying the man would die before he gave up smoking, fornication or the BQQ-5. Any other man would find his Navy career dead, but there was a quality in Albanese that stayed his execution, because Albanese was born to be a sonarman. He had qualified in submarines in record time and had mastered the Q-5 in an even shorter interval. As a young second-class petty officer on his previous sea tour, he had been more expert than his first-class petty officers and rivaled his senior chief. Beyond that, Albanesc had almost supernatural abilities to detect submarines, sifting the meaningless jumble of static with his mind, melding with the computer's subroutines to reach out into the sea around them and pick out the submerged needle from the ocean's haystack. The more Dillinger knew him, the more he wanted to promote Albanese's career, moral turpitude notwithstanding.

"Conn, Sonar, new sonar contact, Sierra Twelve, bearing zero seven eight, definite submerged warship, French Triomphant-class!"

"Coordinator," Dillinger barked into his microphone as he turned to look at Flood, the relief pumping through his veins, "get a curve and a firing solution."

"Get a curve and a solution, Coordinator, aye," Flood snapped. "Plots and Firecontrol, get a curve."

"Plot, aye," Merc said.

"Pos Two, aye," said Lieutenant Mickey Selles on position two.

"Two minutes on the leg, Coordinator," Dillinger said, reminding Flood that he was waiting for the firing solution. Flood leaned over Selles' Pos Two and stepped quickly over to Mercury-Pryce's plot, then turned to Dillinger.

"Captain, we have a firing solution. Recommend launch."

"Firing point procedures," Dillinger said loudly into his mike and to the room. "Tubes one and two, Master One, horizontal salvo, one degree offset, one-minute firing interval."

His team would report in to him, by procedure confirming that all was well with the ordered release of weapons.

"Ship ready," OOD Scottson snapped.

"Weapon ready," Tonelle said from the weapons console.

"Solution ready," Flood said.

"Tube one, *shoot on generated bearing!*" Dillinger commanded. His heart hammered in his chest. It was like the second before a race began, his ears awaiting the gunshot.

"Set!" Selles called, hitting a fixed function key on his firecontrol console that would send the final solution of the computer over to Tonelle's panel, and from there to the torpedo in tube one, locking it into the weapon's pursuit computer.

"Standby!" Tonelle said, taking the stainless-steel trigger lever from the noon position to the nine o'clock STANDBY position. This would divorce the torpedo from any further instructions from the tube and fully arm the propulsion system, making it ready to start its engine.

"Shoot!" Dillinger ordered.

"*Fire!*" Tonelle confirmed, rotating the torpedo trigger all the way to the right to the three o'clock FIRE position.

There was a sudden loud swishing, then an explosive, booming roar that thumped the deckplates and reached up to clap both of Dillinger's eardrums. He yawned, equalizing the pressure in his eustachian tubes, the air vented back into the ship from the launching ram piston causing the ship's atmosphere to spike momentarily in pressure.

"*Conn, Sonar,*" Albanese said in his ear. "*Own-ship's unit, normal launch.*"

"Tube two," Dillinger called, "shoot on generated bearing!"

A second time the whoosh and the bang erupted in the room, a second set of heavy fists smashing Dillinger's ears.

"*Conn, Sonar, second-fired own-ship's unit, normal launch.*"

"Very well, Sonar," Dillinger said, yawning again, his ears crackling and clearing.

Dillinger stood back, almost smug. Two weapons on their way to the target. Ten minutes from now there would be two mock detonations to mark the end of this exercise. After that all he'd need to do would be to write the patrol report, go to a two-hour debriefing, then get home to Norfolk and take his place beside Natalie. After

they got home he promised himself, there would be no
more operations until the baby and Natalie were safe.
The next one, Steve Flood could take out the damned
boat.

Capitaine de Frégate Jean-Paul Gardes smiled at Executive Officer Courcelle in the crowded space of *Le Vigilant*'s control room.

"Isn't that something, *Ours Blanc*?" Gardes said.
"They've stumbled right into our trap."

"Good work, Captain." Courcelle leaned over the
firecontrol display, then looked back at Gardes. "Original tactical plan alpha is tracking, Captain," he said quietly. "Withdrawal vector is clear after evasion device
launch. Recommend you launch the evasion device."

"Firecontrol personnel," Gardes said into his boom
microphone, "firing point procedures, tube two, evasion
device on alpha program."

"Evasion device, tube two, ready, sir," De Lorme
announced.

"Tube two, shoot on programmed bearing," Gardes
ordered calmly, his eyes on the sonar repeater display.

"Conn, Sonar," Albanese's voice called on the circuit.
There was something wrong, Dillinger thought, detecting
something in the sonar chief's voice. Dillinger looked up
at the sonar display. The 266-hertz tonal was still there,
although it had become a doublet, twin towers rising
above the jagged noise level below.

"Go ahead, Sonar," Dillinger said when Albanese
was silent.

*"Conn, Sonar, we have a transient noise from Master
One and the two-sixty-six-cycle tonal has become a
doublet."*

So, Dillinger thought. What did that mean? "Very
well, Sonar," Dillinger responded. Flood held up two
fingers, confusing Dillinger even further.

"Conn, Sonar, we have two Master Ones."

"What? Say again, Sonar."

"Sir, believe Master One has launched an evasion de-vice. A countermeasure decoy. Sounds just like him. That explains the transient."

"Sonar, do you have any bearing separation?"

"Captain, Sonar, yes, and possible zig Master One. Master One's signal-to-noise ratio has increased, he's get-ting louder, aspect change."

"Dammit. Sonar, designate your left contact Master Two, the right contact Master Three."

"Conn, Sonar, aye, possible zig for both Master Two and Master Three. One is upshifting frequency, Two is downshifting. Believe Master Two is turning toward and Master Three is turning away."

Flood shook his head. "Pos Two, track Master Two as a new contact with range at time of zig equal to Mas-ter One's generated range. Pos One, track Master Three the same way."

Lieutenant Philly Breckenridge at pos one was now being fed data from sonar to track the right target at bearing 071. Selles at pos two was tracking the left target at bearing 067. Dillinger looked over Selles' left shoul-der, between positions one and two. Both dot stacks were ugly, the data from sonar going all over the display. Neither stack would settle down until the enemy stopped maneuvering.

"Very well. Attention in the firecontrol party; I intend to track Master Two and Master Three as they settle from their zigs. As soon as they steady on a new course, we will steer the weapons. Since we have two units in the water, we will steer each to a target. That way it won't matter which is the evasion device. After the tar-gets steady on their new courses, we'll execute a maneu-ver across the line of sight and nail down the range. Weapons Officer, apply torpedo power to weapons in tubes three and four and make tubes three and four ready with the exception of opening outer doors."

Dammit, the flaky French submarine was trying to dodge them with this evasion device fraud, but it wouldn't help the sons of bitches. It was a good thing there were two torpedoes vectoring in on the target, or Dillinger would have to make the decision of which to prosecute.

"Conn, Sonar, bearing separation increasing."

"Sonar, Captain, aye," Dillinger said tersely, fuming. In a few moments they would need to steer both torpedoes, or else they would miss both targets. "Coordinator, status of zig procedures?"

"Still integrating on this leg," Flood said, frowning at the firecontrol consoles. "Recommend slowing both torpedoes to slow-speed approach while we get a curve."

"Very well," Dillinger acknowledged. "Weps, downshift units one and two to slow-speed transit. Sonar, Captain, slowing own-ship's units pending firecontrol recommendation."

"Conn, Sonar, aye."

Dillinger waited. A bead of sweat formed at his hairline and moved slowly down his forehead.

Selles spoke into the circuit. "Pos Two has a curve." Then Breckenridge. "Pos One has a curve."

Dillinger turned to Merc. "Plots have a curve," Merc said, not looking up from the plotting table.

"Captain, we have a curve, recommend maneuver to course two eight zero, turning to the right."

Dillinger glared at pos three. He tapped Selles on the shoulder, who toggled his display from a dot-stack on Master Two to the geographic view. It was certain that the westward motion of both targets had ceased. Master Three's bearings and downshifted Doppler were consistent with him withdrawing northward, while Master Two had turned toward the *Hampton*, perhaps going south. Turning the ship to the west would drive the sonar sphere across the line of sight and nail down the two targets' true motions. Meanwhile, the northwest-traveling torpedoes had slowed to eighteen knots— walking speed for a torpedo—conserving their energy and awaiting orders to turn.

"Helm, left full rudder, all ahead two-thirds, steady

course two eight zero. Sonar, Captain, maneuvering to two eight zero, turning toward the targets."

"Conn, Sonar, aye."

"Sir, my helm is left full and Maneuvering answers, all ahead two-thirds."

Dillinger had ordered the ship to speed up through the turn to hurry through the maneuver. He'd order the ship to coast back down as they steadied up on the new course. He tapped his Academy ring on the periscope handrail, the tension making his hand shake. He stared at it as if it belonged to someone else. *Steady*, he commanded himself.

"Passing course north, sir," the helmsman reported.

"Very well," Dillinger said, slurring the words together.

"Passing course three zero zero to the right."

"Helm, all ahead one-third," Dillinger ordered. The ship slowed in the turn.

"All ahead one-third and Maneuvering answers, all ahead one-third. Passing course two nine zero to the left, ten degrees from ordered course."

"Vr'well."

"Steady course two eight zero, sir."

"Sonar, Captain, steady two eight zero, report all contacts."

Once again Albanese had emptied his frequency buckets, waiting for fresh data. It took endless seconds, but finally Albanese reported.

"Conn, Sonar, hold Master Two and Master Three on the towed array."

"Coordinator, get a curve, both targets," Dillinger ordered. The math should work out perfectly now, as long as the enemy didn't maneuver again, but God knew the bastard had launched the evasion device because he had heard them.

Ninety seconds later Flood nodded up at Dillinger. "Captain, we have firing solutions on Master Two and Three. Master Three range fifteen thousand yards, bearing zero four nine, course north, speed eight knots. Master Two range ten thousand yards, bearing zero seven two, course south, speed also eight knots. We have calculated steers for units one and two, with one turning to pursue on course zero four zero at high speed, unit two turning to course one one zero at high speed. Request to steer the units."

"Very well, Coordinator, insert steer commands."

Dillinger waited as Tonelle steered the torpedoes and sped them up.

"Conn, Sonar," Albanese's voice crackled in Dillinger's headset. *"Loss of Master Three."*

Dillinger nodded. The target that had turned north had receded until they lost his signal. It didn't matter—they had plotted his track and put the torpedo on him. He'd be dead soon anyway.

"Conn, Sonar, Master Two has shut down."

Dillinger swallowed. They should have easily heard the south-bound contact. He looked down at Flood.

"That was the evasion device," Flood said slowly. "Should we turn unit two? And maybe we should give chase to the north."

"Conn, Sonar," Albanese said loudly over the circuit, "torpedo in the water! Bearing zero six five! Second torpedo in the water! *Bearing zero six four!"*

There was no time to take recommendations—Master One had just launched two torpedoes at them, or else he had launched them some time ago and only now could they hear them. Dillinger should have seen this coming—if the boomer was aware enough of their presence that he had the presence of mind to launch this spooky evasion device, then he knew enough to launch two torpedoes down their bearing line.

There was only one tactic that the secret-classified *Submarine Approach and Attack Manual* said could save the ship—run from the torpedoes at maximum speed.

"Helm, all ahead flank!" Dillinger hoisted the 7MC microphone while the young helmsman acknowledged. "Maneuvering, Conn, cavitate!"

"Cavitate, Conn, Maneuvering, aye!"

"Helm, left twenty degrees rudder, steady course two one five. Sonar, Captain, evading to the southwest."

The deck began trembling as the screw came up to flank revolutions. The deck tilted suddenly as the ship executed the snap roll. Dillinger's knuckles became white on the periscope stand railing.

"We can turn unit two back to intercept Master One," Flood said.

Dillinger nodded. "Insert a steer to unit two and put it on Master One," he said. "Once that's done, we'll cut the wire and launch units three and four down Master One's last bearing line." If nothing else, a torpedo shot down the hostile bearing line might scare the boomer enough that he would let the *Hampton* escape. Over beer back in Norfolk, Peter Vornado called the tactic "using the fifty-three-centimeter evasion device."

"Steady course two one five, sir, and Maneuvering answers, all ahead flank," the helmsman called.

"Unit two is steered," Tonelle called.

"Weps, cut the wires units one and two and shut outer doors to tubes one and two!"

Tonelle acknowledged while Dillinger stared over his shoulder.

"Wires cut, doors closing on one and two."

"Weps, make tubes three and four ready in all respects."

Dillinger wouldn't go down without a fight, he thought. But how shameful it was to lose this exercise to the French. They weren't even driving an attack boat, for God's sake. How could they have gotten the better of the *Hampton*?

"Conn, Sonar, incoming torpedoes confirmed to be French ECAN model L5 Mod 3 torpedoes."

The L5 had a pursuit speed of only thirty-five knots. The *Hampton* was hauling ass away from the incoming torpedoes at 39.5 knots. With the L5s astern, they would soon be left behind. That was the good news. The bad news was that running from the torpedoes meant they were rapidly leaving the area of *Le Vigilant*. It also meant they needed to send a Code Four SLOT buoy to the NATO task group commander, letting him know that the damned French boomer had fired two shots at them, but before he did that, Dillinger would get off two more torpedoes at the boomer.

"Tubes three and four ready in all respects, Captain," Tonelle reported.

"Coordinator, you got Master One's last solution in pos two?"

"Yes, Captain."

"Very well. Attention in the firecontrol party. I intend to fire three and four blind, over-the-shoulder shots while we continue running to the south. When that's done, I intend to pop a Code Four SLOT. Carry on. OOD, prepare a SLOT buoy with Code Four and our present position."

"Aye, Captain," Scottson said.

Dillinger pulled Flood over. "Any chance these L5s are hotrodded? That they can go faster than thirty-five knots?"

Flood shook his head. "No way, Skipper. Nothing in the op brief about that."

"Good. We'll get away clean, then."

"Conn, Maneuvering, steam leak in the engineroom!" the 7MC crackled, Schluss' voice sounding muffled—he was wearing an EAB emergency breathing mask, Dillinger realized.

Scottson got to the 7MC mike before Dillinger could reach it. "Maneuvering, Conn, report location and severity!"

"Conn, Maneuvering, leak is aft of maneuvering on aft compartment upper level! We're having trouble with the port turbine generator dropping load, believe the leak to be from the port turbine throttle that was repaired by squadron."

"Fuck," Dillinger cursed. A real casualty in the middle of an exercise meant that the exercise was over. *Hamp-*

ton had just lost. But worse, the steam leak could become a fatal ship-killing emergency unless he allowed Schluss to act. "Helm, all stop!" He grabbed the 7MC microphone. "Engineer, Captain, downshift main coolant pumps and isolate the port side of the engineroom!"

"Downshift pumps and isolate port, Conn, Maneuvering, aye!" Schluss called.

"Steam leak in the engineroom," Dillinger announced on the 1MC shipwide announcing system. *"Casualty assistance team, lay aft!"*

A sudden whistle could dimly be heard in the room, coming from the aft port quarter. It almost sounded like a dolphin call.

"Conn, Sonar, incoming torpedoes are going active," Albanese reported, his voice flat as he delivered the bad news, because the torpedoes switching to active probably meant they had gotten a faint detection on the *Hampton*'s hull and were confirming their solution with active pinging. Unlike human operators, the brains of most torpedoes were effective at the use of active pinging sonar, but then it was usually only used once passive detection had succeeded. Anyone could read tea leaves when the answer had already been revealed. The use of active pinging would allow the pursuing torpedo to follow an evading target.

"Sonar, Captain," Dillinger said harshly, "are the torpedoes close or distant?"

"Torpedoes are distant."

"Engineer, what's your status?" Dillinger barked on the 7MC.

"Conn," Schluss shouted breathlessly through his air mask on the 7MC circuit, *"port side of the engineroom isolated, steam leak has stopped, propulsion limit, all head standard, turns for twenty knots."*

Twenty knots wasn't enough to evade the torpedoes, but what the hell, Dillinger thought. Maybe if he went to twenty knots he could keep the French units in pursuit long enough for them to run out of fuel and sink.

"Helm, all ahead standard," Dillinger ordered, then clicked the 7MC mike. "Maneuvering, Conn, make turns for twenty knots."

"Turns for twenty knots, Conn, Maneuvering, aye."

"Conn, Sonar, torpedoes are distant but pinging continues."

Dillinger glanced at the speed readout on the ship control panel. They had slowed from almost forty knots to twenty and were still coasting down.

"Conn, Sonar, torpedoes are closing."

The thought crossed Dillinger's mind that one of those evasion device decoys that the French boomer had used would come in handy right then.

"Officer of the Deck, load forward signal ejector with a Mark Nine evasion device." The aft signal ejector would be useless while the crew tried to recover from the steam leak. Scottson turned to the task.

"Conn, Sonar, torpedo signal-to-noise level increasing." Albanese's way of reminding Dillinger that he had done nothing to evade the torpedoes, but with propulsion limited to the slow speed of twenty knots, there was little Dillinger could do.

"Skipper, what about an under-ice tactic?" Flood asked. He frowned. "Or going upstairs?"

Dillinger thought quickly. At this point, there were only two tactics that would evade incoming close torpedoes—one was the under-ice tactic, hovering motionlessly in the sea, hoping that zero speed would make them invisible to the torpedo active pulses, but that would only work if the torpedoes had sophisticated Doppler filters that would make them blind to return pulses at the same frequency as the transmitted ping. And he had no idea if they had the filters or not, so he would be damned if he would hover here dumbly and helplessly, waiting to be hit by the boomer's weapons. The second tactic meant emergency surfacing, a total admission of defeat for a submarine, and expressly prohibited by the operation order, but which might evade the weapons if they had a similar ceiling setting to the

Mark 48 torpedo. The operation briefing hadn't given much intel on the torpedo at all, which meant he would have to guess.

Dillinger looked at Scottson.

"Status of forward signal ejector?"

"Mark Nine loaded, sir."

"On my mark, launch the forward signal ejector. Chief of the Watch, stand by to emergency blow both groups. Attention in the firecontrol party, my intentions are to conduct an EMBT blow of all main ballast tanks and proceed to the surface to get above the torpedoes' ceiling settings. Carry on."

A sudden whistle shrieked from aft in the room, the sound coming from outside the hull. It was joined by a second groaning, piercing, high-pitched whistle, from the second torpedo. They were close now, perhaps only a mile away.

Dillinger took a deep breath. Should he violate the op order and blast to the surface, or lose to the French without a fight? Either way it would be a failure. He might as well fail boldly, he thought. "OOD, launch the Mark Nine! Chief, *emergency blow both groups!*"

Martinez stood and pulled down the operators on both stainless-steel "chicken switches," and rotated them both into the overhead. The roar of the air system was immediate, the sound of it slamming Dillinger's already sore eardrums. The room filled with white fog and visibility shrank. By feel, Dillinger was able to find a periscope platform handrail. Just as he got a grip on it, the deck began to angle upward steeply. He couldn't see the inclinometer, but they must be at a twenty degree up-bubble. Dillinger looked at the fog, suddenly feeling a dreamlike, disconnected state. The sound of the alarm klaxon startled him back to the moment. Martinez's voice blared over the 1MC, *"Surface, surface, surface!"*

Behind them, at the one-thousand-foot depth they had just left, the Mark Nine evasion device would be erupting into a huge cloud of bubbles while transmitting a loud 300-hertz tonal and a noise that a loud screw would make. Between the two noises and the bubbles, a less sophisticated torpedo would see a target and be confused, perhaps for long enough for them to get above the ceiling.

"Four hundred feet, sir," the diving officer, Senior Chief Mechanics Mate Fred Davies, called. "Three hundred. Two hundred feet."

"Chief of the Watch, secure the blow fore and aft," Dillinger ordered. Martinez pulled the blow levers back down, but without the fans and air conditioning, the fog in the room lingered.

"Conn, Sonar, loss of signal on both torpedoes," Albanese reported.

The angle came suddenly off the deck.

"Surfaced, sir," Davies announced.

"Raising number two scope," Scottson announced. The periscope hydraulics thumped as the unit rose out of the well. Dillinger needed to get the ship submerged again, but those two torpedoes were still down there.

"Conn, Sonar," Albanese announced. *"Loss of contact on both torpedoes."*

"Did you lose them from the layer or because they've shut down?"

"Captain, believe both torpedoes have stopped pinging."

Dillinger smiled, but then bit his lip. They'd avoided losing the exercise to the torpedoes—if Albanese were correct—but the enemy boomer was still out there. What if the torpedoes were in some sort of "reattack mode?"

"Sonar, Captain, are you certain the torpedoes are shut down, or just that your signal faded?"

"Conn, Sonar, we have the sounds of two torpedoes imploding and breaking up."

A cheer rang out in the room.

"Quiet," Dillinger snarled. "Helm, all ahead two-thirds. Diving Officer, submerge the ship to six hundred feet." They had to get deep, before some unaware supertanker ran them over, or a NATO radar picked them up and considered them the enemy. It was bad enough losing the boomer, much less taking friendly fire for having had to surface.

"Conn, Sonar, we have a transient from bearing zero four nine."

A "transient" was a fleeting noise—a hatch slamming shut against its hatchway, a dropped wrench banging on the deck, a torpedo tube door opening.

"OOD, train the scope to zero four nine," Dillinger said, glancing up at the periscope video. It was too dark to see anything except the lights of a ship, but the transients could be coming from surface shipping approaching their darkened, surfaced hull.

Flood looked at Dillinger. "Another torpedo launch?"

"We wouldn't hear that," Dillinger said. "We didn't hear the first two, and the boomer was in weapons range then. Now he's way over the horizon, dammit."

"Submerge the ship to six hundred feet, Dive, aye. Chief of the Watch, open all main ballast tank vents and announce the dive over the 1MC."

"Open all main ballast tank vents, Chief of the Watch, aye, opening all MBT vents," Martinez called. The klaxon rang out through the ship. Martinez's voice boomed over the speakers: *"Dive, dive."*

"Depth five-four feet," Davies said. "Depth five-five feet. Sail's under, sir."

It was taking too long to submerge, Dillinger thought impatiently. His mind turned to attacking the boomer, his gaze on the geographic plot. The transients reported by sonar had come from the same direction as their last bearing to Master One. His next thought was interrupted by Albanese.

"Conn, Sonar, loud transient, bearing zero six one!"

Scottson shouted suddenly from the periscope, "Captain, we have a missile launch, bearing mark!"

"Goddammit," Dillinger cursed as he shot a look at the periscope video. "Hit the high-power doubler," he ordered Scottson.

The image jumped in the view, but it was

unmistakable—the bright white flame trail led from a
ballistic missile launched from the sea, beginning to arc
slightly over.

"Helm, all ahead one-third! Diving Officer, make your
depth six-eight feet. Sonar, Captain, remaining at periscope depth. Mr. Selles, lay to radio and prepare a flash
OPREP-3 message notifying NATO ComTaskGru Two
of the missile launch. Attention in the firecontrol party!
Master Three has launched a missile. He may have gotten one off, but our job is to put him on the bottom
before he can launch any more birds. Snapshot, tube
three, bearing zero six one, insert range forty thousand
yards, high-to-medium active snake, run depth eight zero
feet. Sonar, Captain, launching snapshot." In snapshot
mode, none of the usual status calls were required. Dillinger was shooting from the hip, but there was nothing
else he could do until he had Master One back on sonar.

"Set," Vickerson called.

"Stand by," Tonelle said. "Fire!"

The tube barked as the heavy torpedo left the ship.

"Snapshot tube four," Dillinger ordered, "bearing
zero six zero, range forty-five thousand yards, high-to-
medium active snake."

The second torpedo launch shook the ship as Mikey
Selles ran into the room with a clipboard with a draft
message printout. It was the panic call to the task group
commander that the French ballistic missile sub had gotten off a shot, the news relayed using preformatted al-
phanumeric fields rather than words. Dillinger signed it.
"Transmit," he ordered. Selles disappeared with the
clipboard.

"Conn, Radio, request the HDR."

"Chief of the Watch, raise the HDR mast," Dillinger called.

The thump of hydraulics sounded as Martinez raised
the radio mast so the radiomen could transmit the admission of defeat.

*"Conn, Radio, message transmitted, HDR coming
down."* Hydraulics thumped again as the mast lowered.

"Dive, make your depth eight hundred feet, steep angle," Dillinger ordered. "Helm, all ahead full, steer course zero two zero."

"Lowering number two scope," Scottson called.

The deck plunged below Dillinger's feet as the ship dived deep.

"Conn, Sonar, second loud transient from Master One, suspect second missile launch."

"Dammit," Dillinger muttered. "Sonar, Captain! Report status of two own-ship fired units!"

"Conn, Sonar," Albanese said, his voice sounding almost back to normal, with his neutral, slightly cocky tone. *"Units three and four going active at this time."*

"Any sign of the target's detecting the Mark 48s?"

"Conn, Sonar, no." There was a pause. *"Conn, Sonar, we now have transients from Master Three. He's cavitating, speeding up."*

Scottson looked over at Dillinger. "He's the one running like a scared rabbit now, Skipper."

"Like we were ten minutes ago," Dillinger said dryly. "Sonar, Captain, any sign of a counterfire by Master Three?"

Albanese's response was immediate. *"Conn, Sonar, no."*

"Captain, unit three, is—is," Tonelle stuttered uncharacteristically.

Dillinger jumped off the conn platform, wondering if the *Hampton*'s torpedo had turned toward them. He hurried to the weapons control console.

"What, Weps?"

"Detect, unit three, sir!" Tonelle said. "The weapon is homing."

The control room crowd cheered. It wouldn't be long now.

"Unit four, detect, Captain."

Dillinger looked at Flood. The exercise had finally broken their way, although the damned boomer had gotten off two missiles. At this point, there was nothing Dillinger could do about that.

"Loss of wire guidance, unit three!" Tonelle announced. "Loss of wire continuity, unit four.

"Conn, Sonar, we still have contact on Master Three. He's running at his flank speed to the northwest, but both Mark 48s are beeping. We're confirming two hits on Master Three."

Dillinger nodded. They'd lost the objective of sinking the boomer before he launched, but at least they'd saved the *Hampton* and sunk the French ship. The question was, would his op order–violating emergency surface nullify the exercise result?

"Conn, Sonar," Albanese called. *"Aircraft engines, bearing northeast, believe to be possible ASW helicopter."*

"Well," Dillinger said. "Cavalry's here." He looked at Flood. "Hopefully they won't claim they got the kill."

"Conn, Sonar, helicopter bearing zero three five is dipping a sonar." The helicopter had hovered and lowered a hydrophone into the water.

"Dammit," Dillinger grumbled. "I hope he doesn't think we're the boomer."

"Conn, Radio, we've received the first letter of our callsign on the VLF loop."

"Very well, Radio," Dillinger answered. The brass obviously were calling them to periscope depth. The exercise had ended.

"Conn, Radio, second letter of our callsign is aboard. Recommend transit to periscope depth."

"Helm, all stop. Diving Officer, make your depth one five zero feet, steep angle. Sonar, Conn, proceeding shallow in preparation to coming to periscope depth. Report all contacts."

Two minutes later the periscope broke the deep blue waves of the eastern Atlantic in the brilliant, cloudless morning.

"Conn, Radio, request the HDR mast."

"Chief, raise the HDR mast," Dillinger ordered as he made a slow surface search on the periscope. The sea was empty except for the hovering helicopter, which stopped its sonar transmission and raised its hydrophone when it sighted *Hampton*'s periscope.

"Conn, Radio, we've got immediate message traffic aboard from the satellite. We're also being raised on UHF Nestor from the helicopter."

Dillinger reached into the overhead above the diving officer's station to the red handset for the UHF Nestor circuit, a satellite secure voice radio system.

"Radio, Captain, what's the satellite message read?"

"Conn, message reads, 'Format Alpha Victor Nine, item one, Delta Tango X-ray, item two, Whiskey Fox-trot Lima.' "

"Very well. Navigator?"

Mercury-Pryce furiously thumbed through the NATO codebook. While he did, the UHF circuit made blooping noises from the overhead speaker until a human voice came through, a Carolina accent blasting into the control room.

"Victor Mike, this is Lima Charlie, over."

Dillinger glared at Merc. "Navigator, what does the message decode to? It'd be nice to know before I answer the telephone."

"Captain, message reads, 'terminate exercise, transfer commanding officer to flagship.' "

"Like I thought." He picked up the red radiotele-phone handset. "Lima Charlie, this is Victor Mike, over."

"Victor Mike, Lima Charlie. From ComTaskGru Two, immediate execute as follows: Terminate exercise and surface for helicopter transfer of commanding officer to the flagship, over."

"Lima Charlie, Victor Mike, roger, out." He replaced the handset and reached for the 1MC microphone. "Attention all hands. This is the captain. The exercise is terminated with the *Hampton* alive, the boomer dead, but with a ballistic missile launched." Better to say that than to demoralize the crew by announcing that they had lost, even though they had. It could have been worse, with the loss of the *Hampton* itself to the boomer's exercise torpedoes. "Carry on."

Dillinger turned to Scottson. "OOD, secure battlestations, surface the ship and station the helicopter transfer party. XO, station the command duty officer. I'll be in my stateroom changing."

In his stateroom, Dillinger glanced at his picture of Natalie. "Hold on, honey. I'm coming home."

8

Commander Burke Dillinger stood in the massive, spotless, white-painted aircraft hangar deck of the French aircraft carrier *Charles de Gaulle* and tried to concentrate on the drive-in-movie-sized projection screen showing the unfolding battle of Exercise *Urgent Surge*, looking down from forty thousand feet. The cultured English accent of the Task Group 2 operations officer droned on, the man's voice rising in excitement at the decisive moment in the encounter—when *Le Vigilant* launched the L23 fifty-three-centimeter evasion device that sounded exactly like her and turned in a choreographed dance move to the north while the evasion device's path curved to the south, and seconds later, the launching of the two ECAN torpedoes toward the bearing line of the *Hampton*.

Dillinger heard distant laughter, then realized the crowd in the room—NATO staff types, aviators, captains of the surface ships and half of the officers of *Le Vigilant*—was staring at him.

"Commander Dillinger?" the British ops boss said again. "Are you with us?"

"Yes, Captain," Dillinger answered.

"At this point in time, Commander, when you have detected the incoming ECAN torpedoes, you failed to eject a Code Four SLOT buoy to inform the flagship that you were under attack. As I am certain you are aware, this was a serious violation of the op order. Can you explain yourself?"

A thundercloud crossed Dillinger's face for a moment.

"We were kind of busy with a major steam leak in the engineroom while running from the torpedoes. Unlike the scenario of the exercise, the steam leak was real. It threatened the ship. I know the task group needed the information on the counterattack, and a Code Four was loaded and ready to shoot, but I needed the forward signal ejector for the Mark Nine evasion device and I needed it immediately. I withdrew the Code Four, loaded the Mark Nine and emergency blew to evade the torpedoes."

"I say, couldn't you have just launched the Code Four, then loaded the Mark Nine?" the Royal Navy officer asked, his brow knitted.

"That would have taken valuable seconds away from saving the ship," Dillinger said. "Are you saying you'd have me communicate with you as a higher priority than saving my command?"

"Commander," the Brit said coldly, "that's precisely what I'm saying."

The discussion went on for the next ten minutes about Dillinger's failure to follow procedures and communicate with the flagship. The real failure, he thought, was in being fooled by the evasion devices long enough that *Le Vigilant* was able to get off two missile launches to the South Atlantic European Union missile test range. The briefing hadn't gotten to the point of the French boomer's missile launch. Dillinger was certain the room would enjoy barbequing him over that failure as soon as they got done blaming him for violating the submarine ceiling by emergency blowing to the surface. His mind wandered as the excruciating briefing continued for endless minutes. As he had suspected, his every action was dissected, examined and found wanting. The lesson learned would appear to be that anyone who violated battle procedures—as by turning toward the submerged target—had damned well better win the battle. Out of Dillinger's peripheral vision he saw a figure. He turned and saw Peter Vornado.

"Hey," Dillinger said from the side of his mouth while appearing to pay attention to the debriefing.

"Hi, B.K.," Vornado said quietly. "What do you think?"

"Fuck these guys," Dillinger muttered. "Goddamned boomer cheated with that evasion device trick."

"They always do. Classic SecEx."

"I can't believe they made us come up in the middle of Helen for this."

"I heard you took casualties."

Dillinger nodded. "Petty Officer Murphy died of his injuries. And the other three wounded will be hospitalized for some time."

"What the hell happened?"

"Inboard induction valve operator handle came out of the overhead at a fifty degree-up bubble. Murphy took it in the forehead."

"I met him once. He seemed like a great kid."

"Yeah. He was married and had a one-year-old. My first order of business is visiting his widow. What do I tell her? It was just a game to make the French feel better about their boomer security?"

"I don't know why the French are crowing so loud about *Le Vigilant*'s 'victory.' If this happened for real, Paris would be cinders."

"They're psyched because they made us look like monkeys."

"What happened out there?" Vornado asked. "Did you do the active sonar tactic from the op brief? That's what we found out in our SecExes. It's the only way to defeat the evasion device tactic. If you'd pinged at this asshole he'd be at the bottom."

"Now you tell me," Dillinger grumbled. "Only one problem. My sonar genius has no idea how to interpret active sonar."

Vornado nodded quietly. "Mine too. Fleet-wide problem. Better get him trained."

"Yeah." Dillinger paused. "Did you ever get a sniff of this guy?"

"Not one. And the debrief showed us within ten miles of the son of a bitch. He's quieter than a hole in the ocean."

"Well," Dillinger said, nodding, "at least my sonar chief detected and held on to him." He bit his lip, going back to the moment when he decided against using the active sonar gear.

The debriefing continued with the detailed dissection of Dillinger's mistakes. He couldn't help noticing that his engineroom emergency was not treated as extenuation, and as he suspected, the British ops boss was furious over Dillinger's emergency ascent to the surface, which could have caused a collision with a friendly surface ship.

"What would you have me do, Captain," Dillinger said, "take the torpedoes up my tailpipe to avoid scraping some paint off one of your out-of-position skimmers?" Dillinger's use of the derisive term for surface ship deepened the frown of the Royal Navy officer.

"You don't seem to have an adequate appreciation for the gravity of your repeated procedural violations, Commander Dillinger," the Brit said coldly. "I assume that will be remedied after our briefing of your commanders."

"Just to set the record straight here, Captain," Dillinger said, knowing he should just keep his mouth shut, but unable to stop himself. "Absolute adherence to your rules of engagement and op order procedures would not have won this battle."

"We disagree, sir. Had you employed your active sonar in accordance with the op brief, this battle would have been yours."

Dillinger frowned over at Vornado but said nothing.

Finally the debrief wound down. The French admiral took the podium and commenced his wrap-up speech by congratulating the crew of *Le Vigilant* while scolding the antisubmarine warfare forces of the French and British fleets, but piling on with a particularly harsh assessment of the performance of the *Texas* and the *Hampton*.

The briefing broke up and the officers vanished to their staterooms to dress for the formal reception being given by the officers of *Le Vigilant.* Vornado lingered behind with Dillinger, their backs to the projection screen that still depicted Dillinger's loss to the French SSBN.

"So, Peter, anything new with Rachel?"

"Worse. There were e-mails from her. She's already had three meetings with her attorney. There are papers waiting for me when I get back. I can barely believe it. It's over. It just seems like a bad dream." Vornado looked down at the deck, his face flushing.

Dillinger clapped him on the shoulder, feeling his friend's pain. "I'm so sorry, Peter. God, I would never have thought it would come to this. Look, you always have a place at my house."

Vornado shut his eyes and rubbed them with his fingers, sniffling. "Thanks, but won't Natalie be annoyed at me being underfoot?"

"She'll love having you with us, I mean that, but that reminds me. I need to call her again."

"How is she?"

"I haven't gotten her yet. Just messages on the house phone and her cell." Dillinger's face became a mask of worry, the lines of fatigue deepening.

"Any e-mails?"

"A few, but the latest was three days old."

"Go call her, B.K. I'll meet you at the reception."

Dillinger hurried to his borrowed stateroom in the bowels of the gigantic aircraft carrier, in this odd parallel universe where passageways were painted the wrong color, and the labels and signs were in a different language. He unwrapped the dinner dress white uniform sent over by the squadron, wondering how well it would fit him. It was fully rigged with commander's shoulder boards and medals. He pulled on the black pants and the tuxedo-style shirt, the studs already inserted and ready. The starched white jacket fit perfectly. He grabbed the black bow tie, the act of tying it inevitably reminding him of his father, General Dillinger, former deputy director of the Defense Intelligence Agency, now lying quiet in his grave these last ten years. When the bow tie looked presentable, Dillinger hurried up two levels to the island structure and the communication center.

The French lieutenant on duty broke into a wide smile. "Commander Dillinger," he said in genuine pleasure. "Good to see you again. Let me see if I can get the satellite connection back for you."

"Thank you, Pierre," Dillinger said, handing him the card with Natalie's numbers on it.

Once again there was no answer at the house or on her cell phone. Dillinger tried the number for Natalie's mother, but it rang four times and clicked into voice mail. Dillinger frowned and scribbled a new number on the card. The lieutenant punched the key sequence and handed the phone to Dillinger.

"Kraft here," the voice of Smokin' Joe Kraft boomed in Dillinger's ear.

"Commodore, it's Dillinger."

There was a slight pause. "Hold on, B.K." Dillinger waited. When Kraft returned his voice was gentler. "B.K., how are you? I heard about the exercise. Even though this thing didn't break your way, from what I saw you did a hell of a job."

"Thanks for the consolation prize, Commodore, but we fucked up. Should have used the active tactic, but we're rusty. I'll fix that, sir. It won't happen again."

"Ah, it's our fault, B.K. When was the last time we emphasized active sonar? We're supposed to be stealthy. Anyway, you should be turning the ship over to Flood and getting ready to be flown home. Are you ready to leave?"

"Yes, sir. But I need a favor." Dillinger described his trouble trying to get Natalie on the phone. Dillinger could hear Kraft snapping his fingers and muttered conversation with one of his aides.

"Okay, B.K., there's a staff car on the way right now. Give me the number where I can get you back."

Dillinger took the number from the lieutenant and read it to Kraft.

"Got it, B.K. Go enjoy the reception."

"Thank you, sir."

Dillinger thanked the French communications officer and the radiomen in the space, then left to go to the officers' messroom. As he hurried down the passageway he checked his watch. In two hours he would change and take a helicopter to the American aircraft carrier USS *Nimitz*, then a fighter jet to Virginia Beach's Oceana Naval Air Station. Within an hour of landing he'd be by Natalie's side. It couldn't come soon enough, he thought. When he opened the door of the carrier's wardroom he felt like he'd stepped into the lobby of a five-thousand-dollar-a-night hotel. The room was cavernous, able to seat at least two hundred officers, with mahogany paneling on the bulkheads, bright, gleaming white paint, polished brass fixtures and starched linen tablecloths. The room was lit by candlelight, with the flags of the NATO participants hanging from the overhead. Dillinger frowned at the room, wondering if his Royal Navy detractors would approach him to continue their complaints. He looked for Vornado, but there was no sign of his friend. He found himself at an hors d'oeuvre table. He shrugged and hoisted a plate, unsure of which exotic food to load it with. While he was deciding, a French naval officer in a resplendent starched, formal uniform walked up to him.

"Commander Dillinger?" he said in heavily accented English, the words seeming melodious coming from him, compared to the harsher pronunciation of the senior French staff. Dillinger turned to look at the officer. He was slightly taller than Dillinger, and thinner, with dirty blond hair that would have been too long for American regulations. He wore a white uniform with black shoulderboards, each with three thin gold stripes, with white stripes between the gold ones, the insignia of what would be a full commander in the U.S. Navy. He had a round face with defined cheekbones and a strong chin, gleaming white teeth and green eyes, with crow's-feet that curled into smile lines. He held out a large hand to Dillinger.

Dillinger shook his hand. "Call me B.K. And you, sir?"

"Commander Jean-Paul Gardes," he said warmly, his smile growing wider. "It is a deep honor to meet you, Commander. I mean, B.K. I want to apologize for the rudeness of my command structure. You rattled them, sir. Oh yes, you scared the hell out of them. You were one sonar ping from sinking the entire deterrent force of France. Actually, you did sink us, but just two missiles too late."

"I'm sorry, Captain Gardes," Dillinger said. "Did you say you were on staff with NATO?"

"Me? Oh, no, B.K. And call me Jean-Paul. I'm the commanding officer of *Le Vigilant*."

Dillinger stared at the French officer. "Congratulations on your win."

Gardes waved off the remark. "Please, B.K. We were nearly stopped while you had to keep your speed up. Of course we could hear you first. Had the roles been reversed, you would have put me on the bottom. Besides, I couldn't sink you. It was a draw."

"Yeah, except you got your missiles launched."

Gardes tilted his head. "Only by seconds. We got hit a moment later. I would not call that a decisive win."

Dillinger nodded. "May I buy you a drink, Jean-Paul?"

Gardes grinned. "Absolutely, my friend." They walked to the bar, where Gardes ordered them both a glass of an exotic French wine, but then, anything not out of Napa Valley was exotic to Dillinger.

"Anyway, B.K., let me apologize for the NATO task group's rudeness. You rattled them badly."

"Why do you say that?"

"Because you threw the procedures out the window. They can't predict a captain like you. That keeps them awake at night."

"But it almost worked."

"Precisely, but until they can make your tactics their procedures, they will feel threatened by you."

"B.K.," Vornado said from behind him.

Dillinger smiled at him. "Peter, may I present Commander Jean-Paul Gardes, the captain of the victorious *Le Vigilant.* Commander Gardes, this is Commander Peter Vornado, the captain of the USS *Texas.*"

Vornado smiled politely and shook Gardes' hand. "Pleased to meet you, Captain," he said formally in his authoritative baritone voice. "And congratulations to you and your crew."

"Thank you, Commander."

After a few minutes of conversation between the three officers, Dillinger grinned over at Vornado. "If I weren't leaving in two hours I'd propose we stay up all night and get drunk with Jean-Paul."

"Jean-Paul and I will carry on after you go," Vornado said.

After his second drink, Gardes had withdrawn all his wallet photos. "This is my wife Danielle."

Vornado whistled. The blond woman smiling from the picture was breathtakingly gorgeous.

"And this is my daughter, Margaux." The four-year-old in the picture had blond hair and blue eyes, reminding Dillinger slightly of Vornado's daughter Erin. "The older boy is Marc. The infant is my second daughter, Renée."

Dillinger glanced surreptitiously at Vornado, wondering if Gardes' enthusiasm for his family would make Vornado feel maudlin, but Peter withdrew his own photos, the two men talking and drinking as if all were right in the world. Dillinger grinned, shaking his head, thinking about how lucky he was—a world disaster had turned out to be just a dream, and the very adversary he had sweated and bled to defeat turned out to be a proud family man who knew his wine and loved to tell a good joke.

"And you, B.K.?" Gardes asked. "Do you have children?"

"One on the way," Dillinger said, smiling and reaching into his own wallet. "This is Natalie, my wife. She's due now with the baby."

"Oh, she is *exquisite*," Gardes said, whistling. "What a magnificent specimen of American beauty, my friend."

A sudden worry made Dillinger glance at his watch. "I should go check at the comm center and see if I can reach her," he said. "Gentlemen, if you would forgive me?" Dillinger looked at Gardes and Vornado, who both seemed startled by a figure behind Dillinger. Dillinger turned to see what they were looking at.

Admiral Amaury Devereux stood beside Lieutenant Pierre Dardin, the communications officer. Devereux had closed the briefing in the hangar deck with disdainful comments about the lacking performance of *Hampton* and *Texas*, but there were only sorrow and concern in his lined face. Pierre's face was drained of color, and he merely stared at the deck. Dillinger felt his heart pounding and his pulse roaring in his ears.

"Commander Dillinger, I have a matter of extreme urgency for you," the admiral began in his clipped accent. "There is an emergency at home. You must leave at once. Lieutenant Dardin will accompany you to a waiting helicopter to transfer you to the *Nimitz*. We will send your personal items separately. There is no time for you to pack."

Dillinger's stomach plunged as he blinked at the senior officer.

9

An emergency at home, Dillinger thought. *Natalie*.

No matter how hard he tried later, Dillinger could remember nothing of the next minutes. He knew he had said something to Vornado, then was guided by Pierre through the labyrinthine passageways of the ship until they emerged into the darkness of early evening and the shrieking noises on the flight deck. A deck crewman handed him a jacket and an aviation helmet with a boom microphone and built-in headset, then hurried him to a huge, idling helicopter with the markings of the French Navy, the European Union and NATO painted on it. In seconds Dillinger sat strapped into an aft seat, still wearing his dinner dress whites beneath a combat fatigue jacket. He shivered in the cold. A noise crackled in Dillinger's headset, a heavily accented voice drilling into his eardrums.

"Commander, are you strapped in?"

Dillinger couldn't find his voice. He saw the pilot turn to look at him, then back to his panel. The noise roared in Dillinger's ears. He was barely aware of the lights of the *Charles de Gaulle* fading beneath them or of the time it took before the USS *Nimitz* came into view.

The engines whined to idle as the door opened and two helmeted crewmen of the *Nimitz* pulled him out of the French helicopter. He felt the sweaty French helmet pulled off his head and the new U.S. Navy helmet replace it. The walk to the waiting F-14 was only a few steps, but the fabric of reality was badly wrinkled. It seemed as if Dillinger blinked and he was inside a tight rear seat in the supersonic fighter's cockpit, in a cocoon of instruments and displays under a bubble of Plexiglas, and as he looked around himself in astonishment he felt the thunderous roar of two huge jets on full afterburners and he was instantly on his back staring up at the instrument panel as the world outside became a blurred tunnel.

The deck of the aircraft carrier was no longer beneath him. There was nothing but the cockpit around him and the dark sky overhead and the screaming roar of the jets and the airflow outside the cockpit. He couldn't be sure if the wait was minutes or hours. The cockpit faded for a moment and when he opened his eyes the sky overhead was filled with a million bright diamonds of stars. From deep inside he dimly remembered seeing this sky from the bridge of one of his submarines, but it seemed as if that were a different time in someone else's life. There was blackness for long moments or hours after that. The buzzing in his mouth brought him back to reality and he tried to open his eyes. The sky overhead was dark as crude oil and the stars were gone. The noise of the jets howled one second and quieted the next.

A hard thump and the jet vibrated. Lights zoomed by outside the cockpit as the jet noise returned, the cockpit shuddering. The world rotated outside. The canopy opened slowly. Cool, salty air flowed into the cockpit. Two hands reached down to his harness and unbuckled him. Dillinger stood, crouching under the canopy, the technicians placing his shoes onto the ladder rungs. He lowered himself to the concrete taxiway, glancing at the huge fighter jet. His helmet was removed, his hair matted to his scalp. A hand on his upper arm, hurrying him to a waiting sedan, a large dark-painted Ford Crown Victoria. Beacon lights flashed from the headlights, mirrors, tail lights and rear window. An unmarked police car. He was in the front seat. A state trooper with a Smokey Bear hat put the car in gear and gunned the engine. The roads of the base gave way to the interstate. The interstate faded to a side road. The car stopped at an emergency room entrance. The door opened and a Navy petty officer stood outside and guided him to the automatically opening door. The white corridors moved past him. An elevator door closed. He looked at the petty officer. She looked familiar. As the elevator came to a stop he placed her as the one who had knocked on his door in the storm, a thousand years ago, but he couldn't remember her name.

Down the corridor. It smelled of antiseptic cleaners and floor wax. Harsh white lights overhead. A door opening. His fatigue jacket pulled off him. His hands in hot water, a nurse scrubbing his hands. A cap over his sweat-soaked hair. A green gown wrapped around his body. His feet guided into the pant legs of green surgical scrubs. Green sterile booties wrapped over his shoes. Latex gloves placed over his scrubbed hands. Clear safety glasses on his eyes. A hand on his shoulder, guiding him past two sets of glass doors into a large room crowded with medical machines and lights and equipment. An operating table. Someone on the table. Left arm stretched out, IV tubes snaking into the bare skin. Green sheets covering the abdomen, lifted up into a tent. A green cap covering the patient's head. An oxygen mask over the patient's face. Two men and three women in surgical scrubs concentrating on their work at the end of the table. Dillinger looked at the patient's face. The nose under the clear plastic of the oxygen mask belonged to Natalie. Above the mask were her eyes, her lids closed.

Without thinking he found her hand. It was warm, but limp and sweaty. Without consciously saying anything, he heard his own voice say his first words since Admiral Devereux had found him.

"Natalie. I'm here."

Her eyelids opened slowly. Her eyes were unfocused at first, but then, as she turned toward him, she registered recognition.

"Burke. You made it." She smiled slowly into the oxygen mask, as if drugged.

"You'll be okay, baby," he said, putting his face close to hers and gripping her hand in both of his.

Her eyes filled with tears and her hand trembled. "I'm so glad you got here in time."

"I know." He smiled. "With not much time to spare." He looked over at the surgeon, a tall, thin woman who frowned at him. "Doctor, how long?" he asked.

The surgeon looked up at him, then back down at her incision. That was odd, Dillinger thought. It was as if she deliberately chose not to answer him. He looked back at Natalie. "Was there trouble with labor, honey?"

She shook her head slowly. "No," she said drowsily. "It was planned."

Planned, he wondered. Why did they wait to fly him here? Why was it called an emergency?

"Thank God." He smiled at her. "I'm so excited."

Natalie shut her eyes and opened them slowly. More tears had come. A shiver ran down his spine. Something wasn't right.

"I'm so glad you came back," she said.

"I am too, baby," he said, stroking her face. Her skin was clammy. He'd be glad, he thought, when she recovered from this and got her strength back. Her face seemed pale and drawn. The lines under her eyes were deeper, the dark circles under them darker. He looked down at her arm. She had become so thin that he could see every bone. The skin of her arm seemed unnaturally white. Even the freckles on her skin had seemed to fade. He looked back into her eyes. Her pupils seemed larger than usual. Perhaps the effects of the drugs.

"Burke, don't . . . don't be angry with me."

"Honey," he said soothingly, "Caesarian sections are done all the time. There's no dishonor in it. And we're protecting the baby."

"Will you name the baby 'Burke'? For me? And tell him I love him?"

Dillinger stared at her, unsure of what to say, when a flurry of activity happened at the end of the table. The male obstetrician removed the baby, carrying it carefully to a side table. Alarmed, Dillinger stopped breathing, because the baby was purple as a grape. *There's something wrong with the child*, he thought. *That's the emergency.* He looked down at Natalie, knowing he had to keep his expression controlled or she would panic.

He stepped around Natalie's head to the table and craned his neck. He muttered to the nearest nurse, "Is the baby okay?"

The nurse shot him a glare and turned back to the baby. Odd, he thought. That was the second rude act of the medical team in as many minutes. On the table the baby's color eased from dark purple to a light pink, and the infant cried once, a heartrending sob that moved Dillinger more than any sound he'd ever heard. A new, unfamiliar emotion swelled in him, a desire to hold the child and comfort and protect it.

"Mrs. Dillinger," the obstetrician said, turning to see her and leaning over to look around Dillinger as if he were an object in the way, "the baby's a healthy boy."

Natalie's face was covered with tears. "May I hold him?"

The nurse gently put the bundle on Natalie's chest. The baby had a small stocking cap on his tiny head. His eyes were shut, his face blotchy. He was wrapped in a soft blanket. Natalie used her good arm to hold him, looking down at him. She seemed to tire quickly of holding her head up, and slowly she dropped her head to the pillow. The nurse was right there to take the baby away.

"Why don't I hold him for a moment?" Dillinger asked.

The nurse turned her back and took the baby away to a heat-lamp table.

He turned to Natalie, who was still crying. He held her hand again.

"He's beautiful." Dillinger grinned.

Natalie's eyes shut. Dillinger stroked her forehead, her skin clammy and wet. She opened her eyes again. The tears gathered in them, one of them spilling down her cheek. He wiped it with his hand, thinking she was crying in joy and relief.

"Burke," she said, pausing. "I love you. Please take care of little Burke for me. Tell him I'll always love him."

A copper taste burned in his mouth and he could feel his hands shaking. What was she saying?

"Honey, we'll take care of him together. You can tell him that yourself."

Her eyes widened for a moment. "Will you tell him?" she asked intensely. Dillinger's smile faded, a frown taking its place.

"I'll tell him, Natalie," he said quietly.

"Burke," she said, then coughed, a dry, rattling cough.

"Yes, dearest?" he asked, close to her, his heart hammering in desperate fear.

"You know I love you? I do, I love you so much."

He nodded. "I know," he said slowly. "And I love you, Natalie."

She nodded weakly, her eyelids closing. He stroked her forehead, then heard the alarm of the monitor on the other side of the room. One of the nurses snapped the unit off.

He looked at the nurse. The surgical team had left; only the female obstetrician and the male nurse remaining in the room. The nurse powered down the medical equipment, then began to disconnect Natalie's IV tubes and oxygen mask. The obstetrician scribbled into a file.

"Are you going to stay with her?" the doctor asked, her voice hard.

As if in a dream, Dillinger stared at her. He knew something was deeply wrong, but he didn't know what to do. "What's going on here?" His fist rose to his mouth, and he noticed that his hand shook.

"What's going on?" she asked, pulling off her scrub hat, a mop of kinky auburn hair falling to her shoulders. "What's going on is what you were told would go on."

Time had slowed to a crawl. "Why isn't she being sewn back up? Why did they take away her mask?"

"Because, *Commander* Dillinger, she isn't with us any more."

Dillinger stared at Natalie, unable to move. Finally he reached out to touch her forehead. It was less clammy, but colder. She didn't respond.

"She's right here," he said, his voice coming from a tunnel ten miles deep.

"Her body is. But you got what you wanted, a healthy baby boy."

He tried to regain his commanding voice, his eye moving toward her nametag. "Dr. Kipling, what the fuck is going on?"

She stared at him. "As you were told seven months ago when Natalie discussed the choice, this is the result of not aborting the fetus and turning down the stem cell regime and the radiation and chemotherapy. We might have saved her, you know. But you wanted the child instead. Well, congratulations, Commander Dillinger. You have your new son and your life. Now you just need to bury her and you can move right on."

Dillinger stared at Natalie, dumbstruck. He touched her cheek. It was rigid and cold. He shook her, trying to wake her up. He looked back up at the doctor, but she was blurry through the tears. "She's *dead*?" The incredulity in his voice seemed to irritate the obstetrician.

"Yes, Commander. Just like she told you she'd be. When Natalie came to me, I made her choice clear. Fight the pancreatic cancer or try to carry the baby. I told her if she tried to give birth, there was no guarantee she'd survive to bring the fetus to term, and that if she turned down the cancer treatment odds were both of them would die, but she insisted on trying. She said it was important to *you*. Especially since it was a boy."

Dillinger tried to look at the doctor, but the light seemed too bright. He had to rub his eyes. "She knew it was a boy?" His voice had become suddenly hoarse and trembling.

"Of course," the doctor said. "Why? If the baby were a girl, would you have gotten rid of her and saved Natalie for a second try?"

He tried to speak, but he couldn't find his voice, and there were no words.

"*I think that's quite enough*, Doctor," a hard female voice said from over Dillinger's shoulder. "Are you in the habit of being abusive to the family after the patient's death? How would that complaint look in your file?"

The obstetrician pursed her lips, spun on her heel and left the room.

Dillinger turned slowly. Rachel Vornado stood in the entranceway, the sadness and compassion in her face bringing up the tears. He moved toward her. Her arms encircled him. He put his face on her shoulder and the tears came full force then. As if from a distance he heard himself crying, the sound of an animal caught in a trap. He wasn't sure how long he stood there, but finally he found his voice.

"*I didn't know.*"

"Oh God, B.K., how could you not?" Rachel asked gently. "She got worse every day. That's why I was so mad at you when you left for the hurricane."

"I swear, I didn't know."

Rachel shook her head. "I'm always amazed how a man can be so capable, and yet be so clueless. Look at you; you're the captain of a nuclear submarine. Less than a year ago, you and Natalie survived a nuclear accident. Then she gets pregnant and yet loses weight. You didn't figure that out?"

He shook his head slowly, feeling like a fool. "She kept telling me she was okay. That the doctors said she was just a little tired." He looked at Rachel's face. "Whenever Natalie said something, I always believed her."

Rachel shook her head, her expression part sympathy, part accusation. Finally she turned, took his arm and led him toward the door.

"Wait," he said. He walked back to Natalie. He picked up her hand. It was so goddamned cold.

"I love you," he said. He leaned over and put his face in the nape of her neck. God, how many times had he put his face right there while making love to her, her body moving under him, her eyes looking almost sleepily up at him as her hands ran through his thick hair? He kissed her neck, then put his arms under her body and held her. She was so bony, he thought. Not like that early morning in the Barents. He remembered how incredibly long her legs were, how he ran his hand down her naked, smooth thigh, expecting to feel her knee two hand lengths higher than it was. Her kisses had been so hot and deep that it had made him boil in passion. Now she felt like she'd just come in from a winter swim, her skin rigid and cold. "I love you, Natalie."

Rachel reached for his hands, pulling them away from Natalie's body. She stood him up and walked him, like a sleepwalker, away from the operating table. The walls of the corridor moved toward him as he floated down the passageway. Elevator doors closed on him, then reopened. Windshield wipers on Rachel's big GMC Yukon, the rain beading up, then vanishing. Distant lightning. His house. Still standing. One of the trees knocked over, the fence broken there. Natalie's Mercedes in the driveway. She must have rescued it from the officers' parking lot. The front door opening, shutting. His shoes off in the foyer. Stairs coming toward him.

A light coming on in the bedroom.

"Do you have to go to the bathroom?"

He shook his head, looking at the room. The bed was made and it seemed tidier than he'd ever seen it. Natalie had cleaned it up, he thought dumbly. She had prepared. *She knew.*

The bedclothes pulled aside. Rachel pulling the studs out of his tuxedo shirt, then opening the buttons below. The shirt pulled off and on the floor. Her fingers on his zipper. When was the last time feminine fingers opened his pants, he thought? The fingers had belonged to Natalie. She always did this the same, undoing the zipper, pushing the pants to his thighs, unable to wait until they were on the floor before reaching for him *there*, the heat rising from him as he would surge into the cool skin of her palm, ready for combat, and within seconds she would be on the bed and he would be deep inside her, trying to find the center of her, and her naked thighs would circle him, her hands on his ribs, urging him deeper. The memory made him twitch, but it seemed an obscenity with Natalie lying cold on a morgue table. Rachel pulled the pants quickly off, then his socks. She stood again, a dark cloud on her face. She lowered him to the white field of linen, touching his ankles to get them under the covers. She pulled the covers over him and patted them, then reached for the lamp. The room plunged into darkness.

"Don't go," he heard a male voice say.

"I'll wait for you to fall asleep," Rachel said from nowhere. "Now shut your eyes."

The pillow was wet and he heard sobbing from the distance. He wondered where she was right then. Was she all right? Was she taken care of? Would she be okay, wherever she was? The tears ran down his cheeks and he shook in the bed.

Will you tell him I love him? she said from the other end of the room. *You know I love you? I do, I love you so much.*

Natalie, he thought, his eyes clamped shut. *Why didn't you tell me? I would have told you to fight this and live.*

I know, she said. He opened his eyes. She sat at the end of the bed, her legs crossed in that way she had, when she wanted to make a point to him. Her expression was intense, as if she needed him to understand her. *That's why I concealed it from you. This was important to me, vitally important, and I knew you'd stop it.*

Why didn't you tell me?

She shook her head, flipping her long hair off her

shoulder the way she did before she answered a question, the way he'd always loved.

You have a son, now, Burke. Our son. You need to be strong for him. I married the strongest man on the planet. I know you can do this.

He sat up and looked at her. The moonlight shone on her hair, the smoothness of it making him ache to touch her. She looked as healthy as the day he first met her, so long ago, in his stateroom on the *Tucson.*

You knew, he said. It was an accusation.

She nodded.

His next words came from thinking them. *I'm sorry I had to be away for the French thing.*

I'm not, she said. *You would have known if you'd stayed. You would have been furious. My last weeks would have just been us fighting. I didn't want to leave you like that. That's why I asked Smokin' Joe to send you out.*

He stared at her, incredulous. *You did?*

He was going to send the Virginia. *I told him to send you and get you back just in time. It was just a two- or three-week op.*

Dillinger's mouth dropped open.

But I was worried I wouldn't make it. I tried not to call him because I thought he'd make you surface in the middle of the exercise, but as it turned out he came to me. It was his staffer who took me to the hospital and called to have you flown in. I held on with all my strength, and I got my last wish. I got to see you one more time.

Dillinger stared at her as she stood up and turned to look at the dozing form of Rachel Vornado.

It's bad with her and Peter, isn't it?

He nodded.

Good will come of it, Burke, she said, looking at Rachel Vornado, then back at him. *You can let it happen. I want you to be happy. At that moment, I want you to know that I approve.*

He replied aloud. "Natalie, what are you talking about?"

She smiled at him with that radiant smile that had made him love her.

Good-bye, Burke.

She slowly evaporated, her slim, lovely body becoming merely the moonlight shining in through the curtains.

"Don't go," he pleaded. "Please come back to me."

Rachel blinked, startled. "You're talking in your sleep, B.K." she said.

"Did you want to sleep in the spare room?" he asked. "It's late."

"You sure you're okay?"

"I've had better nights," Dillinger said. "But no sense both of us losing sleep."

"I'll make you coffee in the morning," she said sleepily, "but then I have to get back to the kids."

"Oh, Rachel?"

"Yes, B.K.?"

"Did you know anything about this operation? This French thing?"

Rachel nodded, a guarded expression on her face. "A little."

"Did Natalie ever say anything about talking to Commodore Kraft about sending me out?"

Rachel looked at the hardwood floor. "That was for Smokin' Joe to tell you, B.K., not me. But yes, she wanted you at sea for the last few weeks, so you wouldn't worry or criticize her decision. She talked to Kraft and he changed the orders so the *Virginia* would stay in port and you and your *Hampton* would make the op."

He stared at her. "How," he asked slowly, "how did she get to the hospital?"

Rachel shrugged. "One of Kraft's aides found her here, called 911 and got her to the emergency room, and got Kraft to recall you from the operation."

Dillinger nodded as if the news weren't a surprise. "Good night, Rachel."

She tapped on the doorjamb twice and waved, leaving him alone.

He stared at the column of moonlight from the window, wondering how a dream could be so real. He shut his eyes and tried to sleep. In his dreams, the French sub captain Jean-Paul was in the grip of a huge octopus, and in one of the tentacles was Dillinger's baby. Dillinger woke with a start, wishing his next dream would be of Natalie again, but there was nothing but blackness.

BOOK 2:

▼

Dead Calm

10

The crosshairs of the sniper scope reticle intersected over the guard's left chest pocket. The magnified view was clear and steady enough to see the bead of sweat rolling slowly down the man's forehead, past his eye socket and down his nose. The sweat had less to do with the hot Algerian sun than with what was about to happen.

The guard stood at the fortified entrance of the French *Chancellerie Diplomatique.* He glanced surreptitiously left, then right, while wiping the sweat off with his sleeve just before waving the waiting heavy truck through the barricade. The big diesel roared as the truck's ten wheels rode over the security barrier's retracted steel tire shredders. The truck, loaded with a hidden cargo of diesel oil and nitrate fertilizer, rolled down the inclined ramp that led to the new stone-and-concrete parking-and-utility structure that had been built adjacent to the embassy's east service entrance, the edifice intended to increase the physical security of the main building. The stark shadow of the overhanging upper platform swallowed the truck whole. The guard turned away after the truck vanished, but then the fool swiveled back and glanced nervously toward the parking building. After he turned back toward the street, he looked nervously at his watch.

Through the moments of the guard's fidgeting, the crosshairs of the high-powered rifle scope remained frozen on the man's heart. The sniper scope's eyepiece was tucked snugly into the eye socket of the dark-robed rifleman whose large, bony hands steadily and unflinch-

ingly held the rifle. Other than his olive-toned hands and
one eye, there was nothing more revealed of his face or
body, all of him concealed by the black hooded cassock
and black linen bandana. After a few moments of waiting, the man slowly and smoothly reached up to pull
down the bandana and lift off his hood, revealing a thin,
sinewy forearm. His face would constantly gather second
looks, perhaps because of the ghostly resemblance to his
father. But those who had never known the old man
stared at him as well, a result of the peculiar coexistence
of hardness and softness in his features. His skin was an
olive shade, his jawline strong and dark with a day's
stubble. His full, almost feminine lips arced slightly
downward as he attended to his task. Above the lips was
a smoothly curving nose, a woman's nose, the man often
thought, and when he saw it in a mirror the almost forgotten face of his mother would return to him, which
was another reason to avoid the images in mirrors.
Strong cheekbones framed his light gray eyes, which he
had overheard being described as cold and lifeless, the
eyes of a merciless wolf.

During moments when he was calm, the sniper's eyelids seemed to droop over his eyes, making it seem as if
he were half asleep, the effect adding to the peculiar
cruelty his face seemed to convey, an image that he was
careful not to alter. But when he was excited, his eyes
opened so wide that stark white appeared above and
below the eerie gray of his irises, the expression seeming
almost maniacal, which also had its purposes. Not wanting his thoughts or intentions to be revealed through his
expressions, he kept his eyes hidden behind impenetrable wraparound dark glasses, which had become his
trademark, and which he wore even inside dark, smoky
meeting rooms, but which he had raised to his forehead
so that he could press his eye to the sniper scope. His
hairline was a curving arc above his thick eyebrows, his
hair an oily black, perhaps too long, but controlled and
brushed straight back over his scalp, with not a single
strand out of place, which reflected his intentions that

every molecule of himself yield to his own control. It was a display to the world of the resolve in his heart, a heart that pumped the same blood as the man who had commanded and led the holiest brigade of warriors in the nation, the *Groupe Islamique Armé*.

Four years ago, in a stunning bloody ambush, the ruling Algerian political party, the *Front de Libération Nationale*, which was suspiciously connected to the French government, and the French intelligence agency, *Direction Generale de la Securite Exterieure*, assassinated GIA leader Antar Zouabri, leaving the organization headless. It also left Antar's only son, Issam Akzer Zouabri, fatherless. Six months later, during the raid by the DGSE that had captured Antar Zouabri's replacement, Issam's mother got hit by a stray bullet in the thigh, leaving her wounded and bleeding. She could have survived, but she'd turned down all medical help from the FLN medics. Issam, who then had been twenty-five, begged her to get help, but she had refused. He had spent the next four years wondering if she had allowed herself to fade away from hatred of the FLN or from grief over the loss of her husband.

After Antar Zouabri's blood painted the street as he lay dying, Issam had been recruited to join the GIA. Though he was young, he was driven, talented, ruthless and creative. There were no official titles within the GIA, but had there been, Issam would have been named the director of operational planning. The best ideas were his. Before he arrived, the best the GIA could do was slash the occasional throat of a French journalist or bomb a French bistro. Since Issam had been working, he had been responsible for the creation of five major operations, including the kidnapping of three French billionaire industrialists—one of whose family had given up twenty million Euros before he bled to death—the execution of a high-ranking DGSE official, and now the French embassy operation. If the embassy plan went well, it was almost assured that Issam would take over as the leader of the GIA two years before his thirtieth

birthday. He made a sound in his throat as he wondered
what the chances were of his living so long, particularly
after today's holy task was complete.

The truck would be nearing the kitchen supply doors
about now. Issam wondered if the guard would seem
surprised. Certainly he would be tempted to duck down
below the hip-high stone wall near the guard building.
Were he to do that, it would no doubt be remembered
later by survivors.

For the next long moments Issam stared unblinkingly
through the scope at the guard, his mind empty of
thought, an icy calm descending upon his soul. His mind
opened wide, his senses recording every millisecond as
if he would one day recount it to his descendants. There
came the final moment when the guard stood facing the
street, his hand raised to his face to wipe away sweat.
The next instant a second sun burst into existence where
the embassy had been. The light was blinding. He had
thought he could watch the event from the scope, but
he had not counted on the violence of the explosion.
The shock wave hit him a fraction of a second after the
burst of light and blew him backward. His experience
seemed interrupted, because later he would realize he
remembered every nuance of time leading to the explosion and every detail from when his body slammed onto
the roof three meters from where he had been crouched
at the parapet, but in between there was nothing, as if
he had blacked out while flying backward. He found
himself staring at the details of the surface of the roof,
the oddest sensation the quiet. It should have been loud,
he thought, but there was nothing. The detonation had
deafened him, leaving him in an odd, dreamlike world.

Slowly he rose to his feet, the smell hitting him next.
It was a brew of the chemical stench of the explosion,
burning wood and paper, smoke and something else—
the scent of cooking meat. Human flesh on a barbecue,
he thought. He turned slowly, his eyes still cast downward to the roof as he sought his rifle. He bent and
picked it up, examining it quickly to see if it had been

damaged. Satisfied, he stepped back to the parapet and looked over at the conflagration in the wreckage of the embassy. It was a slice of Hell, and it was gratifying to imagine that within its fires all of the French burned in torment for all eternity.

A black-and-orange cloud rolled upward, boiling from the point of the original detonation. The embassy was sheathed in dark smoke for several long minutes. When it slowly cleared, Issam could see that chaos and wreckage had taken the place of the beauty of the eighteenth-century building, its grandeur replaced by a five-meter-tall pile of burning rubble taking up almost a city block. The formerly groomed grounds of the embassy were scorched black for five hundred meters from the explosion point. The trees had been blown to splinters. There was no sign of the lush bushes other than a cluster of blackened sticks. There was broken glass everywhere. Where the original embassy building and the parking structure had stood there was now a mountain of concrete chunks, masses of granite, pieces of scorched wood and thousands of floating, drifting pieces of paper. A few wandering survivors came into view, one of them staggering down the street with his clothes on fire, unaware that he was burning.

A secondary explosion rocked the bank building. Issam's hearing suddenly returned, as if shocked back into perception by the second blast. The roar of the fires was loud, a rushing, violent noise. Perhaps it had been the diesel tank for the emergency generator that had exploded, or the oxygen tank that sent the medical gas down hoses to the ailing ambassador's office suite. As if suddenly remembering his mission, he took his eyes away from the burning rubble and searched his field of vision for the guard. He wasn't sure which of the street figures was the guard, but a body lying facedown in the street looked like he might be the one.

The sirens began to wail through the noontime city streets. A sudden worry troubled the sniper—what if the medics took the guard? What if he talked? Fortunately, after a few minutes, the prone figure suspected of being the guard slowly rose to his feet and stared at the wreckage of the embassy. It was him. The next problem was the rifle itself. The sniper scope was probably out of alignment. Issam tightened his jaw and squeezed off the first shot, aiming for the center of the guard's head, but hitting his neck. The man spun around, stunned, blood spurting from the hole in his throat. Had the shot hit the carotid artery, the guard would be on the ground. Issam aimed for the heart and pulled the trigger. This shot was also low, the blood staining the man's shirt. He took a deep breath, then aimed a few centimeters above the guard's left shoulder. This shot slammed into the center of the man's heart, and he fell to his knees, stunned. The fourth bullet crashed through the man's right eye, entered his brain and blew out the back of his skull, taking liquefied brain matter, bone fragments and skin with it, the momentum of the bullet knocking him backward in an uncoordinated sprawl. A second later, a fifth and final projectile slammed into the guard's already lifeless body, the bullet crashing through his ribcage and ripping apart what was left of the now silent heart, exiting through the corpse's back and embedding itself into the pavement.

Calmly, one eye on the street below, Issam disassembled his rifle, unscrewed the barrel and the sniper scope, stowing the pieces of the rifle in several inside pockets of this cassock. He stood, brushed the dust off his garment, and calmly returned to the roof entrance door.

Moments later he emerged from the building's rear service entrance. He climbed quickly into the passenger seat of a battered and rusted Toyota sedan idling a few feet from the entrance. The engine of the sedan purred smoothly as the driver put it into gear and rolled the vehicle slowly down the alley until it emerged onto the street a block from the carnage of the embassy explosion. The driver kept the car away from the main streets until he reached the safe house.

Issam Akzer Zouabri climbed out of the car and drew

himself up to his full height, his black sunglasses obscuring his eyes. For a long moment he let himself feel the warmth of the sun and the warm glow of knowing he had achieved his strike at the heart of the French infidel bastards who had raped his country for so long. If the GIA could spill the blood of Paul Chiraud, the French foreign minister, Jacques Mirault, the number-two man in the French DGSE spy agency, Jon Pierre d'Ortall, the French ambassador to Algeria, and the FLN butcher and Algerian vice president, Aszher Uthal, could complete victory evade them for long?

The vision of a Muslim theocratic state was so close he could touch it. The word of this would spread to the ends of the Muslim world, and soon *mujahedeen* would pour in to join them in this jihad against the FLN and the forces and comfort of the French. And it would have the secondary effect of placing him, finally, in command of the GIA, the organization that held so much meaning to him, the group he would gladly die for.

He sniffed the air, almost able to smell the burning flesh from the embassy explosion. It was a good smell, a smell blessed by Allah, he thought.

11

Issam Akzer Zouabri stubbed his cigarette out in the tin ashtray and, behind the dark lenses of his sunglasses, squinted at the man his intelligence deputy had been working on in the year after the embassy explosion. It was Ramadan in Mecca. The café was crowded as night fell and it became allowable to eat a light meal or drink a cup of tea. He allowed his stare to bore into the man across the small table. Youssef Tagreb, if recruited, could fulfill every objective of the embattled GIA and change the face of the map. Algeria could become an Islamic state, and France could become a smoking ruin.

Tagreb was older than Zouabri, his fortieth birthday coming up soon, but he seemed much younger than his years. He stood medium height, almost a head shorter than Zouabri. He was solid in build, his years in the military having counted for more than mere brainpower. Tagreb's face was open and affable, hardly the face of a killer. Zouabri decided that was a fortunate thing, making the older man able to be led, and recent history had shown that leading the older generation—when the leader was not yet thirty—could be a challenge. Tagreb had thick, arched eyebrows, large, liquid brown eyes, a handsome round face, generous lips and a wide smile that displayed uneven teeth. Zouabri had only seen the smile once, he thought, because Tagreb was an extraordinarily sad man. When Tagreb spoke, his voice was a deep baritone worthy of getting him an audition with an opera house, but he seemed hardly conscious of it, his tone hushed as if the two of them were conspirators, which in this case they were.

"So, your operation succeeded? You took out the ambassador and the French officials?"

Zouabri waited a moment before he spoke, making sure his companion was listening.

"The death toll was a hundred and eighty-seven, although thirty-four of the wounded died later, with another fifty or so seriously wounded." Zouabri paused to pull a silver cigarette case from his cassock's inner breast pocket. He withdrew a cigarette and produced a silver lighter, the flame rising a full five centimeters over the tip. He sucked in the smoke and exhaled through his nostrils, the twin smoke trails curling slowly upward to the darkening sky. "The operation was a failure."

"A failure? Why?"

"Where shall I begin? The operation targeted four men: the French ambassador to Algeria, the deputy director of the DGSE, the FLN vice president, and the French foreign minister. All of them lived, because none of them were in the embassy. Their limousines arrived, but the men who got out of them were imposters."

"Body doubles?" Tagreb asked, his eyes widening.

"Exactly. The purpose of the DGSE and the foreign ministry's visit was to deliver to the FLN all the intelligence they'd gained on us. The embassy bombing was foreseen."

Tagreb frowned. "If French intelligence knew about the bombing, why didn't they stop it?"

"Think about it, Youssef." Tagreb raised an eyebrow as if not used to being addressed by his first name, perhaps, Zouabri thought, because he had been called "captain lieutenant" for so long. "The DGSE and the French use the bombing against us, as a way to demonstrate what brutes we supposedly are—not just to the Algerian public, but to the world. Once that happened, the French influence could become stronger. In addition, the FLN and DGSE apparently knew I would be posi-

tioned as a sniper and observer. And then, does it
even matter?"

"This was a year ago?"

"Yes," Zouabri said, knowing that Tagreb had been
at sea when the embassy exploded. He would not have
seen the news clips of the carnage or the wreckage in
Algiers that day. Or, for that matter, the crowing of the
FLN and French governments over the survival of
their officials.

"Did French intelligence and the Algerian government go on a hunt for you?"

Zouabri laughed without mirth. "A hunt? *Crusade*
might have been a better word. The FLN and the DGSE
rounded up so many of my GIA comrades that the organization became fragmented. You probably do not know
much about the French, my friend, but they use torture
routinely. My intelligence chief came for me a half hour
before my door was blown in at three in the morning.
If I were not removed forcibly, I would be in an Algerian prison—or worse, a French cell block—watching
myself bleed with my bones broken."

Zouabri paused, then withdrew his cigarette case
again. He stared at Tagreb, then looked up at the smoke
as it drifted up high above them. "The worst part is that
history repeated itself. Four years ago the FLN, using
their French intelligence assets, conducted a series of
brutal and bloody raids on the holy *Groupe Islamique
Armé*. The satanic forces of the FLN assassinated my
father and fatally wounded my mother. My sister was
taken to the back of a police station and raped by two
men at once. The second-in-command under my father
was Rachid Abou Tourab. The ruthless torture of
Tourab led to the arrest and killings of nearly a thousand
GIA operatives, as well as the infiltration of the GIA.
When I ascended to take over what was left of the organization, I did my utmost to root out the spies and infor-
mants." That was an understatement, Zouabri thought.
He had personally dispatched seven of the worst of the
turncoats, all of them in the way that sent the most elo-

quent message—he slit their throats as they begged for mercy, finally completely decapitating each of them, holding their heads up to the video camera so that the captured film could be sent to the informant's family. The work of purging the GIA had taken over a year, and Zouabri had been certain that all of them had been taken care of, but perhaps he had been wrong.

"So, my friend," Zouabri said, his eyes still on the smoke trail. "That is my story. You now know enough about me to get me killed. Or worse. Now, perhaps you would share your story with me." He paused, glancing at Tagreb, then stubbed the cigarette out and reached for his silver case.

Youssef Tagreb put his teacup down in its saucer. The daylight fasting of Ramadan made him feel weak by this time in the afternoon. Tagreb glanced around him for a moment, as if surprised where his life had taken him. There was no doubt, Mecca was much different than northern Russia.

"I don't quite know where to start," Tagreb said, stirring uncomfortably in his seat. He genuinely liked his new acquaintance, whom he had met a week before, and their conversations had covered ground he'd never expected, but it was only today that Zouabri mentioned that he had run a terrorist organization. By the time he did, he obviously knew how Tagreb would react. But for Tagreb to speak of his own experiences, that would be a first.

It had been a year since Tagreb's father had died peacefully in his bed in their home village in Turkmenistan, the former Soviet republic that was now a poor Islamic state north of Iran and Afghanistan. Tagreb had thought time would ease the ache over losing his father, but the anniversary of his passing had made it worse. To what extent had the old man's faith brought Tagreb to this place, he wondered. Perhaps it was not just Tagreb's father's faith that had influenced Tagreb's own life, but the way Tagreb had disappointed the aging imam.

"You have been a police officer, perhaps? Or in the military?" Zouabri asked. "An officer, perhaps?"

Tagreb frowned, reluctant to speak. "Why would you say that?"

"It is in the way you carry yourself. The Russian Republic Army?"

"No. The navy. I am—or I should say, I was—an officer in the submarine force."

Tagreb's use of the past tense stabbed at him for an instant. The entire time Tagreb had worn the uniform of the navy of the Russian Republic, it had been blasphemous to his father. The younger Tagreb had been identified at an early age as intelligent, perhaps even gifted, and through what at the time had seemed incredible good fortune but now seemed the result of the hand of Allah, Tagreb had attended the University of Moscow, his academic career paid for by the Russian Navy. While today, such a thing might have been unthinkable, in the late 1980s Turkmenistan had still been part of Soviet Russia, and serving in the Russian armed forces would be inevitable for someone with Tagreb's intellectual gifts. In a matter of three years he had earned his nuclear engineering bachelors degree. It took three more to earn his doctorate. Tagreb's true love had been languages, the foreign tongues seeming to be more remembered than learned. He could speak, read and write English, French, Spanish—and, of course, Russian—as if each were his first language. Tagreb's spare time in the university had been spent reading history texts written in his favorite foreign languages, ever aware of how differently each culture saw the great current of human progress.

While Tagreb had incurred an obligation to serve the navy after graduation, he had never thought too much about what he would do. He had assumed he would be an engineer in the civilian support staff, or perhaps a shipbuilder. His courses in naval architecture had sparked a slight interest in the craft of ship design and construction, but it had seemed that was not how his life would turn out. Again, perhaps the hand of Allah could be seen in the turns of his life's path. An older naval officer, Fayyad Ghassab, who was also from Turkmenistan, had taken an interest in young Tagreb. The officer was a junior admiral in the Russian submarine navy. At Ghassab's suggestion, Tagreb took a trip to the secret and mysterious submarine bases in Murmansk, in the north, just before his undergraduate studies were complete. Tagreb had barely been twenty years old at the time, and already he seemed to know where his life was pointed. Without much more thought devoted to the future, Tagreb's career brought him closer to his destiny. Tagreb had been recruited to a postgraduate program, and had studied the reactor physics and dynamics of a core used in the Russian fleet. At Ghassab's urging, Tagreb had hurried up his doctoral studies, all the better to get himself into the submarine training program.

Transitioning from the world of academics, with all its stimulation—experiments on a live reactor core during the day, reading French history at night—to the dreary world of the submarine force training "pipeline" had been emotionally difficult for Tagreb. There had been something missing. His colleagues had suggested that he should seek a wife, or at least a comfort woman. He had thought about it seriously, but after a long year the training ended and his assignment to a fleet submarine came through. He received orders to a submarine named the *Krasnoyarsk*, a sister ship of the ill-fated *Kursk*. In the two years before *Kursk* sank, Tagreb became one of the few Russian submarine force officers who were well versed in both engineering and tactics. He routinely stood the command post watch and knew, not only how to "fight the ship," but how to teach tactics to the younger officers reporting aboard.

After two years on the *Krasnoyarsk*, Tagreb rotated to a ballistic missile submarine, the *TK17*, of the 941 Akula-class, the gigantic submarine named "Typhoon" by the forces of the West. That two-year assignment trained him in the ways of strategic deterrence and stealth, despite the fact that much of his work was in the engineering compartments. When that assignment ended, Tagreb returned to his beloved *Krasnoyarsk*, where he progressed from his climb to first engineer to becoming the chief lieutenant to the weapons-and-tactics officer. Those were amazing days, he thought as he stared at his now-cold tea.

Tagreb told the bare bones of the tale to Issam Zouabri, slowly and haltingly at first, but then, as his passion began to fill him, he related the entire story. Zouabri's dark glasses revealed nothing, and later Tagreb would wonder, had Zouabri's eyes been visible, would Tagreb have been able to tell the story? When Tagreb was finished, it was after two in the morning, and the café had long since closed. Zouabri nodded in understanding, but Tagreb knew he had questions by the incline of his head.

"So, with that success," Zouabri said, "what was it that made you leave your navy?"

Youssef Tagreb made a sound of dismissal from deep in his throat. "It was no longer my navy. I was the protégé of my first commanding officer. My first captain. When he went on to command a new attack submarine, his replacement was my former executive officer, who was promoted from second-in-command to captain. Unfortunately, there was an incident at sea—a collision in the Barents Sea when we came to periscope depth before a routine surfacing to return to port. I was asleep at the time, since my watch did not begin until five hours later. The collision caused only minor damage to the *Krasnoyarsk* but the ship we hit was an oil tanker. For some time it seemed it would sink, and after floundering there, we managed to hook a tow line to it and get it closer to Murmansk, where a seagoing tug was able to get it—finally—into port. The oil spill was tremendous and quite an embarrassment to the navy. My new captain found himself in deep trouble, and was relieved. We never saw him again. Officially, he was sent to a shore duty station somewhere, but the rumors held that he was a broken man."

Tagreb looked up at the stars. A gathering of clouds was slowly moving in from the west.

"I was discouraged by the incident. It stained the reputations of every officer and rating aboard. I was also disappointed at the navy's treatment of Captain First Rank Fiskov."

"The new captain who hit the tanker?"

"Yes," Tagreb said. "That was when a 'fixer captain' was appointed—a man who was brought aboard for one reason—to whip our crew into shape. But there was nothing wrong with our ship. The collision could have happened to anyone, particularly since the tanker was running without lights. The investigation acknowledged that but failed to exonerate Fiskov or the rest of us."

"But you were asleep. You didn't escape blame?"

"It made me seem as if I were asleep during a moment of need. It was a routine surfacing, conducted on another officer's watch. Yet, despite the official reprimand that ruined my future in the navy, I was not a careerist; I was still entirely ready to serve the fleet. But the replacement captain, Captain First Rank Dostoyev, the fixer, took a disliking to me." Tagreb laughed without mirth. "It was worse than that. He decided to make discharging me for incompetence his personal mission.

"But I suddenly had no more time for the politics. My father became ill almost as soon as I realized that my career was over. I left Murmansk to go to my father in Kushka, Turkmenistan. Once I arrived there, I found him suffering from stage four lung cancer." Tagreb sighed. "He had a deep fundamentalist faith. I confided in him what happened to me in the navy. I thought he would be disappointed in me, but his face lit up. He told me that all that had happened to me was a sign from God. He said Allah wanted me to see the light, that we are all involved in a holy war against the unbelievers. At first I found this difficult to accept, but as my father died in the peace of the faithful, I began to hear the old man's voice in my head. In that moment of supreme aloneness, I realized that I had been a servant to the unrighteous. When my leave expired, I decided to desert the Russian Navy. I made my way here, where I met you."

Zouabri watched Tagreb for a long time. Finally he spoke, his voice flat and quiet.

"Youssef, do you believe in the healing power of vengeance?"

Tagreb answered carefully. "I just told you I considered myself one of the faithful. It is Ramadan. As a man of God, how could I turn to any kind of violence?"

"The ending of your navy career was not just a coincidence, Youssef. There was deep purpose there. Allah planned your navy experience in the centuries before your birth. In fact, Allah only allowed your time of success so that you could feel the bitterness of the betrayal by this man you spoke of, Captain First Rank Dostoyev. It is a fact, Youssef, that Dostoyev was personally responsible for your downfall. In doing that, he was an agent of God. He was only delivering the message that God wrote to you long before you drew breath on this earth. Do you understand?"

Tagreb stared through the candlelight at Issam Zouabri and shook his head. "Destiny? Dostoyev's professional jealousy a message from God? It is difficult to believe. The man was vicious and violent, both things I abhor now that holiness has returned to my soul."

Zouabri slowly removed his dark glasses and placed them on the table. Tagreb had never seen the younger man's eyes. His mouth opened slightly as he stared into the cold, pale gray of Zouabri's eyes.

"This man, Dostoyev. Do you see him as God's holy messenger?"

Tagreb frowned slowly, the expression darkening his face. "That would be a leap of understanding that perhaps I am not capable of making."

Zouabri leaned closer. "I have two gifts for you, Youssef. But first, a confession. As the leader of the *Groupe Islamique Armé*, I have some measure of power. Reporting to me is a small but dedicated group of fighters who specialize in intelligence. I admit, they were overcome by the skills of the FLN and DGSE in the embassy bombing, but for the more routine tasks they have been excellent. They are capable of more than simple information gathering." Zouabri paused to light a cigarette, his deliberate lighting of the tip making Tagreb impatient.

"You said you had a confession?"

Zouabri blew smoke out his nostrils as he put his lighter away. "Yes. I know your story, Youssef. My friendship with you is part of my destiny as I walk in the paths laid for me by Allah. Your story was brought to me by a friend of a friend of a relative of your father. It traveled a thousand miles to reach my ears. It came to me for a reason. For a deep purpose, in fulfillment of prophecy."

Tagreb hesitated. "Why did you let me tell the story, then?"

"It was important not for my ears, but for yours. It was Allah's purpose that you remember what happened to you at the hands of Captain Dostoyev. And by extension, at the hands of the most holy God."

Tagreb waved the idea away. "Dostoyev, an agent of Allah? It is hard to believe."

"Do you hate him?"

"Does it matter, Issam? I haven't thought about him in almost a year."

"I told you I had two gifts." Zouabri reached into his cassock, unstrapped an object from his calf and placed it on the table. Tagreb looked down at an ornate jeweled knife, rubies and diamonds shimmering in the light of the flames of the candles. Slowly, as if his hand were moved by an outside force, he reached out and touched the handle. The knife came out of its sheath, the blade a full twenty centimeters long. The blade was a dull gunmetal gray, its lethal utility contrasting starkly with the decorative handle. It came to a sharp point, but half of its blade surface was serrated. The knife felt balanced and lethal in Tagreb's hand. He was reminded of the

first time he had ever held a firearm; the heaviness of
the pistol and its potential power infecting his mind,
leaving him wanting to aim at something and project a
killing force across a distance. As that thought crossed
his consciousness, he quickly put the knife back in its
scabbard and put it back on the table.

"It's beautiful, but why are you doing this? Why did
you spy on me?"

"It is the second gift that is important," Zouabri said,
producing a leather belt inlaid with gold. "Put the knife
on and follow me." Zouabri rose from the table and
walked out of the café.

Tagreb put on the belt and strapped on the knife while
following the GIA commander out to the narrow street,
the thought occurring to him that he could turn and walk
back to his room, but he was intensely curious. The walk
did not take long. They passed by several men who
stood at the entrance to a confined alleyway leading
around a corner to a massive door, where three large,
unsmiling men stood. The biggest drew himself into a
rigid posture of respect, unlocked the door and held it
open.

Tagreb walked into deep gloom, following Zouabri
down a flight of stone steps. The air became cooler as
they descended into a deep basement. There was an
acrid smell, Tagreb realized, a horrible mix of urine and
vomit, and for an instant he wondered if he were safe
in the company of the GIA leader in what seemed to
be a dungeon, the man surrounded by his bodyguards.
The thought passed as a door opened and bright lights
clicked on in the room. Tagreb's jaw dropped.

There was a man huddled on the floor, restrained by
chains at his wrists and ankles that were bolted into the
stone wall. He obviously had not bathed in days, perhaps
weeks, and his disheveled hair hung into his face, his
month-long growth of beard scraggly. But there was no
mistaking his identity.

The pathetic creature on the floor was Captain First

Rank Dostoyev, Navy of the Russian Republic, commanding officer of the *Krasnoyarsk*.

"How in God's name did you do this? And why?" Tagreb stood in front of the prostrate navy captain, noticing that his left eye was black and swollen shut. Perhaps he had resisted his capture or Zouabri's men had decided to beat him.

"We knew about him when you were still approaching your faith."

Tagreb held his hands open, not understanding.

"Your father was one of the faithful for many years. Through his friends, my organization heard about you. My own father began the initiative, to seek out the faithful who are or were members of a sophisticated military. The idea is simple. If we can swell our ranks with faithful technicians, we will eventually find ourselves in a position to take over the equipment of Satan himself. We watched you, and many others, as you encountered the inevitable abuse the infidels deal out to our people, to the anointed of Muhammad."

"And him?"

"My second gift," Zouabri said, smiling for the first time since Tagreb had met him a week before.

In front of him Captain First Rank Dostoyev stood, a wreck of his former self. The first time Tagreb had met the man, Dostoyev had been lean and balding, his skin stretched across his bony face except at his mouth, where his lips seemed to hang when they weren't curled into a mean smirk, revealing uneven, tobacco-stained teeth, his squinty lids revealing cold blue eyes. There had been an insubstantial nature to Dostoyev, as if he were trying to weigh more, to be more, the attempt irritating him. But now, Dostoyev seemed unhealthily swollen and pudgy, but not from being well fed. Dostoyev didn't move, but stood frozen, his eyes clouded over behind folds of skin. His coloring, previously pale and creamy, was now ruddy. There was no doubt Dostoyev had been beaten and poorly fed, and as Tagreb stared in shock at his former captain, the Russian suddenly leaned forward and spit at him. Spittle landed on his cheeks, and a huge wad of slime ran down his chest. Tagreb could smell Dostoyev's stench, and the man's breath could stop a clock. Dostoyev looked up, as if arising from a deep sleep, his dreams clearing. With one bleary eye he looked at Tagreb. Recognition dawned in him, then panic. He rattled his chains as he rose unsteadily to his feet, trying to back away from Zouabri and Tagreb.

Tagreb glanced up at Zouabri, who stood with his arms crossed, his eyes hidden by his dark sunglasses. He nodded his head at his large bodyguard, who stood behind Tagreb.

"Tagreb, Wafeeq, behind you, will film the ritual with a digital video camera. The film will be posted for the faithful, and we will ensure it reaches this pig's family."

"I don't understand," Tagreb said, frowning at the bodyguard.

"Your first gift," Zouabri said. "Use it to remove the head of the man who both betrayed you and brought you to Allah, and by doing so, you show him mercy, delivering him from his life of sin against the Prophet."

"Use it to . . . remove . . . his head?" Tagreb stuttered.

At first Tagreb was surprised by the feeling tingling inside him. Since he had deserted the Russian Navy, he had insisted to himself that he was no longer a violent man. And in his mind, he had never been. True, he had served in the navy of a military force able to level a third of the planet. On the Akula-class ballistic missile submarine *TK-17* he had personally been the battlestations missile control officer, and his the very index finger that would press the fixed function key that would have unleashed nuclear death and destruction upon millions of men, women and children. But still, the world would never have come to that, and his finger would never have been called on to press the button. Besides, even if some world crisis had loomed large, some horrible circumstance that required firing nuclear ballistic missiles that would level a city, if Tagreb himself refused to press the LAUNCH button, he would have been pulled from the missile control console seat, handcuffed to the bulkhead, and he would have watched while another officer pressed the firing key. It was not like he himself was causing a nuclear holocaust, he had always told himself, nor was he even a cog in the wheel of that machinery of destruction, but rather he was a simple contributor to the country that had put him through college. He was not now nor was he ever a warrior. He was a sailor, a seafarer, a technocrat. An honorable man. A man of the faith.

Tagreb felt something touch his hip. In surprise he felt pressure on his belt where he had strapped Zouabri's gift, then the sound of metal on metal. Zouabri's hand held the knife, offering it to Tagreb. Tagreb's fingers closed on it, his intention to put it back in the scabbard. But instead of returning the knife, he stared at it, an alien feeling blowing into him. He looked up at Dostoyev, who had shut his eyes again and hung limply from his chains.

Whatever Tagreb's conflict with Dostoyev had been, it would never be something that would justify killing. He looked up at Zouabri, who slowly removed his sunglasses, revealing the coldest look Tagreb had ever seen.

"This is a holy moment, Youssef," Zouabri said slowly. "In this time you can move to deeper waters in your life. You can transform this man's polluted infidel soul into an instant of pure deliverance for yours. And when you do, your heart will beat with mine. There is a future for you in the *Groupe Islamique Armé*. We have great things planned. Planned for you. Planned for us. Planned for the GIA. And for the future of Islam. It is time. Put the knife on his neck and cleanse the earth of his evil spirit."

For a long moment Tagreb held the knife and stared at Dostoyev. A slight tingle formed in his palm and ran to the tip of each finger, and from there up his wrist, not stopping until it reached his throat. He glanced at his hand, and noticed that his hand trembled. He sensed motion in front of him and saw that Dostoyev's eyes had opened slowly, the Russian glaring at him balefully. Tagreb moved slowly forward until he could smell Dostoyev's scent even without breathing. He put the knife point under Dostoyev's chin, a gesture to scare his old enemy, but Dostoyev just laughed and pulled his head away. Tagreb reached up with his left hand and grabbed Dostoyev's hair tightly, forcing his head back. He moved the knife to the left, to Dostoyev's right side, the razor-sharp edge near the tip resting on Dostoyev's soft skin over his carotid artery. Dostoyev's eyes grew wide for a split second before Tagreb sliced his knife violently to the right, digging as hard into Dostoyev's flesh as he could.

The knife was sharp, but the human neck is filled with dense tissue, strong muscle and tendons. The knife cut two centimeters into Dostoyev's throat, an immediate spurt of arterial blood spewing out to the left. Dostoyev's struggle away from the knife pulled the instrument away from the right side, his throat intact on that side. Dostoyev's movement loosened Tagreb's grip on his hair, the greasiness of it making it slippery, but Tagreb reached in as hard as he could, grabbing handfuls of hair down to the Russian's scalp, and he pulled Dostoyev closer and put the bloody knife in for a second slice, starting it more behind Dostoyev's right ear, retracing the knife's path through the neck until he reached Dostoyev's trachea. Odd, Tagreb thought, that the Russian hadn't made a sound, but then he realized that in the adrenaline of the moment, Dostoyev had been screaming in a panicked, high-pitched howl. With Dostoyev's neck open, his head tilted back, his good eye bugged comically outward—the bloodshot lines running through it making the man seem even more immersed in madness—he screamed so loudly that it rattled the windows. Tagreb's knife paused at Dostoyev's blood-drenched trachea for a slow instant before he brought the serrated edge of the blade to bear on the cartilage, and began sawing Dostoyev's windpipe open. It seemed to take a dozen saw cuts until the man's frightened howling stopped. In the sudden silence of the room, Tagreb could hear Dostoyev sucking wind wetly into his lungs, his airways pulling in the blood, making him cough. Tagreb moved his knife to the right, under Dostoyev's ear, and sliced harder into the carotid artery and jugular on that side, the as-yet-unharmed flesh opening and spewing forth even more blood, a fire hydrant of gushing blood wetting the wall behind Dostoyev, and suddenly, finally, as Dostoyev's blood pressure dropped, he gave one last cough, one last haunted look into Tagreb's eyes, and went completely limp.

For the next minute Tagreb sliced what tissue remained holding his head to his shoulders, then concentrated on the spine, finding a space between two vertebrae and sawing hard until eventually he felt Dostoyev's head free itself of his body. The head hung by the hair in Tagreb's hand, and for a long moment Tagreb just stared dumbly at the slowly rotating head, the face coming into view with one eye swollen shut, the other open and almost completely red. Blood dripped steadily from the chin and throat onto Tagreb's feet. As the face turned out of view, Tagreb seemed to come back into the moment. Slowly, as if in a dream, he turned to face Zouabri and looked into the GIA commander's eyes. The cold look had softened into an expression of approval and brotherly love. Tagreb smiled slowly, not knowing why this act had felt so amazingly right. He held Dostoyev's head up to show the video camera, a small smile on his face.

"Come," Zouabri said. "Let us clean you up. We have much to talk about."

Tagreb dropped Dostoyev's head as if it were merely a rotten head of lettuce. He wiped his hands on his robe as he turned at the door. He gave the blood-spattered room one last glance as he wiped his knife on the robe and replaced it in the scabbard. Here, he thought, here was the place he came to be. There were no thoughts of regret, no feelings of revulsion, no thought of the life he had just taken, only joy and a feeling of having been freed. Freed of all the fetters of false morality that had tied him down to the ideals of the infidels. He smiled again at Zouabri and followed him up the stairs.

"It is in the natural scheme of the fabric of history that we strike out at France," Issam Akzer Zouabri said quietly as he sat on the roof of the building overlooking the holy city. Mecca gleamed below in the dark of the Saudi Arabian night, the shimmering lights of it calming. "It is our destiny."

Youssef Tagreb nodded. "I can see that."

"With a bold stroke at France, with the world's understanding that it was Algeria's dagger in France's heart— and with the French understanding the same—we will commence the dawn of a new day in Algiers. The FLN dogs will be thrown out of office the moment they are no longer supported by the DGSE intelligence agency of Paris. As soon as evil departs our capital, the GIA will resume control of the Algerian government in the name of the Algerian people."

Tagreb nodded.

"I'll need your help. No, more than your mere help, Youssef. Without you there is nothing."

"I am not sure what you mean," Tagreb said slowly. How could he have any part of Issam Zouabri's attack on France?

"It is your background, your blood, your memories and your heart I need."

"I don't understand."

Zouabri laughed without humor. "Tagreb, what is your military background?"

Tagreb's brows came down in an expression of confusion. "I was a submarine officer in the Russian Navy."

"What kind of submarine?"

"An SSGN. The *Krasnoyarsk*. It fired ship-killer cruise missiles. What possible good could that do for you?"

"What other ship did you sail?"

Tagreb registered shock. "*TK-17*. An Akula-class ballistic missile submarine."

"The West calls your Akula-class a 'Typhoon,' which fits perfectly. This is how we will punch our fists into the face of France. They will be overcome by the typhoon of our implacable will."

Tagreb was thunderstruck. "But Issam. That is completely impossible." His next words stuck in his throat. He stuttered through the thought. "The base where the Akula-class submarines are home-ported is in northern Russia, on the Kola Peninsula. It is completely sealed. All of the province is on alert. A terrorist taking an Akula? A 'Typhoon' as you call it? He would have more chance reaching out and grabbing a bolt of lightning during a storm. Issam, there must be another way."

Zouabri seemed completely calm, as if Tagreb had said nothing. For a moment Tagreb thought his words had been ignored. He was about to open his mouth to continue his argument against the insane idea of taking a Russian nuclear submarine when Zouabri held up his hand.

"I suspected it was thus." He paused. "We had immense troubles taking your friend Dostoyev when he was hiding within the great Russian satanic state. We had to lure him entirely out of the country."

Tagreb nodded, his thoughts returning to Dostoyev's decapitation, the strongest memory the feeling of how warm Dostoyev's blood had been flowing over Tagreb's fingers.

"But you still want a ballistic missile submarine for your use against the French."

Zouabri nodded slowly, his eyes fixed on the horizon.

"The American submarines would make perfect weapons for your war."

"It is also your war now, Youssef."

"Yes," Tagreb said, surprised at how strongly he felt about helping Zouabri. There was just something about the man that inspired loyalty in the extreme.

"Tell me about the American submarines."

For the next half hour Tagreb spoke of the Ohio-class submarines with their city-killer missiles. While they seemed perfect for the mission, there was something in Zouabri's voice, some doubt, perhaps even disinterest.

"The trouble goes to how we execute taking the submarine," Tagreb concluded.

"That has been taken care of," Zouabri said, a calm, smooth certainty in his voice.

"But you have reservations," Tagreb said.

"What other nation has ballistic missile submarines?" Zouabri asked.

"Britain. China. The Chinese submarines are as guarded as the Russian ones, and would take time to get into range, and would probably have reliability troubles."

"Any other nation?"

Tagreb thought. "France."

Zouabri smiled. Of course, Tagreb thought. It would make a complete circle to use France's own weapons of mass destruction against their own scourge.

"I do not know much about the French Navy's ships or weaponry, Issam. I would have to study their fleet."

"When the sun rises, go to work on finding out all you can about the French ballistic missile submarines," Zouabri commanded.

At daybreak Youssef Tagreb smiled at Issam Zouabri, despite his crying need for tea or coffee, and Ramadan was five days from being over. Until then, there would be no breakfast, and no morning caffeine.

"You have a report for me?" Zouabri asked.

"It is amazing," Tagreb said. "The new class of French submarine is perfect for us. They have the latest technology and the most accurate weapon systems. And the security of French systems is far relaxed over British and American naval bases. Issam, we could do this."

"Of course," Zouabri said.

"Let me tell you about the missiles," Tagreb began.

Zouabri waved his hand. "It is not for me to know, Youssef. It is enough that you know. Just tell me this. If we were to take one of these nuclear submarines, would we be able to lay waste to the major cities of France?"

Tagreb nodded. "That and far more, Issam. There will be missiles to spare."

"Good," Zouabri said in satisfaction. "All the better. We can use the reserve weapons to hold off retaliation from other nations of the West, perhaps even target London and Washington at the end of the mission. But we will save that for later."

"Issam, how do we accomplish the taking of this submarine?"

"We learned much during our operation to bring in Dostoyev. It will be difficult and challenging, but achievable. And destiny and divine providence will deliver the prize to us as long as we exert ourselves with all our spirits."

Tagreb bit his lip. Zouabri was prone to talking in spiritual riddles, and often in an obtuse sort of way they answered the question, but this time he needed details. "But, Leader Zouabri, how?"

"Wait, Youssef. You will see."

12

Jean-Paul Gardes pulled up to his house in a quaint suburb outside Brest. The debriefing at headquarters had gone late, and after the admiral was done he'd called Danielle and told her that finally he was finished, and since their month of reward vacation began that evening, he wanted to take her out for dinner with the children. Gardes stood outside the townhouse, wondering why the lights of the house were darkened. At this hour—shortly after sunset—the place was usually pure chaos, with children scampering to their baths and arguing that they did not want to go to bed. Jean-Paul unlocked the door and walked in, the scent the first sign, the second the flickering mellow glow of two dozen candles. As his eyes adjusted to the dimness, he saw a slight motion in the back of the room. He blinked, seeing her there on the couch, the large pillows moved from the couch to the floor and surrounded by more candles.

Slowly she stood to greet him. She wore black heels, the pumps making her five centimeters taller. Her long and shapely legs were clad in black, thigh-high fishnet stockings held up by a black lace garter belt. She turned around slowly, as if inviting him to consume her with his eyes. The stockings had lines running up the backs of her legs. Her curving hips and rounded bottom made him want to lunge for her, but as he knew she liked, he stood expressionless, absolutely quiet, his hands at his sides. He looked downward, seeing that her only garment below her slim waist was the garter belt, her blond, downy fur glistening in the glow of the candles. Her long, slender arms were relaxed, her hands touching her thighs, fingers elegant and long and feminine, nails a cream color, in contrast to her golden tan. As she sensed his glance light on her hands, she brought them slowly up to her breasts, which were barely contained in a push-up brassiere that exposed her gorgeous nipples, her twin nipple erections protruding as if they were two apple red pencil erasers. Her fingers closed over the fullness of her breasts, her index fingers stroking her nipples. Gardes stared at her throat, which was long and graceful. Her light blond hair was as straight and silky as her four-year-old daughter's, which made him shake his head in wonder that this woman of thirty-five, with such a body of perfection, had ever had children at all. Her jaw was square, her cheekbones and bone structure framing the beauty of her achingly full lips. Her nose was small and well formed, with a slight upturn to it. But of all her features, it was her eyes that were the most bewitching—they were ocean blue and incredibly wide, and capable of a million expressions. Gardes had always thought that he could know Danielle's exact mood by seeing only her eyes. And tonight there was an arch, mysterious mischief in those eyes, and the realization made him twitch inside his pants, in a place where he had already been responding to Danielle's beauty for the last full minute.

He followed her gaze to his crotch, smiling as he realized how absurd he must look in his full *Marine Nationale* summer white uniform with his erection pointing bravely forward like a battleship's large-caliber gun. Danielle's lips curved into a smile of delight and her tanned fingers made a stark contrast on his white trousers as she slowly unzipped his zipper. Slowly, one centimeter at a time, she sank to her knees, reaching a kneeling position as the zipper finally reached the bottom. She unclasped his belt and pulled his trousers and boxer shorts down, just barely enough that his erection came flying out, the organ seeming to strain toward her, as if his sexuality were stretching outward toward hers. Her moist red lips parted, a filament of wetness momen-

tarily suspended between her upper and lower lips. Her
hand reached out to him, her single fingernail running
gently over the length of his penis. He could see the
long vein in it pulsing in pleasure and longing. The sensation of her fingertips came to him then, the incredible
softness of her hands the only thing in the universe for
a moment. Her mouth opened wider and her soft tongue
came out, and it was the next sensation he felt, the wetness and heat of it running from the engorged tip of him
down the length. His breath caught and he felt his eyes
begin to roll back in his head as he felt her lips close
on the end of him, and then the wet suction of her.
Slowly she moved her head toward him, more and more
of him vanishing into her mouth as she pulled him
deeper. She made the slightest sound in her throat—not
a gagging sound, but just a slight click, the sound she
always made as she sucked him as deeply into her throat
as she could, and soon there was nothing more visible
of his organ. He could feel her lips, then her teeth biting
him slightly where the base of him met his abdomen,
her throat clicking slightly again. There was something
about that sound of her deep-throating him that made
him feel like he enlarged and became even bigger.

As slowly as she had swallowed him, she withdrew, the
strong tumescence of him appearing again in his veined
excitement, his organ surging with excitement and pleasure. Again she sucked him in deeper, her mouth forming a delicate *O* as she brought him deeply into her once
more, and this time as she pulled back she turned her
head just slightly and moved forward again, but now she
sped up until her rhythm made her take only a second
to go from his erection being fully, wetly exposed to
vanishing entirely into her mouth and throat. She
pumped her face back and forth, her wet mouth sucking
on him slightly harder with each stroke. He felt his
hands reach down to her hair, feeling it in his hands, the
smooth cornsilk texture of it so incredibly beautiful. As
if awakened by his touch, her blue eyes opened slightly
and gazed upward at him, as if attempting to see into

his soul as she sucked on him. She always waited to
open her eyes to look up at him, perhaps knowing that
when she did it sent him reeling over the edge, and this
time, as ever, it was those gorgeous eyes and their long
dark eyelashes that did it to him. He began to spurt
inside her mouth when she had him deeply lodged in
her throat, and as if relishing what was happening, her
eyes closed in pleasure and she moved back, his organ
exposed again, and on this stroke she moved deliberately, slowly down on his shaft until he was all the way
in her throat. The spasms shook him, his legs trembling,
the violent orgasm spraying his come into her loving,
receptive mouth, her tongue curling around the tip of
him on the final back-stroke, and he could hear her swal-
lowing. Her eyes opened then, her expression different.
Where before she had gazed at him in urgent lust, now
she seemed as happy as a schoolgirl as the afternoon
bell rang, her eyes curving upward at her cheeks, the
slightest wrinkles forming under them—something she
hated, but which he thought made her even more beautiful. His breathing slowed as the last of his passion
poured into her, the flow weakened now, her tongue
moving through the liquid of it, as if she loved the taste
of him, her eyes closing again. One final time she moved
to his abdomen, her teeth on the base of him, then withdrew slowly, and she froze then, holding his organ in
her mouth silently, motionlessly, as he shrank inside her.
When she opened her mouth finally and released him,
it was with obvious reluctance, as if she were disappointed that this had to have an ending.

His hands moved down her shoulders, her hands rising
to clasp his, and he pulled her to her feet. Her lips
parted and he kissed her then, his tongue entering her
where the other part of him had been, and as always,
there was no trace or taste of him there, so completely
had she swallowed him. He kissed her for long minutes,
her tongue entering his mouth and teasing between his
teeth and his lips, then withdrawing as he chased it back
into her mouth, his tongue seeking out her secrets. His

breathing had calmed as the kiss continued. His hands rose to her shoulders and he held her away from his face so he could stare into her eyes. As she always did, and as he had always adored, her eyes flitted from his left eye to his right, as if she were attempting to see into him and find his love for her.

"Danielle," he whispered.

"Yes," she replied, her whisper even softer.

"I love you," he said, his left hand stroking her hair, his right cupping her breast, the warmth and softness of it perceptible through the material of the lingerie.

"I know," she said, smiling, her white teeth visible for the first time, her smile worthy of a toothpaste billboard. Gardes smiled back, knowing she never told him she loved him in reply to his declaration, but only when she initiated the thought.

He let go of her to take off his shoes, then pulled off his trousers and tossed them to a chair, then began to unbutton his shirt. She pouted. "I'll do that," she said softly. He dropped his hands and felt her fingers slowly take off his shirt. Reverently she draped the shirt over the back of a chair, then turned to pull off his T-shirt. When he stood naked in front of her, she slowly removed her brassiere, then reclined on the floor among the pillows.

Her fingers ran through his hair, then her nails scratched their way down his naked back and around to the front of him. Her cool fingers found him then, and he was as hard as stone. He turned her body to be under him on the couch. The opening of her seemed hot, almost feverish, the wetness coating the head of him, as if inviting his entry. Her breath caught in her throat, and he could see the vein on her right temple pulse as it had before. He pinched her right nipple and moved up to kiss her, her mouth reaching out to bite his lower lip, and just then, in one surging, lunging motion, he thrust into her, her gasp a mixed brew of pleasure and pain, and like a crash test car hitting the barrier he slammed himself into her so deeply that he hit bottom hard, the moan torn from her lips, *mon Dieu*, and he slowly withdrew all the way, the tip of him again teasing the lips of her, and her eyelids fluttered open for a half second and her blue eyes looked at him again with that adoring yet volcanically lusting look, the one that always made him climax. He fought the sensation, intent on driving her deeper and deeper into the surface of the couch, as if hammering a nail.

She began her moans then, the sounds he would always cherish and had heard from no other woman on earth, the squealing of her rising to a crescendo as he forced himself deep into her hot, enveloping wetness again and again, until her scream was ear-piercing, then crashed to a deep howl of pleasure as her pelvis shuddered rapidly, her nails scratching his back, her hands urging him more deeply into her. When the noise of her climax ended in a sound in her throat, her eyelids came open again, and the look she gave him this time was deliberate, and he felt almost as if she had cheated, for there was no way he could go on with her looking at him with that naked feminine lust, a drug that would always hold him hostage, and the sensations swept him away. He clamped his eyes shut as his own climax shook him, clutched him, squeezed him and emptied him into her, his rhythmic spasms shaking him until he couldn't keep himself from saying, *mon Dieu, mon DIEU,* feeling as if he would lose consciousness, but finally he came back from the beyond where he'd been and the room returned, and with it the couch beneath him and his beloved Danielle. She looked up at him, a serene, shining happiness glowing from her face, her wide eyes filled with adoration, but with no sign of the molten lust that had been there mere minutes before, that emotion extinguished for the moment.

When his breath returned, he kissed her cheek, feeling himself still inside her, but defeated and shrinking, the female always the eventual victor of this battle. Her skin was warm on his lips, the scent of her perfume an olfactory melody. He blinked, remembering he had wanted to ask her something.

"Children?" he said, feeling like a neglectful parent for having not asked until this moment.

"Overnighting at your mother's," Danielle said slowly, dreamily. "You'll have all of a month to play with them. Tonight I wanted you to just play with me."

He took her upstairs and laid her on the bed. He had meant to make love to her again, but they had both been exhausted and satiated by their first encounter, and when Jean-Paul returned from the bathroom, Danielle lay deep in sleep, snoring gently. He smiled to himself, thinking about how she could fall asleep in the middle of a sentence—her own sentence—and begin snoring within seconds, sleep always coming to her like a switch being thrown. She woke up the same way, as if she'd never been asleep, her eyes coming open every day at four in the morning. She would lace up her running shoes, and no matter the weather, take the stairs two at a time and blast out the front door for a seven-mile run. Gardes had stopped trying to keep up with her—she didn't just jog, she *ran*, her body as fit as an Olympic athlete's. Gardes never could understand how she spent seven miles in a sprint, but she had been that way since the beginning and had never changed. The day she had given birth to Margaux, she had run five miles, and had been disappointed that she had had to cut two miles off her course.

Gardes kissed her cheek, but Danielle didn't stir. He unfastened her garter belt and removed it and her stockings and bra, putting them and her stiletto pumps away on a high shelf of her closet. It would be a rare pleasure to hold her slender, naked body all night, he thought, without two or three children crowding the bed to get to their mother, who had obviously long since stopped sleeping in the nude.

13

Jean-Paul Gardes whistled to himself absently as he started his car to drive to headquarters. A month had passed since *Le Vigilant* had returned to port for the Blue crew's rest and relaxation. It had gone back to sea with the Red Crew, then yesterday again made landfall in the missile loading facility, where it would remain for only two days until Jean-Paul Gardes' officers and men took her back to sea for an abbreviated one-month-long strategic patrol. The next morning was the change-of-command ceremony, when the exhausted *Rouge* crew turned over the watch to Gardes' Blue crew. That afternoon, he would drive *Le Vigilant* to sea, and for thirty days and thirty nights he would not see his precious children or dear Danielle. He hated the thought of a month without his babies or his wife, but he thrilled to the thought of again taking the behemoth submarine to the deep ocean, where no one could find them, harm them, deter them or stop them from their sacred mission to the Republic, for its safety and defense.

The black Mercedes stretch limousine's black windows revealed nothing of the inside. Its engine purred quietly in the crisp September morning. The sea breeze from the Atlantic blew between the buildings of the cross street. The school was one block in from the ocean, in a section of Brest, France, where the well-to-do lived, which made even the opulent Mercedes unobtrusive. In the back, on the right side of the rear seat, Abdul-Azim Fakhri sat holding a twelve-centimeter-long, razor-sharp stiletto in his left hand and the door handle in his right. Nestled in a holster slung from his left shoulder was a Glock 9 mm semiautomatic pistol, fully cocked, the safety engaged, mere thumb pressure the only thing that kept it from being ready to fire.

Fakhri was a nondescript man of Arabic descent, his thinning hair cut extremely close to the scalp. He had a curving, slightly bulbous nose, somewhat uneven teeth, and gray eyes with eyelids that drooped, making him seem as if he were half asleep. His eyes never showed any emotion, the same dead look in them whether he was raping a prostitute, reporting to a superior or taking out the garbage. He rarely spoke, and the few times he did, his voice was jagged and cutting and guttural. He had deep, ugly red scars on the backs of his hands, the result of the hundreds of knife fights he had had with his men to combat the boredom of waiting during an operation. Fakhri had been Issam Zouabri's chief of staff since his beginnings in the *Groupe Islamique Armé*, assigned there by Issam's father. He was ten years older than Issam, and at first had been reluctant to be a babysitter, but Issam's vision and talent had made Fakhri his most loyal subordinate. He rose with Issam as the young man took over as commander-in-chief of the decimated, nearly defeated GIA. Today, he was Issam's vice-commander, his second-in-command. He and Issam had handpicked their circle of principal leaders of the GIA. Each one of them was an operative, able to execute an assassination or a kidnapping, and they were all ruthless to the core. Had Issam commanded any one of them, he would have obediently hacked off the head of his own mother. And yet, they were not mere soldiers. Each one could handle paperwork, hack into computer systems, design weapons from assorted items in a junk drawer and be deemed worthy of a battlefield promotion, able easily to assert the kind of leadership that would allow one of them to take over for Issam or Fakhri at a moment's notice. And though they were ambitious, Issam knew enough not to appoint men who were too ambitious, as that could lead to the assassination of the leader.

Fakhri glanced at his expensive Baum & Mercier watch, his face showing no expression at all. He looked out the window, betraying no impatience. It was a few minutes later than the forecast time, but, five minutes after he expected her, the pretty blond woman came walking over the crest of the hill behind the car. She pushed a baby stroller, its occupant a one-year-old brunette girl. Beside the mother, a four-year-old girl walked, dressed in striped leggings beneath a matching dress, her hair as platinum blond as her mother's. Lagging behind the four-year-old was a five-year-old boy with his hands in his pockets, dressed in jeans and a sweatshirt, a New York Yankees baseball cap worn low over his eyes. Fakhri waited, his heart pounding in his chest. The mother walked closer, oblivious to the Mercedes, the car just another of the luxurious automobiles parked on the tree-lined boulevard. The mother and her children came closer, now a block away from the Mercedes.

The door of the townhouse opposite the car's rear bumper opened, and out of the house poured four affable-looking men wearing paint-splattered T-shirts and jeans, all of them chatting and joking happily, as if they were leaving a job they'd been working on all night. They turned to walk down the sidewalk in the direction of the woman, moving slowly, seemingly more interested in good-naturedly joking and punching each other than making progress down the street. They paused to smile and greet the woman as she drew even with the car just behind the Mercedes. One of the men doffed his baseball cap and humorously bowed to the lady, a large grin on his face. She smiled tolerantly at the painters and pushed the baby stroller past the man who had saluted her.

The next tenth of a second seemed to take an hour. The two men behind the woman blurred into motion, the man who had smiled diving for the mother's legs, the other snaking an arm around her neck. Fakhri pulled the door lever and opened the door as wide as it would go, then lunged all the way forward into the cabin. He reached under his sportcoat and withdrew the Glock, keeping the stiletto in his left hand. In the next second the mother was hurled into the car, her screaming much too loud for Fakhri's taste. He reached over and jabbed the stiletto into her upper arm, drawing blood, then put the point of the knife in front of her eyes, the pain and shock stifling her shout. The children were shoved in next, the youngest howling in pain and fear, the older boy making a brave show of fighting.

The baby stroller was tossed into the door, then the boy's baseball cap, which had fallen off in the fray. The four "painters" dived into the car, the last in slamming the door behind him. The thump of the doors locking came just before the big Mercedes' engine roared to life, the eight people in the back scrambling for handholds as the car accelerated away from the curb. The townhouses where the car had been parked shrank into a blur in the distance as the limo gained speed and crested the next hill. By then Fakhri regained his balance, his Glock leveled at the woman, his stiletto pointed at her left eye. Bandar Qadir, who was Fakhri's well-chosen second-in-command on this operation, the painter who had bowed to the woman, snapped handcuffs on her slim wrists and ankles, then latched the handcuffs onto special restraints in the backseat so that she was completely immobilized, sitting up in the middle of the seat. Her eyes filled with tears as she looked at him. She began babbling that she would do anything if he would only let her children go. Fakhri leaned closer, a look of compassion on his face, just before he smashed his fist into her jaw, smacking her head back on the seat, a scream of fear and pain filling the car.

"French cunt," he said emotionlessly in French, as if it were a fact rather than an epithet. He motioned with his eyes to Qadir, who slapped duct tape on her mouth.

It took less than a minute for the other men to similarly bind the children. When the interior of the limo was finally under control, Fakhri sheathed his stiletto and holstered his Glock, and looked into the eyes of the woman, his expression completely reasonable, as if his violence from the moment before had never happened.

In perfect French, he said to her, "Good morning, Mademoiselle Gardes. Or should I call you 'Danielle'— seeing as how we are about to get very intimately acquainted? Please don't give us any trouble, and you and your children will be completely unharmed. If either you or they attempt to escape or attract attention, I will regrettably be forced to cut off the finger of one child and feed it to one of the others, while you watch, of course. And should I run out of fingers, eyeballs are next. Then genitalia. Do I make myself understood?"

She nodded quickly, the tears now wetting her cheeks, her nose running as well. It was a shame, Fakhri thought. She had awakened on this day such a beautiful woman. When the sun set, she might not be quite as beautiful. And depending on how much or how little she cooperated, she might be the mother of fewer children.

Fakhri found his cell phone and clicked into the speed dial.

"Operator forty-three." Issam Zouabri's expressionless voice sounded metallic on the connection.

"We have the first pickup," Fakhri said. "It was routine. Delivery will be on time."

"Very good," Zouabri said before hanging up.

The limousine drove on for some time while Fakhri stared out the darkened windows. He glanced at his watch and thought of the dozens of things he would like to do to these children if Zouabri allowed him. The mere idea of it made him tingle, but as he glanced at the frightened eyes of the wife of *Capitaine de Frégate* Jean-Paul Gardes, he came back to the moment. It was dangerous to fantasize now. There were still a hundred things that could go wrong with this errand.

Issam Zouabri walked slowly along the long corridor of the darkened, grimy warehouse in the far outskirts of

Brest, his boots clicking on the concrete floor. Beside him, Youssef Tagreb walked.

"Do not forget, Youssef," Zouabri said, his voice smooth and in command. "Until we gain access to the submarine, my name is 'Salah al Din.' The story of our being Chechen rebels *must* remain credible. The French must believe with all their hearts that these weapons will be aimed at Russia, not their own soil. And they must never think the missiles will be used, they must believe they will only be seized as a threat. The moment we lose this illusion, it won't matter what our leverage is, our operation will fail. Any of these men will gladly trade their families for the lives of eighty million countrymen, but there is no way they will offer up their children and wives for a mere threat—a statement—toward Moscow."

Tagreb nodded unhappily. The two continued walking. While Zouabri's eyes remained facing front, Tagreb craned his neck and looked around, seeming nervous and out of place.

"So, Youssef, your spirit is not at peace. Why are you worried?"

"Obviously, Issam—Salah al Din—I have never done this before. Or anything remotely like it."

"Ah, but you were a weapons officer on a Typhoon submarine. You held a hundred million lives in your hands, your fingers on the trigger."

"Hardly," Tagreb said. "No such use of the missiles would have happened. The weapons are there to prevent war."

"But had your country—nay, not even your country, the country that fed and sheltered and educated you— had that country called on you, you would have launched the missiles."

"Yes," Tagreb sighed. "I was trained to do so. I had the aptitude. I would have obeyed. But no matter how many people died, it was distinctly different from killing at close range."

"But you killed your former captain at close range.

His blood spilled down your hands. I saw your face. Your spirit was free at that moment."

"That was different. He was an enemy. Not a woman. Or a child." Tagreb sniffed. "This is difficult, Issam."

"Salah," Zouabri corrected gently. "No, I tell you truly, my friend. This is the easy part. This is the enjoyable part. Executing a carefully thought out plan—a plan agonized over with its every detail called into question—that is the hard part. Now, all the creative work, the heavy thinking is behind us. The 'what' is determined, the 'how' is decided, and now there is simply action."

"I suppose," Tagreb said. "I'm also worried about myself. I think it will be impossible for me. Does the fact that they are innocent women and children mean nothing to you?"

"Ah," Zouabri said. "Again, that is the easy part." Issam stopped. "Do you own a toolbox, Youssef?"

"What?" Tagreb seemed surprised at the question.

"A toolbox. Filled with common tools. Hammer, screwdriver, tape measure; certainly you possessed one at one time in your life?"

Tagreb shook his head. "Yes, of course. Why?"

"Unless you have possessed and used the various tools in a toolbox, Youssef, you will never truly understand leadership. It goes first to understanding your lieutenants, peering into their characters, finding out what motivates them, drives them, focuses them. Next, it is the commander's responsibility to know what each one is good at. The hammer's function is to slam nails into wood. The screwdriver's function is much more subtle, but similar if you think about it, since it subtly rotates the screw into the wood with more or less the same end result. The tape measure's job is much less glamorous, but then, would the hammer or screwdriver truly achieve greatness without the utility of the tape measure? Once the commander knows the tools, and if he knows the job, it merely becomes the almost mindless task of deploying the tools to their separate tasks. Do I make myself clear?"

Tagreb stopped. "Listen. *Salah*. I appreciate parables as much as the next disciple. But I know you are not talking about hammers and tape measures. Please speak clearly. Please believe that I am capable of understanding. I was a captain-lieutenant in the Russian Republic Navy. I know leadership. I know equipment. I know people. Don't treat me as if I am a ten-year-old apprentice."

Issam nodded. "And in speaking thus, you have taught me much more than I set out to teach you in the first place, Youssef. I am truly blessed to have you with me in this mission. I do not often speak of my gratitude or my affections. They are dimly perceived by me in the moments before I fall asleep at night, and I constantly remind myself to commend my subordinates, but then the next day begins and I am in the flow of time, my commitment forgotten. Please forgive me. I am lacking as a leader."

Tagreb put up his hand as if to stop Zouabri's speech. "Go on, Salah. I told you I was apprehensive about the operation's impact on women and children. That was the point that you went off about hammers and screwdrivers."

"Yes, I did, didn't I?" Zouabri smiled, then continued his slow walk. "Youssef, these are never pleasant things for men like us. We believe in the protection of women from the ugliness of the world. Children, the very children of the living god, we believe should be shielded from the conflicts of our *jihad*. We have allowed ourselves to be blinded by an important fact in believing this way, Youssef, and that fact is, these women and children have infidel French blood running through their veins, blood that would someday spill ours, extinguish the heartbeats of our own children. That does not make our actions any easier, but we need not hammer in the nail ourselves, only to select the hammer. You see, my vice-commander, Abdul Fakhri, is an expert at such matters. It is as if he were created by Allah himself to solve such nagging problems for us. We are fortunate indeed."

"So," Tagreb said, "we leave all this to Fakhri?"

For a moment Issam did not speak. When he did, he inclined his face toward the ceiling. "No. Fakhri is our hands, but our eyes must still see. We will not be in the blood-splattered rooms with him, but we will regrettably be required to watch the same scenes that our targets will watch." Issam put his hand on Tagreb's shoulder. "It will not be easy for any of us, this thing we do, Youssef. But it must be done."

"Yes, I suppose so," Tagreb said.

Far behind them, down the wide corridor between the rooms of the warehouse, a rollup door began to open, the bright sunlight of the morning shining into the gloom of the interior.

"The first delivery," Issam said, a pleased look on his face, as the black limousine rolled into the building.

Jean-Paul Gardes pulled into the garage and shut off the engine. He whistled as he entered the house. He had been thinking about the discrepancy list for most of the drive home, the list of pieces of equipment that were out of service or out of commission or were somehow not fit for duty at sea. The list was broken down into categories; the first priority the things that would absolutely prevent *Le Vigilant* from going to sea, but fortunately that list was empty. It was the secondary and tertiary lists that bothered Gardes. He didn't like to harbor thoughts like the one stubbornly sticking in his mind at this moment, but he was beginning to believe the evidence—when he and his Blue Crew turned the ship over to the Red Crew, the list of discrepancies was short, and none of them included things that could be fixed at sea. When Commander Laurent Hurst III turned over command of *Le Vigilant* to Gardes' *Équipage Bleu*, the discrepancies were just short of major. Gardes had complained, gently, to his opposite number, but Hurst seemed to be as much a victim of the *circuit de mesure préventive de pénis-cerveau*, the "penis-brain interlock," as any of his crewmembers. The penis-brain interlock was a phenomenon as old as seafarers, and occurred as a ship made its way back into port from a long voyage, when the minds of the crew were so taken up with re-uniting with wet and willing wives or girlfriends— thinking with their penises—that routine seamanship went afoul. Simple tasks like uncoiling heavy mooring lines became difficult, and more difficult tasks like calculating tides and currents became nearly impossible. It took enormous discipline to keep one's mind on task in such a situation. Gardes himself was subject to the same problem, particularly with Danielle, in all her glory, waiting for him, their first night back usually resembling what had happened last night, he thought, smiling.

He smiled to himself as he shut the door behind him, that once again his beautiful wife had displaced unpleasant thoughts from his mind. He put his keys in the bowl on the kitchen counter, near the door they entered and left by most of the time, and put down his slim briefcase. Very little paperwork came home with him, seeing how it was entirely too classified.

"Danielle?" he called, wondering if she were upstairs. It would be just like her to wait for him, naked, for his second-to-last sexual encounter with her before he left for two months. But she was nowhere to be found on the second floor. Probably shopping for the meal she'd cook him for lunch, he thought, or at his mother's house arguing over how the children were being raised. He looked out the front window of the master bedroom, just to see if she were returning, when he saw the black four-door Mercedes pull up in front of the house.

Abdul-Azim Fakhri waited in the back of the sedan in the left rear seat behind the driver, Bandar Qadir, the man who had played the painter in the abduction of Danielle Gardes, and who might be called by some measures her new boyfriend. Fakhri chuckled at the thought. The sound of his laugh elicited a whimper from the passenger in the right-hand seat, which angered Fakhri, so he gave her a hard elbow to the face, making her choke back her sounds. She had learned something this morning, he thought.

The walkie-talkie radio function on his cell phone beeped. He hoisted it to his mouth.

"Yes," he said.

"He's in the house." It was the voice of Kaliq Hafeez, Fakhri's man on foot. Kaliq had French blood in him and could even be mistaken for a Westerner. Fortunately, there was no French in his attitude.

"Good," Fakhri said, putting the phone away. "Go," he commanded Qadir. The Mercedes accelerated gently around the block and came to a halt in front of Gardes' townhouse. The car they were using on this part of the operation was not as attention-grabbing as the stretch limo, but, Fakhri had to admit, he missed the roominess of the bigger car, especially when it came to maneuvering around the hostage. As the car came to a full stop in front of the Gardes home, Qadir hit the automatic lock button, unlocking the right rear door. Fakhri lunged past his prisoner to the door handle, opened the door wide, and with one mighty thrust, pushed her out onto the sidewalk. As she rolled away from the sidewalk, he took a brown paper-wrapped package and tossed it on top of her. She had learned her lesson from a few minutes before, he thought, as she didn't make a single sound, or perhaps her encounter with the sidewalk had knocked her out.

Not that it mattered, he thought, the goddamned French cunt. Were it up to him, he would have left her here, cut in half, with her tits sliced off and stuffed in her mouth, but Zouabri had outlined this part of the operation carefully, and there was to be no deviation from his plan.

"Roll," Fakhri spat.

The car accelerated again, this time just as slowly as before, as if nothing were unusual. Two streets over, Qadir sped up a bit. Once they were at the coastal highway, the trip would be smoother. Fakhri glanced at his watch. In two hours they would be in the Atlantic on the chartered yacht. He hoped he wouldn't get seasick.

"What?" Gardes uttered in disbelief to himself. A bloody body had just rolled out of the black Mercedes, which took off down the street. Gardes stared out the window at the blood-spattered victim, thinking that he or she had been murdered and the Mercedes had dumped the corpse. Then pure shock made him freeze for just a moment, as something about the body clicked in his mind.

Danielle!

Gardes bolted from the room, his mind bifurcating the way it did during an emergency at sea, and just as in a life-threatening disaster, he felt time perceptibly slow down to a crawl. In the slow-motion dash down the stairs, he could feel one part of his mind, now divorced from the rest of him, processing, thinking, rationally if not calmly, and the thought was—

Where is the damned cordless phone? We can never find it when we need it. I have to call the ambulance, the police, the authorities, the Judicial Police!

The second part of his mind was far less logical. It spun ahead, a whirl of emotions and impulses and reflexes, none of it able to be verbalized, as most of it was coming from Gardes' reptilian brain. The adrenaline pumped into his system, further slowing down time, and it seemed to take forever to get to the foyer of the house. Gardes fumbled with the lock to the front door and slammed it open, then dashed out into the street.

If he lived to be a hundred and thirty, he would never forget the images of the next few seconds as he came close to her. She was draped in what had once been a white bedsheet, extending from her throat to her feet, making Gardes think that it was a death shroud. The sheet was soaked in blood, with some of it dried to a dark red, some of it slick and wet. On her backside the sheet was brown, where she had eliminated inside the shroud, and on the front below her throat it was covered in vomit and blood. The sheet was secured around her with turns of gray duct tape; a turn around her ankles, then above her knees, a band of tape about her waist, two wraps around her chest, immobilizing her arms, and the final wrap at her throat, where the sheet had been torn off to reveal her face and hair, but the ripped fabric made Gardes wonder if she had spent time with the sheet all the way over her head.

There was duct tape over her mouth, and blood and mucus clogged her nostrils. Gardes ripped the tape off and forced himself to be calm enough to check her breathing. She was breathing on her own, barely. Suddenly she stiffened, then dry heaved. He held her forehead, her skin hot to the touch. When she was done, her eyes slowly came half open. He realized they were both swollen almost shut, both of them bruised nearly black. There was a sound as she croaked something.

"What?" he asked her, his mind racing as he eyed the car and calculated the distance to the nearest hospital, wondering if it would be quicker to rush her to the emergency room in his car or wait for the ambulance.

"Get . . . me . . . inside," she said weakly, her voice a strained, tortured whisper before she coughed. "Inside, Jean-Paul. Before anyone sees me."

"Inside?" It would be faster in the car, he decided, but if she had trouble on the way, there would be nothing he could do for her. The ambulance might take an extra minute to get here, but the paramedics could help her immediately when they arrived. He reached a decision—the ambulance.

"Jean-Paul!" she shrieked.

"I hear you, honey," he said, trying to sound comforting. "Don't worry, I'll get you help. We shouldn't move you—"

"Get me in the house now, before someone sees me," she commanded.

He blinked at her, uncomprehending.

"Now," she whispered intensely. Her eyes opened

wide, despite the swelling, almost as if they had bugged out. He could see how bloodshot her eyes were—there was barely any white left. "And bring that package."

"Danielle," he said, standing, his voice authoritative, "I'm going to get the phone, don't move." He'd already turned to run into the house when he heard her voice. This time it was plaintive, a begging moan.

"They have the *children*, Jean-Paul."

Gardes froze, his heart hammering painfully in his chest as a renewed panic rose in him. *Where were the children?*

"They're animals, they'll kill the children—no, they'll dismember and torture them—if you don't listen to me *right now*." She began to cry, her sobs the saddest thing Gardes had ever heard in his life. He turned back to her. Her eyes were still wide open, the eyes of someone going mad. "*Please* . . . get me inside!"

Without thinking, he bent and scooped her body up, then stood, his legs straining slightly as he forced himself erect.

"The package," she moaned. "Get the package!"

Dumbly he turned, saw the brown box and put her back down. He picked it up, clamped it in his teeth, and picked her back up and hurried into the house. He laid her gently on the couch, ran into the kitchen for a sharp knife, then returned and began cutting off the duct tape binding her.

"We need to call the police," he said, suddenly thinking it was foolish to concentrate on the duct tape instead of picking up the phone. Danielle's arms came free just then, and she pulled them free of the shroud. The sight of them made him freeze—her skin was covered with cigarette burns and deep cuts, with severe bruising on every square centimeter.

"My God, what happened to you?" he asked. "Where are the kids? Who has them?"

Just then her hands clamped on either side of his face. "Listen to me," she said angrily through clenched teeth. Some of them were missing, the others caked in dried blood. "If you pick up the phone to call the police I swear I'll kill you."

Gardes stared at his wife. "What did you say?"

She took a deep breath. "Armed terrorists kidnapped me and the children on the way to school. They want your submarine. They're Chechen rebels. They want to threaten Russia to get the Russians out of Chechnya. They aren't going to use your missiles—they don't have the knowledge and they don't care to have it. But if you don't do what they ask, they'll torture the children. Slowly, Jean-Paul." She took a breath, exhausted, the tears beginning then, tears of fear and frustration and pain. "They already did horrible things to them," she said, her voice rising in panic. "They did terrible things! They'll do far worse! They'll die in terrible *agony* if you don't listen!"

"Okay, okay, calm down—"

"Don't tell me to be calm, Jean-Paul. *Listen!* They have the others, too."

"What others?"

"Emmanuelle Courcelle, Serge and Christelle. Michéle Teisseire and Juliette and Claire. Véronique De Lorme and her kids, Marlene and Matthieu, and Anaïs Molyneux." She sobbed, then choked, then coughed. Her voice softer, she said, "They murdered Michéle."

"Danielle," Gardes said, his hands shaking as he placed them gently on her shoulders. "Are you sure about this?"

Her eyes shut, the tears washed down her battered and bloody cheeks. "I saw them, Jean-Paul. They were doing things to the children, terrible things. Fingers cut off. They fed them! They fed them to the other children, choking them, making them eat *body parts* of their siblings, while their mothers watched! They taped Emmanuelle's eyes open to force her to watch! They made Michéle's children watch as they raped her, then slit her throat, then *cut her head off*!"

Danielle dry heaved again as Gardes held her forehead. Somewhere, something cracked deep in his mind, making that strange detachment of his rational self much more pronounced. In that part of his mind, he was no longer emotional. Within that part, he looked down at his beloved wife and felt nothing. The fear and panic and loathing for the men doing this terrible thing, all that was in his other self, on the other side of a blast-proof wall from his logical side. His love for Danielle was on the other side as well. Even his love for his children became isolated from him for just a split second as he realized the implications of what Danielle was saying, and as his time sense slowed even more than when he saw her out front, he realized he was in front of a fork in the road, perhaps the hugest decision of his life.

The Republic was in danger. Armed terrorists had hijacked the women and children of the senior officers of the most powerful warship on Earth, with enough killing power to level half of Europe. It could be even worse than Europe, he thought. This could even be a coordinated strike at the entire West—France, Britain, Germany, Spain, America, Canada, the entire civilized non-Muslim world. He deliberately took a deep breath, turning his head to look into the kitchen, where the cordless phone handset lay in its charger.

Call the police, a voice in his head commanded. Call the DPSD. The *Direction de la Protection et de la Securite de la Defense*, the Directorate for Defense Protection and Security, responsible for the security of the Republic's military forces, they would know what to do. Call the DST, the *Direction de la Surveillance du Territoire*, the Directorate of Territorial Security. They would know what to do. No, the first call should go to DCPJ, the *Direction Centrale Police Judiciaire*, the Judicial Police— they could coordinate and make the calls to the other alphabet-soup organizations.

Danielle raised her head, her expression miserable. "Jean-Paul, play the DVD they made. See for yourself."

He stared at her, suddenly not knowing what he should do. The rational part of his mind seemed to vanish, and he was back, submerged in panic and terrible fear for his children and an unbearable anger for what had happened to his wife.

"Play it," she said. Her screaming began then. *"Play it,"* she shouted, over and over.

As if in a dream, Gardes stood and opened the brown package. As he did, Danielle grabbed the knife he'd used and cut away the remainder of her duct tape bindings, and pulled away the sheet. Underneath it she was naked. He stopped and stared at her. Every part of her body was either bloody, bruised, burned or cut, or all at once.

"Oh, dear God, what happened to you, Danielle?" he heard himself whisper.

"They raped me, Jean-Paul," she said, in a frightening, emotionless tone. "Two men at once. They made the children watch. They held Marc's eyes open as they both raped me, one after the other." She sank to her knees and put her face in her hands and began sobbing silently. He dropped the DVD case and rushed over to her, but she reared up on him like a raging, wounded animal. *"Play the DVD!"* she shouted. "This isn't about me, it's about the children, and not just ours! There are ten children at risk, Jean-Paul, *ten!* And four women. No, only three, now . . . Jean-Paul, it isn't just that they'll die, they'll be tortured!"

For just an instant he remembered his father's legal pad with the word *torture* scrawled on the canary yellow page, then he bent, picked up the DVD and put the disk into the entertainment center. *Oh, dear God*, he thought, *my children could be being tortured or killed right at this instant and I'm watching a fucking movie.*

The screen cleared of static and revealed the face of a young man with a thin face, perhaps no more than thirty, wearing a black garment and dark black wraparound sunglasses. They made him seem insectlike. He had black hair, a pointed chin, defined cheekbones. He would be considered handsome, Gardes thought. The background was a stark, featureless white. The man on the screen didn't move for long seconds, just stared at the camera. In the background, a bloodcurdling shriek suddenly sounded. It was the scream of a young child, but mercifully did not sound like one of the Gardes children. The man suddenly held up his hand, and instantly the scream died down to an agonized crying.

"Captain Gardes," the man said. His voice was a deep tenor, smooth and authoritative, not used to being questioned. As he said Gardes' name, he inclined his head slightly forward, as if he were meeting Gardes in person, the gesture giving the oddest and out-of-place impression of respect. "It doesn't matter who I am," he said, then paused. "It doesn't matter whom I represent." Another pause. "To you, my cause and my motivations have no meaning. I do not expect them to have meaning to anyone but me and my men. And my countrymen, far away." The man raised his hand, and immediately another agonized child's scream came over the audio. The shriek continued for three terrible seconds, then ended when the man dropped his hand. "What is important is credibility. Belief. Belief in reality. Qutuz," the man said, speaking to someone off camera, "rotate the camera if you would, please. Show the room."

The view on the screen changed slowly, the man in black leaving the picture. The scene began to show red on the white background. Gardes could tell the walls had been draped in clear plastic. The surface of the plastic sheeting was drenched in blood and gore. In one place it seemed as if the blood had splattered, as if under pressure.

"Stop the camera there, Qutuz. You see the blood, Captain?" It seemed surreal to hear this abomination of a man address him with his office, a mark of respect he was owed not because of his rank, which was only a commander, but because he was in command of a ship. "I'm afraid that creating the pattern left one of your friends, a Mademoiselle Michéle Teisseire, rather in pieces. In fact, her head has been irreparably separated from her body. Naturally, we captured it all on film. That segment will air later on this disk, which I've included for your use, Captain Gardes, but I will explain in due time. Qutuz, if you would frame me again." The field of view rotated again to bring the man into the center of the screen.

"It would not do to keep going without knowing at least my name. You may call me by the name of *Salah al Din*. Obviously, that is not the name my dear mother gave me, but it is an ancient name, Captain. It means 'Righteousness of the Faith.' It is also the name of the Muslim leader who liberated Jerusalem from the Crusaders. This will have some meaning for you shortly, because, you see, I come from a small village in Chechnya. Not long ago, Russian soldiers crashed into my home. My mother was fifty years old when this happened. I say 'was' because she is no longer living. The Russians raped her and beat her while they raped her. They made me and my sister watch. When they were done, they clubbed her head until her brains lay on the wood floor of the kitchen. Then they started on my sister. They said they saved the best for last. There was not an orifice of my sister's body that was not drilled into by the disgusting penises of the Russians. At one point they took a knife to open up her nostril, and one of the Russians used his sex organ on that orifice as well. All the while, you understand, they had a knife at my throat and made me watch. Finally, they told me that their unit commander would take her from behind, and that at the very moment he climaxed in my sister's rectum, his men would cut her throat. It took him a long time, Captain Gardes. A very long time. Apparently he had spent all morning performing such brutal things. But finally he reached his point of no return. His eyes shut, his body shuddered, he pumped his disgusting fluids into my sister's bowels, and just then his lieutenant sliced my sister's throat. Have you ever seen what it looks like when both carotid arteries and both jugular veins are sliced open in one ruthless cut?"

Gardes looked over at Danielle, but she lay on the carpeted floor in front of the television, still naked, still bleeding, cradling herself and rocking back and forth. Gardes moved to comfort her, but she snarled viciously at him, *"Just fucking watch!"*

The man who had called himself Salah al Din continued. "Blood splashes everywhere. You might think of it as a blood firehose. For your purposes, Captain, I have filmed your chief engineer's wife being treated the same way as the Russians treated my sister, just so you can visualize what it must have been like for me to see it. Oh, you say you don't want to watch? Fine, then let your chief engineer, *Capitaine de Corvette* Aymeric Teisseire, watch. We chose Mademoiselle Teisseire very carefully, Captain, because of all our fourteen hostages, she was the least valuable. Yes, that is true. She was cast off by your engineer, yes? He begged her to return to their marriage because she controlled the children, not because he loved her. Ask him, he will admit it to you. Interesting, isn't it, Captain, what a man will do when someone controls his children? And now, it is more than an academic point, because now it is I, Salah al Din, who controls *your* children, Captain, and the children of your beloved *Cadre Dirigeant,* Vincent 'the Polar Bear' Courcelle. Oh yes, we certainly did do our homework.

"I will waste no more of your time and get to the point, Captain, but before I do, let me just list for the record the hostages we hold. Your children, young Marc. Your sweet young daughter, Margaux. And your favorite—I know, it is impolitic to name favorite children, isn't it, Commander, yet still, she is—young Renée." For ten seconds the film showed the terrible torture of Gardes' children. Gardes brought both hands to his mouth in horror. It was the longest ten seconds of his life.

"And now the others. The offspring of your executive officer. The young daughters of your chief engineer, the ones he sought so hard to regain. The daughter and son of your weapons officer—they are older, aren't they, Captain? The daughter, thirteen is her age? I believe my men described her as, how would you say it in French?

'Juicy'? Yes, I believe that over the coming hours my men will content themselves with the many delights of young Marlene."

Gardes clenched his fists, his sole impulse to punch the television. The stray thought entered his head that he wished that he had never awakened to this terrible day, but had died in his sleep, back in another lifetime when life was so good.

"Although, I have to say, while I don't see it myself, some of my troops have been much more interested in fifteen-year-old Matthieu. There simply is no accounting for taste, now, is there, Captain? Ah, well, that is simply the way it goes. Oh, how could I forget? The women, of course. Let us have a look at beautiful Emmanuelle."

Gardes shut his eyes, but the voice from the screen was a nail pounded into his eardrums: *"Suck me, French whore! You know you love it!"*

Gardes was unable to take any more. He reached for the remote to turn it off, but Danielle screamed at him again, *"Don't turn it off, just watch!"* He froze as Véronique De Lorme appeared on screen, her body slowly mutilated as they watched.

"Oh my God," Gardes cried, tears streaming down his cheeks.

"Shut up, Jean-Paul," Danielle hissed. "If it is hard to watch, imagine how terrible it was to experience!"

Gardes ran his fingers through his hair, an old habit of anxiety he had broken in his midshipman days.

"And Anaïs, the lovely bride of your *navigateur*. But then, I suppose she used to be lovely. Once my men finish cutting out her eyeballs, she will be far less attractive, don't you think, Captain?

"And finally, our first and foremost hostage, your gorgeous and prized wife, Danielle. She used to be a fashion model, didn't she, Commander? You may wonder at my choice of words, calling her a hostage, since we have deliberately released her. But, you see, Jean-Paul, we forced her to witness everything that is in the second part of this message. It was difficult keeping her eyes open for all of that, but duct tape is an incredibly useful thing, we've found. We set her free with this DVD to convince you of what will happen if you go to the authorities. You see, it matters little if our hostages die, at least, it doesn't matter to us. To you, you fathers and husbands, it matters greatly. But we've added an additional element to the equation. Torture. If you should fail in the task I am about to assign you, not only will your little ones die, they will pray that they died *much* sooner. There are a thousand ways to suffer, Captain. Maybe ten thousand. We can prolong agony for weeks if need be. We have IV bottles to keep these young ones alive while we keep them in so much pain they are at the bare edge of consciousness."

Without warning, Gardes suddenly rushed to the kitchen sink and explosively vomited, leaning over the sink while Salah al Din continued.

"Now to business, Captain. It is time to convene your senior officers. I'm afraid you're just going to have to watch this film all over again, and it will be required of you that you watch it to the end, so that your officers can see what we have been spending the day doing with their loved ones." Salah al Din smiled. "Once they have been informed of the situation, you will of course discuss the merits and disadvantages of going to the police or the intelligence agencies. Certainly that must be part of the agenda, because, after all, you are human. You have blood flowing through your veins, you are a thinking and feeling man, yes? So discuss it. Air out the issue. Fantasize about getting the authorities involved. You would feel far less alone, I believe. Armed agents buzzing about your homes, taking evidence, making it feel as if progress is being made. But we will know almost immediately. How will we know? Your homes are watched. Your phones are tapped. We are watching your submarine. We have agents everywhere. Even in your prized police agencies. We will know. And what happens when a single one of you goes to the police?

"I'll tell you what happens. We will begin to cut your

little ones to pieces. Slowly at first. I'm afraid there will not be much left of your sons and daughters by the time the authorities arrive. Not even much to bury, I'm afraid, as we've been keeping some fairly vicious dogs quite hungry for some time. And in the end stages, we will just turn over the still-living children and women to the dogs and let them finish. Do you ever have nightmares about being eaten by a hungry beast, Captain? It is not a pleasant dream, no, not at all. And the thought of the last thing your loved ones see being the sharp, bloody teeth of the animal eating them." Salah shook his head. "So distasteful. So unnecessary. So insane, I know. Let us then believe for a moment that your fantasizing about calling the police is over.

"You are asking yourself, what do we want? We want FS *Le Vigilant* of course. We want you to allow us aboard once you depart for the deep Atlantic. What do we want with your ship? The missiles, you imagine. You are not correct. We do not want to *use* them, simply to *possess* them. We aim to get Russia out of Chechnya, permanently. We will keep your ship for some time, hidden away in a secret location. The Russians, faced with a nuclear threat, will withdraw from my homeland. Of that, I am certain. What I am not sure of is whether they will stay out. Our objective will be to keep *Le Vigilant* ready to launch its missiles at a moment's notice at the Russian cities. You have seen the strength of our purpose demonstrated on your family and those of your officers. Certainly, there can be no doubt that if we can be this ruthless with women and children, in person, we can push a button that will send millions of the Russian animals to meet Allah, who will have the wrath of fire waiting for them. Now, once we have *Le Vigilant* in our possession, we will release you and your crew, with a sealed envelope."

Salah al Din held up a large, white envelope. "Inside this you will find details of the location of this warehouse. At that point you may contact the police, your spy agencies, anyone you want. Your authorities will find them all alive. They will be bruised, with broken skin, contusions, a concussion or two." Salah chuckled. "Well, certain of their orifices might be somewhat enlarged for some time, but that will heal. If you obey this video, no eyeballs will be removed. There have been a total of four toes and small fingers removed, but nothing that will leave too much of a disfigurement. We had to make sure Danielle knew how serious we are. So, other than Mademoiselle Teisseire, all of our hostages will be right as rain. Two weeks in a hospital and they will be good as new."

For the first time Salah smiled, a ghastly, horrifying expression.

"But, Captain, let me warn you. A contingent of my team will remain here until *Le Vigilant* is in our hands, for two main reasons. First, to carry out my threat in case you do call the authorities at any time before the ship is ours. And to provide medical aid, food and comfort to the hostages the moment we posses *Le Vigilant*. All this pain—" A sudden screen collage of the hellish torture and pain of each of the hostages flashed across the screen. Gardes felt his stomach clench for the second time, but he was empty. "—will end, the very moment we have *Le Vigilant*. Now, we are aware that you do not sail until tomorrow. It will be a stressful night for you, knowing that we are making life uncomfortable for your loved ones. But we must do it, if for no other reason than to hurry your thoughts to the hour you give us your submarine.

"So, tomorrow, Friday, at eleven in the morning, you will cast off your lines and make for the Atlantic. By noon, you will be far clear of Brest and ready to submerge this magnificent weapon system. We will be here."

A chart flashed up on the screen, showing the traffic separation scheme entering and leaving Port Brest, the very outer buoy shown on the right, and a point due east of it marked with an *X*. Below the mark, the latitude and longitude were shown in block lettering.

"Make a note of this position, Captain. Go ahead, write it down now."

Gardes grabbed a pen and ripped a section of the morning newspaper off and scribbled down the latitude and longitude.

"We will be there, waiting for you in a white yacht. You will slow down your vessel and let us aboard. When you do, the senior officers may take the yacht back to port. Don't worry about reprisals. The moment your bosses see this video, they will completely understand. You had no choice. What could you do, watch your children have their eyeballs cut out? Watch your eyeless daughter hang from the intestines of your still horribly alive son?" Salah chuckled. "Of course not. I can almost sense your next thought. You worry about the remainder of your crew. We will have no need for them, but the yacht is not big enough for all hundred and eleven of your crew, so we believe they should wait for rescue in the ship's rafts. Is this acceptable, Captain? I know you cannot speak to me, but you will speak with your actions.

"And finally, Captain, part two of this disk, our documentary of what each of your loved ones has suffered. I will allow you to stop the video here so as to summon your senior officer cadre to your home. I imagine you will encounter resistance from them to turn over such a powerful weapon system to violent men. Worry not, Jean-Paul. Their resistance will dissolve as you show them this. And remember, we are violent, but we are not your enemies. We are the enemies of the foul, loathsome Russians. Remember it is they we seek to humble, not you."

Salah stared at the camera again, as he had done at the beginning.

"I will see you at sea, Captain. Until then, the peace of Allah be with you."

The screen went blue, then changed to a view of Michéle Teisseire being dragged into a white room. Gardes stopped the video, the image of the Rhino's wife frozen on the screen, her face a mask of terror.

Gardes turned and cradled Danielle in his arms. His touch made her twitch, then scream.

"We need to get you to a hospital," he said, feeling more helpless than at any time in his life.

"Help me upstairs," she said, her body shivering. "Put me in a warm bathtub. Then call your officers."

Gardes never got the chance. The jangling of the phone made both of them jump. He hurried to it and picked it up.

"Gardes," he said, his voice trembling.

"Captain!" Lieutenant Commander Vincent Courcelle's voice crackled over the connection. "Something's terribly wrong!"

If he only knew, Gardes thought.

14

"How do I look?" Issam Zouabri asked, standing in front of Youssef Tagreb wearing the dress blue tunic, pants and officer's cap of a *Marine Navale* lieutenant commander's uniform, the stripes circling his sleeves.

Tagreb shook his head in admiration. "Resplendent, Salah." Tagreb looked at his own uniform in the stained mirror, the sleeve stripes those of a *capitaine de vaisseau*, a full captain. He could carry off the illusion because of his age, but it was a double or triple promotion from the equivalent rank he had held in the Russian Republic Navy. The strange uniform carried a foreign navy's symbols, but it reminded Tagreb of his past. Was it his imagination, or did the uniform make him seem taller, straighter, more a man?

Zouabri nodded, donning his black wraparound sunglasses. Abdul-Azim Fakhri, Zouabri's vice-commander, stepped into the enclosed warehouse office that they had commandeered as a command center, wearing the uniform of a *capitaine de corvette*, a lieutenant commander.

"Is everything prepared?" Zouabri asked.

Fakhri nodded as he pulled a powerful automatic pistol—a Heckler & Koch HK MP-5 10 mm submachine gun—from a small duffel bag and snapped a huge clip full of lethal ammunition into it.

"Only one thing left to do before we leave," he said. "Although it's a shame. We are turning our backs on another week of amusement."

Zouabri nodded, seeming distracted. Tagreb took in the pistol with alarm.

"Salah? Issam? What is going on here? What's the gun for?"

Fakhri shot Tagreb a quick glance of contempt, then shook his head and moved to leave.

"Issam!" Tagreb shouted. "Stop that man now, or else I'm not going anywhere! You know as well as I, this mission fails without me."

Zouabri held up his hand to Fakhri, who paused, a look of disgust on his features.

"What is it you want, Youssef?" Zouabri asked, his expression unreadable behind his black shades.

"I want what we promised. That the hostages would be given aid and released," he said, irritated that his own voice sounded shrill.

"And, my friend, why is that?"

"Because, Issam, they are children. And innocent women. And they have suffered enough."

Issam laughed. "They will all be dead in a day or a week from our missiles, Youssef. Is it not more merciful to release them from their lives this day rather than that one?"

"No, it is not merciful," Tagreb said, more emphasis, a deeper timbre in his voice. "When they perish with their countrymen, they deserve to die going about their lives. In their schools, their churches, sleeping in their beds, dressing their children. Not tied up like animals, waiting for a rescue that will never come. You yourself taught me that there is meaning in how a person dies, Issam. *It matters.* Look at how Dostoyev died. His death reflected what he deserved from his miserable life. These innocents, they do not require such a death as you are extending to them. Should they die—no, *when* they die—from the missiles, that is different. In that case, they die as they were meant to. Together. As a nation." He shook his head. "This is my demand, Issam. Let them go."

Zouabri stared at Tagreb for a long time, and Tagreb's impulse was to look down, but he had severed the head of an enemy with his bare hands, hacking into the man's spine, and after an empowering experience like that there was no longer fear. Zouabri was correct to change Tagreb's soul with that gift, but now he must deal with the very reality he had altered. As Tagreb was now partly a creation of Zouabri's, it became Zouabri's lot to face that creation. A complete circle had been formed, Tagreb thought, seeing how in some ways he was beginning even to think like Zouabri.

"If we let them go," Zouabri said slowly, logically, rationally, "they will alert their families and the police. Our operation will end. Before it begins. And all their suffering, which had meaning, after all, because it led to a greater purpose, you will have neutralized. Their suffering would be in vain."

Tagreb was growing tired of the younger man's metaphysical manner of speech. These were real people. Women and children. They did not deserve to die like dogs.

"We promised them we would leave, but then notify the authorities in time for their rescue. I insist we honor that promise."

"I have no desire to hurt them or spare them at this point. I am indifferent, except as it affects our operation. And it goes to the methods, Youssef. How would you propose we spare these infidels so that our holy errand is not compromised?"

"We have a duplicate copy of the video disk you made. Mail it to their police with the address of the warehouse. It will take a day to arrive. By Monday they will come here and liberate the hostages. We will be three days gone by then."

"Think about the implications of what you are saying, Youssef. If we do that, the French Navy will know we have *Le Vigilant*."

"So what?" Tagreb said. "They will know anyway."

"How?"

"A hundred ways, Salah. A submarine has routines, ways the command structure knows that things are in order. In some cases another submarine—one of their

SSNs, an attack hunter/killer sub—shadows the SSBN to make sure no enemy submarine does likewise. In other circumstances, the submarine passes over a specific hydrophone array in a specific ocean location so that the command-and-control officers know that all is well. In other procedures, the submarine will eject a time-delay radio beacon with an 'all-okay' signal. We don't know their exact procedures, but the procedures do exist. Certainly they did for *TK-17* in the Northern Fleet. Because, at all times, the heads of state must know that their oceangoing missile silos are still in existence and have not fallen prey to a mishap, a stuck hovering system valve, or even a mutiny. Notifying their police ourselves will make no difference anyway. *Le Vigilant* has won the 'war of silence.' It is the most quiet submarine in the hemisphere. No antisubmarine warfare forces will find her. The submarine is invulnerable. Not even their own navy could find her if she intends to slip away." Tagreb had learned from Issam, he thought. One of the things he had learned was when to stop speaking and use silence as a tool of negotiation.

"But certainly, by Monday, our missiles will have flown."

"We don't know that, Issam. Salah. It depends on how long it takes me to go through the technical data and find a way that one man alone—or a group of men—can override all the interlocks to launch these without authorization, and further, it goes to the amount of time it will take me to understand how to target the missiles precisely. And the procedures for launch. This is a tremendous body of knowledge, Salah. It can be done. It will be done. How long it will take is in the hands of Allah. It could be a week. Perhaps two. Three weeks is entirely possible. And bear in mind, it shall fall on me to instruct your men in the operation of this colossal vehicle. It is not like flying a plane, under the total control of one man. It is not easy driving a submarine, even for an expert or a group of experts. No matter the extent of automation, it takes many skilled hands. The vessel has a normal crew of one hundred and eleven men. We will sail it with fourteen landlubbers and one submariner—a submariner who is not qualified on this ship. Our first hours will be spent safely submerging the ship and understanding her propulsion plant, ballasting systems, even her navigation systems. Without exact navigation, no missile can hit a target, for the launch point must be known. Salah, it will not be Monday or a week from Monday."

Zouabri stared implacably at Tagreb from behind his glasses. This was obviously news to the GIA commander-in-chief, but that was because this had never come under discussion. And, Tagreb thought, what choice did Zouabri have at this point? Keeping the French crew alive long enough to guide the ship, or even target the weapons? Or was that his intention all along? A doubt occurred to Tagreb, that Zouabri intended to use the crew of the submarine to control the ship rather than Tagreb himself. If that were true, Tagreb would be obsolete the moment they submerged. Issam would have no further need for him. If that turned out to be the case, would Issam kill him? The thought made Tagreb's stomach grow a cold, heavy spot in its center. He felt suddenly nauseated, but he stood erect, trying not to show his emotions.

"So you change the operation completely, Youssef," Issam finally said slowly. "We are at sea for many days before we fulfill our destiny. We let these hostages return to their families. We intentionally notify the authorities that we have taken the submarine. We dare them to find us." He paused, his face a mask of angry stone. But then he smiled. Tagreb stared in astonishment. The man's smile could light up an arena, Tagreb thought, and yet he never used the gesture. "Youssef, my friend, I cherish the way you think. This is even more bold than taking the submarine in the first place." He placed both his hands on Tagreb's shoulders and squeezed them. "Thank you, Youssef. You are truly sent to me from Allah." He turned to Fakhri. "A change is occurring to the plan, Abdul. The hostages will be left here, alive, as well as we can leave them. Make sure they are restrained, but not unduly uncomfortable. Place fresh IV fluid bottles on their stands, and check the needles. Refill the water bottles. Sponge them down with antibiotic fluids and dress their wounds. Employ all the men. Be thorough. Not one of these women or children shall die for the next seventy-two hours. Do I make my orders clear? Let not any omission I have made from my order to you stop you from taking all initiative to fulfill the intent of my meaning. Do it with the force of Allah, Abdul."

Fakhri blinked his eyes obediently, his expression open and receptive, as if the order were one that he was completely enthusiastic to follow. "It shall be exactly as you say, Salah," he said, bowing slightly. He put the weapon back in the carrying case and left the room to do Zouabri's bidding.

"Youssef, prepare the mailing to the French with the video disk. We are late." He paused. "Be sure to make it sufficiently convincing that this is a Chechen operation. No sense frightening the French. I don't want them to evacuate Paris, after all. That would cause unnecessary panic, perhaps even loss of life, don't you think?"

Tagreb bent to the task, wondering for just an instant if Zouabri would prevent him from mailing it. He wrote the note longhand, describing who was held hostage and the location of the warehouse, then sealed the note and the disk in an envelope. There came the issue of whom to mail it to, but Tagreb simply wrote it to the Judicial Police in Paris. He could get the specifics in the post office.

Zouabri climbed into the front passenger seat of the van and pointed his finger to the driver, Qutuz Madari, instructing him to roll. The van started.

"Qutuz," Zouabri said, "find a post office. It is important."

"There's one a kilometer down the main road," Qutuz said.

"Good."

At the post office, Tagreb himself got out with the envelope. He asked the clerk the official address of the *Direction Centrale Police Judiciaire*, the Judicial Police—the national police force and investigative agency—and scrawled the address on the envelope, then reached into his pocket for sufficient funds to ship the package.

"We can arrange for Saturday delivery if you would like," the clerk offered.

Tagreb considered. It was Friday morning. The hostages might well not last until Monday. He had mentioned Monday to Zouabri, but then, even if the package arrived on time on Saturday, there was no guarantee that anyone at the Judicial Police would open it, read it, understand it, or begin to act on it. And at least that way, it would be ready to be opened Monday morning rather than still in transit. It was not a violation of his agreement with Zouabri, Tagreb decided. He nodded. "Yes, that would be perfect," he said to the clerk, paying for the shipment, then leaving and walking out to the van for the ride to the marina.

He may have only given the women and children a few more days—at most a few more weeks—to live, but there was meaning in the gesture. At least they wouldn't expire in that dirty, pain-filled warehouse. They would die within the comfort of their lives. It made a difference, he thought, and Allah would smile on him for the gesture.

15

Lieutenant Emile Everard put the binoculars to his eyes and spotted the bright, featureless white hull of the FOST personnel transfer boat. It flew a French flag and the flag of *Force Océanique Stratégique*, though it wasn't the usual drab gray, beat-up equipment they usually used. Admiral D'Aubigne must have arranged for a new flag transfer vessel, Everard thought. He had no idea why the admiral had wanted a personnel transfer so soon after they departed for the mission, but the operation order change had come just as they were departing the pier.

That was, by far, the least of the things that made this voyage so strange. Since Everard had reported aboard for the underway, the department heads, the executive officer and the captain had all been in foul and distracted moods. Everard wondered if the FOST party to come on board might be doing some kind of inspection or evaluation of the captain and his senior officers. It did fit the facts. He shrugged. They would know soon enough.

"Personnel transfer boat is in sight, Captain. Request to station the personnel transfer party on deck."

Gardes nodded, clearing his throat. "Station the personnel transfer party on deck. The chief engineer will be leading the deck party."

"Aye, Captain," Everard said. Usually the *chef du bateau*, the chief of the boat—the senior noncom onboard, reporting directly to Courcelle and in charge of all the enlisted ratings aboard—would lead the deck team, but it made sense to have a senior department head on deck.

With a FOST team arriving, with all the tension this was causing, it would be the obvious decision. A mistake could make a bad situation worse, such as dropping one of the staffers overboard. Well, Everard thought, the sooner they got the riders aboard, the sooner they could get this over with.

"Control, Bridge, station the personnel transfer party on deck. The chief engineer is ordered to be man-in-charge topside."

"Bridge, Control, aye, station the personnel transfer party on deck, chief engineer in charge."

The shipwide announcing circuit clicked as Turnock's voice boomed out. *"Now station the personnel transfer party on deck, chief engineer in charge topside."*

Apparently Teisseire had been ready for the order, Everard thought, as he was the first man out the missile compartment hatch, already dressed in his weatherproof coveralls and his safety harness. The rest of the deck seamen followed him out the hatch, maneuvering around the sail to the foredeck. All twelve of them assembled there, their safety harnesses latched onto a safety groove set into the deck.

"Helm, Bridge, all stop," Everard ordered as the personnel transfer boat maneuvered closer. He could see the FOST officers on the deck of the boat, which looked like it was a fifteen-meter, dual-diesel-engine craft, obviously brand-new, with curved back lines. A nice piece of equipment—FOST must have reached deep into their budget for this, or gotten a special funding. The boat was worthy of being a pleasure cabin cruiser. That would have been a nice way to spend the day at sea, Everard thought. It could have supported some outstanding deep sea fishing. He wondered if any of the staffers had brought fishing tackle to use while they waited for *Le Vigilant* at the rendezvous point.

Something seemed to strike Everard wrong suddenly. He held up his binoculars. The officers were in the wrong uniforms, wearing dress blues instead of summer whites. It was September, but the change of uniform was

still a week away. Unless they intended to be onboard
for some time, meaning they would disembark in October, for God's sake. That would be par for this damned
run, a rider team making themselves at home, taking
over the officers' staterooms, commandeering the officers' mess, drinking their coffee and taking fucking hotel
showers until there was no hot water. Fucking staff rats.
Everard shook his head, the second possibility occurring
to him, that Gardes' sins had been so severe that a board
of inquiry were being convened. In that terrible case,
the officers would have arrived in dress blues even in
the middle of the summer to convey the gravity of their
errand. He glanced again at Gardes, who seemed to be
getting more nervous with every passing minute.

The personnel transfer craft heaved to on the starboard bow and passed over its lines. Everard picked up
his microphone.

"Navigator, Bridge, personnel transfer craft is tied up,
port-side-to, on our starboard bow." Molyneux would
need to make a deck log entry about it. He could see
this out the periscope, but in case he was as off his game
as the captain, Everard thought he would make the
announcement.

"Bridge, Navigator, aye," Molyneux said, his voice flat
and emotionless.

On the foredeck, Engineer Teisseire was hanging suspended from his harness, his hand outstretched to the
first of the FOST team. He pulled the man aboard and
passed him up to the other deck party, who steadied the
officer and assisted his walk aft around the sail. That
was odd, Everard thought, noticing that the FOST team
didn't have the usual regulation life jackets. Perhaps this
board of inquiry—or whatever the hell it was—was convened so hastily that they didn't have time to equip
themselves. Or the new FOST boat hadn't been fully
outfitted yet. That at least made Everard feel better. The
staff rats had made a seamanship mistake themselves, so
how could they stand too righteously in judgment of his

captain? Unfortunately, Everard realized glumly, staffers had their own sense of navy regulations and tended to forgive themselves of major gaffes while accusing a ship's force for the slightest infractions. Just another reason to get rid of these riders as soon as they could.

The second and third staffers came aboard, until Everard counted fifteen of them. The most senior was a *capitaine de vaisseau*, a full captain, who outranked Gardes, but he seemed diffident, as if he had never been aboard before. And it was strange—Everard was familiar with D'Aubigne's staff, having been invited to a FOST luncheon on Tuesday, the day before their attack simulator examination. That captain was a newcomer, but then, new officers rotated in all the time. The rest were an unfamiliar lot, and obviously there were no Parisians among them. They were all dark in skin tone except for the captain, but that wasn't completely out of the ordinary. The navy always had recruited heavily from the Mediterranean coast, where the old submarine base at Toulon had been, back when the Med had been a Cold War battleground.

Then a chilling thought occurred to Everard, that the captain might be Gardes' replacement. Maybe that's what this was about—Gardes had done something wrong, and he was about to be fired and a new captain would be replacing him. Everard chanced a glance at Gardes, but if anything the captain seemed relieved. On the foredeck, *le Rhino* was manhandling the staffer's sea bags onto the deck from the boat. Finally the gear was aboard, and the deck crew began carrying it into the hull. It wasn't long before they all disappeared down the hatch except for the Rhino and *Maître* Marcel Follet, the chief of the boat, who passed the personnel transfer boat's lines back. As the engineer strode past the sail he shouted up at the ship control crew.

"Personnel transfer craft shoved off!"

"Very well, *Ingénieur*," Everard acknowledged. "Captain, the FOST team is aboard."

"Very good, Deck Officer," Gardes said. "I'm going below. Proceed to the dive point. Rig down the flying bridge. Notify me when the deck is rigged for sea."

"Yes, Captain," Everard said, moving aside so Gardes could pass and go down the access tunnel into the ship.

"And secure the maneuvering watch. Convene the department heads in the officers' mess. We'll be meeting with the riders."

"Yes, sir," Everard replied.

The personnel transfer boat should have turned and proceeded back to Brest, but instead it floated, tossing in the waves. For just an instant Everard had the strangest impression that no one was aboard. He put the thought out of his mind as the captain climbed down the ladder into the ship.

"Bridge, Control, deck party aboard, last man down, hatch rigged for sea."

"Control, Bridge, aye. Helm, Bridge, all ahead full, left five degrees rudder, steady course two seven eight." It wouldn't do to hit the FOST transfer boat, he thought, ordering it to be given a wide berth.

"Lookout, lay to the flying bridge and rig it for sea," he ordered.

The ship accelerated smoothly in its turn back to their base course, the wind and the bow wave picking back up. It was usually a wonderful moment when the captain laid below and left full command of the ship in the deck officer's hands, for a thrilling surface transit to the dive point, but as with all things today, there was no joy in any of it. Everard sighed under his breath as he scanned the horizon with his binoculars.

Captain Jean-Paul Gardes hurried down the ladder, emerging into the control room. Courcelle and Molyneux had already left. They were probably waiting for him in the officers' mess. Gardes wiped the sweat off his forehead. The operation, so far, had gone far smoother than he could have imagined. The best thing they'd ever done was get Everard on the bridge. He hadn't suspected anything. Legard would have had a heart attack over the use of a civilian yacht for the supposed FOST team, with their ragtag incorrect uniforms, their missing life jackets, flying the flags incorrectly—but at least they'd had the presence of mind to get a *Force Océanique Stratégique* flag, although it was the obsolete one. And then to abandon their yacht completely and leave it floating at sea; Jesus, Legard would have sounded the general fucking alarm. And every one of the "riders" was obviously not a Frenchman, each of them sloppily wearing their out-of-season uniforms like they were costumes, but at least none of them had opened their mouth to speak, or else their accents would have given them away. There was no way Salah al Din could ever pass for a Frenchman, not with that horrible accent in his accursed voice. But at least they had concealed their weapons well, which was probably why they had chosen the winter uniforms with their suit jackets, which could cover a pistol in a shoulder holster. Gardes felt the pistol tucked under his pants, the thought occurring to him that with only fifteen of the terrorists aboard, the senior officers might be able to take them down, but then the same thought came to him that had brought him to this horrible moment—his wife and children, and those of his men, were still being held captive, still possibly being tortured.

The only thing on his mind was getting to Salah al Din and asking him if he'd fulfilled his promise to release the families. If Gardes got the wrong answer on that—if these Chechen bastards claimed to have killed their hostages, he would reach into his pants, grab the 9 mm and commence firing, and he didn't give a damn if they killed him before he killed them. After all, why would he want to live another day if Danielle, Marc, Margaux and little Renée were dead? Dying would be an honor at that point, and if he could die in the act of reversing this terrible sin, this despicable treason, then all the better. He clenched his jaw, his old feelings of command certainty returning to him for a merciful moment.

But the feeling was short-lived. He turned the door-knob of the officers' mess door, but it was locked. The cover over the red, round window lifted, and the door was unlocked and opened. A massive dark-skinned paw pulled him into the room and slammed the door shut after him. The Chechens had already taken off their uniform jackets and thrown them aside, wearing white shirts and black pants, their epaulettes missing any sign of insignia. The leader of the band, Salah al Din, sat in Gardes' captain's chair, looking completely relaxed and serene. He wore his wraparound black sunglasses even in the relative dimness of the room. Surrounding him were his thugs, all of them armed with automatic rifles. There was no way, he realized, he could go for his pistol and get off more than a round before they emptied fifty shells into him, and he had to know the answer to the one question that had kept him alive up to this moment.

Seated around the table were Courcelle and the three department heads, each looking as hopeless as Gardes felt, their hands outstretched on the tabletop.

"Come in, Captain," Salah said cheerfully, motioning Gardes to a seat opposite him, the supply officer's chair, as if he were a host at an opulent party. As if for punctuation to his invitation, one of the Chechens grabbed him and threw him into the seat. Gardes looked up, trying not to appear helpless, and pulled his chair up to the table so that he might be able to withdraw his pistol. Perhaps he could at least get off a shot at Salah al Din before they killed him. Escaping the ship in their boat, as they had promised, was obviously not going to happen.

But as if Salah read his mind, he commanded sharply, "Please put your hands on the table, Captain Gardes. Fayyad, please disarm Commander Gardes as you did the others."

One of the larger of Salah's men, a cruel-looking man with the facial bone structure of a great ape, handed his weapon to a comrade, pulled Gardes bodily out of his chair and unzipped his coveralls, reaching into his belt for Gardes' pistol. Gardes winced, the Chechen roughing up his groin as he pulled out the weapon. Fayyad put the weapon in his own belt, then threw Gardes back in the chair before taking back his rifle.

"What have you done with our families?" Gardes asked, trying to inject menace into his voice. It didn't work, as his voice cracked on the last word.

"Youssef," Salah said to a man in his forties, the thin, tall one who had worn the captain's uniform, who seemed younger than his years, both physically and psychologically. Gardes bit his lip, wondering where his clairvoyance for people had been when he had needed it most, when it might have helped him fight his way out of this miserable situation. "Tell the good captain what you did with the children and women."

Gardes' stomach tensed. He felt a terrible dread that this Youssef character would say how horribly they had mutilated his dear children—and Danielle—before killing them. But Youssef leaned over the table.

"I sent a package to the Judicial Police this morning with the same video disk that Salah sent to you, Captain. I enclosed the address and location of the warehouse." The man's voice was a smooth tenor, caring and compassionate. It had to be a trick, Gardes thought at first, but he looked into the man's eyes, searching for signs of deception, praying that his "second sight" would come to him now, and the man was definitely telling the truth. "We disinfected and dressed their wounds, we refilled their IV bottles, we gave them fresh water. The authorities will be there shortly. None of them experienced any permanent injuries, except for the finger and toe amputations that Salah told you about, and those wounds were all expertly treated. Other than Mademoiselle Teisseire, they will all survive. They will all return to full health. And Michèle Teisseire, well, we had to do that so that you would know we were serious."

"That's enough, Youssef," Salah al Din said gently in his heavily accented French. "There is no need to apologize to *them*." There was contempt in his voice on the last word. "It should be enough for them that you spared their families. I tell you truthfully, Captain Gardes, it was my intention to dispose of the hostages. You have Fighter Tagreb here to thank for the lives of your off-spring and your women. He insisted. As to your fate, we made you a promise, but Youssef will not be able to intercede for you in this moment. I am afraid, gentle-men, that this is your Judgment Day." Salah delivered the news as calmly as if he were discussing the weather.

Gardes' reaction surprised him. He looked again at Tagreb. He felt suddenly light as a feather, despite his just being given a death sentence. At least the little ones and Danielle would live. And truth be told, after com-mitting this terrible, treasonous act, dying here, today, would be far preferable to being executed by his own countrymen, or worse, rotting in a military prison the rest of his days, carrying the terrible burden of guilt for his betrayal of the Republic. He couldn't help speaking. He nodded to Tagreb and said, "Thank you, Mr. Tagreb. I thank you and my officers thank you."

Tagreb looked embarrassed. He said nothing.

"That leaves us with a few matters of business, gentle-men," Salah continued, as if he were at a board meeting. "You see, although I've just informed you that your hopes for living are extinguished, I can't have you lead-ing a revolt aboard this ship. My ship." He reached into his pocket and withdrew a silver cigarette case and lighter. He lit up and blew the smoke into the overhead. "Unfortunately for you, I have the same leverage on you that I had with your families. Let us confine ourselves to the men in this room for just a moment. I have gained access to the submarine, which is certainly helpful, but all we control is this tiny part of it. Significant, yes, but we have hardly accomplished our mission."

Gardes wondered why Salah was pointing out his own vulnerability. It was true, they had automatic weapons, but outside the walls of the officers' mess were 105 men, each of whom would resist these men, down to the last man.

"Fayyad?" Salah said. The beefy terrorist who had

taken Gardes' pistol reached into one of the duffel bags and withdrew a large automatic pistol and a long silencer. He efficiently screwed the silencer onto the barrel, then turned the weapon and handed it grip first to Salah. Salah al Din hoisted it, the barrel pointing to the overhead.

"Captain Gardes, I need one more thing from you," he said. Calmly he leveled the pistol at the engineer and fired the weapon into Teisseire's forehead. There was a whooshing sound, then a thud. Gardes stared openmouthed as Teisseire's head exploded, a shower of bones, hair and brains hitting the outboard bulkhead of the messroom, what had been a stereo console now red and gray and covered with gore. Teisseire's expression of shock remained frozen on his face for just an instant, two trails of blood running down his forehead from the small entrance wound, before he toppled to the deck, his heavy body hitting the carpeted floor with a loud thump.

Gardes rose half out of his seat, then found himself staring down the barrel of the huge pistol. His heart pounded in his chest. It was like looking into the maw of a cannon.

"What," Gardes said, finding his voice, "what do you want?"

"I want what you want, Captain. I have told you that today is your dying day. Your only choice now is the manner of your death. Do you want to die like your engineer here, ignominiously with a stupid expression on your face while your men see your brains on the walls, or do you want to die together, mercifully, as a group, with a measure of dignity? I have the power to offer this to you. And it goes to your crewmembers as well, you see."

Gardes shot a look at De Lorme, for a moment remembering his bravery of five years ago, the fugitive thought that perhaps the weapons officer could pull a second rabbit out of his hat, but De Lorme's eyes remained hollow as he stared dumbly at the brains and blood on the stereo console.

"So, Captain, what will it be? Will you extend to me and my men one final gesture? Will you help us give you all a merciful and dignified death as a group, or will you force me to execute all hundred and eleven of you one by one, as I have Engineer Teisseire?"

"What do you require?" Gardes asked, his eyes becoming wet. He wiped them quickly, misery flooding into him.

"Step aside with me, Captain," Salah al Din said. "Let us speak as two commanding officers, one captain to another, yes?" Salah stood and walked calmly out the forward door to the small officers' galley. Gardes stood uncertainly and followed him, aware of the baleful eyes of the Chechens and his officers on him.

The outer door to the galley was shut, locked and guarded by one of Salah's other formidable fighters. The cover over its circular window was also in place, the covers designed so that classified briefings could be held in the messroom without any of the crew seeing charts or other classified data. Salah shut the door to the messroom. Only Salah, his guard and Gardes stood in the small space.

"Yes?" Gardes said, wishing Salah would just get on with it.

"I appreciate the depth of your pain, Captain," Salah said, his voice gentle. "Were I in similar circumstances, I would feel it just as you do. But I have learned many lessons in my life, Captain. One very important one I learned mere hours ago, and that is that it matters how a man leaves this earth. Youssef taught me that when he convinced me, against my original intentions, to allow your family members to live. It is significant. And he is correct. Dying with a bullet to the brain is a shameful way to go. For all we know, Captain, it is unbearably painful for those microseconds it takes for a bullet to traverse the brain. Perhaps that interval of time expands to feel like a century, and during that horrible instant, all you think and feel is the misery of how you are dying."

Gardes took a breath, wishing the terrorist would hurry up and get to the point.

"And it is not just *how* you die, Captain, but whether you die alone or with your men. From what I know of command, watching your men die is a miserable prospect. It is inevitable, Captain, that each of your men will die today. It may even take three days to execute them all. True, some may fight back. Some may unite against us. Some of my own men may die in the fighting. But eventually, we will prevail. We have the superior weapons, and we live to fight, we glory in *jihad* and we pray for a warrior's death. For us, it will be an entryway into heaven. For your men, it will just be a disrespectful bullet blasting through their heads. But let me offer you a much better alternative. It is in your power to change this fate, Captain Gardes. As a man who cherishes the men under his command, it is up to you to make the decision. I can allow you to change this hard reality so that every man in your crew dies at the same moment. Quickly, efficiently, mercifully, finally. With no terrible bullet. No terrible execution. It will be as if a veterinarian puts a beloved pet to sleep. Will you help me deliver your crew to Allah in such peace, Captain?"

Gardes felt the water in his eyes again. He dropped his gaze to the troweled stone floor of the galley. The next second seemed to take an hour. If his second sight told him anything, it was that Salah was being absolutely serious. It came to him that if his men did fight, and if only one of them survived, perhaps the fate of *Le Vigilant* would be different, but how could one of his own survive against the kind of weapons—and the sheer fierce will—of these men? All that would happen is that his men would withdraw to the secret, grubby, oily places in the ship, the potable water tanks, the bilges, the stinking sewage holding tanks. An image came to his mind, of a child hiding from the Nazis in the stinking, fetid well of an outhouse. Would he want that for his men, to hide like animals, and then still be hunted down and executed? He took a deep breath.

"What is it you require, Salah?" he asked, his will and his strength at an end.

"My lieutenant, Tagreb, will go with you. With him will be my vice-commander Abdul. They will don their uniforms for this. They will look completely and utterly official. You will lead them to your fan room. I trust, as the captain of this vessel, you know where that is?"

Oh my God, the ventilation system, Gardes thought. That was how they planned to take the vessel. But he merely nodded, his eyes still on the deck.

"Once again, I promise it will be quick. I know I have made promises to you in the past that I have not kept, but you must admit, the most important promise I did keep. And Tagreb, he saw to that. He will go with you. It will not be too hard for you. Consider him your personal angel. You could not ask for better, Jean-Paul, the man has a golden soul. And the canisters are on a two-minute time delay, which means if you hurry, you can even make it back here before the gas begins to act."

"The emergency breathing air system," Gardes heard himself saying. "My men will sense gas and get into their masks."

Salah shook his head. "It is odorless, tasteless, Captain. It will drop your men in their boots in one breath. The second breath will shut down their central nervous systems. Within seconds their hearts will stop. They will have no idea what happened. It will be as if the lights have been turned off. One moment they will be happily standing their watches. The next, they will be in heaven with their ancestors. There to watch over their children. Just as you will be."

"You would make me an angel of death for my entire crew," Gardes sniffed. "You would have me deliver them to you to die."

"I would," Salah said, his voice even softer. "It is your choice, your final command decision, Captain. But simply listen to one final fact. If we compare the two means of death—one in which your men die instantly, with no knowledge of the terrible thing that happened here today, the other in which they realize they will die violently, without dignity, with that horrible gun at their temple, surrounded by the blood and gore of the comrades who were executed before them—which death allows them to leave this earth the happier? By gas or by bullet?"

For a terrible ten seconds Gardes stood there, unable to respond. He choked back a sob, finally, and looked up at Salah. "I can't do it. I won't do it."

Salah nodded thoughtfully, as if he were not surprised. "Of course I understand, Captain. Well." He smiled suddenly, Gardes startled by the incredible flood of warmth that came into his features. "It was worth a try. Let us return to the others, shall we?" He held out his hand like a maître d' pointing the way to a table. Gardes put his head down and reentered the messroom.

The officers looked up at him searching his face for hope. He shook his head, barely able to meet their eyes. While his back was turned and he walked toward the end of the table, he heard the supersonic crackle of another silenced bullet and turned to watch Bertrand De Lorme collapse from his chair, gore covering his shoulders and chest and the messroom table. In Salah's hand was the smoking pistol. Across from De Lorme, Adrian Molyneux's eyes bulged and he cried out in fear and pain, his fist flying up to his face. The pistol in Salah's hand came down slowly until the tip of the silencer was poised exactly between the navigator's eyes.

"Captain," Salah said, "I presume you want me to pull the trigger? That is what you told me in the galley, yes?"

Gardes turned to face Salah al Din directly, the vision in his right eye suddenly blurring. He wiped the tear away, furious at himself that it betrayed his emotions. "Sir, I cannot lead you to the fan room for you to poison my crew. It would make me complicit with you. Do what you will to me and my men. My crew, however, will fight you."

"Very well, Captain," Salah said, and Molyneux's head detonated, the blood splashing all the way to the overhead, the top half of his skull missing as his head lolled back on his neck.

"I'll show you where the fan room is," *Ours Blanc* Courcelle blurted, his eyes wide. He turned sadly to Gardes. "It's right by frame CP-4, Captain. I will show them." He blinked four times, then stared significantly at Gardes.

But the fan room wasn't at frame CP-4. Frames were the hoops of steel that formed the skeleton of the ship, and started at the nosecone and extended all the way aft to the screw, numbered sequentially. The fan room was at frame 214.

No, "CP-4" meant something entirely different. CP stood for *circuit principal*, or main circuit. Circuit CP-1 was the shipwide announcing PA system. CP-2 announced within maneuvering. CP-3 announced in the missile compartment and the missile control center. And CP-4 was the emergency circuit, in which any of the hundreds of sound-powered phone handsets scattered throughout the ship could be tied into the CP-1 main announcing speakers through a toggle switch labeled CP-4. They drilled using it constantly. Sometimes the first notification of an emergency was the characteristically faint call of "flooding in the engineroom" coming over the CP-1 speakers from a CP-4 panic announcement.

Courcelle was speaking in code: use the CP-4 to notify the crew of the emergency and get them to fight.

It was so obvious that it slammed into Gardes's consciousness like a hammer striking the hull. He had caused the unnecessary death of Molyneux by not thinking on his feet, but then, how much had he always relied on his officers for advice? Courcelle was completely right. If Gardes could take Salah's men to the fan room, but lunge for a phone handset and get an announcement out—even if he took a bullet while he did it—it could be the one crucial thing that could alter the equation and save the ship.

"No," Gardes said emphatically, raising his gaze to Salah. "I'll show you. My options are out, Salah. If my *cadre dirigeant* would so quickly help you, I can do no more." He purposely made it seem that he was furious at Courcelle. The slightest change came over Courcelle's face—they had understood each other.

"I'm ready," Gardes said, visualizing the path to the after machinery room and the sound-powered phone handsets on their way there.

"Excellent, my friend," Salah said, nodding. "It is not something you should regret."

"Youssef? Abdul?"

Salah al Din's two lieutenants entered the cramped galley. Fakhri carried a heavy duffel bag. Each had put their uniforms back on, including their officers' caps.

"Take off your caps," Gardes said. "No one wears them inside the hull."

They dropped the caps to the floor.

"Follow me," Gardes said.

Salah opened the door.

"This way," Gardes said, trying to maintain his composure. He led the two "officers" aft down the central passageway and through the hatch to the missile compartment. A few crewmembers walked the passageway, each cheerfully acknowledging the captain and the riders, but no one challenging them. All the phones were further outboard then their central walk, except for the phone stand at missile eight, but the two men were hurrying him so much that pausing would get him shot or expedited. He bit his lip, wondering if he would be able to wait until they reached the auxiliary equipment room, where there were three phones with CP-4 toggle switches.

They hustled past three crewmen, all of whom nodded respectfully, quietly, but avoided eye contact. Gardes tried to bulge his eyes out, to create suspicion in them, but no one saw him. They hurried to the aft bulkhead of the middle level, stopping at the door to the auxiliary equipment space. Gardes remembered that a watchstander would be there.

"There's a mechanic on watch," Gardes said to Fakhri. The terrorist nodded and reached under his coat, withdrawing an automatic pistol. Hurriedly he screwed on a silencer, then nodded.

Gardes opened the door. The auxiliaryman of the watch, a tall, chunky youngster, looked up in surprise. It wasn't often the commanding officer visited the machinery spaces, not without the engineer or the damage control assistant with him.

"Captain," he said, confused, but respectful. He stared in uncomprehending shock at Fakhri's pistol.

Two shots whistled through the air, one hitting the mechanic above his ear and splitting open his head, the second in his neck. He went down without a sound, bleeding furiously onto the deck.

"There," Gardes said, pointing to the chamber of the fan enclosure, his hand slowly reaching for the black plastic phone handset. Through this metal box all the ship's air flowed. It occurred to him that until recently the hatch to the bridge tunnel was left open on the surface, but since an incident on the last patrol when, in a high sea state, they had taken blue water down the hatch directly into the control room, with all its delicate electronics, Gardes' standing orders required the lower hatch to be shut, no matter how balmy the weather was topside. At sea habits died hard, and if the crew got used to shutting the hatch, it would always be shut when it needed to be. But that standing order meant that the ship was sealed, even on the surface. That gas would kill everyone, a mere three minutes from now, unless he could get the word out on the CP-4.

"Pull the dogging latches open by turning them to the right," Gardes said while Tagreb manhandled the latches and Fakhri stood watch on the room. Gardes had the phone in one hand while his other hand stabbed down the CP-4 toggle switch. He lifted the phone quickly to his lips.

"Nuclear weapon security violation! Messroom and aux machinery," Gardes shouted as loudly as he could,

his voice faintly piped through the overhead speakers, yet clear and distinct. *"The ship has been taken by—"*

Tagreb froze and turned, his mouth open in dismay. Fakhri didn't hesitate. His MP-5 was already pointed at Commander Jean-Paul Gardes. His face hardened as he pulled the trigger, the bullets flashing across the compartment at the captain's chest. As Gardes collapsed, his throat came into the stream of 10 mm ammunition, the bullets ripping his throat open and nearly decapitating him, then blowing off his right ear, his right jaw and opening the right side of his head. As the French officer dropped to the deck in a splattered pool of blood, Fakhri released the trigger.

Gardes twitched and convulsed as the lead flew through his body, two of the bullets ripping open his heart and aorta. As he fell, he saw the deck coming up in slow motion, but the room grew dark much faster than the deck rose. The darkness washed over the room and over Gardes' reality like a black tidal wave washing over his head, his consciousness submerged and crushed in an instant.

The darkness lasted only a minute or an hour or a day, and soon the unbroken, infinite blackness lit up at the outer reaches of his awareness, until a greenish hue took over, the green moving smoothly and swiftly toward the center of Gardes' vision. At first the green was a blur, but then it cleared, a lush grass spreading out for kilometers on either side of him, and directly in front of him he saw Danielle, the way she had been the evening after the simulator exercise, tall and slim and shimmering, her hair long and straight and gorgeous, her mouth smiling at him, her eyes shining. He wondered, was this some sort of message transmitted across time and space? Was she thanking him for saving the children? Or was this a communiqué from beyond the grave? Her sexual attire melted into a dark, long gown of shimmering material, and then little Marc stood next to his mother, looking up at Gardes, wearing his prized possession, the New York Yankees baseball cap, then Margaux appeared with her blond hair and wide blue eyes, the precious carbon copy of her beautiful mother, and finally Renée was there, except she was older, a grown woman in her twenties, just as lovely as her mother, and the expression on her face was one of gratitude and forgiveness.

As quickly as the images came they blinked out of existence, and Gardes stood alone on the grass. He looked down, the ground becoming translucent, and immediately below him he saw the deck of the auxiliary machinery space, where the horribly mangled body of a pitifully mutilated corpse slowly bled out, gore and blood staining him all over. Gardes felt shock as he peered down at the poor man. The grass slowly disappeared, melting away, and reality was the auxiliary machinery room and the dead body. Gardes sank down on one knee next to the corpse, his fingers gently, sadly, stroking his bloodstained hair. He wondered who it could be before the realization dawned on him that he was staring at his own body.

Then he suddenly understood everything.

He put his hand down on the body's bloody chest, over his heart, the body cooling rapidly, the tissue hardening. *Good-bye, old friend*, he thought.

He stood, still staring at the corpse, then turned away, and the surroundings of the submarine that had once been his command left him and the ancient reality returned, the landscape from before he had come here.

He looked up to see the four grinning young men walking toward him, and he broke into a delighted smile.

Vincent, he said in greeting. *Adrian. Aymeric. Bertrand. Was it painful?*

They shook their heads.

I'm glad.

Tagreb and Fakhri heaved, and the door to the fan compartment came open. Tagreb held it open while Fakhri withdrew eight canisters from his bag, each resembling a medium-sized fire extinguisher. He rotated the tops to the two-minute mark, clicked a button under a protective cover on each, and tossed them in. Tagreb shut the fanroom hatch and redogged it.

"Hurry," Tagreb said, turning to face Fakhri. "The masks."

Abdul reached into his duffel bag and withdrew two heavy air bottles, each twenty centimeters long, each with a long black hose valved into a regulator, and a large black rubber face mask connected to the hose.

Tagreb shoved his face into his mask, tightened the straps and opened the J-valve. He strapped the bottle onto his back and took an experimental breath. The air was hot, coppery and dry, but otherwise satisfactory. Tagreb prayed for a moment that the seal on his mask held.

"The emergency announcement that the captain made before he died," Tagreb said quickly, his voice trembling in fear. "Do you think they are coming for us?"

"They are seconds from hell," Fakhri said. "Does it matter?"

The canisters in the fan room made a clunking noise as they exploded. This was it, Tagreb thought. Either his gas mask facial seal held and he lived, or the gas killed him. He eyed the door leading forward, thinking about the crew now that Captain Gardes had sneakily alerted them with his little phone system. He had been sneaky after all. Tagreb reached over to the door and rotated the deadbolt lock, thinking it odd that a machinery space even had a bulkhead that wasn't watertight, and then a door with a lock. On *TK-17* or the *Krasnoyarsk* such an arrangement would never have happened—there had been no locks on the stateroom doors, much less doors on machinery spaces.

Just as he withdrew his hand from the deadbolt, a resounding booming sound came from the door. Tagreb jumped, alarmed and startled, feeling completely naked without a weapon. While Fakhri raised his weapon, Tagreb dived into the duffel and withdrew a second MP-5, rummaging furiously for a clip. Fakhri readied his weapon, but he had to be nearly out of ammunition. *Where was the Allah-cursed clip?* Finally, with trembling fingers, Tagreb found the clip.

A dozen things happened within the next half second.

Tagreb rammed the clip into the MP-5.

Four men, in frighteningly slow motion, burst into the room.

Fakhri opened fire, his last four rounds flying from his submachine gun.

Tagreb raised his weapon and pulled the trigger.

Big as a hand cannon, one of the French lifted his Glock 9 mm pistol and opened fire.

Nothing happened with Tagreb's MP-5.

A second French Glock came to bear.

Red stains bloomed on the chests of two of the raiders.

Tagreb realized his safety was engaged.

A bullet whizzed by Tagreb's ear.

He frantically reached for the safety.

Fakhri's animal shout emerged as he realized he was out of rounds, his MP-5 exhausted.

The four men from the ship's crew ran further into the room, one of them leveling his Glock at Tagreb's eyes.

It was over, Tagreb thought. *After all this, today he died.*

He felt Fakhri's fingers close on his MP-5 as the Algerian's own weapon began to fall in slow motion toward the deck.

Even before Fakhri could open fire the crewmen in the space began to change.

One instant they stood there in poses of action, nearly frozen in time by the adrenaline rushing through Tagreb's system. The next, the two with red on their uniforms let go of their Glocks, their hands moving toward their chests. But the other two froze, their mouths open, their eyes suddenly even wider. And all four began a slow-motion trip toward the deck.

Tagreb watched as they collapsed. Finally Fakhri got his fingers into the trigger guard of Tagreb's MP-5 and disengaged the safety. He opened fire, the bullets ripping open the shoulders of one man already on his knees on the deckplates. The second uninjured crewman remained untargeted, but he hit the deck first. Fakhri stopped shooting as all four men hit the deck, the unharmed single crewmember's body convulsing furiously.

"The gas!" Tagreb exclaimed in delight. "The gas got them!"

All four invaders were still, three of them bleeding, the fourth still shuddering, his body finally quiet.

They had done it! The submarine was theirs! Except that it was still on the surface with a dead helmsman at the wheel, perhaps circling stupidly on the ocean's surface.

Fakhri found a spare clip and reloaded the exhausted MP-5, then waved Tagreb forward. Tagreb glanced at the dead captain of the French submarine. It was too bad, Tagreb thought. He seemed like a nice man.

Capitaine de Frégate Jean-Paul Gardes' body functions had long since shut down. As he lay on his side on the deck of the auxiliary machinery space, a final trail of blood escaped his nostril and ran down to join the rest of the pool of congealing blood on the steel deckplates. His body was already growing cold and stiff.

Throughout the vastness of the warship *Le Vigilant*, the only creatures alive were Salah al Din—Issam Zouabri—Youssef Tagreb and Zouabri's thirteen armed men.

16

Youssef Tagreb dashed up the steep stairs to the upper level as if he were being chased by the devil. There was no telling if he would be able to get this done in time. The canned air in their bottles was good for twenty minutes—if they were breathing gently, and rushing up stairs was no way to conserve oxygen.

If he failed at what he was about to do, all of them would die just as surely as the crew had. He arrived in the transverse space leading to the small hatch, blinked through the foggy mask of his breathing apparatus, then charged aft through the door to emerge into the control room. It was a slaughterhouse. Bodies lay everywhere. Men still wearing headsets with boom microphones slumped over consoles. One man stood at the periscope, his arms draped over the horizontal grips, grotesquely held up by the unit as if it were a cross he'd been nailed to. Tagreb's trained eye turned forward, to the ship control console, were the planesman and helmsman slumped in their seats, restrained in them by seatbelts. Tagreb's second priority would be to get one of Issam's fighters on the wheel. God knew they didn't need to be wiggling through the sea, doing a huge, uncontrolled, high-speed slalom, or else some aircraft seeing their wake or a merchant ship would call in that something very wrong was going on with a submarine.

He looked over the displays, reading the French technical terms, translating them in his mind to English and from English to Russian. It was a damned frustrating thing, but it was the only way he could comprehend the foreign labels. But what he sought was not there. He found a worn, slim three-ring notebook in the heavily instrumented wraparound console aft of the ship control station and pulled it out. The cover announced that it was the *Submarine Standard Operating Procedures, S616-Class*. Thank Allah, he thought. He rifled through it, but there was no table of contents. He had to go through each tab and, in his panic, his reading was slowing down.

Trim Dive, he read. Initial Submergence. Surfacing. Dive to Test Depth. Snorkeling. Equipment Lineup for Submergence. Normal Battery Charge. Dammit! None of them were what he needed. He kept reading. Fire. Flooding. Collision. Emergency Ventilation—yes, that was it. He opened the page, reading frantically. The main induction mast needed to be raised, but there was no description of where that was on the panel, so it must be self-explanatory, he thought. He looked up, his foggy mask making him all the more frantic, his face close to the panel so he could read the labels. If he couldn't ventilate the ship in the next—he glanced at his watch— seven minutes, they'd be the next casualties of the nerve agent. Quickly! he commanded himself. Finally, on the lap section of the console, above the collapsed body of the man who had sat there, he found a section of the panel marked MAIN INDUCTION. It was a lever, next to several others such as RADIO 1, RADIO 2, DIRECTION FINDER, RADAR. This must be the mast hydraulics controls. He reached for the main induction lever and lifted it. Immediately the thump of hydraulics sounded in the overhead. The mast was coming up. An indicating light on the panel turned from a green bar to a red circle. The mast was up.

Suddenly a loud sound startled Tagreb, the overhead speaker rasping.

"Control, Bridge! Why is the induction mast coming up?"

Lieutenant Emile Everard stared at the top of the sail behind him. Why was the induction mast rising out of

the sail? Without permission from him? Who was con-
ning this submarine? At first he was irritated. He picked
up the Circuit 7 ship control microphone and barked
into it.

"Control, Bridge! Why is the induction mast coming
up?"

He waited, his irritation becoming more intense. If the
captain heard that things were going wrong on Everard's
watch, it would not be a good day, particularly with riders from FOST aboard. When there was no answer, he
glared at the phonetalker-lookout.

"Pass the word on the phone circuit—ask why the
induction mast was raised."

"Yes, Lieutenant."

While he waited, Everard contemplated yelling again
into the Circuit 7, but held back, waiting for the reply
from the control room.

The enlisted lookout looked up at him. "No reply
from control, sir." He frowned, an expression of anxiety
flashing across his young face. Everard shook his head.
What a day for a screwup.

"Control, Bridge, *what's going on down there?*"

Tagreb frowned. There was still a crewman—or several
of them—up in the ship control crow's nest on the fin,
Tagreb thought. Issam would not be pleased at that.
What if one or more of them came down the ladder?
Tagreb pulled out his radio.

"Issam, I need help here! Bring weapons."

"On the way," Issam's voice crackled.

"Control, Bridge, what's going on down there?"

Tagreb turned to the procedure. The manual told him
which automatic valves to open to drain the induction
manifold. It was much simpler than on his old submarines.

"Helm, Bridge, circuit check, acknowledge!"

"Nuclear Control, Bridge, circuit check." The officer
was getting less angry and more forlorn, Tagreb thought.

"Control, Bridge, pick up the A-circuit sound-powered

phone!" How long would it be before the frustrated officer sent men down the access tunnel?

Just then Issam and Fakhri arrived.

"What's wrong?" Issam asked through his mask.

"There's someone up in the fin," Tagreb shouted, his voice distorted by the rubber mask. "He keeps calling down. He may come down or send someone down."

"Got it," Issam said. Fakhri aimed his rifle at the hatch in the overhead.

"Still no answer, Lieutenant."

Everard shook his head, partly out of concern, partly out of frustration. He looked at his junior officer of the deck, *Enseigne de Vaisseau de 1re Classe* Roland Beauvais. "Obviously a drill. Go below and investigate."

Beauvais nodded. "Going below." He handed his binoculars to the lookout while Everard held the hatch grating open, then lowered himself down and vanished into the darkness of the tunnel.

"Dammit," Everard muttered. It figured, an unannounced drill on his watch. Below, someone obviously had a stopwatch and was timing his reaction, the riders from FOST taking notes on how well he did.

He waited, tapping his fingers on the cockpit coaming. After a minute, with no word from below, he glanced at the phonetalker.

"Pretty sinister drill scenario, eh, Lieutenant?"

Everard nodded. "Yeah, but it'll be complete soon, as soon as Ensign Beauvais reports on the phone or shouts up the tunnel. You hear anything?"

The lookout shook his head solemnly. "Nothing."

"The hatch wheel is moving," Fakhri reported. "Hatch wheel is spinning fast now. Hatch is opening."

Tagreb froze. A boot came down from the hatchway, then a second. Two legs became visible as the man from above lowered himself down the ladder. He turned and looked at Fakhri and saw the bodies in the room, the standing men in their gas masks and shouted the word

"Lieutenant!" before Fakhri pumped a dozen rounds into his chest. The man collapsed to the deck like a doll, but Fakhri had made a thunderous noise. But at least, Tagreb thought, opening the hatch let outside air into the space, and allowed contaminated air up the tunnel. The nerve agent in the air might even neutralize the others up above, and perhaps give Tagreb more time to ventilate the ship.

"What was that?" Everard asked.

"I don't know, Lieutenant. Sounded like a crash."

"Damn." Everard thought for a moment. "You'd better get below. You may need to station yourself halfway up the tunnel and relay communications by shouting if all the circuits are down."

"What about the induction mast, sir? Is it possible there was a fire or toxic gas emergency?"

Everard considered. "There's an emergency air mask storage cubbyhole about two feet from the hatchway. Hold your breath and put on the mask as soon as you get below."

"Lieutenant, this isn't my idea of fun, going into a hull filled with toxic gas."

"Hell, it's probably just a drill. If you were doing a toxic gas emergency drill, you'd have a loss of communication to the bridge go along with it."

"Maybe, sir, but I've never heard of a drill like this before."

It was useless speculating, Everard thought. He felt like going down the hatch himself and punching whoever came up with this drill scenario, the cruel bastard. "It's a drill. Just get below, and don't forget the mask, or the drill monitors will pronounce you as 'dead' as Beauvais. Get word to me as soon as you can."

"Yes, sir," the lookout said. "Here's the phone headset, in case you hear anything."

Everard took the headset and pulled the grating at the hatch aside one more time. The lookout clambered down the ladder, leaving Everard feeling more alone than anytime in his life.

He looked down at the cockpit. Every communication device was built to talk to the interior of the submarine. Only the VHF radio in its holster at his belt had the capability of transmitting radio signals to the outside world. And it would only work at short range. If he couldn't see a ship, he couldn't be heard by one. And the ship would be out of control. All the steering mechanisms were in the control room and the far aft engineroom. If a toxic gas emergency had taken down the crew, the ship would simply keep going until it hit something.

Everard grimaced. His imagination was obviously running away with him. Any moment the lookout would be shouting up the tunnel.

"Another man," Issam announced.

"Let him in," Tagreb hissed. "See if he goes down from the gas!"

"Hold your fire, Fakhri," Issam instructed.

The second man came down. Tagreb waited, the oddest thought occurring to him, to ask him where the manual inboard exhaust valve was located. Issam and Fakhri allowed the Frenchman to come all the way down the ladder. He looked around the room in complete and utter panic, unable to find his voice as he stared at Fakhri's leveled automatic rifle. For long seconds he stood there under the hatchway. Perhaps, Tagreb thought, the nerve agent had lost effectiveness. Or maybe it had dispersed from the access tunnel to the fin.

No sooner had he thought that than the Frenchman's eyes rolled up into his head and he spun on his way down to the deck, his feet flying upward as his head hit, then the body bouncing and lying quietly.

Tagreb found the LP POSITIVE DISPLACEMENT COMPRESSOR label over a switch on the panel. He turned the rotary knob to the START position, then to the RUN position. A furious noise rattled the control room, the sound of a huge motor or fan. He looked up at the ventilation duct, which suddenly began blowing air much harder. The ship's toxic air was being ventilated, but the question was, how long would it take to evacuate the contaminated air from the ship? Did they have three minutes left on these puny portable systems? Could the air be cleaned up enough that they could switch to the ship's emergency air breathing masks without being killed by residual nerve agent?

The roaring of the low-pressure blower was loud at the top of the sail, the noise of it booming back up the ductwork from the induction mast. Well, at least the crew were alive, he thought in relief. There had to be someone down there to operate the ballast control panel. But that begged the question—with no word from below a full minute after the lookout went down, what should Everard do now?

Well, it was obviously a drill. Everard took a look around the horizon with the binoculars. There were no ships in sight. For the moment it would be safe to go below. And there had to be a drill monitor on the periscope for ship safety. Everard looked up. The periscope hadn't rotated for some time. But the radar mast was rotating. The crew in the control room could avoid collision with that, at least.

Another long minute. The blower was going, but there was no sound on the headphones or on the communication circuit. Everard made a decision. He would go below. What else could he do, stay up here helpless and stupid?

He pulled aside the grating and lowered himself into the tunnel.

"Third man," Fakhri murmured, his eyes on the ladder from the hatch.

"Let him enter," Tagreb said. "He is our canary!"

"Roland?" a voice called. It was a younger man, perhàps in his twenties, the same voice that had been on the squawk box speaker. "*Maître* Bruyere?" Tagreb, Issam and Fakhri all remained quiet, allowing the man to climb all the way down the ladder.

He emerged into the room, a handsome blond-haired, blue-eyed youth. He had the same reaction the others had, dumbfounded shock as he stared at the bodies, the terrorists in their masks and the rifles.

"Hands up," Fakhri finally said. For another moment the man stared at Fakhri, then finally raised his hands.

Excellent, Tagreb thought. He didn't fall to the deck. The atmosphere was clearing up.

"You aren't from *Force Océanique Stratégique* after all, are you?" the youngster asked.

Issam shook his head. "I'm afraid not, young man," he said.

"And that's why the captain was so upset?"

"Precisely," Issam said. "My friend, please step away from under that hatch."

The Frenchman looked up, then gingerly stepped over the bodies, his hands still over his head.

"Now, walk over here," Issam commanded.

A frown on his features, the youth complied, going over toward the starboard side.

"Now here." Issam led him to the navigation room. When he survived that, Issam marched him to the corners of the control room. He looked up at Tagreb. "Excellent job, Youssef. You have saved the ship."

Tagreb tried to inhale, but his bottle had gone completely out of air. He pulled the rubber mask off and took a tentative breath. There was no doubt, the ship stank of death, and something else, perhaps the residual effects of the nerve agent, but Tagreb was still standing. He grinned at Issam.

"Abdul," Issam said to Fakhri. "Did you want to take the last hostage and use him to take care of your, shall we say, raging fires?"

Fakhri considered the question, taking a long look at the blond Frenchman, but finally he shook his head. "I am not in the mood. And I had my fill with the younger ones back at the warehouse."

Issam nodded seriously. "Of course. Well then, send him to Allah."

Before Issam even completed the sentence, Fakhri opened fire, the stream of his bullets nearly slicing the youth in half.

"Hey!" Tagreb shouted. "Stop it! Cease fire! This is a delicate electronics room! You want to sink us, you fool?"

By then the last Frenchman, the very last of the crew of the warship *Le Vigilant*, lay dead, half on the elevated periscope platform, half on the deck, his blood flooding the deckplates of the room and making Tagreb's footing slippery.

"Issam, no more use of the weapons!" Tagreb said. "They all need to be put away. We could jeopardize the entire mission. And kill ourselves at the same time. This is a dangerous business."

"I agree," Issam said.

"Next, I need one of your men to take the wheel at this panel."

"Does it have an autopilot setting?" Issam asked. "Like the yacht did?"

An interesting question. Tagreb leaned over. There was an autopilot panel. Not certain how complex it was, he examined it up close, which was much easier to do without a foggy mask on. It mostly consisted of a dial to insert the ordered heading and an engagement/disengagement set of buttons. He glanced up at the compass rose, which showed them on course 270, due west. He dialed it in and pressed the ENGAGE button. A green light came on. The steering was on autopilot. *Krasnoyarsk* had had nothing like this, but it did seem obvious.

"What now?"

"We need to submerge. And to do that I first need to slow down the ship. I'm going aft. I need one of your men. And at some point, we need to gather the bodies in the torpedo room."

"Why the torpedo room?"

"Our only options are to fire them out the weapon tubes or put them in frozen stores," Tagreb said. "The ship was loaded for a long voyage. There is probably no room in the freezers." Issam nodded.

Tagreb left the control room, wiping the sweat from his brow and taking a deep breath. That had been close, he thought. Too damned close.

It took several hours and what seemed a gallon of sweat for Tagreb, working with the unschooled terrorists, to submerge the ship and to start up the atmospheric control systems, then to make sure the navigation systems were working. But finally it was done.

"How long until we can launch missiles?" Issam asked.

Tagreb shook his head. "I'll let you know when I'm deep into the technical manuals. But I know why it's urgent. We won't take a second longer than we need to."

The formerly French submarine *Le Vigilant* sailed on, submerged and quiet, heading southwest, away from the coast of Europe and from the forces that would threaten her. Down at her depth, nothing on the planet could harm her, other than the sea herself. They were invulnerable, although still somewhat disarmed, but Issam nodded to himself in satisfaction. In ten days, or twenty, this ship would become a steel avenging angel of Allah. In ten days, or twenty, Paris would burn and the infidels would meet Satan.

BOOK 3:

▼

Sea State

17

Saturday morning had always been the day that Vice Admiral Thibaut D'Aubigne was at his best in the office. The staff was gone, the phones were quiet, the brass were mercifully silent, and all the work that had piled up since the weekend before could be sliced through efficiently and quickly. Sometimes D'Aubigne wore his uniform, especially if he were going to dinner with any visiting flag officers or general staff. Other days he would come in wearing civilian clothes, perhaps jeans, or even shorts, and a golf shirt, particularly since that communicated to everyone that he was not open for business. Other occupants of the headquarters building who didn't know him assumed he was simply coming in briefly to pick up something he'd forgotten Friday, which was exactly the way he wanted it. And those who did know him, knew him well enough to leave him alone on Saturday.

D'Aubigne set his briefcase on the polished, massive, antique mahogany desk that had once been used by a fleet admiral during the Napoleonic Wars. He pulled out a set of clear plastic folders, each one labeled with the title of its project. After he spread the papers neatly into piles on the otherwise completely empty desk surface, he spun around and booted up his computer. As it came online, he walked over to the bar and started the coffee machine, its boiling and humming filling the room for a few moments, the aroma bringing back happy memories of his youth, his seafaring days. He pulled out a cigar from the humidor, clipped the torpedo end of it and lit it with the ornate FS *Le Vigilant* lighter given to him by the ship's captain after her commissioning ceremony. As he stoked it to life, his mind wandered to the NATO exercise, and how completely the French SSBN under Jean-Paul Gardes' brilliant tactical command had gloriously evaded the hundred-warship task force frantically searching for her.

When the coffee was ready he poured a cup and sat back in his leather executive chair. Two cups of coffee and half a cigar into the morning, he had disposed of the action required of him on seven of the files. As he finished each one, he tucked its paperwork neatly back into the dossier and put it in his principal aide's in-box. *Capitaine de Corvette* Guillaume Swithin had been working for D'Aubigne for two years, since D'Aubigne was appointed as ALFOST, the *Force Océanique Stratégique Amiral Aux Commandes*. "Admiral-in-command," D'Aubigne thought, smiling slightly, had always sounded good before a man's name, but it was the authority, autonomy and the chance to change the submarine force for the better that had been the rewards of the office. That and the chance to work with subordinates like Swithin, who would be next in line to take over as executive officer of *Le Vigilant*. It would be career-enhancing for the fiery redheaded lieutenant commander, because to date Swithin had sailed only in the attack submarine force— the ideal place to hone an officer's aggressiveness and ability to attack, but the future-admirals' ranks would be filled with officers who had excelled on both sides of the equation—attack and strategic deterrence—as Jean-Paul Gardes had.

D'Aubigne checked his handheld tablet computer and clicked to the duty roster. If he remembered correctly, Swithin had the duty today down in the *Force Océanique Stratégique* Command Center, which was perfect, because if D'Aubigne had any questions on any of their paperwork, he could call down to Flag Plot and engage the mind of the bored officer. Bored, because on a sleepy Saturday during a time of low world tension there would be little going on in the strategic submarine force. And that, ironically, was their mission, to protect the Republic without firing a shot.

The admiral lost himself for two hours, occasionally refilling his coffee and chomping on the long-cold cigar. He checked his watch—he might finish early today, he thought. Perhaps he could get his daughter and her fiancé out to dinner with him and his wife, Anastasia. There were a hundred things to do before the wedding, and he had been decidedly missing in action for the planning. If he showed a bit more effort, it might increase his recent standing in Anastasia's eyes. She had been distracted, annoyed and stressed over the coming affair, and it wasn't that D'Aubigne had been withdrawn in his work, but things had been busy lately. He had been looking at the framed oil painting of Anastasia mounted on the opposite wall. Beautiful woman, he mused, and she just got better with age.

The shrill bell of the secure phone line made him jump. That was odd, he thought, as he reached for it.

"D'Aubigne," he said in his gravelly baritone.

"Admiral," the voice said. It was Lieutenant Commander Swithin. "Duty Officer, sir. We have a situation. Request your presence in Flag Plot."

"On the way." D'Aubigne dropped the phone on its cradle, locked his office behind him and hurried to the elevator. He pressed the button to the command center deck and scanned his badge into the permissive lock. The elevator seemed to take forever to make the trip. D'Aubigne kept his mind neutral, as this was probably not good news, but he would know soon enough. He didn't remember the walk down the corridor, checking in with the security guard or the walk into Flag Plot. Swithin looked up at him from a computer screen, then stood to greet him.

"Le Vigilant," Guillaume Swithin said, frowning. "She missed her delouse rendezvous with the *Amethyste*."

That wasn't good, D'Aubigne thought, and there was almost no innocuous way to explain it away. Per routine procedure, the fast attack submarine *Amethyste* had been waiting in a slow, silent pace pattern, awaiting the arrival of *Le Vigilant* at a secret coordinate in the Atlantic. Between one and two days out of port, a ballistic missile submarine would transit through an area where a friendly attack submarine lurked. The attack boat would know the exact time that the SSBN would be transiting through the area. If the SSBN were trailed, shadowed, by an enemy submarine, the French attack submarine would detect the uninvited guest. It was merely a precaution from the days of the Cold War, when Soviet attack submarines would endeavor to covertly follow a ballistic missile submarine, because, if they could, then the secret locations of the Republic's at-sea missile silos would not be so secret. A trailing enemy submarine could conceivably neutralize a French ballistic missile submarine by merely lying in wait for the SSBN to come to missile firing depth. The slightest indication of an impending missile launch could then be reacted to by firing a salvo of torpedoes, and the French attack—or more likely, counterattack—could be stopped before it began. The tactic could be defeated by "delousing" the SSBN with a French attack sub, because once the missile submarine was notified that it was being followed, it could take the kind of decisive evasive action that had allowed *Le Vigilant* to disappear from the sonar screens of the *Texas* and the *Hampton* during Exercise *Urgent Surge*.

Urgent Surge had proved that France's attack submarines had definite problems detecting the Triomphant-class submarines, which had been one of the reasons the exercise had been conducted, because NATO had wanted to know to what extent the American Virginia-class submarines could find and trail one of the new Triomphants, and as they had shown, the U.S. Navy's submarines were far more acoustically sensitive, with both better sonar electronics and a quieter listening platform for the employment of the sonars, but it still had not helped them prosecute an attack in time. The Rubis Amethyste-class submarines were less acoustically capable than the Virginias, as well as the Improved 688-class vintage submarines, but in a delouse scenario, in which the exact location and time of rendezvous were known, the Rubis Amethyste submarine would be able to detect a Triomphant at close range and to determine if it were being followed.

The implications of *Le Vigilant* failing to meet her expected transit through *Amethyste*'s delouse area were serious. The SSBN could have experienced one of a hundred emergencies at sea that could have proved fatal. That was the worst case. Alternately, she could have succumbed to a power plant casualty that had limited her speed, or that degraded her navigation system, though it was hard to imagine a navigation error serious enough—with all the equipment redundancy—to put the boat off course enough to miss the *Amethyste*.

"How late is *Le Vigilant*?"

Swithin glanced at the full-wall electronic chart display. The *Amethyste* operation area was shown outlined in flashing red lines. The track of *Le Vigilant* crossed through it, the bold line shown in green. Fifty nautical miles on the other side of the rendezvous location, the track of *Le Vigilant* stopped at a green dot labeled POINT DELTA. This was where the submarine's location became intentionally unknown even to headquarters. At the point of departure, or point delta, the SSBN's orders were to transit the ocean based on a randomly generated pattern from her onboard computer. Not even *Le Vigilant*'s captain or crew were to know where she would go next. She was ordered to stay within the boundaries that allowed her missiles to reach their targets, but otherwise she could be anywhere in the deep blue sea. The thinking was that if headquarters remained in the dark about her location, so would any potential headquarters spies. It was the entire point of having the sea-deployed missiles hidden away at a secret location at sea, where only the crew knew where they were and where they had been, but couldn't say where she would be six hours in the future.

"Two hours, Admiral."

D'Aubigne nodded. Six hours could not be explained away, but two might be. A spurious reactor trip may have required them to proceed slowly at periscope depth while they attended to the problem, and might not have been reason enough to radio headquarters. A bigger problem, something ship-threatening or mission-critical that held them up longer, would usually result in a trouble-message being transmitted despite the SSBN standard operating procedure of maintaining radio silence if at all possible. The phrase *If you're going to be late, call your mother* flashed into D'Aubigne's mind, then a momentary flutter of anxiety—what if something catastrophic had happened to *Le Vigilant*?

"Who's been notified?"

"*Marine Navale* command center and you."

"Very well," the admiral said. The decision of what to do next was still his. If *Le Vigilant* remained missing four hours from now, the procedures called for the mobilization of the attack submarines in port to scramble to sea and initiate a search for her. The antisubmarine forces of the surface navy would get underway as well, and the maritime patrol aircraft would be launched to search along *Le Vigilant*'s known track. D'Aubigne had the option to call for that action now ràther than waiting, but if *Le Vigilant* showed up an hour from now, the mobilization would prove a waste of effort and he could be perceived to have acted in panic, which was never good for a flag officer's career.

It came down to his own instincts. How did he see this situation? What was his intuition? On the one hand, if *Le Vigilant* had gone down in water shallow enough for a rescue, every minute counted, and every minute he failed to act was one less minute of oxygen for a trapped crew, and on the other, if he knee-jerk reacted and sent out the entire fleet for nothing, he might as well hand in his admiral's stars.

He tapped his chin as he looked up at the wall display. The green track going through the *Amethyste* op-

eration area made him bite his lip. There was
something that didn't add up. He thought of Captain
Jean-Paul Gardes and the kind of commanding officer
he was. To a great extent, a submarine captain was as
much in a gray area as Admiral D'Aubigne. If he were
late by two hours or three, would Gardes break radio
silence and transmit a trouble-message to headquarters, or would he keep his head down and solve the
problem in the dark?

D'Aubigne had known Jean-Paul for seventeen years.
Gardes would know that *Amethyste* would be waiting
and that, if he missed the rendezvous, *Amethyste* would
sound the alarm, and he knew that D'Aubigne himself
would be notified immediately and would have to decide
what to do. It was not like Gardes to operate in the dark,
D'Aubigne realized. If Jean-Paul had had problems, he
would tell HQ and eliminate their doubts. Which was
good news, because it made D'Aubigne's decision con-
siderably easier, but it was astonishingly bad news because it meant there was something seriously wrong with
Le Vigilant.

"Call out a Code One to all ASW forces, submerged,
surface and air," D'Aubigne said to Swithin. "Then notify Admiral Devereux's duty officer and ask him to get
Devereux on a secure connection."

Swithin stared at the admiral for a moment, then nodded, acknowledging the order, then hurrying to carry
it out.

Admiral D'Aubigne remained in the command center
for a few tense moments, then became aware of his
shorts and golf shirt. He decided to return to his office
and change. It looked like this would be a longer day
than he had thought. A tight ball of anxiety had formed
in his stomach, and seemed like it had no intention of
leaving. He clenched his jaw, attempting to betray none
of the fear he felt inside.

Jesus, Jean-Paul, he thought, *what the hell happened
to you?*

*   *   *

D'Aubigne opened his office door and rushed to his closet, where he always kept a fully rigged, pressed uniform for those occasions when the work went on through the night and into the next day. He was buttoning up his shirt when he noticed the flashing on his computer screen. He had never been much of an enthusiast for the fleet email system, or any email system for that matter. He had insisted that anyone who reported to him specify the level of importance of their email traffic, and he was ruthless about enforcing the priority system. Woe be it to the officer who elevated the priority of an administrative piece of drivel so that D'Aubigne read it and wondered why he'd wasted his time. Similarly, he'd be damned if a message that contained something vital he'd need to know lingered unread in his queue, then caused him to get an embarrassing phone call from Admiral Devereux asking him about the matter. Once D'Aubigne's subordinates understood how to communicate with him by email, he'd arranged to have his computer flash bright messages on his screen the moment a high-priority email came in, so that no time would be wasted. When such an email was received, the screen would display a flashing red screen with the green, bold word PRESSANT—*URGENT*.

The screen was flashing now.

D'Aubigne wondered if this could be something from Devereux's staff about the Code One alert he'd just ordered, though they would be more likely to use the secure phone. It might have been from his opposite number, the admiral-in-command of the attack submarine force, Philip Pierpont, or from any of a hundred commanders affected by D'Aubigne's sounding the alarm.

He decided to open the message, scan it to find out what it was about, and get back down to Flag Plot. Still standing, he leaned over the computer keyboard and clicked into the software, then froze when he saw the summary, with only the message sender's name and the subject line. The email was from five minutes ago. The sender, impossibly, was Jean-Paul Gardes. But it was the message subject, in bold capitals, that made D'Aubigne collapse into his chair.

EMERGENCY//EMERGENCY//EMERGENCY//SSBN HIJACKED//CMDR J. GARDES SENDS

While D'Aubigne opened the message, he picked up the secure red phone handset and pressed the button to buzz the duty officer in Flag Plot.

"Yes, Admiral."

"Duty Officer," D'Aubigne said formally, trying to keep his voice from trembling, "notify the president's office, *Marine Navale* command center, Admiral Devereux and Admiral Pierpont. *Le Vigilant* has been hijacked."

18

Commander Burke Dillinger picked up the phone, knocking the base to the floor. *"Dillinger,"* he barked irritably over the sound of the hysterically shrieking baby he carried in a "football hold," the boy draped facedown on Dillinger's forearm. The boy had been screaming like this for two hours, so Dillinger had been bouncing him in the hold to try to ease the pain of the colic. Dear God, he thought, would it be possible to be any more miserable?

Two weeks ago he had buried Natalie. Practically the entire squadron—no, almost the entire East Coast Submarine Force—had shown up for it, even a group of three-star admirals arriving from D.C. Natalie had been an aide to a senior officer before she reported aboard the *Tucson*, and she'd had a wide network at the Pentagon. Dillinger had looked around him at the crowd packed into the church, marveling at how few he knew. And it occurred to him that the woman he'd been desperately in love with had died a complete mystery to him. Despite the depth of their relationship, he'd known her only for the month of the northern run op that had ended in the disaster in the Barents, then the downhill months afterward when she had been happily but unhealthily pregnant. So many of her friends he'd never known. Even her sister was a stranger to him, and he'd met her for the first time in the funeral home for the viewing. Vera D'Assault looked nothing like Natalie, nor did she have any of Natalie's lionhearted character, he thought as he shook the limp hand of the mousy, slight, almost frail thirty-year-old woman.

Natalie's sister had brought what seemed like a thousand photographs of Natalie, pictures Dillinger had never seen. Natalie as a baby, as a young child, in her track outfit, her hands reaching for heaven as she won a track race, wearing her high school medals, a gowned and high-heeled teenage Natalie at her prom, then the Navy years. Natalie as a plebe, an upperclassman, then a firstie, her sword carried jauntily as she led a company to the parade field. Then her surface-Navy career, a photo of her in a blue ball cap leaning against a compass alidade on the bridge of a destroyer. Then her years at the Pentagon, including photos of her with the Marine Corps major she'd been engaged to during that shore tour. In those photos she seemed radiantly happy, and that expression made him think of how her face had seemed in the hour that he had first made love to her. The last pictures were of the days just before Dillinger met her, her exotic, dark good looks shining out from the picture.

He stood there and looked at the photo, the day he met her returning to him. The yeoman who told him she'd arrived, and he remembered his frown of displeasure at accepting a woman as a second-in-command when his previous XO, Mikey, was in the hospital. The stateroom door had opened and there stood the most beautiful woman Dillinger had ever met. *What is this, a joke?* he'd thought, thinking Vornado had sent over a stripper from their gentlemen's club wearing a uniform as a prank, but she was genuine and every bit the professional. He'd stuttered as he greeted her, then scolded himself and forced himself back into his commanding persona. The development of their relationship seemed, looking back, like a dream. And yet, when he remembered Natalie, it seemed as if he had known her all his life, maybe longer. He turned from the pictures and looked at Vera D'Assault and her scowling mother, who apparently had no use for Dillinger, a husband who had allowed his wife to die so he could claim a male heir. She didn't say it, but it was in her eyes and all over her face. The two women were nothing like Natalie, he thought, and wondered what her father had been like.

During the church service, Dillinger had cradled Burke in his arms, refusing help from Vera or her mother, bouncing the gurgling baby comfortingly while he waited in the front row of the church for Smokin' Joe Kraft's eulogy. Rachel Vornado had advised him to leave the boy home with the nanny she'd hired for him, since he was a newborn and shouldn't be outside or exposed to the myriad germs of five hundred attendees at the funeral, but this was little Burke's last connection to his mother, a mother he'd grow up knowing only from the pictures of her on the wall and the stories of Dillinger and his friends.

When the church service ended, Dillinger walked into the daylight, his puffy, dark eyes shrouded in black impenetrable Ray•Bans, then rode in the limo to the burial site. He watched the casket emerge, the odd thought lingering in his mind that he needed to ask Natalie about something. This had been happening to him since she died, he realized. He'd have a thought he'd mean to share with her, and only then realize she was gone, and the sadness would bear down on him all over again. It must have occurred two dozen times a day. She was his last thought as he tried to fall asleep at night; she was his first thought in the morning. The worst part about waking up was that as he initially returned to consciousness he didn't remember she was dead, and then a second after waking it would all return to him and the weight of that heaviness was crushing. Finally he seemed conscious enough of her death that the lapse of memories had begun to ease, but here in the stark sunshine he forgot again.

The thing he'd wondered and wanted to ask Natalie was, would Rachel and Peter Vornado be able to heal their rift? Peter stood immediately to the right of him, almost as if he were ready to prop up Dillinger. Rachel stood on the other side of the crowd, looking at Dillinger with liquid eyes. Not once did she acknowledge Peter. He found himself staring into her face, his mind far away, remembering happier days. He dropped his gaze to the casket and watched as the people lined up to walk by it. A decorated, dress-uniform-clad Marine colonel, Natalie's ex-fiancé, lingered at the casket, his hand pressing on the walnut surface of the lid for several long minutes, his eyes shut. Finally he crossed himself, then moved on, glancing momentarily at Dillinger, the same shadow crossing his features as Natalie's mother had worn.

After the service Dillinger went numbly through the motions, greeting people at a reception at his house, hosted by Rachel. What would he have done without her, he wondered dully. Rachel was a ball of energy, mobilized into action by Dillinger's terrible need. She rarely spoke to Dillinger, but her quiet presence seemed everywhere. For the first week Peter Vornado had lived in the basement bedroom while he searched for a bachelor pad suitable to entertain his three children and, while he camped out, he'd managed to avoid his estranged wife, but his USS *Texas* had been called to sea by the Monday after the funeral with no sign of a return date. Rachel had interviewed three dozen nannies and had selected a short, chubby twenty-two-year-old girl with a meek manner and a steady hand in taking care of Burke. Rachel promised to help her with Burke if Dillinger himself got called to sea, but it was as if Smokin' Joe Kraft knew that Dillinger needed time. While the other boats of the Squadron deployed for exercises or routine duty, the USS *Hampton* lay tied up, bow out at the furthest berth from the shore, Dillinger's favorite spot. Dillinger went to work, sleepwalking through his days, the normally boisterous wardroom lunches pin-drop silent. He didn't eat, and other than the single glass of scotch that put him to sleep at night, he didn't drink, forsaking the usual happy hours at the Dolphin Pub. The weight had begun to drop off him, his uniforms hanging on his once-bullish frame, his cheeks becoming hollow, his face turning gaunt. The empty days melted into gray weeks. Other than the rhythm of the house, run by young nanny, Hannah, and overseen by drill-sergeant Rachel, nothing seemed to happen, and the bleak sameness of the days made Dillinger wonder what day of the week it was. More than once he'd reported to the ship on a Saturday or Sunday, wondering where the crew was.

But tonight, a September Saturday, things seemed particularly unsettled. Hannah had the flu and was being attended to by her mother, leaving Dillinger with the baby, with no sign of Rachel. Burke had a severe case of colic, and had been screaming all afternoon. Dillinger was two seconds from taking him to the emergency room when the phone rang, and the only reason he had picked up was the thought that Natalie was returning his call.

"Hello?" he shouted. There was no answer. "Dammit, I can't hear you." He squinted at the caller-ID window, but the light was too dim. He was about to hang up when he heard her voice.

"Burke, it's me," Rachel Vornado said. She had a smooth, sultry, musical voice, even on a cell connection, with a pitch just slightly deep for a woman, which irritated her, and which she blamed on all the shouting at the children she'd been forced to do over the years, but she had spoken with a buttery tenor the night he and Peter met her, and like so many things about her, that hadn't changed. Dillinger only knew two women with voices comparable to Rachel's, and those had been to Dayna Baines, his newscaster ex-girlfriend, and Natalie. He shook his head, frustrated with himself, wondering when he would stop using the present tense when it came to Natalie. *You're gone*, he said to her in his mind.

"God, where have you been, guardian angel?" he asked Rachel, his voice irritated. "Your wings fall off?" He was both annoyed at her and grateful to her, he realized. She had swooped in to help him the moment he'd come home from the hospital with Burke, sometimes bringing little Erin with her, but often leaving Erin at her next-door neighbor's. She said helping with Dillinger's baby helped keep her mind off the divorce from Peter. He tried to ask her about it, but she would say nothing, as if knowing his loyalty would be divided.

"Oh, I hear him," she said with affection toward the baby. "God, he's so cute. Takes after his mother."

"Thanks, Rachel, but he's screaming bloody murder."

"It's just the colic. Tell him Rachel is in his driveway."

"Oh, great," he said, hanging up. He met her in the foyer. She walked in, wearing a dark suit with a skirt a few inches higher than her knees, dark pumps, a cream-colored blouse and a silver chain with a single pearl. He realized he hadn't seen her in anything but blue jeans since Natalie died. Her black hair, so short when Peter was sick last summer, had grown down to her shoulders, and it shone in the light of the room, and for a moment he was reminded of Natalie's hair, which had always been longer than Rachel's, and which Rachel had always envied. He stared at her, the realization coming to him that Rachel was beautiful, and the simultaneous guilty thought that he was being scandalously disloyal to Natalie.

"Back at work?" he asked, suddenly disappointed. If she were returning to her marketing job—which, frankly, had paid more than her husband's—it meant bad news for him with this newborn. How would he cope without her?

"Here, give that angel to me," she said soothingly, taking the child from his grip. Burke continued his scream as Dillinger handed him over, then, sensing Rachel's embrace, his screams changed to whimpers and finally settled into the occasional mewling noise. Rachel bounced him on her forearm just as Dillinger had done.

"How the fuck do you do that?" he asked, peeved. He'd been doing that for an hour.

"He knows who knows what they're doing," she said soothingly, as if addressing the baby.

"What's with the suit?" he asked again. "Work?"

She glanced up, the flecks of green and blue in her brown eyes catching the light from the overhead chandelier, which was brighter now as dusk approached. Dillinger sensed something different. She was wearing perfume, he thought, an exotic scent that made him want to smell more of it. Irritated at his reaction, he backed up two steps.

"No, not work," she said, a mysterious smile gracing her lips as she set down her purse and breezed into the kitchen.

"So, why the outfit?"

"You don't like it?"

"No, actually," he said, stuttering slightly, "you look great."

"So I'm ugly in jeans and a sweater?" She smiled, mocking him.

"You know what I mean." He scratched the back of his neck, wondering if he should offer her a drink. "Get you a beer?"

She shook her head. "I think tonight we'd better have coffee."

"Sure," he said, moving to brew a pot. When she didn't answer him, he asked again about her suit.

"God, you're so relentless," she said, smiling at him slightly, then looking back down at the baby. "I was going to tell you anyway. I was in a SCIF." She pronounced it "skiff."

He froze at the sink, then turned to look at her. A SCIF was a special compartmented information facility, like the ones they had at CIA headquarters or ComSubLant HQ, a room sound-isolated from the world, with the ventilation ducts specially trapped to avoid sounds from voices leaking out, the room screened for bugs, and even the wires going to the outlets and network connections sanitized against eavesdropping devices. Usually built underground, a SCIF was a place where matters seven levels more classified than top secret could be discussed.

"It was a CIA debriefing," she added, rising to find the changing mat for Burke's soiled diaper.

He frowned. "Are you going to make me drag this out of you one word at a time?" His voice betrayed his irritation.

"No," she said, glancing up at him. "Commodore Kraft brought me. It's because I know about your northern run."

Dillinger stared at her, the implications of what she'd just said flashing through his mind. She knew about the Barents operation and what had happened to Vornado, Dillinger and Natalie. "Jesus, Rachel, you called Smokin' Joe Kraft? You realize that could ruin Peter's career?"

She shrugged. "It was Peter who called Kraft to tell him there'd been a possible security violation. Kraft called me over to talk to the CIA operations people. I told them the truth. Peter talks in his sleep on the rare occasion when he's completely wiped out, and I heard some things."

Dillinger filled the coffeemaker with water. "Yeah, I suppose he did. Is that what your separation is about?"

Her expression darkened. "Not a separation, B.K., a divorce, and it's partly about that, yes."

"Dammit, Rachel, he would never have done that if not for the operation."

"It's not about that," she said, but didn't elaborate.

The pot began to brew. Dillinger sat at the kitchen table across from her as she settled back down, the diaper changed.

"Just tell me what you know."

"They told me it never happened," she said. "At least, not unless I'm in another SCIF." She laughed, the sound melodious. "Now I get to tell *you* for once that what I know is too classified to discuss."

He nodded. "So is Peter in trouble?"

"No." She shook her head. "They were happy that he wanted to contain the leak. And I'm certainly not going to discuss it."

Dillinger looked down at the table. "So Peter being with another woman on that op has shut the door on your marriage forever?"

Her expression was dark. "It's not the girl, B.K. That I understood. It was that he lied to me about what he was doing. He was supposed to be in a shipyard in South America, not taking a fucking supersub to sea on a suicide mission." She never cursed, Dillinger realized, but she was now.

"Rachel, he had to deceive you. CIA told you themselves. It was too classified. How could he have told you about that without going to prison?"

"B.K.," she said gently, "you know I'm a devout Catholic. Every night Peter was at sea, submerged, I would say a special prayer and I'd light a candle. It sounds silly, maybe obsessive-compulsive, but to me, those prayers and candle flames kept him alive until the sun rose the next day. Then, after being fed a damned cover story before he left, I find out that he's at sea fighting for his life. And losing." Her eyes drilled into Dillinger's. "I was furious. I don't take well to being lied to. Not about that. I hope you'll bear that in mind, in the future."

Dillinger blinked at her. What the hell was that last warning about? "So, it was the lie about the op that split you up?"

She shook her head. "A divorce, just like a marriage, is made of a billion elements, B.K. It was the final straw. The last of a thousand cuts, but the one that woke me up. I fell out of love with him, B.K., because he chose to go into danger every day as a profession when we have three children." She glanced at little Burke. "Maybe you'd best think about what you're doing with your own life."

He shot a quick look at her while he poured the coffee, but her eyes were on the child. She looked back up at him. "You won't finish the cup. I'll be upstairs." She stood, cradling the baby gently.

"Where are you going?" he called after her.

"You have company," she said from the stairs.

That was a strange thing to say, he thought. Rachel was more like family than company. The moment of peace was a godsend after all Burke's crying, he thought, sipping the brew. The jangling of the doorbell startled him, and he heard Rachel's last line echo in his mind as he walked to the foyer. He opened the door to the tall, imposing, blond-buzz-cut, blue-eyed presence of Commodore Joseph "Smokin' Joe" Kraft. Dillinger smiled uncertainly, one eyebrow raised.

"Come on in, boss. I just brewed a pot of coffee, and you're catching me in a rare quiet moment."

Kraft didn't smile and he didn't move. Behind him his black Lincoln Navigator idled in the driveway, its headlights and foglamps glaring onto the porch. In the street in front of the house was a Virginia state trooper's cruiser with its beacons on.

"B.K., you packed?" he asked.

"Commodore, what's going on?"

Just then Rachel hurried down the steps with the baby in one hand, the other clutching Dillinger's green sea bag and a fresh, fully rigged khaki uniform on a hanger, his polished black shoes hanging by their laces from the sea bag's handle.

"Sorry, Joe," Rachel said sweetly to Kraft. "I just got here."

"You've got thirty seconds to get in character," Kraft said seriously to Dillinger, his jaw clenching.

"Commodore," Dillinger said, glaring at Rachel Vornado. "You want to tell me what the hell is going on?"

"Yes, yes I do. In the truck. Let's go."

There was no arguing with Kraft when he was like this. Dillinger nodded and took the uniform from Rachel, ducked into the powder room and dropped his jeans and T-shirt to the floor, emerging a few seconds later as a naval officer and submarine commander. Kraft and Rachel were talking in low tones in the kitchen. The commodore looked up, stood, kissed Rachel on the cheek and walked briskly to his truck. Dillinger picked up his bag and looked at Rachel.

"Not sure when I'll be back," he apologized. "You've got the kid?"

"Don't worry," she said, approaching him close enough that he could smell her scent again. She looked up into his eyes, her own wide and shining. "Come back when you can." Her voice trembled. "And be damned careful."

What the hell is going on? he thought. Suddenly it felt like the afternoon of the hurricane run. Another emergency. Another woman telling him to come back alive.

"I'll be right there, Commodore," Dillinger called. He looked down at Rachel. "Do you know what this is about as well?"

She nodded, her eyes large and unblinking as she looked up at him. He had the sudden impulse to kiss her, and the thought made him furious. What was going on inside him? Could he be this disgracefully disrespectful of Natalie's memory?

"I know because Peter knew," she said softly. "It was part of what he said in the middle of the night."

What was she talking about? Then he remembered what Vornado had said in the rain as they hurried to the pier that day. *A French ballistic missile submarine gone bad.* Dear God, he thought.

"I'll be careful," he said to her. He leaned down and gently kissed the cheek of his son, who had fallen asleep in Rachel's arms. He stood erect, seeing her seeking his eyes. Not sure what to do, his hands rose to her shoulders. He could feel the silky texture of her suit jacket and the tautness of her shoulder muscles underneath. There was a warmth from her. Her lips parted, just slightly. He drew her into a tight hug before he did something stupid, and he could feel the warmth of her chest and her scent filled his nostrils, an unwanted storm churning inside him. As suddenly as he embraced her he released her and stepped back to leave. "Thank you, Rachel," he said, his voice hoarse.

"Burke, I'll light a candle for you," she said softly. "Every night."

She'd never called him anything but "B.K." since he'd met her. He stared at her for a long moment, the confusion tearing at him, and, not knowing what to say and not trusting his own voice, he slowly nodded once at her, his eyes on hers, then turned and walked into the foyer and out the front door. When it shut behind him he felt the impulse to touch the door with his left hand, the way he had that day he left as the hurricane bore down on the East Coast, but instead he forced himself to walk to Kraft's truck.

Commodore Kraft threw the truck in reverse and roared backward into the street, the tires shrieking as he threw it in drive and followed the state trooper. Dillinger's gaze didn't leave the house until Kraft rounded the corner. Once on the main street, the trooper accelerated rapidly, his beacons flashing in the darkness.

Dillinger wondered how to ask the commodore to tell him what he already suspected from Rachel. "We gonna be gone long, sir?" he asked.

"I won't. You will."

"Where's your staff car? And driver?"

"I need to talk to you on the way in," Kraft said, reaching for the cigar case on the console. "Want one?"

"No thanks, but I'll cut it for you." He took the cigar cutter and clipped the end off the Cohiba, and handed it to Kraft. Kraft fired the tip up, the truck filling with mellow smoke. "You couldn't talk to me in the staff car?"

"This is too classified for his ears," Kraft said.

"Why the cop?"

"You didn't guess? It's urgent. Your crew is being hauled in."

"I guessed," Dillinger said.

"B.K., there's a problem. A big hairy problem. You and the *Hampton* are being mobilized for Operation

Crashing Eagle. 'Crashing' as in not invited to the party."

"Okay," Dillinger said, his tone inviting Kraft to continue.

Kraft glanced over at Dillinger, the cigar clenched in his teeth, the look one of undisguised appraisal. "A group of terrorists have hijacked the French missile submarine *Le Vigilant*. Newest ship of the French submarine fleet. Same class as the guy you were up against in Exercise *Urgent Surge*."

Dillinger was silent for a moment. "So, that exercise," Dillinger asked. "That was for *real*? The brass anticipated this?"

Kraft shook his head. "Not exactly, B.K. Life imitated art. They thought it was a British SSBN that was going to be taken. Exercise *Urgent Surge* was to demonstrate to the Brits that they'd better tighten up security. The French were just working with us."

"So who took the submarine?"

"An Algerian Islamic faction called the GIA. They've had a beef with the French for generations. Their agents were watching the UK submarine bases and we were watching them watch. At the last minute they changed targets from the Brits to the French. Maybe the British thing was a diversion. Or maybe the Brits tightened up their security too much. At this point, it doesn't really matter. There's a terrorist group that has it in for the French—and maybe the rest of the West as well—armed with enough warheads to level every key city in the Northern Hemisphere."

Dillinger swallowed hard. "Jesus. How'd they manage to steal a ballistic missile submarine?"

"CIA didn't say. I guess we don't have the need to know."

"So why not just call me in the usual way? And brief me with an op order? What's with the chauffer job and the state trooper?"

"It's complicated," Kraft said. "Look, to get this Frog

boomer they need the FY08 sonar system. We already surged Peter and the *Texas*. And McDonovan and the *Virginia*. But Mac's got a primary-to-secondary leak with the engineroom getting hotter by the minute, so we're brining him into the Faslane, Scotland, submarine base for emergency repairs."

"Commodore, this is a tactical situation. Fuck the radiation, keep him out there."

"Can't, B.K., it's too severe. Mac's got life-threatening levels of radiation in the enginehouse. He's gotta shut down, cool down and depressurize. Then a complete steam generator repair."

"Sorry to hear that."

"Fuckin' machinery always bursts into flames in its hour of need."

"What about Peter?"

"Brass is worried about him. He's off his game."

"You know about Rachel divorcing him?"

"Yeah. It's too bad but it happens. Happened to me."

Dillinger looked down at his boots. "I'm off my game too, sir."

Kraft's voice grew even more gravelly than usual. "I know. You've been flat since the northern run. You would have gotten *Le Vigilant* if you'd been your usual self."

Dillinger wasn't so sure. The French SSBN had been damned good.

"You still haven't told me why the odd way of deploying us."

"I'm not there yet. See, this whole thing—the French don't know we know. They're an independent lot. They're trying to solve this by themselves, with French assets. NATO didn't get the call."

"Good God, didn't we talk to them?"

"We can't. We know this is going on by the use of intelligence methods and sources we're not supposed to be using on our allies. But shit like this—this is why we spy on our friends."

Dillinger didn't say anything, but still wondered about the strangeness of Kraft picking him up. He decided to ask the question a third time.

Kraft sighed. "CinCLant staff's gonna try to put all the eggs in Peter's basket, but I'm worried about him. This French boomer's captain—you know how good he is from the way he kicked our asses in *Urgent Surge*."

"But don't you think the crew of the boomer is dead by now if the Algerians took the boat?"

Kraft shook his head. "CIA says no. They won't say why."

"That means the Algerians have leverage."

"Whatever. The Agency thinks the Algerians deceived the French into believing that they are Chechens threatening Russia. The Algerians will get to the point of missile launch and then kill the crew, then retarget the weapons for France. Bad news is that they'll be ready to launch. Good news is that once the French crew is dead, the Algerians will be easy to take down."

"It'll be too late."

Kraft gave Dillinger a significant look. "For the French. Not for us. The Algerians are Islamic terrorists. They hate America half as much as they hate France, but they hate us all the same. You've got to go get these guys."

"I can guess what my mission is."

"It's not what you think, B.K. I'm surging *Hampton* on advice from Admiral Worth at ComSubLant. Orders from CinCLantFleet aren't in yet. But ComSubLant wants you in the central Atlantic on the way to East-Lant. You've got four days to get in position. By then the French will realize they're in trouble. When they call for help, you and Vornado will be there. With your FY08 sonars, your quiet platforms and torpedo rooms full of weapons. When you get the word, take this motherfucker down."

Dillinger nodded, deep in thought. That was why Kraft was bringing him in personally. The orders weren't official. The op order hadn't been conceived yet, much less written. And Dillinger wondered whether it was Admiral Worth advising Kraft or the other way around. Not that it mattered. An emergency like this was bigger than personalities and political ambitions.

"I'm worried about something," Kraft said, hesitation in his voice.

"Yes, boss?"

"It's you, B.K. You gotta get your head out of your ass. You sail like you did on the Barents run, there's no problem. But you operate like you did in August, you're dead. And your crew is dead too."

Dillinger nodded sullenly. "Yes, sir."

"Your Squadron Eight op order puts you on course zero five zero at flank. I don't have the authority to order you to emergency flank, but you may get it once you're out. Keep going and don't slow to come to periscope depth until you're in position at Point X-ray. You'll get called to periscope depth by ELF radio. At that point you'll get your final orders."

"Aye, aye, sir." Dillinger paused. "Anything we can do if one of these birds flies? What about the Space Command's ballistic missile shield? We poured billions into it. Won't it work?"

Kraft frowned. "I asked CIA that. Let's just say the ops boss over there has very dark circles under his eyes and he's aged ten years since the Barents operation."

"What if the French don't ask for help?"

"They will. They're emergency deploying their entire navy. That we can see without spying on them. We'll ask why."

"They'll say it's an exercise."

Kraft looked over at Dillinger as he stubbed out his cigar. "Their government is evacuating Paris as we speak."

"Holy shit," Dillinger breathed. "Holy fucking shit."

"Exactly. We'll ask about the evacuation. CIA thinks in four days the French will see reason, especially if— quite conveniently—you guys happen to be in the area."

"Won't that seem suspicious?"

"By then they won't care. Four days from now means four nights of waking up screaming from nightmares. Besides, if they stay stubborn, the president won't wait. You'll be released to take down the SSBN in any case."

"Four days," Dillinger said. "If the Algerians have the crew and they have leverage, what makes you think they won't launch now?"

"CIA thinks the crew'll hold out for a week before they crack. Apparently this has been studied with our own forces. After a week held hostage, even a crew totally loyal to the French can't withstand torture even at moderate levels. At more intense levels, they'll crack faster, but the stakes are high here. The crew will know that a hundred million people could die. They'll hold up to higher levels of torture."

"What if the crew are dead? What if some Algerian sub expert is on board? Operating the ship?"

"Not likely. You know any Algerians who can operate a nuclear submarine?"

"You know what I mean, sir, they could be well funded. They could have gotten a bitter British expatriot or a Russian or Chinese boomer sailor to help them."

"B.K., could you walk onto the deck of a foreign ballistic missile submarine and operate it on day one? You've always been an attack boat sailor. You think you could launch ICBMs?"

"It would take me some time, but yeah. There are tech manuals on board. I'd figure it out."

"In less than four days?"

"No," Dillinger said, shaking his head. "No way."

"Which is why the crew being held hostage is the more severe scenario and the one we're assuming. If an ex-Chinese boomer expert is leading their actions, he'll fight the ship poorly and we can kick his ass. That'll be an easy day. It's the hostage situation that is keeping the brass sleepless."

"I understand."

The truck had reached the gate of Norfolk Naval Station. The state trooper turned off his beacons and turned around, waving to Kraft. As they showed their identification, Dillinger thought about the mission. Kraft was taking a risk putting him and the *Hampton* out there, particularly with Dillinger's recent sluggishness. Not to mention Peter Vornado's problems.

"Listen, Commodore, I won't let you down. And I appreciate your vote of confidence."

Kraft nodded, but said nothing until he reached the pier security building. "Go with God, B.K.," he said.

Dillinger reached out and shook Kraft's hand, then withdrew his sea bag.

"Thanks again, sir."

"Good luck and good hunting."

Kraft watched as Dillinger carried his bags toward the security shack. He had the terrible feeling he had just seen the younger man for the last time. He tried to shake off the feeling, then drove on, deciding to park and spend an hour in his office on the tender ship.

19

Youssef Tagreb poured his fifth cup of coffee and sat back down at the messroom table. It had been so long since he'd slept he was no longer sure what day it was, and when he looked at the bulkhead chronometer, he wasn't sure if it was reading the morning or evening hours. The clocks on *TK-17* and *Krasnoyarsk* had had twenty-four-hour faces, taking away the doubt. He had set the clocks to Greenwich Mean Time, as he had heard the West did, because if any of their submarines came for him, he wanted to be synchronized with them. Back when the chronometer was set to Moscow Time, the submarine never ran during the wee hours with the sharpness it did during the day. The point of vulnerability was always the back-watches, he thought, but then, the only capability on this vessel was his, and he was afraid to sleep, not until he got things under control.

For the first time the thought came to him that this was a suicide mission. How would they ever launch all these missiles without being detected and sunk? It was unrealistic, but stealth and surprise were on their side. For the moment. Once the missiles began flying, their position would be advertised. Perhaps he could convince Zouabri to launch them in four-missile salvos. But that was a future argument.

Navigation had been the first problem after the mechanical systems were stable. It had taken hours to assemble all the technical manuals he needed, and he was missing some. The inertial nav system was functional, and he knew where the ship was, but the system would need an update from the overhead satellite system, and odds were the French government would get it to be scrambled as a countermeasure to Tagreb's launch. Which meant he would have to shoot the missiles on the inertial navigation system without a final correction, and accuracy could suffer. He wouldn't mention that to Zouabri. What difference would it make if they missed the Eiffel Tower by half a kilometer? Or three? Or seventeen? Either way, Paris would burn. Tagreb left the manuals piled in a corner and went on to the next priority—training the crew.

It took him three times as long to train Zouabri's men on the operation of the ship control station as it should have taken. Even then, he had doubts that they could perform. He'd kept the system in autopilot, but someone needed to watch it constantly. A failure of the computer could send them plummeting to the deep and kill them faster than Tagreb could react. The trouble was, the men fell asleep while doing nothing but sitting watching the panel. Submariners they would never be.

He got two hours of sleep, until Asad Javadi woke him up. It was the most painful feeling Tagreb had felt in years, rising out of the cot in the executive officer's stateroom after so little rest, but there were chores to do. Tagreb dragged himself to the officers' messroom, where the tech manuals were arranged for the sonar systems. Once he mastered the French sonars, he would go on to torpedo firecontrol. Then he would stand his vigil in the sonar room, making sure they were not fired upon by an enemy intruder. He'd take the ballistic missile firecontrol manuals there and study how to operate the system. Somehow he would have to train Zouabri how to use the two-man trigger, or he'd have to jumper it out. Probably the latter. A few modifications in missile control and he would be able to launch a missile by himself. He'd also study the missile tech manuals and understand how they worked.

All this technical study, while he was this fatigued, was making him more tired. He found himself reading and rereading the same page over and over. He needed more sleep. He was just rising to return to bed when Zouabri came into the messroom, refreshed and relaxed. Tagreb gave him a warning look, as if to say, *Don't ask me about how long it will take me to launch the missiles.*

As he pulled the covers back over himself, he wondered, would it even be possible to do this? Could one man—even as brilliant a scholar and engineer as he— really manage to launch nuclear missiles at France, mastering a behemoth weapon system he'd never seen or been trained on? Could it be so different from the weapons on the Akula-Typhoon submarine he'd understood in his youth? The answer was, it was different. The Western and Russian systems were developed in complete isolation from one another. Being on this ship was akin to walking into a parallel universe. So alike, yet so dissimilar. He shut his eyes and tried to clear his mind.

He was so tired he didn't remember falling asleep. It was fifteen hours later when he woke.

It seemed as if it had been mere minutes since the door of Commodore Kraft's truck slammed shut behind him. The pier had seemed to float toward him, his disembodied spirit drifting down the concrete jetty until he arrived at the black hull of the *Hampton*. The words of the officer of the deck barely registered. Had he been asked later who the OOD had been, he would have frowned in concentration, the faces of the junior officers melting into a single entity. He stood atop the sail, his safety harness latched to the flying bridge handrails, the flag flapping behind him in the darkness. The bow wave below foamed up over the hull, its roar painfully loud. To port, their running light made the foam red, the starboard light turning the waves on the right green. The lights of the buoys approached on either side as the ship roared down Thimble Shoal Channel. The Bay Bridge flew by next. The OOD turned the ship at the traffic separation scheme, the bow plowing into the sea as it headed due east. This was the first time Dillinger had been to sea since Natalie died. There was something missing from it, he thought. It was no longer the mystical, spiritual experience it had been, like the day he had taken *Hampton* out for the hurricane run. It was just another task to perform, no more significant than taking out the garbage or changing one of the baby's diapers. Just another errand: *Go out and take down the French boomer.* Sometimes the minutes lasted hours as he thought about Burke and Peter Vornado and Natalie D'Assault Dillinger. Or about the upturned face of Rachel Vornado as she had looked into his eyes and said, *I'll light a candle for you.* Why would she say that, he wondered. Other times an hour melted away, as two of them did as he rose suddenly to consciousness as Lionel Tonelle called up to him, "Captain? We're ready to rig the bridge for dive."

Had he really spent the entire five-hour surface transit standing dumbly on the flying bridge? He never did that. He had always gone below and monitored the crew's performance during the hazardous operation of driving the submarine on the surface. He nodded, disconnected from the bridge handrails and lowered himself down the ladder into the ship. In his stateroom, he didn't remember removing the safety harness or showering off the salt of the sea spray, nor donning his at-sea coveralls. He blinked as he stood in the control room giving the officer of the deck permission to dive. An instant later he sat at the wardroom table surrounded by his officers, a steaming cup of coffee in front of him as he glanced up at the chart of the Atlantic projected onto the aft bulkhead as Navigator Matt Mercury-Pryce gestured with his laser pointer. As if he'd seen the chart in his dreams, Dillinger nodded in recognition. It was so obvious, he thought. It was the warplan he would have sketched out. An image came to mind of him in his youth, the quarterback of a pickup football game scratching out a play with a stick in the dirt in the huddle, briefing his receivers and linemen.

The chart was labeled *OPERATION CRASHING EAGLE//*

CINCLANTFLEET OP PLAN 2201. The theater of battle was the Atlantic north of the equator. The target, the French ballistic missile submarine *Le Vigilant*, wouldn't have time to transit south of the equator, not if the plan worked. Emerging from Norfolk, Virginia, home of the most vicious forces of America's fleet, were three arrows. They diverged at the continental shelf, one arrow moving northeast, the middle one continuing due east, the southern one going southeast. The northern arrow represented Atlantic Fleet Commander Task Group 2.0 built around the aircraft carrier USS *Nimitz*. The middle thrust was LantFleet CTG 10.0 under the USS *Reagan*. The southern sortie was from LantFleet CTG 1.0 under the *Eisenhower*. On the chart's far right, a dual range circle was drawn around Brest, France, the origin of *Le Vigilant*. One of the circles assumed a speed of twenty knots—entirely too fast for tactical stealth, but physically possible. The second circle was the ten-knot curve, which made more sense. Mercury-Pryce clicked the slide to the next time interval. The upper and lower arrows curved and turned east, the shape on the chart looking like a pitchfork. The range circles around Brest had moved outward. Two dotted-lined curves appeared, one in blue, the other in red, each depicting the 3,240-nautical-mile range of *Le Vigilant*'s nuclear missiles from all possible locations of *Le Vigilant*; the red curve from the ten-knot circle's locations, the blue from the twenty-knot curve. The next click of the chart showed the southern force, CTG 1.0, dividing into two task forces; CTF 1.1 under *Eisenhower*, heading eastward over the southern Atlantic, and CTF 1.2 under the *Carl Vinson*, which headed far south to the equator as a contingency. Each of the task groups included two nuclear submarines, there to defend the surface forces against attack from hostile subs, but in this battle they were ordered to stay close to their battle groups rather than head out ahead in search of submerged contacts. The forward deployed submarines in this operation would be Vornado's USS *Texas* and Dillinger's *Hampton*.

In the middle of the Atlantic, a bold north-south line showed the mid-Atlantic sound surveillance system SOSUS array, a linear bank of hydrophones originally built as a trip-wire to detect incoming Russian submarines. The array had been upgraded over the years, but was not considered sensitive enough to detect a ship as silent as *Le Vigilant*. But then, even a quiet ship eventually emitted transient noises—hatch slams, dropped wrenches, opening missile doors—and the computers of the SOSUS system were straining for just such transients. The sound pattern of a thousand transients unique to submarines had been entered into the processors' memory, and the system, while flawed, could pick up a poorly operated submarine. To the northeast, a diagonal line showed the SOSUS array that followed the line from Greenland to Iceland to England, the famed "GI-UK Gap" of the Cold War days, a pinch point for Arctic Russian submarines to emerge into the North Atlantic, which would now be used to see if *Le Vigilant* transited north to hide under the polar icecap. A third SOSUS line was drawn two hundred miles off the continental shelf of the U.S., the final line of defense for close submarines, but there was no way it would be of use in this operation.

Dillinger yawned as the track of the *Hampton* flashed up on the screen, the curve showing them headed into the twenty-knot curve and then the ten-knot curve of the French boomer at the latitude of northwest Africa. The patrol area of the USS *Texas* flashed up next, Peter Vornado executing a northwest-to-southeast pace pattern between the ten-knot and twenty-knot curves off Gibraltar. Dillinger stared at the *Texas* pattern, his mind drifting again to Vornado and his falling out with Rachel, the bright sunny day of their wedding rising in Dillinger's memory, the light of her eyes back then reserved only for Peter. He saw Rachel's face again, this time remembering how she'd looked at him in the operating room as Natalie lay cold on the table, her lifeless body still hooked up to the IV tubes and vital sign monitors, and how she had pulled Dillinger away from that last embrace. What had her eyes shown then? Grief? Reflected suffering?

"What do you think, Skipper?" Steve Flood asked.

"I'm sorry, what did you ask?" Dillinger said, hoping his distraction wouldn't upset the officers, but they were a bright lot. They had to be thinking the same thing Smokin' Joe Kraft had thought—*You gotta get your head out of your ass.*

"The U.K. submarine force, sir," Lionel Tonelle said. "Won't they deploy in support of the operation?"

Dillinger looked up at the chart. There was nothing on it depicting the Royal Navy's attack submarines.

"This must still be too classified," he said, blinking, thinking that was a huge mistake.

"There's no mention of NATO forces," Engineer Pat Schluss complained. "NATO could have deployed the new German U-boats with their air-independent propulsion, not to mention the diesel U-boats, and there are some damned quiet diesel subs out of Norway. It's a crime not to write a coordinated op plan."

"And the French antisubmarine forces aren't shown," Mercury-Pryce said. "And the sound signature of the French nuclear attack boats, the Amethyste class, is somewhat similar to the Triomphant submarines. If we don't coordinate with the French, Captain, we could be hunting for the wrong ships." The young navigator who no longer looked so young frowned at the chart. "It's a glaring omission, Skipper. Maybe even a fatal flaw."

Dillinger waved his hand in dismissal. "The plan will be updated every day," he said. "Britain will be brought into the mix, I'm sure. And we'll coordinate with the French and NATO. This op order just gets the fleet out of Norfolk and on their way. Not that it'll make much difference to us. We need to realize something, gents." He looked up, his officers all staring into his eyes. "Every asset, every warship on that chart, is going to form a circle at the theater boundaries. All the LantFleet task forces are doing is making a big net, and somewhere inside it is the French SSBN. The only ones going inside, forward deployed, to get this son of a bitch, are us and the *Texas*. Meanwhile, the task forces will tighten the noose, hoping only to grab the French boomer if it tries to escape the theater. The brass may think his plan is to get out of his own missile range—trying to lie low for months to wait for the heat to die down, then reemerge to kill Paris—so he'd head for the South Atlantic or the Arctic Ocean, and our barrier forces will hear him and vector us toward him." Dillinger shook his head. "That just won't happen. I think he'll stay quiet and slow and in comfortable missile range of French targets."

"Why do you think that, sir?" Flood asked, his eyebrows raised.

Dillinger shrugged. "It's what I'd do if I walked onto an unfamiliar submarine. Going fast risks sinking. A jam dive, for example. Or a reactor trip from an improperly operated high-power run. And going fast makes noise, which invites detection and getting attacked. This guy doesn't want a face-to-face encounter with any of us, trust me. He just wants to figure out how to target these missiles and get them launched, and then to disappear."

Flood nodded. "Any word on whether the French crew is held hostage and launching missiles under duress, or if they're dead and the Algerian terrorists are in charge?"

"Nothing," Mercury-Pryce said. "Does it matter, XO?"

Flood shrugged. "I guess I thought the French crew would be better equipped to fight off an attack from an incoming SSN, like us. The Algerians—even if they have an expatriate SSBN expert—would be shorthanded and unskilled at a submarine-*versus*-submarine dogfight."

Dillinger nodded. "But then, a captive French crew might *try* to lose a battle with a 'hostile' SSN, their way of knocking off the Algerians."

"A suicidal way," Merc said.

"So what?" Schluss added. "Better to die than have eighty million of your countrymen nuked. This happened to me, I'd be banging on the hull with a wrench to give away our position. Or I'd open a main seawater drain valve and scuttle the fuckin' ship right under the terrorists' noses."

Suddenly Dillinger felt a heavy fatigue settle on his shoulders. He hadn't slept much in the last two nights, not with Burke crying every hour Friday night and not sleeping at all on Saturday night. The lack of sleep was contributing to the floating feeling of unreality, or perhaps it was this nightmare of a mission, and the pressure of being one of the two submarines capable of taking down *Le Vigilant*. During the Barents run he'd experienced severe insomnia, but the drifting feeling had never been this bad. There was something terribly wrong with his sense of time, some minutes almost freezing, others whipping by so that a day barely existed. Maybe some real, uninterrupted sleep would help, he thought. He owed it to the mission to be on his game, Kraft's words still echoing in his mind.

"Anything else, Nav?"

Merc shook his head. "That's it, Skipper."

"Good. This briefing is concluded. XO? Meet me on the conn."

The officers stood as Dillinger rose and made his way to the control room. In a few minutes Flood joined him. Matt Mercury-Pryce came up to relieve Phil Breckenridge, the most junior OOD, who had taken the conn so the more senior officers could attend the op-brief.

"Yes, Captain?" Flood asked.

"Station the command duty officer and tell the OOD you're taking over for me during the mid-watch," Dillinger said. "I'm going to try to get some sleep. But don't hesitate to get me up if there's anything emergent. Or if we get an update to the operation order."

"Aye, aye, sir. Good night, Skipper."

Dillinger turned and entered his stateroom. He darkened the overheads, dimmed the ship control instrument panel gauges, took off his coveralls and climbed under the covers. He shut his eyes and tried to sleep. But his mind seemed to chug on, sluggishly but stubbornly, and he tossed and turned.

He hadn't realized he'd fallen asleep until he woke himself, screaming, at two in the morning, from a nightmare. He sat up, his forehead wet with sweat, and tried to remember the dream. All he could recall was a nameless evil far at sea, lurking and waiting for him. The door to the head opened. Dillinger looked up, expecting Natalie to come into his stateroom, until he remembered. *Natalie was dead.*

"Captain?" Flood asked. "You okay?"

"Just a bad dream, XO," Dillinger said. *Like my life is now*, he thought. The door shut and he tried to return to sleep.

Colonel Auguste Guischard had been named the senior Judicial Police Commander of the Terrorism Interagency Tactical Task Force six months before. He was young for the position, which had been meant as a senior leadership post. No one else named to that office would be standing out here in full assault gear, but his theory was that one led from the trench. The thought of spending the rest of his career in an office absent of the slightest danger other than a paper cut made him nauseated. Which was why the moment he got the call, he turned the day-to-day over to his deputy and rushed out to the scene with the boys. But once he got here and saw the full briefing details, all thought of excitement left him. This was no longer something one did for risk and thrills and excitement. This was something that made a man sick to his stomach.

Hostages. An urgent rescue. Torture. Guischard bit his lip and made his face look as commanding as possible. The men would need to see resolve on his face.

He crouched down, his hand poised to give the signal. He wore a black body suit of heavy nylon covering Kevlar bulletproof armor, making his bone-thin, wiry frame seem bulky. Even his gloves were heavy nylon holding Kevlar armor panels in place. In his right hand

he carried an Uzi 9 mm automatic pistol. On his belt
were ten grenades—the five on his right the flash-bang
smoke units, designed to shock, frighten and confuse,
but cause no harm; the five on the left fragmentation
grenades powerful enough to knock down a two-story
house. Strapped to his right thigh were five oblong cylindrical tear gas grenades, and on his left were five pepper
gas units. In his right shoulder holster was a cocked
black Mark VII Desert Eagle .50 caliber pistol, able to
take off a man's head. In the right holster was a DeMarc
87-T peppergas pistol that could drop an assailant to the
deck, blind him and close his throat, with a good shot
leading to a kill if an ambulance weren't standing by.
Guischard wore a black helmet, burnished to a flat, unre-
flective surface, with a full face shield that likewise reflected no light. Beneath the shield his air mask was
fitted, the mask covering his eyes and fed from two black
air bottles on his back, the supply giving him thirty minutes of air inside a building full of smoke, tear gas or
pepper gas. In front of Guischard's right eye was a light-
activated infrared sensor, allowing him to peer through
darkness and smoke, but clear when there was sufficient
light. Behind him were thirty of his men, all of them
equipped and trained as he had been. They lived on the
edge, training hard and drinking hard, each of them as
vicious as the evil forces they combated.

He could feel his pulse rise as he gave the signal with
his left hand. His second-in-command hit the detonator
button on the remote, and three hundred kilos of Sem-
tex RDX/PETN moldable explosive suddenly lit up the
darkness at what had been the shut garage door entrance
to the huge, neglected warehouse. The shock wave was
deafening, the blast sending metal fragments of the door
flying over their heads. A huge cloud of smoke erupted
from the doorway, and as soon as the blast stopped hurl-
ing shrapnel, Guischard and his men sprinted into the
warehouse, fanning out, their weapons at the ready. The
infrared sensor came on, allowing him to see where he
was going and the warmth of the people a few dozen

yards ahead. His weapon leveled at the figures, he stepped quickly to the door of the first room, a flash-bang grenade in his left hand. He tapped his partner on the shoulder, and together they kicked in the door so hard that it came off the upper hinge and hung there crazily, swinging back and forth. Guischard rushed into the room, then froze.

The scene in front of him was a nightmare. A naked woman hung from chains, her body covered with sores and knife wounds, pus and blood oozing out of what had once been an attractive body. In front of her were three naked children restrained in duct tape, each bruised and bloody, though not as bad as the woman. At first Guischard was uncertain whether any of them were alive, but his training kicked in, and he realized that there was no threat in the room.

For the next five minutes they broke into all the rooms of the warehouse, finding seven scenes of abject horror, the seventh room a charnel house lined with what had once been a white sheet but was now splattered with blood. The decapitated corpse of a young woman lay on the floor, both of her arms removed. There must have been some sort of torture video being shot by the criminals, or perhaps a satanic ritual that made these monsters torture the women and children in such a horror show.

A half hour later the warehouse was cleared—whoever had done this was long gone. Guischard holstered his Uzi, pulled off his helmet and his gas mask and returned to the first room he'd invaded. The medics were working on unchaining the suspended woman and had already removed the children. A hollow, sick feeling rose in Guischard's stomach as he smelled the fetid air in the warehouse for the first time. Something made him look at the woman more closely. There were blood and vomit on her lips and chin, but, oddly, also on her cheeks. He looked down and did a double take at what appeared to be a human arm, a female arm, on the floor, an arm with bites taken out of it. The monsters, he thought, had made this poor woman eat the flesh of one of the other hostages. He felt his stomach roll sickeningly, so he looked away and took a long puff of air from his tanks, the nausea slowly fading. When he regained control, he looked at the medic.

"Are they all dead?" The medical supervisor was clad in Kevlar armor identical to Guischard's.

"No," the medic said, shaking his head. "But I think it might have been better for them if they had died."

"Bastards," Guischard said. "Anyone conscious?"

"Not one."

Guischard walked out of the building to make his secure cell phone report to the task force's headquarters. He passed twenty ambulances, each of them hurriedly loading the bodies of the former hostages. One of the children was being brought over on a gurney, the girl barely four years old, three of her fingers sliced off, her face covered in blood. Guischard shut his eyes for a long second, then resolutely moved toward the command truck. Off behind a bush, one of his men was bent over double, vomiting furiously onto the grass. For just a second he felt an urge to join the man, but fought it off.

Jesus, he thought as he donned his phone headset. *Who were these men and why had they done such a terrible thing? And where were they now?*

20

"Something's horribly wrong!" Abdul-Azim Fakhri shouted as he rushed into Youssef Tagreb's stateroom, the commandeered executive officer's sea cabin. Tagreb sat up, choking down panic as his heart hammered in his chest.

Without asking what the problem was he pulled on the at-sea coverall uniform he'd found that came closest to fitting him, threw his feet into a pair of boots and followed Fakhir out of the room. In the passageway he could feel the tilt of the deck downward, and the air was growing hotter by the second. *They'd tripped the reactor* he thought in panic. Prayers to Allah, recovering from a reactor outage was one of the most complex operations on the ship, and Tagreb had studied it in detail, reviewing the location of every switch and button and inverter and keylock. But studying reactor recovery was one thing—actually doing it was entirely different, and there were a thousand ways that restarting a reactor that had shut itself down could cause even more severe problems than what had actually tripped it in the first place.

Tagreb ducked through the hatch to the missile compartment and sprinted down the long central aisle between the forestlike crowd of vertical missile tubes until he reached the machinery compartment where the captain of the vessel had died. He could hear the wailing of the reactor siren, the nuclear control space's most serious alarm, all the way from the missile compartment. He dashed down a ladder to the middle level, then through the heavy hatch into the reactor compartment

shielded tunnel, and through that to the engineroom. By
the time he climbed up into the engineroom upper level
he was drenched in sweat. Tagreb burst into nuclear control and lunged for the siren cutout switch, which
plunged the room into silence. Too much silence—there
was not a peep from the turbine generators, which usually shrieked like full-throttle jet engines, and there was
no sound of rushing steam through the headers. And the
air handlers had shut down, a result of the ventilation
tripping off as the air conditioners dropped out of the
circuits. Great Allah, the temperature was fifty-five degrees Celsius and climbing, almost enough to roast flesh.
About the only thing normal was the overhead lighting,
but the battery had picked that up, and Allah alone
knew how long the battery would hold the massive ship's
loads before shutting down. And the ship's angle downward was frightening—they could be sinking toward
crush depth.

"What is it?" he asked Bandar Qadir, who stood
watch in nuclear control beside Kaliq Hafeez. Qadir was
a ruthless warrior, and perhaps the most comfortable
around equipment, but generally clueless and over-
whelmed by the complexity of the nuclear machinery.
His main function was just to watch the plant and call
Tagreb if anything went wrong. The question was mostly
rhetorical. Tagreb scanned the panel as Qadir babbled
about the sirens wailing.

All the controlling rod group's bottom lights were on,
Tagreb saw. Reactor power on the power range meter
was zero. On the intermediate range meter, the needle
was falling slowly, far below the power range point. The
rate meter showed reactor neutron level dying at negative one-third decade per minute. Tagreb reached over
to the main engine throttles, and they were shut, as he'd
instructed the men to do if the sirens went off. The battery discharge meter was clicking away, much too fast.
Tagreb reached down and snapped open the electrical
breakers for the nonvital buses, then shut them again,

which would drop all the nonessential gear and conserve the battery energy.

"We noticed the boiler level gauges going crazy," Qadir said. "The needles went up, then down, then quickly up and down. Then the siren sounded."

Tagreb nodded. It was as he thought. He'd known he should have done the steam generator blowdown, but that operation was just too damned noisy, and now they'd have no choice. With impurities building up in the secondary coolant, the boiler level gauges had gotten clogged with dirt, which made them fail, and they controlled the feed valves that opened or shut to fill the boilers with water from the condensers. And if the main feed valves had gone full open, they could have filled the boilers suddenly with enough cold feed water to cause the reactor power to skyrocket in an instant, and the protective circuits shut them down on power-to-flow scram. It wasn't good, but he might be able to recover from this. The trouble was, it would take a while, and they needed to maintain depth control while Tagreb recovered. The ship was obviously heavy forward, so he needed to pump the forward variable ballast aft, but it would be quicker to get the emergency propulsion motor online.

"Qadir, come with me," Tagreb said, just as Issam Zouabri appeared outside nuclear control.

Tagreb hurried to the aft area of the engineroom, where the emergency propulsion motor lay aft of the reduction gear. He found the clutch operating mechanism, checked that he had hydraulic pressure, and operated the valve. A clunking sound came from the huge drivetrain, the sound of the clutch disengaging the reduction gear and main engines from the driveshaft. Now only the emergency propulsion motor controlled the screw. He shut the breaker to the EPM, then moved its throttle to the dead-slow-ahead indicator. He watched as the shaft slowly turned, faster and faster, then stabilized. The tachometer read thirty-one RPM. Perfect.

"Qadir, run forward to the control room, tell them they have three knots, and tell them to control the ship's angle!"

Qadir ran forward, Tagreb hurrying after him to the nuclear control room. There at the door Zouabri waited. Tagreb waited, the angle slowly coming off the deck— Qadir had done his job, thank Allah. Now there remained the serious matter of blowing down the steam generators and the level gauges.

"Well?" Zouabri asked.

Tagreb rubbed the sweat off his brow. "I can recover the reactor, but to do it I need to blow the bad, polluted, sediment-laden water out of the steam generators. The boilers."

"So? Do it," Zouabri said.

"You need to realize the implications. It is the loudest thing we will ever do other than launch a missile."

"Can't you do it quietly?"

Tagreb shook his head. "The water is superheated. At extremely high pressure. When it leaves the ship and hits the cold seawater, it makes a noise like—well, you can't imagine what it sounds like." Tagreb had wracked his brain to figure out a means to blow the generators down into the ship, but it had been prevented by the ship's design—the energy of the secondary coolant blasting into the hull could kill crewmen and damage equipment.

"What does that mean for our mission?"

"Maybe nothing. Maybe everything. It depends how close the forces hunting us are."

"What is the worst-case scenario?"

"An attack submarine is sent to the source of the noise and torpedoes us, ending us and our mission."

"Haven't you been studying how to detect such an attacker and to kill him without us being sunk?"

"Yes."

"Are you confident?"

No, Tagreb thought. In a fight with an attack submarine he would be outgunned, unless he could master the use of the evasion device, and so far he hadn't gotten to its technical manual. The torpedoes he'd understood, spending almost all of day two on studying the torpedo firecontrol systems and the weapons' computer guidance systems. He had gone to the torpedo room and practiced ramming torpedoes into the tubes and moving them around the room. An evasion device was loaded into the number one tube, which had made him think about how to use it, but there had been no time. And still, he hadn't gotten to the missile firecontrol system, which Zouabri insisted he hurry up and understand. Today Tagreb had planned to learn the ship's sonar system, so that he could detect an enemy, and assuming he could have understood it in a day, he had planned the next day to get into the missile systems. And as he had learned from the first protracted time without sleep, unless he slept at least six hours, learning the new systems made him incredibly fatigued, and he ended up reading the same technical manual page over and over.

"It doesn't matter if I'm confident. We don't have any choice on this. We have to do the blowdown or we can't restart the reactor and keep it up."

Zouabri nodded. "Then do it."

Tagreb nodded. He went into nuclear control, scanned the gauges, his gaze lingering on the battery discharge meter. Using the emergency propulsion motor would exhaust the battery in less than half an hour. He had to hurry. He found the reactor plant control manual and opened it to the blowdown procedure, studying it for several seconds. He turned to Zouabri.

"I need you to go forward and have them bring the ship to a depth of thirty meters. Then send four men aft."

Zouabri nodded and disappeared. Tagreb took the heavy manual with him to the lower level of the engineroom, laying it on an equipment cabinet between the huge main feed valves. He found the valves for steam generator blowdown and read through the procedure. This was not good, he thought. He'd have to start one of the main feed pumps and fill both boilers to the top, then open the valves and blow them overboard to the bottom level indication. The pump would exhaust the battery in no time. But then, what choice did he have?

Tagreb hit the start button on the feed pump, over-rode the main feed valve controller and filled both steam generators, which was not easy, as the level indicator needles were moving all over hell, but he assumed the average of the needle swing was correct. After a few minutes of pumping, he shut the feed valves and the pump, praying to Allah that the battery lasted. He stepped to the blowdown valves and opened the hull valve, then the backup valve, and finally cracked open the port steam generator blowdown valve. The noise was deafening as he opened the valve further, his eye up on the level gauge, watching as the generator poured its polluted water overboard. He should have grabbed some of the industrial-strength ear protectors, he thought, as the noise hammered on his eardrums. It seemed to take a long time for the water to go overboard, endless minutes ticking by as the noise roared in Tagreb's ears, but finally the port boiler was nearly empty. Tagreb shut the port valve, then cracked open the starboard boiler's valve and opened it further. The roaring noise returned; if anything, even louder this time. He watched the port boiler drain, then shut the valve and the hull and backup valves. Mercifully, the noise stopped, but Tagreb's ears still rang violently.

He restarted the main feed pump and refilled the boilers, then shut it back down. He'd need to add chemicals to the boiler as soon as possible, since that was the normal operation, but the immediate need was to restart the reactor. With the battery this drained from using the huge feed pump, he'd have to heat up the reactor plant and steam systems with heatup rates severe enough to damage them, but this was a survival effort.

Tagreb ran back to the upper level, stopping at the motor control and switchgear room, where he shut the three breakers to the controlling rod group inverter, then hurried into the nuclear control room. Zouabri was there, wanting to ask him questions. Tagreb held up one hand, shot a glance at the battery meter and the battery bus voltage. It was worse than he thought. There might be only minutes before the battery crashed, and he didn't even want to think what would happen then.

He grabbed the operating instruction book, scanned it for a moment, then glanced up at the reactor plant control panel. Neutron level had fallen through to the bottom of the intermediate range and well into the startup range. He shook his head and grabbed the source range channel selector switch and turned it to STARTUP RATE SCRAM SELECTION, then found the low-pressure cutout switch and switched it to LOW PRESSURE CUTOUT. He exhaled, knowing that he might make a mistake that tripped the reactor again, but all he could do was try.

He selected the controlling rod group selector switch and put the switch to the IN position to latch the rods, then after thirty seconds pulled the rods out. After ten seconds the rod bottom lights winked out—the rods were moving. The rod height indicators began to move, and if they were to be believed, the rods were moving out of the core. The startup was underway! He watched the startup rate meter and startup neutron level. The rate climbed off the negative one-third mark and moved toward zero and beyond, past one decade per minute, then to two. He kept pulling rods until the rate meter needle edged up to eight decades per minute. His heart pounded under his soaked coveralls as the neutron level moved to the top of the startup range. He switched the startup rate channel selector switch to STARTUP CHANNEL CUTOUT and continued his rod pull. The intermediate neutron level meter's needle budged, its rate needle coming off zero and climbing as the startup rate needle had, all the way up to eight decades per minute.

Tagreb prayed as the needle rose higher, the intermediate range needle rising toward the top. He glanced at the battery discharge meter, and realized how bad the news was. Allah be damned, the battery was nearly exhausted! Tagreb had failed.

The lights overhead flickered just before the entire ship was plunged into complete darkness.

The second day at sea had been uneventful, if a hunt for a killer nuclear missile submarine that could threaten half the world could be called that. They had continued down the track line of the chart, the ship shaking violently as the main engines shrieked far aft, pouring out their thirty thousand shaft horsepower. The deck trembled with the ship's travel, a reminder to every soul onboard that their errand was urgent. As the clock clicked past midnight, the ship had crossed longitude 47 degrees west at north latitude 40 degrees, about five hundred nautical miles southeast of the tip of Newfoundland, the opening of the mid-Atlantic. At *Hampton*'s present speed of advance she would be in position a day early, the op order's track ending at longitude 30 west, latitude 41 north, which was five hundred nautical miles northeast of the Azores Islands, the approach to the coastlines of north Africa, Spain, Portugal, France and the U.K. By then the brass expected to get an update to them, to change the plan and get them closer to this stolen boomer.

Burke Dillinger stared down at his coffee cup, the trembling of the wardroom table making rings of waves on the surface of the brown brew. He glanced at the ship control gauges, the compass showing the submarine rocketing east-northeast along the great circle route toward Portugal, depth 654 feet, speed, 33.5 knots. Dillinger had wondered why CinCLantFleet hadn't ordered them to throttle up to emergency flank, which would have gained them another knot or two of speed, but at the cost of contaminating the engineroom with high levels of radioactivity as fuel elements began to melt within the core and spread their contamination to the primary loop. While it was unsafe from a nuclear reactor operational standpoint, if the fate of the hemisphere depended on it, who cared if the fuel melted here or there? Or that the crew absorbed a near-lethal dose of radiation? Dillinger shook his head. It was a sign they were speeding to nowhere, as the brass didn't know where the bad guy was.

The phone buzzed from the conn. Dillinger reached under the table, for a moment remembering back when Natalie had touched his hand as he had reached for the phone on the Barents run. God, he missed her. Where was she, he thought? Certainly not rotting under the earth. Her spirit was somewhere. Had he really felt her the night that she died? Was that really her, or was it just a dream? Hadn't she told him something that no one had known, that Smokin' Joe Kraft had sent Dillinger on Exercise *Urgent Surge* because Natalie had asked him to? And when he asked, he had found that out, and it was something he never would have suspected. Surely that was evidence that whoever Natalie was, whatever her soul had been, still existed? Such a magnificent creation as Natalie D'Assault Dillinger couldn't just disappear from the universe, could she? In one day, in one hour, could she really have gone from a living, breathing, splendid being, to an inanimate collection of rotting meat and oozing fluids? Is that all there was to life? *Natalie, where are you?* He projected the thought out as hard as he could, but there was no answer. He couldn't feel her. It was nothing like the feeling he'd had the evening she died. She was *real* there in front of him that night, as real as she'd been in life. But now there was just emptiness. Dillinger blinked, wondering how someone he had known for such a short time could turn his life so completely upside down, then disappear without a trace. His eyes felt irritated. He rubbed them, his fingers wet, as he answered the phone.

"Captain," he said.

"Officer of the Deck, sir," the navigator, Matt Mercury-

Pryce said. "Ship has reached Point November, sir, and
I've altered course to zero eight seven. Still on the deep
flank run, sir."

"Very well," he said. He glanced at the chronometer.
It had a maddening tendency to spin around, the hands
of the clock blurring as Dillinger's sense of time continued in its crazy, whirling acceleration and alarming mo-
lasses slowing, time sometimes stopping completely as if
captured by a strobe light. The last half hour had happened in an instant, and the coffee in front of Dillinger
was cold. "OOD, I'll be stationing the XO as the command duty officer at zero one hundred."

"Aye, aye, sir," Merc replied. "Good night, Captain."

Dillinger replaced the phone in the under-table cradle,
the action reminding him again of Natalie. God, would
he ever be free of the grief?

Youssef Tagreb felt the hot water of the shower taking
away his troubles, or at least the sweat caused by them.
Each muscle seemed to relax slowly. On the *Krasnoyarsk* the hot water would have been exhausted five minutes ago, but the French had obviously designed the ship
for luxury. There was no doubt about it, creature com-
forts made a difficult journey bearable. Not that this
journey would ever be anything other than difficult, he
thought, and it was getting worse by the day. It hadn't
been six hours since the reactor had tripped out, leaving
the ship on battery power while Tagreb had tried to
clear the steam generators of the sediment that had
made the level controllers go crazy. And just as he had
been restarting the reactor, the battery had died. A dead
battery was normally a catastrophic accident, dooming a
ship with a tripped reactor.

Tagreb had grabbed a battle lantern and turned it on,
shining the light on the reactor plant control panel. The
loss of power had de-energized the entire grid of the
ship, and he had to check to see if the reactor had
tripped again, and fortunately it had. He dashed aft, the
handle of the overgrown flashlight in his mouth as he

vaulted down the ladderway and through the hatch leading forward. The trip through the darkened submarine was frightening, and he collided once with someone feeling their way in the forward compartment. In the control room there was general panic.

"Shut up and listen," Tagreb had commanded. "You still have hydraulic power for ship control. And your panel gauges are still on from their internal batteries." After calming down the men in the room he turned on the battle lanterns, their weak yellow glow showing the ship control panels. The ship's depth was 150 meters. He'd need to get shallow enough to get the snorkel mast up. At the ballast control panel he cursed as he wished he'd had the hovering computer online. He lined up the automatic valves to blow high-pressure air from the tanks in the ballast volumes to the depth control tank. The deck was steady but tilted downward, since there was a balance problem with the ship heavy forward. He'd have to live with it.

He bubbled air into the depth control tank a bit at a time, to avoid overfilling it. He didn't want the ship to roar out of the ocean and surface. The mission would be over the second he did that. It took an hour to budge the gigantic ship slowly toward the surface. The only hurry was that the batteries in the ship control consoles and reactor plant control panel were dwindling, but they should have been designed for six hours or so. Finally the ship's old-fashioned backup depth gauges showed the vessel at a keel depth of fifteen meters. He shone the lantern on the panel where the mast- and antennae-control hydraulics were located, found the snorkel mast, and snapped up the toggle to raise it. There was no power to the switch. With the light in hand, he searched in the overhead for the hydraulic control valve. He couldn't find it, so he'd had to crawl back behind the ballast control console, in a space barely able to hold his slender body.

Finally he found a manifold of hydraulic valves, each of them labeled. When he reached the snorkel control valve he operated it, and the piping groaned as hydraulic pressure pushed the mast out of the hull. He found the dogeared standard operating procedures manual and opened it to the snorkel procedure, which was similar to the ventilation procedure he'd done four days ago, though it seemed lifetimes ago. Finally the control room was ready. He dashed down the ladderways to the lower level, where the gigantic diesel engine awaited. He took a deep breath, shining his battle lantern on the diesel startup procedure. It took some time to line up the valves, but then he was ready. He pulled the air start lever, and high-pressure air flowed from the air banks into the cylinder head and the engine, spinning it slowly, then cranking it faster, the roar of the operation slamming Tagreb's eardrums. With one hand on the operating lever and the other holding the battle lantern, he found the ear protectors, put the lantern down and put them on, just as the diesel engine roared to life. He watched the temperature gauges on the lubricating oil and the seawater injection and exhaust, and the engine warmed up slowly but perfectly. Life was improving, he thought. It was time to make the generator come to life, which would be a trick with no AC or DC power in the ship. At the aft end of the generator casing there was a connection point for an emergency battery so that the generator electromagnetic field could be "flashed" by an external source. There was no battery connected. He searched the compartment for the most important battery in the ship, but couldn't find it. He put his battle lantern on the battery casing. It had the same voltage as his battle lantern. Perhaps that was why there was no battery here—they could use any of the battle lantern batteries. He found two in the compartment and took them apart, withdrew the shoebox-sized battery and dropped it on the tray, then connected the battery to the terminals and found the toggle switch labeled EMERGENCY FIELD FLASH. He clicked it on, and immediately the sound in the space changed, the diesel's roar deepening slightly. Tagreb moved further aft to the local diesel generator breaker, which normally would be operated remotely from nuclear control. He grabbed the heavy lever and pulled it upward. Nothing changed, but the breaker stayed shut. The generator produced DC power, and right now it powered nothing. He had to shut the battery breaker and charge the battery from the diesel. The battery breaker was located further forward, outside the room in a switchgear-and-equipment bay between the diesel and the torpedo room. Tagreb shut the breaker, hoping the massive battery bank beneath the torpedo room didn't explode. If it did, it would be over quickly, because the weapons in the room would detonate immediately afterward. He realized he had clamped his eyes shut in fear.

When he opened them, the lights in the space were flicking on as the battery buses came back to full voltage, the ship's lighting—the most basic load—returning. He turned off the battle lantern and put it down, took a last look around at the diesel space, then rushed back up to the middle level and aft. He barely remembered his sprint through the missile compartment and the reactor shielded tunnel, and up the ladder to the nuclear control room. Four pairs of eyes drilled into him, one of them belonging to a sweat-soaked Issam Zouabri, and if Tagreb weren't mistaken, he sensed that Zouabri had a slight glimmer of fear in his eyes. Tagreb wouldn't blame him a bit, he thought, because the ship was not yet out of the woods. He pushed the electrical operator off his chair and reached for the motor-generator breakers, which automatically started the huge, refrigerator-sized DC motors from the battery buses, which turned driveshafts connected to AC generators, the heavy, industrial way that DC power and AC power could be converted from one form of electrical energy to another. He listened for the sound of explosions and fireballs, but there was no sound in the room at all except the slight hum of the gauges and the fluorescent lights overhead. Tagreb took a deep breath and snapped shut the controllers for the AC vital bus breakers at the AC end of

the motor generators, then shut the breakers linking the
nonvital turbine generator buses to the vital buses. His
eyes on the vertical panel, he scanned the voltage and
current flows. The diesel generator's loud roar could
right then be broadcasting their position to the world,
he thought, but then he suppressed his fear—after all,
the ocean was full of diesel engine noises. Fishing vessels
and merchant vessels everywhere used the diesel engine
for power and generators. There was no way a 1500-
kilowatt diesel would raise suspicion. At least, he
hoped not.

The return of the electrical grid restarted the ventilation fans. He'd need to restart the huge air-conditioning
units. He left the nuclear control room and hurried to
the middle level and cranked up the R114 units and the
lithium bromide unit—the ship would be freezing soon
unless he got the reactor back online.

But there was something important he had to do. The
ship stable for a moment, he dashed back forward, all
the way to the control room, where Bandar Qadir and
Kaliq Hafeez were in charge of ship control, made sure
that ship control was nominal, and then into sonar,
where Jaul Karim and Asad Javadi stood the watch at
the sonar consoles, but the consoles were blank. Tagreb
had restarted the sonar systems, watching as they reinitialized. For some anxious moments he sweated as he
began to think the sonar suite wouldn't come back on,
but finally it restarted and the data began to flow onto
the screens again. With the loud diesel roaring, their
own-ship's noise was too great for the sonar to do much
good at detecting another quiet submarine, which was
all the reason Tagreb needed to return to nuclear control
and restart the reactor.

It took twenty minutes to return the engineroom to a
steaming condition, another twenty to warm up and restart the steam turbine generators. With the diesel online, there was no reason to risk damaging the heavy
equipment with emergency startup rates. Finally, an
hour and a half after the trouble began, *Le Vigilant* was

quiet, moving sharklike through the deep sea on nuclear power, the diesel quiet and awaiting the next emergency. When Tagreb was finished, he was so soaked in sweat that his boots were swamped. He slowly walked to the stateroom and showered, the fright of the last hours washing down the drain.

He had it, he thought. He knew the ship's torpedo weapon systems, the firing mechanisms, the firecontrol computers. He'd mastered the sonar suite, and moreover, he'd been able to teach the men of Issam's crew the bare essentials they needed to act as alarms, to alert Tagreb that there was something wrong that he needed to come see. There was no real way these rudimentary assassins could ever be any more than early warning watchstanders. But in that capacity they would do well.

The ship was becoming an extension of himself. He now knew the minds of the French designers, and he had to admit to himself, much of this ship's design was pure genius. He walked in an odd parallel universe where every problem the Russian naval architects of the Akula/Typhoon *TK-17* had struggled with had been solved with panache. The French approach to engineering problems was truly elegant, Tagreb thought. And now their own magnificent weapon system would reach out and kill them. To Issam there was cosmic, circular justice in that. To Tagreb it did not matter. He knew he would level the cities of the Western power, a civilization he had studied in his youth and admired, back in the days before his eyes had been opened to the ways of the Koran. And with his newfound faith he realized the cleansing power of killing. Had he not removed the head of his former oppressor, Dostoyev, he might have felt differently, but he now realized that the infidels were unworthy of life. Perhaps those French citizens who did survive the nuclear fires about to rain down on the cities of France would see the light of Allah in their circumstances. And in that light might be their salvation.

But what remained was Tagreb's final study of the missile firecontrol system. He had fully digested the mis-

sile technology, and had spent some time on the rudi-
ments of the firecontrol computers, but did not yet have
the technology fully mastered. But with what he already
knew, he knew that bypassing the missile safety circuits
and interlocks would be surprisingly simple. He had
been amazed at first that the weapons would be so easy
to launch by an unschooled engineer, but then the point
of these missiles was that, were France attacked by an
enemy, the crew would have the ability to launch the
weapons with no further instructions, no further cen-
trally controlled warhead unlock codes. There was a cute
little interlock with a firing trigger, a ridiculous little
plastic pistol with a coiled cord, locked in a combination
safe within the missile control center, with another firing
trigger locked in a similar safe in the control room. The
idea was that the ship's captain in the control room
would have to pull the trigger at exactly the same time
as the weapons officer in the missile control pulled his
trigger. Only then would the missile launch circuit be
complete, and only then would its gas generator ignite
to force the missile out of the tube. There was only one
problem the designers hadn't stopped to consider—the
control room trigger could be jumpered out of the circuit
from the MCP-5 panel in the missile control center with
a half euro's worth of wire. With that one circuit shorted,
the missile could be launched by one man. When Tagreb
had realized this, he had laughed aloud. The dual-trigger
control mechanism was obviously a means of making the
system look more safe than it truly was for the benefit
and comfort of the politicians and citizens.

With a few more hours of study he would understand
the entire system, he thought, and when he did, they
would line up and launch the missiles, all of them in one
salvo. The question rose in Tagreb's mind—what would
happen next? He assumed they would use the submarine
to escape. Perhaps take it to one of the deeper ocean
basins close to a coastline, perhaps near the coast of
Africa—Morocco or the western Sahara probably—and
scuttle the vessel, then take one of the rubber rafts with

its electric motor toward shore. A few swift knife cuts, and the raft would sink, the motor with it, and all trace of their mission would be gone.

Tagreb toweled off, dressed and grabbed a box full of missile firecontrol technical manuals, drawings printed from microfilm, and technical bulletins—all top secret—and carried it to the sonar room, where Jaul Karim stood the watch. He greeted Issam's warrior and sank into the deep leather seat in front of sonar console two. He pulled up one of the tech manuals and opened it to the first page, then raised his eyes to the vertical display directly in front of him. The waterfalls had steadied over the last half hour since he had initialized the system, and from what he could see, there was not much there. He lifted his eyes to the upper display, which was a narrowband display, of frequency on the bottom and intensity vertically, the display fed from the towed sonar array. The computer had drawn squares around frequencies of interest, the unit flashing if a frequency arose that seemed tactically important. Every so often the display blanked out as the computer discarded all the data, then began gathering fresh information. A spike in frequency would point to an intruding manmade vessel, and if it failed to correlate to the direction to a surface ship—which would always be loud—then it was the approach of a submerged warship. Tagreb yawned. It was all too easy. *Krasnoyarsk* and *TK-17* had been nowhere near this sophisticated.

The sonar situation under control, Tagreb began reading the tech manual. An hour passed, then a second, his concentration lost in the technical details of the intricate and brilliant design of the French missile firecontrol system. Every few minutes he raised his eyes and scanned the sonar displays. After three hours, with two of the technical publications completely absorbed and put in the discard pile, he stood, stretched, opened the aft door and walked through the access bay into the control room. He nodded at Diya Waqar, who sat at the firecontrol console. Waqar had been one of Issam's lot who

had been disgusted by Abdul-Azim Fakhri's abuse of
the French children, as Tagreb had been. He bit his lip,
trying to vanquish the distasteful memories. They were
infidels, but they were only babies, and hadn't deserved
what Fakhri had done to them, even if they were sen-
tenced to death within days, perhaps only hours.

Issam Zouabri appeared in the forward doorway.

"Ah, Youssef," Zouabri said, getting ready to ask the
question he'd asked ten times a day since they had taken
the submarine. "Are you any closer to missile launch?"

Tagreb nodded. "We launch today. I'm mere hours
away."

"Excellent! What stands between you and complete
readiness?"

"Memorizing three technical manuals."

"You memorize them?"

Tagreb shrugged. "Once I read them, I can see every
page, every circuit, every concept. It is not that difficult."

Zouabri smiled. "You are truly a gift from Allah."

Dillinger once again stood by the operating table, as he
had in every dream since the night Natalie had left him.
In this one, as in some of them, after she died, she still
spoke to him. Usually he just heard her voice in his
head. But in this one she spoke with her mouth, the
effect odd since her dead eyes stared at the ceiling.

"Peter sacrifices," she said. "He is sacrificed in fulfillment."

Are you saying he dies? he asked her.

"His mission is completed. The circle closes."

What happens? Can I stop it? Can I help him?

Natalie blinked suddenly, the film of death evaporat-
ing from her eyes. Her eyes focused on the ceiling, but
she didn't turn or look at him. He remembered her
doing this once before. He'd awakened in the night the
week before the hurricane run, Exercise *Urgent Surge*,
and found her staring at the ceiling, her eyes clear, focused on nothing, tears streaking down her temple into
her hair. He hadn't said anything, but shut his eyes and

tried to go back to sleep, thinking he'd interrupted a private moment. That morning he'd asked her what had been wrong. A brief dark cloud had passed across her face, but she recovered quickly and denied that she had done it. When he'd insisted, she dismissed it by saying he must have been dreaming. He realized now that she must have been thinking about the cancer and how her time was short, perhaps what life would be like for Dillinger and little Burke after she was gone.

"It comes to pass because of your decision."

Why? What do you mean?

But she didn't answer. She just stared at the ceiling.

Natalie?

The sudden loud buzzing of the phone from control startled him awake. He sat up in bed, his forehead beaded with sweat. He reached for the phone.

"Captain." At least his voice was deep and in control. His head spun, nausea rising in his stomach.

"Captain, XO," Flood said. "The OOD reports we've got an ELF radio signal coming in. The first letter of our callsign is received. I've ordered him to slow and come shallow in preparation for coming to periscope depth."

Dillinger held the phone handset down and stared at it as if it were an insect. For a second he felt a severe vertigo. *Peter is sacrificed in fulfillment and the circle closes because of your decision.* Her voice was a mysterious whisper in his mind. He wiped the sweat off his forehead. *Get your head out of your ass*, Commodore Kraft's gravelly voice countered.

"Very well, XO. Meet me in control."

Dillinger stood, changed his underclothes and donned his coveralls, then walked out to control. The deck had steadied from its previous trembling as the OOD slowed the vessel, then inclined steeply upward. Dillinger waved to OOD Matt Mercury-Pryce, then nodded at Steve Flood. He glanced around the room, got a status update, then said to Flood, "I relieve you." He turned to Merc. "The command duty officer is secured."

"Aye, sir."

"I'll be in radio." Dillinger walked aft into the radio room. He entered the combination code on the door lock and let himself in. The radio chief, Senior Chief Marconi, stood at the ELF receiver panel, Communicator Mikey Selles right behind him.

"Evening, men," Dillinger said. "What've we got?"

"Yessir," Selles said, his perpetual grin somewhat drooping. "ELF callsign is aboard. Recommend going to PD and getting our message."

Dillinger turned and stepped back into control. Flood stood waiting at the attack center, as anxious as Dillinger. "OOD?"

"Yes, Captain," Merc said from the railed periscope stand. "Ship is at one five zero feet, steering zero eight zero, speed seven knots, baffle clear completed with no sonar contacts, request permission to proceed to periscope depth."

"Very well, take her to PD," Dillinger ordered.

"Periscope depth, aye," Merc acknowledged. "Radio, Sonar, coming to periscope depth! Diving Officer, make your depth six seven feet! Helm, all ahead one third!"

"Six seven feet, aye!"

"Conn, Radio, aye."

"Conn, Sonar, aye."

The deck angled upward again as Mercury-Pryce reached into the overhead. "Lookaround, number two scope!" he called.

"Depth, one four zero," the diving officer reported.

"Speed six," the helmsman called.

"Up scope!" Merc rotated the hydraulic control ring and the periscope slowly emerged from the periscope well. As the optic module rose he put his face on it, snapped down the periscope grips and began to swing the unit in circles as he searched the waves above them for close contacts. Hitting the underside of a supertanker would be bad form during a combat operation.

"One hundred feet!" the diving officer called.

"Very well," Merc replied.

"Nine zero! Eight zero feet."

"No shapes or shadows," Merc said aloud.

"Seven five feet, sir. Seven zero feet!"

"V'well!"

"Six nine feet!"

"Scope's breaking."

"Six eight."

"Scope's breaking . . ."

"Six seven!"

"Scope's clear!"

There was silence in the room as the OOD made rapid circles on the periscope, frantically searching for close surface ships, any one of which could rupture the hull in a collision. The control room crew held their breath, awaiting the call of "emergency deep," for which they'd take immediate actions to get back to the safety of the deep to save the ship, but Merc said nothing, eventually slowing his search.

"No close contacts!" he said. "Chief, raise the HDR antenna!"

The sound of hydraulics bumping thudded in the room as the chief of the watch raised the high data rate antenna. "Radio, Conn, HDR is up!"

"Conn, Radio, aye," Senior Chief Marconi's voice crackled. There was a pause. *"Conn, Radio, radio messages aboard, HDR coming down, recommend goin' deep."*

"Take her deep and flank it," Dillinger ordered. "I'll be in radio."

Mikey Selles handed him the clipboard with the top secret message printout. He scanned it, read it slower, then read it again. He looked up to see Steve Flood, an expression of curiosity on the XO's face. Dillinger handed over the message board and waited for Flood to read it.

"Fuck," the XO said.

"Exactly," Dillinger said. "Gather the boys in the wardroom."

Again time did its strange magic act, the next hour

compressing to fill mere seconds. The men stood and filed out of the wardroom, a projection screen picture of the Northern Hemisphere still on the screen.

"Leave it on for a minute," Dillinger said to Navigator Mercury-Pryce as he fetched a cup of coffee and plopped back down in his chair. Flood had elected to stay as well, his gaze on his cup as he stirred in some of the heavy cream that the supply officer had stolen before they broke out of port. "What do you think?"

Flood glanced at the chart of the North Atlantic, the image appearing as if taken from high Earth orbit over mid-Atlantic.

"They were all wrong," Flood said. "This guy didn't hump it at all. He cruised slow and silent. Until he fucked up. Now we've got him."

"Yeah," Dillinger said. The situation report caught *Le Vigilant* in a huge mistake. Five hours ago a tremendously loud and long-lasting transient noise was detected in the east Atlantic basin off the northwest tip of Spain. The first series of noises correlated to a blowdown— either the submarine had blown down his steam generators or lifted a relief valve in the primary coolant system and ejected superheated water and steam into the ocean, the resulting noise louder than a rocket engine. If that had been the only transient, the bastard would have gotten away with the tactical blunder and evaded detection, but he had compounded his error. Not long after the blowdown noises, a loud diesel engine had started up and remained on for some time—over ninety minutes, roaring and chugging through the ocean. From the moment of the blowdown transient and continuing through the diesel engine noise, *Le Vigilant*'s position had been triangulated by multiple sonar sources. The first was the sonar sensors of Peter Vornado's USS *Texas*, which had been pacing in a box pattern six hundred miles north of the Azores, waiting for the SSBN to emerge from the east Atlantic basin. With the sonar line from *Texas* pointing east-southeast, they had enough data given the constraints of the French and Spanish shorelines to vector in on *Le Vigilant*, but additional data had been gained from the highly secret mid-Atlantic SOSUS hydrophones strung north-to-south at longitude 45 west, and from the older network extending from Greenland to Iceland, and from Iceland to the northern tip of Scotland. Those three bearing lines nailed the French submarine's position within a few hundred nautical miles. The chart's huge areas defined by the target's ten-knot and twenty-knot curves had made them all feel a sinking feeling that the haystack was much too big to find the needle, but now that *Le Vigilant* had practically broadcast his position, they had him in his front yard.

The *Texas* had been sent toward Brest with the admirals' intention to get her on the east side of the target. Meanwhile, Dillinger's orders changed slightly, his op order updated to move the *Hampton* slightly more north, but his speed orders remained at flank. Between the *Texas* and the *Hampton*, the strategists intended to squeeze the target. The trouble was, now there was little room to maneuver. The original operation plan had the French boomer in the middle of the deep blue Atlantic, where the surface action groups could tighten the net while *Texas* and *Hampton* closed in from either side, but now both American submarines were too far west, and the target had his back to the French coastline. The water in the east-Atlantic basin between the U.K., France and Spain was shallower than the Azores operation area, which would prove better for sonar detection of the target, but the French antisubmarine forces— having joined in on what was now a joint NATO operation—were stirring up a lot of noise off Brest.

"I'd feel better if it were just us and *Texas* trying to find this guy," Dillinger said. "Now that the Royal Navy subs are in the mix to the north and the French outside Brest, we're going to have too many submerged targets in the area."

"Maybe the brass should have ordered us to wait off the Azores for this guy to move farther west."

"There's no time," Dillinger said. "Remember 'T2K'?

Time-to-knowledge? This guy will know how to launch the missiles soon, and from this close, he can't miss."

"*Texas* is going to get to the bastard first," Flood said glumly.

"I don't know," Dillinger said, an odd feeling tingling on the back of his neck, his hair rising. What was that? It was a shaking feeling, the trembling sensation traveling down to his shoulders and down his back. *There was something here.* No, that wasn't it. Not something. *Someone.* Natalie. He could feel her. She was *here.* Right here in the wardroom, 654 feet beneath the Atlantic. He tried to see if he could see her ghost as an apparition, the way he had that night in his bedroom, but he saw nothing. He tried to see if he could localize the feeling—where was she coming from most strongly?

"Skipper?" Flood asked. "What's wrong? Sir, you look white as a ghost."

"What?" Dillinger said. "Nothing, just thinking." The tingling was still there at the back of his shoulders.

"I'll leave you to think, Skip," Flood said. Dillinger barely noticed his second-in-command leaving. He was alone in the wardroom as the chronometer clicked past the hour of 0100.

She was still here.

Natalie? he asked in his mind. *Is that you?* It was one thing to hear her voice in his dreams. Quite another to feel her presence and sense her voice in his mind when he was awake. His hand trembled as he bit his fist.

"Yes," her sweet voice said from nowhere. The tingle flashed up his spine and he shivered. The hair on the back of his neck stood straight up.

Natalie, I've missed you so much.

She didn't answer, but he felt a sense of warmth wash over his body, just for an instant, and then the room grew cold again.

Is there a reason you're here?

"Yes," she said.

Is it to tell me something?

Her presence seemed strongest at the chart. He

looked up at it, the detection lines from the SOSUS arrays and the *Texas* intersection in the east-Atlantic basin four hundred miles west of Brest. At the flashing intersection point, she existed, there and nowhere else.

"At the point of decision," she said slowly.

Yes? What?

"Burke, at the point of decision, don't hesitate. Peter saved your life. You can't save his."

What? What the hell did that mean? Peter Vornado? The Texas?

Natalie, is Peter Vornado going to die?

There was no answer for a few seconds. Then the voice in his mind repeated itself.

"At the point of decision, Burke, don't hesitate."

And then she was gone, and the tingle on his back and shoulders with her. It was as if she had never really been there. He shook his head, wondering if he had fallen asleep at the table, but he had been fully awake the entire time. Dumbly he looked down at his coffee. It had gone cold. He picked it up, his hand trembling so violently that he spilled it on his coverall sleeve. He put the cup in the sink, switched off the screen projection and walked slowly up to his stateroom, reaching out with his senses, trying to find Natalie again, but she was nowhere.

Could this be even remotely taken seriously, he wondered. Or was it evidence that he was losing his mind? Was it a sign that he should turn command of the *Hampton* over to Flood? Seeing—or at least sensing—the ghost of his wife was not a sign of acceptable mental health. But then, what if this were real? What if she truly had visited him? What did her words mean? That he couldn't save Vornado? He shook his head. He would be glad when this operation was over, one way or the other.

BOOK 4:

▼

Attack Plan Bravo

21

Colonel Auguste Guischard, Judicial Police Terrorism
Interagency Tactical Task Force senior commander, adjusted his headset and stared grimly out the window of
the NH90 helicopter as he flew along the bank of the
Seine River over the heart of Paris. The ride was turbu-
lent above the smoking fires of the city below. He shook
his head. It was a terrible thing. He thought the slaughterhouse where *Le Vigilant*'s crew's hostages had been
kept was the worst thing he'd see on his trip to the
grave, but the evacuation of Paris made that warehouse
nightmare fade completely. Below them, shining in the
darkness of the hours before dawn, the red taillights of
Renaults, Citroëns, buses, motorcycles and scooters
choked every road of the city, jammed solid on all lanes
of the highways, going the wrong way on the inbound
lanes. The roads were just as jammed with bicycles and
pedestrians, the mass exodus from the city a ghastly
sight. Since the announcement that Paris was under severe threat of nuclear destruction—an hour after the last
governmental helicopter had lifted off and carried the
politicians responsible for this sad affair to their safe,
cushy underground bunkers—Parisians had frantically
thrown clothes and diapers and bottles of water into suit-
cases, the trunks of their cars, or on the backs of bicycles, and headed in a mad panic to what had been called
the safe zone, a ring around Paris set ninety miles from
the Eiffel Tower, although Guischard knew that even
those in the governmental tents set up for temporary
camps to house the refugees at the ninety-mile limit

would likely die from nuclear fallout and radiation effects. God alone knew which way the wind would blow after the nuclear mushroom cloud bloomed.

The less-evolved members of the population took to looting. The fires at all points of the compass were testimony to that. The panic of the evacuating population took its toll, the traffic accidents jamming the roads soon causing fistfights to break out. The mass fear had led to at least ten thousand deaths and perhaps four times that many severe injuries, but the empty hospitals were useless. Even if the nuclear warheads never rained down from the skies, the damage to the city caused by the panic would take years to repair. Paris, laid out in its horrible wounded, bleeding state, looked like it must have in 1940 when the Nazis invaded.

Below, in the streets, a skeleton force of police, army infantrymen and security officers attempted to patrol the city, left behind to safeguard property in case the attack could be averted, and to try to find those who hadn't heard the warning. Unbelievably, there were some so isolated that they hadn't heard the news. Invalids, shutins, old war veterans. The patrolling force did what it could to evacuate them, and to stop the rioting on the highways. But there was only so much that three thousand men could do in a panic-stricken city of millions. And each of the patrolling officers was deathly afraid themselves. Just before Guischard had climbed into the helicopter he had spoken with a contingent of the remaining force, and every man was trembling with fear, unable to keep from glancing at the sky overhead every few minutes, wondering if they would see the reentry vehicles of the nuclear missiles as the warheads came streaking in at supersonic speed.

Even Guischard himself had trouble keeping the impending disaster off his mind. He was in command of the force patrolling Paris, which meant that he would die with his men. How long would it take, he thought, before the missiles came? Two hours? Two days? Ten? And what would it be like to die under the white-hot heat of a nuclear explosion? Would his nerves even have time to register pain before his body ceased to exist? Would he be awake and conscious one second, mere plasma, subatomic particles scattered to the universe, the next?

He clamped his jaw shut and tried to maintain his outer bravery, directing the pilot to fly to the southeast. But even he couldn't stop himself from glancing out the top window at the starry, smoke-stained sky, wondering if there were any streaks of incoming warheads.

Youssef Tagreb sighed as he shut the last technical manual to the SAD weapons control, the *Systeme d'Armes de Dissuasion* data system for the launching and control of the submarine-launched ballistic missiles. He decided to walk down to the missile control center and drop off the twenty kilograms of technical material there, in case he needed it. He also wanted to get the jumpering of the MCP-5 panel done, so that the ridiculous plastic weapon triggers would be taken out of the launching system's circuits.

He checked his watch—he'd been awake twenty hours, and it might be best to get some sleep before the launch. It was the middle of the night Greenwich Mean Time on Thursday, October 2. Tagreb ducked into the missile control center and put the box of tech data down, then went to the central control console and powered up the entire center's missile control consoles. After a half hour in the room he felt comfortable with his new-found knowledge—it was now "integrated," because he could now correlate circuit diagrams in his mind, with their multiple switches, power supplies, interlocks and relays, to the physical reality of the missile control center's consoles, electronic cabinets and equipment panels. The room was little more than a big trigger, with all the safety protection such a big gun would need. It also fed in navigational data from the upper-level nav center's inertial navigation system, since no missile could hit its target unless the launching point were known to within mere tens of meters. The third input to the room was from the missiles themselves, and the room spoke to the missile computers to instruct them on the targets. The multiple reentry vehicle bus could split the separate warheads as far apart as a hundred kilometers, or could keep them all clustered to form a super punch to a large city. Tagreb had decided that Paris should be targeted by eight missiles, half the payload of the entire submarine, as the city was vast—essentially sixty kilometers in diameter, with civilization going on for tens of kilometers beyond that, and a population within the greater metro area of over fifteen million souls. Two of the missiles would cluster-detonate at the Eiffel Tower, with one supercluster of six warheads going off as a ground burst with detonation at ten feet above the ground. The second cluster would detonate at three hundred meters, and would reach out to destroy anything the first cluster had missed. The other thirty-six warheads would be spread far apart, each detonating with a ground burst over strategic political, demographic and cultural centers.

The selection of the targets had been a favorite subject of Issam Zouabri's. He had papered his commandeered stateroom with charts and maps of France, including Paris, Orleans, Brest, Le Havre, Dunkerque, Metz, Saarbrücken, Basel, Lyon, Marseille, Toulon, Nice, Perpignan, Rouen, Toulouse, Bordeaux, Tours, Limoges and Nantes. The eighteen second-tier cities were each to receive two 150-kiloton warheads, which left an even dozen warheads for the third-tier targets of Vierzon, Le Mans, Moulins, Clermont-Ferrand, Montpellier, Arcachon, La Rochelle, Brive-la-Gaillarde, Montiucon, Besançon, Saint-Dizier and Saint-Nazaire. Within each target city Zouabri had selected ground zero coordinates and burst height, even going to the trouble of compiling exact latitude and longitude figures and launching/clustering order.

Tagreb asked if, instead, Issam would want to hurl some missiles in the direction of Moscow, Washington, Berlin, Frankfurt, New York or London. At first, Zouabri stared at Tagreb as if he had vomited on Zouabri's feet, and Tagreb was about to withdraw his suggestion, but something seemed to move over his features. Zouabri nodded and withdrew one missile to split its warheads between Washington, D.C., and New York, and a second missile to target Moscow, but he would spare no more, reluctant to part with twelve warheads, and returned to his stateroom to decide if the second-tier cities would make do with single warheads or if some of the third-tier targets would be spared completely. Programming the sixteen missiles would take some time, Tagreb realized. He sat at the first console, and with Zouabri behind him—busy making decisions on the retargeting—began the task of programming Missile 01 with the Eiffel Tower supercluster.

Tagreb lost himself in the task, becoming frustrated twice at some of the complexities of the software. The basic problem was that the software engineers for the SAD weapons control system had been either rushed or unimaginative, and the logical software modules were not located where they should be. Tagreb could have rewritten the code in a week to optimize and simplify the target programming modules, but that was obviously not the mission. Once the initial missile was programmed, Tagreb checked his watch. It had taken an hour. As a comparison for his efficiency, Tagreb noted the time and then programmed the second supercluster missile. It took a mere twenty minutes. If this went as predicted, the last missiles targeting the third-tier targets would take less than five minutes each, despite spreading their warheads out over the countryside.

When the third missile was programmed, Tagreb got up and ran up the stairs to the sonar room, just to make sure everything was nominal, and that Karim and Javadi were properly watching the sonar consoles. Tagreb spent fifteen minutes at the console verifying that there were no submarine or surface warship intruders, but the sea was surprisingly empty. For a moment Tagreb felt a twinge of regret at notifying the authorities about the hostages at the warehouse, because this lack of shipping had him worried. Either the sonar gear was malfunctioning—not likely—or the French Navy had cleared the seaway of its normal traffic so that they could find and sink *Le Vigilant*. Tagreb frowned, a dark feeling crossing his newfound optimism. He was two hours away from being able to rise to missile firing depth and launch all sixteen missiles. An hour after the first launch, the whole of French civilization would be dying, and Moscow, Washington and New York would be smoldering cinders. The infidels would be dealt a killing blow, and Issam would take his rightful place as the leader of a new government in Algeria. What about Tagreb himself? What would become of him, he thought? Would Issam offer him a position of power in the new regime, or would he be paid off and sent on his way?

Tagreb stared out over the meaningless jumble of white noise of the broadband sonar display, reaching out with his intuition, trying to find the needle in the haystack, the fatal needle that might be coming for him. Though he trained the monitoring hydrophones toward the bearings of every conceivable noise in the sea, there was nothing but the ghostly cry of a distant whale, the clicking of shrimp and a diesel engine throbbing far over the horizon. He stared up at the narrowband processor output graphs, watching as the computer sliced the ocean into smaller chunks of data and examined them for manmade bell tones, from the higher frequencies to the extremely low frequencies. But the graphs showed nothing of interest. He finally stood up and took off his headset, stepping aft through the access bay to the control room. The ship control watchstanders seemed alert. The firecontrol watchstander, Qutuz Madari, nodded at Tagreb as he adjusted his display, practice-tracking the distant ship making the diesel engine noise. Tagreb leaned over the console and gave Madari a few suggestions, then walked aft to the navigation room. He checked the chart display, making sure their southwest progress continued at four knots. They hadn't covered many nautical miles since they'd left Brest. With the slowing they'd experienced, they'd barely left behind the Bay of Biscay and Cape Ortegal, the northwest cape of Spain, to emerge into the Western European Basin of the eastern Atlantic. They were to turn to the southwest in another twelve hours and make for the gap between the Azores and the Madeira island chain, where his planned track ended. From there, he would have continued south to the Tropic of Cancer. If they were able to launch in the short term, barely off Spain, the best idea would be to speed up and do a maximum-power run south toward the border of Morocco and the western Sahara, where he would scuttle the ship and take the crew to the beach. Figuring out what they would do then was a task for another day, Tagreb decided. He measured the distance from their firing point to the distant targets. Washington and New York were close to the edge of the 6,000-kilometer range of the M45 ballistic missiles, as was Moscow. Had he driven *Le Vigilant* faster down their track the Moscow objective would have become impossible, and that had become important to Tagreb, much more so than the American targets or the French ones.

He decided to go get something to eat, then return to the task of programming the weapons. He would check sonar and firecontrol every half hour, and in two hours the missiles would be ready for launch. Today the sun would rise on the Republic of France for the last time. Tagreb tapped his chin. The missiles would fall on Paris at six in the morning. Perhaps that was too early. He decided to find Zouabri to see if he wanted the missiles to arrive after the hour of the morning commute, which would allow a greater number of kills. But Zouabri had left him a note in the missile control room, that he would take two hours of rest while Tagreb programmed the missiles. Suddenly the long hours and the task in front of him made Tagreb long for sleep. Once the missiles were targeted, they would launch them. With a sixty-second firing interval, it would take sixteen minutes to fire them all, sixteen minutes of pure vulnerability. Then the high-speed run would begin, and the chase of the Western antisubmarine forces, because *Le Vigilant*'s position would be known. He had picked a direction and he would follow it, but it might put him right into the maw of a Western naval force. He would have to fight them, he knew. It wasn't the surface ships he feared. It was their submarines. Tagreb decided to visit the torpedo room, just to make himself feel better. He knew he should stay in the missile control center until his targeting task was complete, but he wanted to make sure the torpedoes were ready in case a lucky hostile submarine found them.

In the torpedo room he found Mubin Sabet and his partner, Latif Vahdat. Both were asleep on mattresses they had laid on the deck between the racks of ECAN L5 Mod 3 torpedoes. Tagreb stepped carefully over them, not angry at their sleeping at their duty station, since not much would happen until the ship got into trouble, and if his instructions had been followed, the ship's torpedo tubes would be cocked guns.

He walked forward to the torpedo tube doors. As he had ordered, the port tube bank had been loaded with Mod 17 antisubmarine countermeasures, a torpedo body built from the ECAN L5 torpedo, but with the warhead removed and a noisemaker and guidance computer installed in its place. The Mod 17 was able to simulate the noise of a transiting Triomphant-class submarine, and, to an enemy, was indistinguishable from the real thing. The Mod 17s were his escape hatch should the worst happen. Tagreb checked them. The one in tube two was powered up with its tube's outer door open. The other, in tube four, was shut down but plugged into power and ready to be activated, its tube's outer door shut. Perfect, Tagreb thought. On the starboard side, the tubes were loaded with ECAN torpedoes. Tube one's weapon was powered up with the outer tube door open. Tube three's weapon was shut down but ready to be started, its tube door shut. Excellent. Tagreb returned slowly to the missile control center, blowing the air out of his cheeks.

Fatigue was starting to come for him, he realized. And fatigue made a man functionally dumber. And made for mistakes. Tagreb yawned again, and ordered his assistant, Wafeeq Algosaubi, to go make some fresh coffee and to bring the entire pot to the missile control center.

As he waited, Tagreb began programming missile three.

The Mark 48 ADCAP torpedo sailed through the ocean water heading south-southwest, at a quiet and leisurely twenty-four knots, its medium run-to-enable speed, which covered ground efficiently yet kept its noise signature down. The unit had been fired six minutes ago. The ten minutes leading up to its launch had been as it had expected. It had lain in torpedo tube number one on the starboard side of the USS *Texas* with the outer door open, fully powered up for the previous half hour, its gyro spinning on the off chance that it would be called to action. Twenty-seven minutes ago, the submarine *Texas*' thin wire-towed array sonar began to feed a narrowband frequency signal down the towing cable into the sonar equipment space, and from there into the computer analyzer of the narrowband processor module of the FY08 BQQ-5E sonar suite. The detection had been nothing unusual, as the entire ocean's frequency spectrum was loaded into the narrowband module for sifting. But this particular "beam" of ocean at this frequency, rather than being mere hay, had turned out to include a needle. On the sonar displays a narrow spike appeared out of the graph at the frequency of the Triomphant-class' turbine generator harmonic. The sonarman on watch alerted the sonar petty officer of the watch, who alerted the officer of the deck, who called Captain Peter Vornado on the JA phone circuit. Vornado had ordered battlestations manned, and within minutes had maneuvered the USS *Texas* across the line of sight to the target, known within the control room as "Master One." The result of the maneuvers was a crude parallax range and "solution" to the target, the rogue submarine *Le*

Vigilant. While rough, the data was good enough to fire a salvo of torpedoes with confidence.

The target solution—the precious package of data containing the target's distance, speed and course—came flashing down the umbilical wire to the Mark 48 torpedo in tube one. The torpedo acknowledged, as if it were a hunting dog taking its master's instructions obediently. The seconds counted down, and external power and signals were disconnected, and suddenly the water pressure at the aft end of the tube rose dramatically higher than the pressure of the surrounding sea, and like a spitwad propelled down the length of a straw, the torpedo accelerated down the tube and emerged into the open sea. The acceleration shut a sensor contact, which closed a circuit that started the fuel pump, opened the fuel valve to the combustion chamber and lit off the ignition circuits in the chamber, and with the propeller windmilling in the water flow, the fuel igniting in the chamber pressurized the exhaust turbine and spun the shaft rapidly. On its own power, the torpedo accelerated rapidly and shot away from the submarine, trailing a long thin data wire, able to tell the submarine what was going on where it was.

The torpedo's course was not pointed to the target, which at the present moment was over the torpedo's shoulder to the left. The torpedo was not sent in a tail chase toward the target, but rather had been sent ahead to a point in the sea where the target was predicted to be twenty-eight minutes in the future.

Eight minutes after launch, a second torpedo emerged from the hull of the *Texas*. Two minutes later, a baseball-bat-sized submarine-launched-one-way-transmitter SLOT buoy was ejected from *Texas'* forward signal ejector. It rose to the surface, its whip antenna springing up so that it could transmit the situation report hurriedly loaded into the unit by Vornado's communications officer. The SITREP reported *Texas'* position, the estimated position of the target, and the current status of the torpedo attack. The message was relayed both by an orbiting maritime patrol aircraft, which was searching for *Le Vigilant* itself, and the orbiting Navy communications satellite. Within seconds the FLASH message was received in the Naval Command and Operations Center of the Pentagon. The watch officers monitoring the battle immediately coded an outgoing transmission to the satellite, addressee USS *Hampton*, with the information obtained from *Texas*. In parallel the watch officers notified the Joint Chiefs and the president. The terror of the theft of the ballistic missile submarine *Le Vigilant* was almost over, or so said the messages.

The ADCAP torpedo drove on calmly, its suicide mission's rendezvous with *Le Vigilant* only another seventeen minutes in the future. Two minutes before that happened, the torpedo would reach the "enable point," where it would arm the warhead and begin its corkscrew-pattern sonar search, seeking the hull of the target with passive sonar, until, after a valid detection, it would shift from a passive search to an active pinging attack, speed up to forty-nine knots and maneuver directly for the target. When it got close to the hull, the magnetic lines of force of the Earth's magnetic field would be so concentrated by the iron of the hull that the magnetic sensors would light up the proximity circuit, and the torpedo's eighteen hundred pounds of HBX high explosive would detonate, blowing the hull of the target open, flooding it, and ruining its day.

So far, there were no new instructions coming down the guidance and data wire from the *Texas*. And no news was good news. The torpedo sailed calmly on, counting the seconds until its destiny arrived.

"What's it say?" Dillinger shot at Mikey Selles from the conn. *Hampton* had rocketed to periscope depth at the first letter of the ELF call sign, the satellite transmission downloaded a few seconds after the periscope penetrated the waves. The message aboard, the ship dived back to the depths where the long-range sonar signals were strongest, at a depth of eight hundred feet.

Selles handed the clipboard to Lieutenant Commander Mercury-Pryce, who stood the OOD watch. He looked up at Dillinger.

"*Texas* has got her. They found *Le Vigilant*. The position and solution are here. They've launched a Mark 48 salvo at it."

"*Fuck*," Steve Flood cursed. "It's over. All this way for nothing."

Dillinger smirked at his second-in-command. "XO, a world catastrophe has just been averted, and was brought to a close by our side, by our old friend Peter Vornado. How could you see bad news in that?" His face grew hard again. "OOD, get us deep at twenty knots. Plot an intercept course to the target, where *Texas* reported it."

"Aye, sir."

"And man silent battlestations."

"Aye, aye, sir," Merc snapped. "Chief of the Watch, man silent battlestations!"

While the crew reported to their battlestations, the room filling up with an absurd number of people, Dillinger glanced at the chart. *Texas* had gotten damned lucky. Vornado's ship had been on the great circle route to the Bay of Biscay from his previous position at the four-day-ten-knot circle. The op order stated that he'd proceed toward Bordeaux, then turn north toward Brest and Britain's Land's End at longitude 5 degrees west, then turn back, heading southwest toward northwest Spain and continue the zig-zag through the ocean looking for *Le Vigilant*. But before Peter got into the pattern, he detected the French boomer, "snapped him up," and pumped out two ADCAP Mark 48s. But Vornado wasn't out of the woods yet.

"How far to the detect point, OOD?" Dillinger's voice was irritated. Merc should have announced that information by now.

"Eighty nautical miles. Intercept bearing is due east, sir."

"Shit," Dillinger muttered. He would have to blast over there at flank speed to be part of this battle, to join the fight. And even at flank, it would take over two hours to get close enough to detect *Le Vigilant*. Which meant Peter Vornado would have to take on *Le Vigilant* alone.

But wasn't the fight as good as over? Certainly the fact that *Texas* had gotten off a dual torpedo shot, having ambushed the unsuspecting French submarine, meant something. He searched inside for his feelings, because all his fears had centered not on the danger to him and the *Hampton*, or to Paris and the other French cities, but to Vornado and his *Texas*. The ghost of Natalie and her dire warnings about Peter dying and something Dillinger needed to do "at the decision point" seemed in the light of day like a silly schoolboy's dream. That was it, he thought. It was just a dream, or a waking fantasy, that carried no weight. There was no Natalie, not in this world. Whatever she had been, she wasn't a Shakespearean ghost wandering through the scenes of his submarine giving him cryptic messages about losing this battle, or Peter and the *Texas* dying. He looked down at the deck, all those images seeming stupid now, and for a long moment he doubted his own sanity. Smokin' Joe Kraft's voice was now much louder than Natalie's had ever been—

You gotta get your head out of your ass.

And Kraft had been right.

"Officer of the Deck, speed up to flank, course east, and code a SLOT buoy to CinCLant telling them we're flanking it in to join the fight, though we suspect we may be arriving too late."

"Aye, aye, sir," Mercury-Pryce acknowledged. "Helm, all ahead flank, right one degree rudder, steady course east. Chief of the Watch, send for the communications officer and step on it."

Dillinger clutched the stainless handrail of the conn, the trembling of the accelerating hull reverberating in his chest. He shook his head. They were too late. Despite his gentle reprimand, he knew exactly how Flood had felt.

After the third missile, target programming became much easier. The repetition made the task quicker each time, until missiles fifteen and sixteen took hardly a minute each. Youssef Tagreb looked up from the missile control master command console at Issam Zouabri.

"It is done. We are ready."

Zouabri smiled. "Excellent."

"All that remains is to line up the hovering computer, rise to missile firing depth and launch," Tagreb said.

"Let it be so," Zouabri said.

Tagreb's belt radio beeped, one of the units he had taken from the second-in-command's stateroom and given to the men in nuclear control, the control room and sonar. "Tagreb," he said.

"Youssef, there is something strange on our sonar screen," Jaul Karim said.

Tagreb ran out of the missile control center, pushing past Zouabri. When he arrived a moment later in the sonar room he saw the screen Karim pointed at. There was a medium-frequency bell tone in the sea. The towed sonar array had an ambiguity in bearing from the conical formed beam, but the sound was loud enough that the waterfall broadband screen showed the same detection to the north, bearing zero one five. The most frightening thing was that the direction to the noise had not changed since the computer had detected it, some three minutes in the past, which was a very bad sign.

"What is it?" Zouabri asked.

"Incoming torpedo," Tagreb said, leaving sonar and stepping aft. "Prayers to Allah," Tagreb cursed under his breath as he punched the portable radio transmit button. "Nuclear Control," he shouted into the radio. Bishr Nassiri stood watch this hour in the nuclear control space. "Nassiri, do you copy?"

"Nuclear Control," Nassiri answered.

"Get ready to shut the throttles and group scram the reactor," Tagreb said.

"We can shut the throttles, but are you sure you want to trip the reactor after last time?"

"Yes, just get ready," Tagreb said. His voice trembled as he sat at the weapon control console. Torpedo tube one was lined up with the Mod 17 evasion device, the torpedo body with the noisemaker and antitorpedo countermeasures in it. The Mod 17 was fully powered up, but not yet programmed. The tube was flooded, with the outer door opened. Tagreb concentrated on the panel, ignoring Zouabri's questions, until he loaded in the same course and speed as *Le Vigilant*. It took a moment for the panel to report back that the countermeasure had accepted Tagreb's presets, but when the lights lit green, he hit the firing key. The tube boomed from two decks below as the countermeasure was launched. He glanced at the panel, seeing that the unit had left the ship successfully.

"What's going on?" Zouabri said. "Will it hit us?"

Tagreb waved him off. "Nassiri, shut the throttles!"

"Throttles shutting," Nassiri said. "Throttles are shut."

"Group scram the reactor!" Tagreb ordered. "Shut it down! Switch off the reactor recirculation pumps!"

"Are you sure you're doing the right thing?" Zouabri said. "Will you have to run the diesel again?"

"No," Tagreb said as he stepped to the forward port console, the ballast control panel. He scanned to the ship control consoles to see ship's speed as he brought up the hovering computer on the display. When the ship glided to a halt, he'd engage the hovering system and stop, motionless in the sea, the old underice tactic he'd been taught in his *TK-17* days. Stopping the submarine, making it motionless in the sea, would avoid being detected by a pinging torpedo that would look for its return echo at a higher or lower frequency, the frequency changed by the speed of the target toward or away from the pinging source, the effect called a Doppler filter. And tripping the reactor and stopping the ship intentionally shut down all the loud, rotating heavy equipment such as the turbines, reduction gear, main feed pumps and the huge reactor recirculation pumps. The noise signature of the already-whisper quiet ship would be even quieter.

Almost immediately the control room grew hot. Sweat beads formed on Tagreb's forehead. It was time for his next tactic. He ran to the navigation room aft of control, where the navigation display showed the ship's track over time extending back behind them. The torpedo was coming from the north. But its bearings had been steady since detection, according to the sonar repeater console hung in the outboard overhead. Finally, now that they were slowing down, the bearing to the torpedo was starting to drift to the left, which meant it was no longer on an intercept course. With luck or skill or both, it would still be on an intercept course to the Mod 17 countermeasure Tagreb had launched.

It was time for Tagreb's next tactic. This one would stop the intruder submarine cold. He stepped back into the control room, the chart memorized, and selected the weapon control panel to the ECAN torpedo in tube two. Like the Mod 17, it was powered up, its gyro spinning, its outer door opened, ready to fire. It took a moment to load in what Tagreb wanted. He programmed the torpedo to continue down *Le Vigilant*'s previous course, two five zero, but faster than the four knots of the Mod 17 evasion device. The ECAN torpedo would travel at twenty knots down the track line of the ship's previous course. Tagreb turned and craned his neck to check the ship's speed. The electromagnetic speed indicator read zero knots.

"Raboud, how is the hovering system?"

"It seems to be working fine," Fayyad Raboud reported.

Tagreb checked the torpedo settings, instructing it to travel down the two five zero heading until it reached a point five miles down the track. At that point, he programmed it to turn to the northeast. That way, before the weapon made for the attacking submarine, it would go to where *Le Vigilant* would have been had Tagreb not put on the brakes. The attacker would detect the incoming torpedo, and if he fired down the bearing line of the torpedo approach, he would be shooting at Tagreb's countermeasure rather than at *Le Vigilant*. It was a hastily improvised technique, but it should work. Tagreb avoided congratulating himself, though, as that would curse the tactic.

When the torpedo readbacks were correct, Tagreb punched the firing key a second time, and the deck jumped again as the torpedo was launched. He checked the panel, watching the unit to make sure it ran down the two five zero bearing line, then turned to course zero two zero fifteen minutes in the future.

There was nothing to do now but wait, he thought as he wiped the sweat from his brow. If he could just keep the sonar system, firecontrol system and hovering computer from shutting down in the heat, he would be able to chase away the attacking submarine.

But that brought up the next question—how would he be able to have the peace he needed to launch the ballistic missiles? If they had not only been found out but shot at by an adversary, it meant their position was known. He'd leave that thought for later. The only thing he could do now was try to protect the ship.

Commander Peter Vornado leaned casually against the edge of the command console, his hands in his coverall pockets, his long, lean form seeming completely relaxed despite the tension of the battle, his posture a deliberate theater for the men and an attempt to communicate to them his confidence, but Vornado was far from confident. The scenario unfolding before them was all too familiar from the exercises they had done in the Va-Capes Operating Area with American SSBNs. No matter how perfect the signal strength to the boomer was,

Vornado didn't trust it. The tendency of the ballistic missile submarines was to launch a countermeasure that sounded more like the target than the target itself.

It had been a tremendous relief to find the boomer on their narrowband sonar system. Vornado had been careful, wanting to drive closer to the target to make sure he didn't lose it, but hanging back enough that the bastard didn't hear them. He looked around the room quickly, taking in the battlestations crew of the *Texas*. He had sailed with a few of the men back on the *Hampton* in the days before the Barents Sea operation. His second-in-command, Lieutenant Commander Henry "the Bull" del Toro, stood in front of the attack center consoles, bullying the junior officers operating the fire-control system. The Bull was a huge man with a surprisingly gentle manner, except when annoyed or at battlestations, when his personality changed and he became frighteningly aggressive.

Vornado glanced at the brass chronometer bolted to the bulkhead above the attack center consoles, then down at the position two display showing the solution to Master One. The position three console was selected to the geographic plot and showed the center of the display as own-ship, the *Texas*. Further south-southwest was a flashing diamond shape, representing Master One, the target submarine. Two thin trails extended from own-ship east-southeast, the torpedoes Vornado had launched, which drove out to intercept the transiting submarine.

"Coordinator," Vornado asked del Toro, "time to intercept?"

The executive officer leaned over the geo plot, checked with the pos two operator, then spoke into his boom mike to the navigator, Lieutenant Commander Harrison "Dick" O'Dea, a recently divorced Notre Dame grad who had once taken a bullet in the abdomen during a drunken brawl in a Chicago sports bar during the Navy–Notre Dame football game. O'Dea leaned over the plot table, then made a report to del Toro.

"Twelve minutes and change, Captain," del Toro said.

Vornado nodded, standing up straight, his hands still in his pockets. Twelve minutes and this fucking nightmare would be over, and he could return to thinking about his broken marriage to Rachel. For a fleeting moment his thoughts returned to her; for some reason the song that was playing when he first saw her had continued to run through his head since he'd manned battlestations.

"Conn, Sonar," the circuit rasped with the West Virginia–accented voice of the humorless sonar supervisor, Senior Chief Dave Simansky, a lanky, tall, dark-haired disciplinarian who was captain of the ship's inter-Navy football, softball and basketball teams, and had rocketed *Texas* to the top of every league. Other than sports, his only interest on earth was the AN/BQQ-5E sonar suite, and when off watch he haunted the crews' mess with his binder of technical bulletins on the intricate sonar system. *"We've got several transients from Master One."*

"Sonar, Coordinator," del Toro barked into his microphone. "Classify."

"Conn, Sonar, believe it to be weapon doors."

Vornado lifted an eyebrow at del Toro. Was it possible Master One was lining up to shoot a torpedo?

"Conn, Sonar, transient detected on bearing to Master One. Believe we're hearing a tube launch."

"Sonar, Coordinator, aye," del Toro answered, his eyes on Vornado.

It could be a torpedo launch or a submarine-duplicating countermeasure.

Vornado waited in the tense minutes while sonar evaluated the noises in the sea coming from Master One.

"Conn, Sonar, more transients from Master One. Conn, Sonar, stand by."

Vornado glanced at the geo plot, then at the chart aft of the conn, evaluating his evacuation route in the event that Master One returned fire.

"Conn, Sonar, no further transients from Master One. No detected torpedoes. But it sounded like several tube launches. We're alert for countermeasures."

"Sonar, Conn, aye," del Toro acknowledged.

Vornado waited, his teeth clenched. The French boomer evidently wasn't run by the terrorists as intelligence had thought. The French crew must still be alive for the boomer to fight like it evidently was. He wondered why, if the target submarine knew their torpedo was closing on him, he didn't speed up and run.

"Conn, Sonar, target zig, Master One, he's speeding up, turn count increasing."

That answered that question, Vornado thought.

"Target zig, Master One," del Toro called to the watchstanders, which caused them to implement new target tracking procedures, since their assumptions of the target's speed and course would immediately fall apart. They would need to understand quickly what the target was doing now, or else both Mark 48 torpedoes would miss. The encounter, so much theirs only five minutes before, was turning the target's way.

"Conn, Sonar, torpedo in the water, bearing two zero two!"

Dammit, that was it, Vornado thought. The bastard had heard him and counterfired. They'd gotten too close, or the son of a bitch had heard their Mark 48s. This was bad news indeed. In the next tenth of a second Vornado would need to make the decisions that would determine the outcome of the battle. He could stand his ground as the torpedo came in from Master One, but that would certainly be suicidal. He could run and withdraw from the incoming weapon, but the noise he'd emit would mark his spot in the sea in case the boomer had fired blindly down the bearing line to the incoming torpedoes. But at least he would live to return to the fight. And he needed to inform the fleet that his ambush of *Le Vigilant* had failed, and that the French SSBN had returned fire.

"Helm, all ahead flank, right five degrees rudder, steady course north!" Vornado grabbed the 7MC microphone. "Maneuvering, Captain, cavitate!" He dropped the microphone. "Radio, Captain, insert SINS position into a Code Four SLOT buoy and load it in the forward signal ejector!" The signal ejector would be better used for a countermeasure to confuse the incoming torpedo, but Vornado had to tell the Pentagon that he'd been fired on. The code four message simply read, "Under torpedo attack by target this position."

As the deck trembled with the ship's acceleration, Vornado felt his heart hammering in his chest. It wasn't fear, it was anger. He wanted revenge. No terrorists fired on his beloved *Texas* and lived to see the sunrise. He leaned over the aft conn rail, stared at the chart and tried to imagine what the boomer captain was thinking.

22

Peter Vornado crouched behind Mario Marchese at the weapon control panel, his expression intense, his jaw clenched. Since detecting the incoming ECAN torpedoes, *Texas* had sped up to her maximum speed of 42.8 knots, slightly slower than the day she'd come out of the building yard. Since the French torpedoes could only go thirty-five knots, they weren't lethal unless something catastrophic happened to the reactor plant that would slow the ship. But in the moments after the sonarmen had detected the ECAN torpedoes, the French target had sped up to thirty-two knots and gone deep, blasting away to the west, as could be expected when it detected the incoming torpedoes. Vornado had immediately ordered his two torpedoes to abandon their programming, since they'd been on a blind run-to-enable, transiting calmly to a point in the ocean where the French sub would have been had it kept up its slow-speed crawl at four knots. Now that it was rocketing away to escape the torpedoes, the units would miss unless they were reprogrammed.

"Both units enabled," Weapons Officer Mario Marchese reported.

"Good, switch to active search mode," Vornado ordered.

"Active search mode . . . selected and confirmed."

"Sonar, Captain, you have own-ship's units pinging?"

"Captain, Sonar, yes."

Vornado shook his head. The weapons were in a damned tail chase of the withdrawing French submarine,

which was less effective than an intercept based on predicted geometry. But unlike the situation with the
ECAN torpedoes, the Mark 48 ADCAPs, in high-speed
search mode, would go forty knots, and if they caught a
whiff of the target and locked on, they'd speed up to
fifty-eight. There would be no escape for the son of a
bitch.

Vornado watched the WCP intensely, the panel's display flashing each time the lead torpedo pinged. After
ten pings, the battle broke their way.

"Homing!" Marchese said. "Homing, unit one!"

The torpedo had gotten three return pings from a single location, each of them passing through the Doppler
filter. It was a hard detect, and only a drastic torpedo
malfunction or the weapon exhausting its fuel could save
the French submarine now.

*"Conn, Sonar, own-ship's first-fired unit has sped up
to maximum turn count. We've lost bearing separation
between Master One and the first-fired unit."*

Vornado looked over at the pos two display. "Sonar,
Captain, aye." The direction to the outbound torpedo
and the target had merged. Always a good sign.

It would all be over soon.

The French Mod 17 countermeasure drove through the
depths three hundred meters below the surface, programmed to run blindly west at thirty knots, but its sonar
module perked up as it detected the incoming pings from
the chasing torpedo. The guidance computer, on recog-
nizing the ping, ordered the Mod 17 to overpower its
turbine beyond the design top speed while two panels
on the flanks of the torpedo body blew off and ejected
twin streamers that flew backward in the flow stream.
The water flow opened both into billowing shapes almost
like parachutes, made of silky material with metallic mi-
crothreads. The foil canopy spread out behind the Mod
17, its purpose to strengthen the signal of the return
sonar ping from the inbound torpedo. The throttled-up
turbine kept the Mod 17 at its normal maximum speed,

but it was burning fuel rapidly and would run out of endurance soon. While it waited for the torpedo to get closer, it powered up the powerful electromagnets that would simulate the magnetic disturbance of an iron hull.

Mark 48 unit one pinged to the target, then listened for the return. It was out there, the range half a nautical mile. The torpedo continued pinging, the guidance computer locked on to the target. The warhead was fully armed and ready to detonate. Fuel level was forty-eight percent, enough to chase the target for quite a while. Closer and closer it came to the target, the distance shrinking. As it homed on the target, its magnetic proximity detector picked up strengthening lines of magnetic force, which correlated to the solid ping return bouncing off the flanks of the target. In its last tenth of a second of existence, the distance to the target return diminished to zero, the magnetic detector output went to maximum, and on command the electrical signal to the low explosive train lit off the blasting cap-like charges, which ignited the high explosive. One thousand eight hundred pounds of highly engineered, extremely dense explosives exploded in a furious fireball.

The explosion reached out and blew the Mod 17 evasion device into a hundred thousand fragments, scattering them onto the ocean bottom. The shock wave from the detonation traveled out at underwater sonic velocity to the sonar hydrophones of the BQQ-5E system of the USS *Texas*, but the sound could easily be heard through the two thick HY-100 steel of the hull. The battlestations crew in the control room cheered.

Commander Peter Vornado glanced at his XO. Henry the Bull del Toro smirked, like a weary teacher dealing with a rowdy classroom.

"Okay, okay, as you were," del Toro commanded on the circuit. "Quiet in control. Let's bear in mind we're still running from an attacking torpedo, people."

The crowd calmed down.

"Sonar, Captain," Vornado called, "have you regained

Master One on narrowband or broadband?" *Did we hit him?* Vornado thought.

"Conn, Sonar," Chief Simansky reported, *"no signal on Master One, narrowband or broadband."*

"Captain," del Toro said, "we have the second unit in the water. We'd better shut it down."

Vornado nodded. "Shut down unit two."

"Aye, sir, Weps, shut down unit two."

"Conn, Sonar, incoming ECAN torpedo number one has shut down."

It ran out of fuel, Vornado thought, smiling.

"Sonar, Conn, aye," del Toro said on the circuit.

"Conn, Sonar, second *incoming torpedo shut down."*

"Now," Vornado said, "everyone can cheer. Helm, all stop. Officer of the Deck, secure from battlestations. Take the conn and bring us to one five zero feet. We're going to periscope depth to pass the word. Communicator, draft a situation report on the sinking."

"Yessir," Selles said, removing his headset and jumping up from the position one firecontrol console.

Vornado leaned over the port navigation plot table as the deck inclined upward, producing a pair of reading glasses from his coverall pocket. They could be home in ten days at a moderate speed, maybe faster if they got a more rapid speed-of-advance in the return trip op order. He exhaled slowly, thinking about how little there was to come home for.

But then, that wasn't all true. He had his friendship with Dillinger. And he needed to make peace with Rachel. And he wondered if he needed to find a new bachelor pad. Dillinger had the new baby there and, with the au pair, he was out of room. True, they were both trying to build new lives, which might argue for Vornado remaining there, he thought as he idly walked the navigator's dividers across the chart. But was he sure Rachel was done? And was he done with her? How could he walk out of the rubble of a destroyed marriage? Was he still in shock? If he were to make the choice of staying with Rachel or leaving her, what would he do? Did he still love her? The writing on the chart blurred in front of him as he withdrew deep in thought.

"Captain, draft message, sir," Lieutenant Fred Easterling, the communications officer, said, interrupting Vornado's reverie. He handed over the clipboard with the message to the Pentagon Op Center and ComSubLant. It was short and to the point. *Le Vigilant* had been transiting at four knots east-southeast in the West European Basin not far from the Bay of Biscay, northwest of the tip of Spain. *Texas* had snapped up the French submarine, pumped out two Mark 48 ADCAPs, run from two counterfires and survived to hear the French sub disintegrate. Mission accomplished.

Vornado frowned at the message and carried it with him to the forward starboard corner of control, through the door into the sonar room.

"Evening, Skipper." Chief Simansky grinned. "Congratulations."

Vornado didn't acknowledge the compliment. "Chief, you have anything on narrowband in the vicinity of the detonation? Or any other tonal from Master One at any bearing?"

Simansky shook his head. "The sea's empty, Captain. We got him good. We shot him dead. He's on the ocean floor and his filthy French nukes with him."

Vornado looked into his chief's eyes and at the sonar screens, trying to reach out with his own senses. What was it that was bothering him, he wondered.

Maybe it was just that it was too easy.

"Very well, Chief. Good work."

Vornado stepped back into control, stepped up next to the conn and looked up at Lieutenant D.K. "Deke" Flynn, the morning watch's officer of the deck now that battlestations had been secured.

"Your report?"

"Captain, ship's at one five zero feet, baffles cleared, two surface contacts, both merchants, Sierra six seven bears east, twelve thousand yards, outside closest-point-of-approach, Sierra six eight bears west, ten thousand yards, also outside CPA and opening. Request permission to come to periscope depth and transmit the contact sitrep."

Vornado nodded. "Very well, proceed to PD and transmit. I'll be in my stateroom."

He couldn't help but feel it was all such an anticlimax. But then, in a disaster like this, would drama be better? He shook his head and walked into his stateroom, seeing it as if for the first time. Rachel's haunting brown eyes with their hint of green stared at him from her portrait, taken last year before the Barents operation. He walked to it slowly and took it off its bolts on the bulkhead and put it carefully away in one of the locker cubbyholes, feeling like he weighed a hundred tons. Cheer up, he told himself. He and the *Texas* had just saved half a continent from nuclear destruction. Not a bad day's work. He smirked and plopped down in his command chair.

Tagreb vaulted down the steep ship's ladder to the middle level from the control room, an ear-to-ear grin on his face as he thought of how he'd just fooled the enemy submarine. Shutting down the reactor had been a touch of genius, he thought. With no rotating equipment, the submarine was making almost zero noise. And with it frozen motionless in the sea, it would not upshift or downshift the frequency of an incoming sonar pulse, which meant they'd be invisible to most torpedo sonars, even as big as the ship was.

"I don't understand," Zouabri said as he tried to keep up with Tagreb's mad rush to the missile control room. "How is it that the first time you lost the reactor, the battery died, and we ended up using the diesel? But this time, we've been shut down three times as long as the first time, and yet the battery keeps working?"

"Main feed pump," Tagreb muttered. He looked at Zouabri. "We had a casualty, a problem that required a huge electrical load. Now we don't. We're not spending our amp-hour budget like we were the first time. That's why."

"How long will it last?"

Tagreb sighed as he sat down at the missile control console. "Bishr," he called on his radio to Bishr Nassiri, who stood the watch in nuclear control.

"Bishr here, Mr. Tagreb."

"Bishr, tell me what you have on the electric plant control panel on the amp-hour meter."

"Sir, it reads five seventy-five."

"Good. Thank you." Tagreb glanced at Zouabri. "Battery will last long after the last missile is launched."

Zouabri wiped the sweat from his hair. The gesture reminded Tagreb that the electronics were roasting without seawater cooling or the air conditioning. And sustained temperatures above fifty degrees Celsius would cause widespread electronic malfunctions and component shutdowns. Which brought Tagreb to the thought that froze his finger over the missile control panel—and that was that, by the time half the missiles were launched, the submarine that had come for them might return, find them from the noise of the missile launches, or the visible streaks of rocket exhaust from the surface, and it would torpedo them straight into heaven. The ECAN torpedoes Tagreb had launched were slower than the submarine they had been chasing, or at least so he had suspected, and there had been no sound of torpedo detonation. Had the weapons gone off, he might have been more confident, but he felt that the submarine must still be lurking out there, searching for them fruitlessly. That is, until the first missile roared from the sea.

Tagreb turned to address Diya Waqar and Qutuz Madari, the two fighters who had some schooling on advanced weapons systems, and who had shown some minimal aptitude for running the missile panels. "Diya and Qutuz, pay attention as I go through this for missile one. I'll launch it, and after that, you will launch number two while I supervise you. After that you will see to the launches while I move between control, sonar and missile control. Do you both understand?"

The technicians nodded, but they were frightened. Zouabri frowned. Tagreb gave him a confident look. "The weapons are all preprogrammed, Issam. They only need to have their computers told to count down and their tubes prepared and fired."

"If you say so," Zouabri said, but he did not seem happy.

Tagreb cracked his knuckles over the panel and glanced up at the depth display. The ship was hovering perfectly at fifty meters keel depth. He brought up missile one on the targeting computer, confirmed it was set to the latitude and longitude of Paris, confirmed that there was to be zero "spread" between the MIRV reentry vehicles so that they would detonate together, and set in the location of the Eiffel Tower as the burst locus with the height at ground level. The next screen of the SAD weapons control *Systeme d'Armes de Dissuasion* missile launching control system showed the status of the Sagittaire/Thales/Thomson-CSF digital inertial-control-and-guidance computer system. Tagreb powered up the computer and spun up missile one's onboard gyro. The missiles on the *TK-17* had taken a full twenty minutes to stabilize their gyros, but the ballistic missiles designed by the French geniuses at EADS Space Transportation, formerly Aerospatiale from Les Mureaux, spun up to stability in a miraculous forty seconds.

An indication flashed on the screen briefly, a cryptic message in all capitals surrounded by a box reading:

NAV01: XR PHASE A SINS FAULT: OUT OF NOMINAL SIGNAL SBR VECTOR

The box flashed for two seconds, then disappeared. Tagreb stared at the display for a moment, then queried the software to try to understand what the error message had said, but none of the error profiles kept the message. He clenched his jaw, annoyed. He knew the missile systems thoroughly, but the error message didn't seem familiar. Since there was nothing in the error registers, the fault had cleared itself, but that was not necessarily good news, because an intermittent error was impossible to troubleshoot.

"I have to perform a system check," he said to Zouabri. "A diagnostic. We have a fault."

"How long with that take?"

Tagreb grimaced. Perhaps too long, he thought, and the longer he went without cooling to the computer systems, the greater the chance of another fault or error creeping in. And eventually they would run out of battery amp-hours. Tagreb needed to launch the missile salvo now, or at least half of it, then start the reactor and get out of the area.

"Never mind," he said. "Diya and Qutuz, we're proceeding with the launch, so watch my panel." Tagreb selected the upper hatch flood-and-vent valve controls and brought seawater into the top of missile one, a thin membrane keeping the water from touching the missile. When the trapped air was gone and the pressure equalized, he punched the fixed function key that opened the missile door. Above and aft of him, the massive muzzle door of missile number one, on the power of the hydraulic system, smoothly and steadily rotated up and open. The missile water protection membrane rupture disc below became exposed, the number 01 shown on it.

Tagreb checked the missile targeting one last time, and it was correct. He selected the LAUNCH AUTO-SEQUENCE fixed function key and pressed it. The screen normally would flash up the symbol WEAPONS OFFICER—COMMANDING OFFICER SIMULTANEOUS INPUT INTERLOCK SIGNAL but that referred to the silly pistol triggers in control and the missile control center that would need to be pulled at the same time. Instead, the software flashed the message SIMULTANEOUS INPUT INTERLOCK SAT-

ISFIED. The missile was fully ready to launch, but there was nothing more to do, as Tagreb had already pressed the autosequence key. The missile countdown numerals flashed on the panel, going from five and rolling down to zero. The deck vibrated for a moment, then just slightly lurched. The noise above and aft of them was loud and rushing for a few seconds, then calmed. The deck sank just slightly again, and all was quiet. On the panel, the status message flashed, MISSILE 01 LAUNCH NOMINAL. The first missile was away, Tagreb grinned. One down, fifteen to go.

Zouabri smiled. "Paris will be a dim memory in fifteen minutes," he said.

On the turtleback hull of the submarine *Le Vigilant*, the rupture disc membrane shattered along prescored seams, the disc coming apart in six wedge shapes. The disk fragments flew out of the way under the pressure of steam roaring out of the tube, the steam formed from a solid rocket engine deep in the belly of the submarine igniting in a reservoir of distilled water. The water flashing to steam increased the pressure in the tube exactly like gunpowder ignition raised pressure in a cannon barrel, and for the next half second the vertical launch tube was simply a vertical cannon and the massive M45 missile was the projectile. In an instant the missile flew out of the tube, not one molecule of seawater touching its flanks, as the bubble of steam from the gas generator followed and enclosed the missile as it rose the two missile lengths to the surface above. As if parted by the hands of a god, the water above separated as the steam bubble blew upward out of the waves.

On the surface above, lazy cumulus clouds rolled slowly overhead on the slight breeze. Sunrise had come an hour before, and the slanting morning rays of the sun painted light and shadows of the slight swells of the Atlantic on the seascape canvas. Far overhead, a seagull orbited above the calm waves. On the horizon, appearing from behind a cloud, a four-engine turboprop aircraft flew northward, oblivious to the rising steam bubble that became visible when it was five meters below the surface. At first the rising steam seemed like a spot of white below the surface, but soon it rose and burst through the waves, and an explosion of foam and spray erupted upward and outward from the ocean. One instant there were only the suspended water, foam, droplets and the bloom of white vapor that had risen suddenly from the sea, but in the next instant a white shape materialized, an oblong, stubby pencil, bluntly tapered at one end, cylindrical through its length, with a steerable rocket nozzle at the bottom.

For a moment the missile continued to rise upward, having been propelled out of the ocean by the steam bubble, but gravity steadily dragged it back earthward, until the missile's upward ascent stopped, and the upward velocity stopped. In that instant the missile hung there, motionless, and just before it began to fall back to earth, a small contact clicked as the missile experienced zero gee at the top of its flight. The zero-gee contact sent electrical current flooding toward the solid rocket fuel ignition circuits, and within milliseconds the fuel at the center of the missile ignited. A few more milliseconds and the fires inside the missile's belly roared to full thrust as the hot exhaust gases poured downward out of the nozzle. The missile's control system took control of the nozzle, rotating it expertly and quickly to keep the center of the thrust vector pointed upward through the missile's constantly changing center of gravity. The missile accelerated from the thrust as the rocket motor forced it abruptly skyward. The ocean and the burst of water at the surface rapidly shrank far below as the missile rocketed to the heavens. A bare moment later the missile pierced the sound barrier and continued in its hypersonic flight as the thick air buffeted its surface, but as it sped up, the air thinned. The blueness of the sky yielded to the black of space. Far below the missile, the Earth's blue-and-green-and-white beauty gleamed, and above it the stars shone in the black heavens.

* * *

Sonarman Chief Dave Simansky stood, stretched and yawned, then cracked his knuckles. His normal watch didn't start until noon. Now that battlestations was secured, he could take a nap and be fresh for the long afternoon watch, which would probably feature the ship getting its orders to return to Norfolk. Simansky and *Texas* had been away a bit too long, considering he had only planned to be out for three days as the hurricane barreled in. But did he feel like a nap or a cup of coffee? As he contemplated the question a flash on the broadband screen caught his attention. It was a momentary bright spot at bearing one nine zero, which didn't correlate to anything—the target had ceased to exist almost due west of them, and this trace was from the east-northeast. Simansky watched the noise disappear on the one-minute history graph, but it was still visible on the five-minute history display. Without thinking he realized he had taken a seat at console zero and donned his headset. He adjusted the ball cursor to the Q5's audio input azimuth. He trained the direction he listened to bearing zero seven five and shut his eyes.

Thunk!

Another noise, sounding like metal on metal. No, not quite, more like the thump of hydraulics moving something heavy. A periscope or a torpedo tube door. From a bearing where there had been nothing.

But after the noise, there was nothing. Simansky initiated a narrowband processor search from the beam to that bearing, but it would be ten minutes of data acquisition before there was anything definitive, which was the problem with narrowband sonar detection.

Simansky shut his eyes and concentrated. When the noise of the gas generator ignition hit his ears, it was loud enough to make him throw down the headset.

"Conn, Sonar, loud transients bearing zero seven five, possible weapon launch!"

The sea opened and ejected the huge M45 missile, the bright orange flames shooting out the rocket nozzle as the unit rose vertically from the sea, leaving behind a column of smoke and vapor. Twenty-four nautical miles to the northwest, a U.S. Navy Lockheed P-3C Update III Orion maritime patrol aviation aircraft, a four-engine turboprop trailing a long, thin magnetic-anomaly-detector probe, had been banking to the south to continue a crisscross search pattern when the smoke trail of the missile came into view out of the cockpit window. For a tenth of second, both pilots froze, their mouths open.

In the minutes afterward, the aircraft came out of its turn and aimed at the point where the flame column met the sea, dived toward the waves and opened a bomb bay door underneath the aircraft's belly. The plane flew low over the waves, its flaps retracting so that it could cruise slowly over the water. The radios of the P-3C lit up with activity across the electromagnetic spectrum as it frantically communicated what had happened to the shore and the communications satellite orbiting high above the mid-Atlantic. The aircraft was five miles from the missile flame trail when the first Mark 50 Barracuda torpedo fell from the underbelly of the plane. As it flew, the aircraft launched two more of the torpedoes. A half mile from the missile launch point, the P-3 ejected several dozen sonobuoys, the sonobuoy field continuing as it overflew the missile launch point, the buoys opening into two parts, the floating portion bobbing on the waves with an antenna raised to communicate to the aircraft above, the other sinking to a preset depth to listen for the submerged target. Beyond the flame trail, the P-3 ejected three more torpedoes, the weapons splashing down into the ocean below.

The P-3's radio communications indicated a high confidence that the ballistic missile submarine would be detected and destroyed. But the antisubmarine commander had his doubts—the six Mark 50s launched had been "snapshots," which meant they were fired blind, with "default" presets, and no information on the target. And it mattered, because shooting a stationary boomer hovering at shallow missile firing depth required the Doppler filters to be disengaged and the weapon to ping actively, while targeting a moving, running submarine required the Doppler filters on, with either active or passive search. The six units launched had mixed default settings, with the first three selected for stationary shallow target settings with active pings at a hundred-foot depth setting, the second three selected to passive search at the deeper stratum. All six were programmed to circle slowly in the sea and search for the target, but it was entirely possible that all six could miss. Getting a hit with a torpedo was a precise science, not unlike shooting down a cannonball with another cannonball. But if nothing else, the commander thought, the torpedoes would force action from the target, perhaps driving him into the widening sonobuoy field being laid by the P-3 as it flew in increasing-diameter circles around the flame trail.

The phone from control buzzed insistently. Dillinger wiped his face at the sink after splashing water on himself to wake up a bit. He picked up the heavy handset, cursing again when he thought of Natalie. When would she be out of his conscious mind, he wondered.

"Captain."

"Sir," Mercury-Pryce reported, his voice trembling, "we have a loud transient. Sonar says it's a missile launch. *Le Vigilant* is still out there."

Dillinger dropped the phone and ran into the control room.

23

Peter Vornado frowned at the position one firecontrol sonar display, trying to keep thoughts of failure from his mind. They'd been fooled by the fucking French boomer, just as they had been during the SecEx exercises. The bloody boomer had launched an evasion device that sounded more like the boomer than the boomer did. And Vornado had bought the deception, despite his training, and stood down after his torpedo detonated on a damned decoy. Which meant that Master One was still alive, alive enough to have just launched an intercontinental ballistic missile.

The terrorists had just won, Vornado thought. And it was his fault. Thanks to his failure, tens of millions of innocents would be paying for his mistake with their lives. He looked up at the chronometer. In mere minutes the missile would be making landfall over Paris. In Vornado's past he had played competitive tennis, and, like many men, many of his life lessons had come on the field of sports. The one he drew on now was what he'd learned from a coach at Annapolis, who had lectured ceaselessly about how to behave when the match was apparently lost, running unending drills on the midshipmen.

"Attention in the firecontrol party," Vornado said to the hastily reconvened battlestations crew. "Obviously the bad news is that we lost the first round. *Le Vigilant* got off a shot at Paris. But we are here to make sure he doesn't get a second missile off. And he's had, because we know his position." The deck began to tremble as

the ship responded to his previous order to come up to
flank speed as he maneuvered the *Texas* toward the
bearing of the missile launch. "We have a bearing from
sonar that correlates to the position of Master One at
the point shortly after our torpedo closed in on him. I
believe Master One launched an evasion device to accelerate to what looked to us like a flank-speed withdrawal,
but I think he stopped and hovered after he fired the
decoy, and stayed there to launch the missile. The intersection of the bearing line to the missile launch and our
previous track of Master One before his flank-speed run
determine our initial position guess at Master One's
launching position. My intentions are to fire a torpedo
salvo at this position. Carry on."

If the crew could hurry through firing point procedures, Vornado could have eight weapons in the water
four minutes from now. Their quick range analysis to
the missile launch point showed it twenty miles to the
northeast. It would take the torpedoes a good twenty
minutes to get there, and a lot could happen in twenty
minutes, Vornado fumed.

"Firing point procedures," he announced, "horizontal
salvo, tubes one through four, target Master One, thirty-
second firing interval."

"Ship ready," the officer of the deck called.

"Weapon ready," the weapons officer announced.

"Solution ready," del Toro reported.

"Shoot on generated bearing!" Vornado ordered.

It was the last thing he remembered.

The missile ignored the beauty of the vista below as the
solid rocket fuel burned out, completely exhausted. A
ring of explosive bolts in the midsection of the missile
detonated, and the first stage separated. Two seconds
later the second-stage solid rocket fuel ignited, and the
missile continued in its upward flight. The sky grew
blacker, the stars became brighter, and the view became
even more beautiful. The second stage soon cut out as
its fuel was completely expended, and a second ring of

explosive bolts fired and separated it. The third-stage engine ignited, and the missile accelerated until the third stage was exhausted and fell away from the main bus of the missile, the vehicle that carried the six hundred-fifty-kiloton TN-71 warheads. The main bus continued to rise from the velocity it had been given by the third stage, but finally it arced over, the Earth's gravity beginning to win the battle to bring the missile body back down. It was completely ballistic now, in a gigantic free fall, no different than a rock thrown skyward by a little boy, flying in a parabolic curve. A third of the way back down, the upper missile body cracked open and what had been the beautifully shaped, aerodynamic nosecone flew apart, pieces of it spiraling and tumbling end-over-end far over the blue Earth, revealing the six warheads of the multiple reentry vehicles, each of them with its own sharply pointed nosecone, all the better to descend at supersonic speed through the air that would grow thick as they fell.

The central reentry vehicle with its hundred-fifty-kiloton TN-71 warhead separated from the main bus first, the explosive bolts kicking it away from its brothers. As all the warheads had the same target locus, they would reenter the atmosphere close together, but not so close that their reentry ionization trails would interfere and cause one to tumble. A small thruster pack moved the first reentry vehicle away from the main bus faster and corrected its trajectory so that it would fall on the correct curve. It arced downward, the earth flying upward toward it faster and faster. A small guidance unit kicked in, checking the stars and telling the thruster pack how to nudge the warhead over just so, to make sure it would land on the precise point in its arc.

The reentry began suddenly, the friction of the air on the nosecone warming it almost immediately as the air grew thicker and began to slow down the hypersonic warhead. For endless seconds, the ionizing flames around the missile and the violence of the shock wave traveling over its flank tossed it in the hellishly hot atmosphere. For that moment in time, it seemed altogether possible that the blast furnace of the air would incinerate the warhead, but as the unit slowed the incandescence grew weaker, until the warhead slowed to the speed of a bullet and the view in front of it cleared. Off to either side and above the first warhead, the other reentry vehicles descended, separated by a hundred meters, falling as if in formation.

The Earth grew closer. Far below, the coastline extended along the horizon. The vista was mostly cloudy, a thin, hazy overcast covering the Earth's surface between the weapons and their target. Not that it mattered to the TN-71 warhead. Its targeting was letter-perfect. The curvature of the Earth seemed to flatten as the unit descended, the tops of the clouds coming closer, until finally the warhead flew into pure fluffy, foggy whiteness. The weapon's altimeter wound down as the target rose invisibly below it. As the altitude approached a thousand meters above ground zero, the warhead's arming mechanism began its clockwork-precise motion, rotating a thick metal plate to allow a passage between the low-explosive charges with the high-explosive, pie-shaped shaped charges. At three hundred meters above ground zero, an exactly precise ignition happened to the six low-explosive train detonators, which were sophisticated blasting caps that blew up the low-explosive charges. The flame front from the low-explosives passed through the passages in the metal safety plate and reached the relatively insensitive and stable high-explosive charges. In a coordinated blast, all six high-explosive charges detonated, imploding the separated conical shapes of pure uranium-235 into a single ball of uranium.

As the first warhead fell through an altitude of one hundred meters, the physics of the uranium shapes subtly changed. When the U-235 cones had been separated, the uranium atoms' nuclei would undergo spontaneous fission, one in a hundred million coming apart on its own and generating either two or three heavy neutrons and a hundred mega-electron volts of energy from the products of the fission having less mass than what had been present previously, the "mass defect" going entirely into the raw energy of heat. Most of the neutrons that resulted from these spontaneous fissions flew out into space—leaked—without causing any more fission reactions. But when the cones of uranium were smashed suddenly together into a compact sphere, an amazing thing happened to these "leakage" neutrons—for the most part, they no longer leaked. A spherical shape had less surface area per volume than any other shape, which so minimized neutron leakage that the neutrons emitted from the spontaneous fissions were absorbed into other uranium nuclei and caused more fissions. This was the chain reaction Einstein had tempted President Roosevelt with, able to level entire cities from the rapid release of energy.

At ninety meters above the fog-shrouded target, the ball of uranium's leakage neutrons were trapped inside the sphere and caused a rapidly escalating chain reaction of fissions. Like a pot of popcorn suddenly going from occasional pops to a frenzied mad roar, the fission reactions climbed with each successive "generation" of fissions, the first causing three, the three each making three more, and those nine each generating an additional three. The uranium in the sphere rapidly underwent billions, trillions, quadrillions of fissions, each one generating the minuscule amount of energy from each fission's mass defect, but as the fissioning increased to a sextillion fissions, the energy was enough to heat the sphere to several million degrees.

What had been the TN-71 warhead was thermonuclear, which meant it was not just a simple uranium device, because the uranium fission bomb—terrifying as it was alone—was merely the trigger. Surrounding the sphere of uranium were canisters of deuterium, or heavy water, rich in protons and neutrons, which in the heat of the fission reaction began to fuse together to form helium, and in the oddball world of quantum physics, the results of the coming together of subatomic particles was lighter than what had existed before the reaction, and the disappearance of the mass resulted in the release of untold amounts of energy, which skyrocketed the bomb's fireball in temperature until the blast had the energy of the surface of the sun itself.

Soon the fireball had released so much energy that it began to separate the reactants that had relied on physical closeness to cause the furious detonation, and the reactions ceased adding to the energy balance as the atoms causing the energy release were blown apart. The fireball grew in diameter, the center of it at eighty-five meters, until the bottom of the fireball touched ground zero, and like the hammer of a Greek god smashing the earth, the fury of the explosion reached out to destroy all that surrounded it. At the blast's center, the fireball grew in width, the other detonations of the five reentry vehicles blooming like stars torn from the heavens. Above the fireballs, the buoyancy of the explosions caused superheated vapor to rise rapidly. As it did, it left a vacuum beneath it, which sucked in air from ground level from all points of the compass and swept it upward into a column, feeding the rising and cooling orange-and-black ovoid high above.

From a distance, there had been nothing but clouds and fog one minute, a bursting sun the next, five more suns joining the first a moment later, the clustered, powerful detonations growing into six tremendous, hideous and awesome mushroom clouds. The heat of the explosions flashed over the landscape, flowing horizontally away from ground zero. After the radiation passed at the speed of light, the shock wave propagated outward at the sonic velocity in air, much slower. Though the radiation effects were severe, the late-arriving blast of the shock wave was severe enough to rip flesh off the bones of anyone standing to watch the detonations.

The miracle of weapon technology elegantly built by the French had had its say in the tremendously destructive nuclear energy release, a release that terrorist Issam Zouabri focused into an avenging angel against the Frenchmen who had subjugated the nation that he loved.

In the moments after the launch of Missile 01, it seemed as if a hundred things happened at once, or perhaps it was simply that Youssef Tagreb's sense of time changed. Tagreb's radio blared out the panicked voice of Jaul Karim, who stood the watch in the sonar room.

"Mr. Tagreb! There are splashes in the water! And the noise of an airplane! And beeping! There are beeping noises! Please come up, hurry."

Tagreb shot a look at his assistant in the missile control center, Wafeeq Algosaubi. "Get ready to line up missile zero two," Tagreb barked before he ran out of the room and took the ship's ladder two at a time. At the top of the stairs in the access bay he vaulted into sonar.

"What is it?" It didn't take long to see the confusion in the broadband sonar panel. The noise of the missile launch blanked out the display for a good two minutes of data, but then there was the trace of something loud and close going from the north rapidly to the south. The only thing capable of traveling past that fast was an airplane, and the only airplane that loud to do that would be an antisubmarine patrol craft.

But that wasn't the worst of it. Along the time axis, at the bearings to the tangent-shaped curve of the airplane flyover, there were loud transients blooming on the broadband display—much too loud for sonobuoys being dropped; these were heavy splashes. And there were light traces extending from the loud transients, which would correlate to . . . torpedoes! So, the beeps Karim heard, were they coming from sonobuoys dropped by the plane or from air-launched torpedoes?

Tagreb grabbed a set of headphones and pulled them on. He trained the cursor to one of the traces on the busy broadband display. There was no mistake; it was the rising and falling siren sounds of a torpedo in an active sonar search.

Which was a relief, Tagreb thought. He searched through the transients and found two more torpedoes doing active sonar searches. One of them was close enough that he imagined he could hear it through the hull with the naked ear. He looked at Karim, but the man Tagreb had put into the sonar space was petrified by fear. Well, at least he had had the sense to alert Tagreb and get him here.

"Don't worry about those," Tagreb said, pointing to each loud moving trace. "Those are active torpedoes. They are pinging at us, but we're invisible to them as long as we're hovering, stopped, in the sea. We won't change the frequency of their pings, so their computers will reject any sound bouncing off us."

"What about the other three?" Karim asked.

Tagreb found the other torpedoes, each of the three quiet. Unmistakably torpedoes, which were loud and not shy about the noise they put out. But these did not put out active sonar sounds. They were passive units, making sine-shaped curves on the display, which meant they were circling in the sea out there, listening for noise. They were trouble, Tagreb thought.

"They're listeners. They could be trouble. But they've got to be shallow-layer weapons only." If the passive circling units were listening for a hovering submarine, they would be listening only in the shallowest fifty meters of the sea. If Tagreb could get the ship deep by adjusting the hovering system, get the boat to the deep water slowly, without much velocity, he could fool both the active torpedoes and the passive ones.

The other noises on the broadband display were a concern. He listened to them. Faint beeps, none of them moving. They had to be sonobuoys, pinging at the hull and uploading a signal to the overhead aircraft. Again, pings were not a problem, because no active sonar sounds were any good against a stationary target, only for something moving. There had to be other buoys out there, passive ones that just listened, but *Le Vigilant* was quiet with the reactor shut down.

Tagreb glanced at his watch. His budget of amp-hours on the battery was being expended while he fought these torpedoes. "Bishr!" he shouted in his radio to Bishr Nassiri back in nuclear control. "Amp-hours remaining on the battery?"

Bishr answered immediately, his voice shaking. The sounds of the sonars coming in through the hull had obviously frightened him. *"Mr. Tagreb, I'm down to one hundred."*

Prayers to Allah, Tagreb thought. The battery was dying. He had to get them deep, and then he'd have to restart the reactor. There wasn't enough battery power to get through five more launches even if the aircraft hadn't come by. Why had he thought he had a full hour?

Tagreb hurried to control, wishing the ship had some countermeasure to use against an antisubmarine warfare aircraft. Back in his *Krasnoyarsk* days, there had been talk about a missile that would fly out of the sail to find an ASW aircraft and blow it out of the sky. But he had found nothing in the technical manuals of *Le Vigilant* about such a system. A shame, he thought. He wondered how long he would have to evade the infidel devils in the airplane. When he started the reactor it would eliminate his advantage of complete quiet. Once there was machinery noise in the water from the reactor systems, the passive torpedoes would be able to hear him. *Only if he stayed shallow*, he thought.

Zouabri stood in control, frowning. "I know you're busy, Tagreb, but what are we doing?"

Tagreb threw himself in the control seat at the ballast control panel at the hovering computer display. It was flashing a warning:

HOV01: DEPTH CONTROL CALC FAULT: PROCESSOR TEMPERATURE RATE

Tagreb frowned. It reminded him of the flashing warning just before he'd launched the first missile. What had the previous warning said? Something about "Nav 01," and "SINS Phase A fault." Could the two warnings be related? He concentrated on the warning, then saw a variable function option labeled DETAILS. He pressed it, and it read:

HOVERING COMPUTER PROCESSOR TEMPERATURE RISING AT RATES OUT OF NOMINAL. COMPUTER PROCESSOR AUTOSHUTDOWN TO INITIATE IN 02:23.

The numerals on the detail message were rolling down toward zero. The hovering computer was too hot, Tagreb realized. He had a little over two minutes before it died. And if the hovering computer were about to fail on high temperatures, so too were the sonar systems and the missile control systems. Perhaps it had been foolish to imagine he could launch the missiles on the ship's battery with the heat of the reactor plant still cooking away the interior. Tagreb realized his hair was soaked in sweat, as was his uniform.

"Tagreb? What are you doing? I need to know," Zouabri said sharply. Tagreb ignored him.

Tagreb dialed in the depth rate on the variable-selection analog knob, rolling the ship's command depth level from thirty meters to three hundred. The second knob was for depth rate, the speed at which the ship would sink. Since the computer would shut down in two minutes, he needed to get the vessel deep quickly. He dialed in the maximum, a full ten meters per second. It would be dangerous, Tagreb knew, because the mammoth submarine would begin plunging to the deep like an out-of-control elevator at the point that the computer died. Absent his quick action, they would continue falling down through crush depth. He watched the panel and saw that the ship had begun to sink. He looked up at Zouabri.

"I'm executing a vertical dive. A soon-to-be-deadstick vertical dive," he said, one eye on the panel. He had wanted to run aft to nuclear control and restart the core, but he needed to be here when the computer shut down in another sixty seconds so that he could recover from the depth excursion manually. Without the computer, the ship could easily become unbalanced and begin to tilt forward or aft. At three hundred meters, that could prove disastrous. He turned to look at Zouabri. The terrorist leader stood between Tagreb and the open door to the navigation room. Behind Zouabri, in the navigation room, there was a flashing light. What was that?

Tagreb got up and pushed past Zouabri and stepped to the door to the navigation room. There on the port row of consoles a red flashing annunciator alarm blinked, large letters spelling:

PHASE A SINS FAULT

Curses to Allah, Tagreb thought. That was what the missile control center's error message had said just before he'd launched missile number one. He hurried to it, part of his mind nagging at him that he stood on the decks of a huge submarine that was plummeting downward at ten meters per second with a dead hovering computer. He looked at the alarm panel, which was an array set up at the number one ship's inertial navigation controller, SINS Phase A. The entire inertial navigation unit was offline. Tagreb scrolled through the software error messages—the damned SINS unit one computer had failed from high temperature. From the reactor being shutdown and no air conditioning or seawater cooling! Dammit, Tagreb cursed.

"Now what's wrong?" Zouabri asked peevishly.

"If this fault happened before the first missile launch, it means our missile missed its target, that's what's wrong." Tagreb looked at the central computer display, hoping that the SINS unit one fault had taken it out of the circuit. The central display read SINS POSITION AVERAGING SELECTED. "Oh no," he said as he left the room and returned to the control room's ballast control panel.

"What?"

"We lost one of the ship's inertial navigation systems. And we lost it before we launched the missile." Tagreb sat in the control seat, one eye on the manual depth indication readout, the other switching off the hovering computer just before it shut itself down. He frowned at the panel, the sweat rolling into his eyes.

"What does that mean?" Zouabri was getting upset, Tagreb thought, but he didn't care. He had bigger problems.

Tagreb turned to him. "Look, Issam, to launch a ballistic missile and get an accurate hit, you must know exactly where on the Earth's surface you are launching from. If your position is incorrect when you launch, the missile will miss."

"Are you saying the missile didn't hit the target?"

Tagreb turned his complete attention to the ballast control panel. He could recover from the vertical dive manually—at least, he thought he could. He selected the central trim pump and turned it on. If the pump failed to start, the ship was doomed and would continue sinking. But the pump came on. Without the computer it was impossible to know when to stop pumping. Tagreb might make the ship too light and it would surface, or he could pump too little and the ship would keep sinking. Mother of Allah, he needed to be four places at once. For the next two minutes he pumped and waited, trying to get the ship's depth to steady.

Finally he was somewhat satisfied, the vertical dive stopped, the ship steady at three hundred meters, but the deck was beginning to tilt aft. They were heavy aft. Tagreb considered pumping from the aft variable ballast tanks to the forward ones, but what he really needed to do was restart the reactor.

"Mr. Tagreb, only sixty amp-hours remaining on the battery," Bishr reported on the radio.

"On my way," Tagreb said into his radio as he flew out of the seat of the ballast control panel and began to run aft to nuclear control.

He was climbing through the hatchway to the shielded reactor compartment tunnel when the explosion hit, throwing him to the deck. His head hit the bulkhead, the pain blinding, dizziness making his head spin. He opened his eyes, but there was nothing to see, because the lights had gone out.

Twenty-five nautical miles southwest of the six rising mushroom clouds, the P-3C Orion maritime patrol aviation aircraft had been banking hard to starboard to deliver another volley of sonobuoys in a frantic attempt to get a better firing solution on the French ballistic missile submarine. The flashes of the six hydrogen bombs came in the windows first, the tremendously bright light causing the pilot and copilot to lose their sight immediately from the flash burns. For a moment they flew the plane completely blind, trying to stop their panic. But seconds later the shock wave smashed into the aircraft, blowing off both wings, smashing the fuselage in half and scattering aluminum, steel and cables over the surface of the sea in the fury of the violent shock.

The blast's shock wave roared over the sea, the southwest portion of it blowing twenty-seven nautical miles from ground zero to the position of the submerged hull of the launching ship, the French submarine *Le Vigilant* and, nineteen miles further southwest, over the hull of the United States submarine *Texas*. The shock wave continued over the sea fifty-eight miles to the west, over the second U.S. submarine, the USS *Hampton*. Over the next minutes the mushroom clouds rose high into the stratosphere, the winds aloft starting to tilt them over to the west, the columns of the mushrooms beginning to mingle together. The force of the blasts smashed downward into the ocean water 297 miles west southwest of Brest in the Atlantic Ocean instead of over the city of Paris, the guidance computers misled by the programming of *Le Vigilant*'s onboard tactical data system, which in turn had been lied to by the averaging function of the two ship's inertial navigation units, since one of them had tumbled badly from the heat of the system in the high temperatures following the reactor shutdown.

In the first minutes after the passage of the underwater portion of the shock wave, the submarine *Le Vigilant* drifted two hundred meters above her crush depth, her lights out, her reactor inert, every electrical breaker tripping open from the buffeting of the ship. The submarine *Texas* likewise suffered from the opening of her electrical breakers, her lights and systems extinguishing, but her crew remained conscious and commenced recovery almost immediately. To the west, the submarine *Hampton* was unaffected by the shock wave except as it registered in the sonar room, making the battlestations sonar-console-two operator's ears ring from his headset. *Hampton* continued on its flank-speed run toward the location of the missile launch, two of her torpedo tube doors open, all four torpedoes powered up and ready for launch.

Commander Burke Dillinger glared at the sonar repeater panel, furious that they had failed in the mission to kill the French submarine. That failure would be reversed this very watch, he promised himself.

24

It was as if time slowed to a halt and every second began to last an hour, and he could tell because the reactor siren, which normally wailed through a complete cycle in two seconds, seemed to be taking a full minute to go from its deepest tone to its most shrill. In the first two seconds after realizing his injury was superficial, Youssef Tagreb bolted to his feet and felt along the reactor compartment tunnel for the battle lantern. He had hurried past here fifty times since they had taken over the submarine, and his seaman's eye had measured and memorized every emergency breathing air station and every battle lantern location. For a moment he slipped on the deck, almost losing his footing and wrenching his back, but he found the lantern and turned it on. It worked, illuminating the space in a harsh cone of light, praise be to Allah.

With the lights out, he would need to hurry to the operations compartment on the lower level near the diesel engine and reshut the battery breaker as he had before. He only hoped he had enough battery capacity to restart the reactor without having to snorkel. Using the diesel in this kind of tactical situation would kill them. He ran across the angled deck of the missile compartment, the inclination from the ship being heavy aft. Tagreb continued through the hatch to the forward compartment and down the ladder to the lower level. He opened the door to the battery breaker cubicle and shut the breaker. The overhead lights flickered, then came on. His radio began to make noise as Bishr in nuclear control began to panic. Tagreb felt the deck, the tilt aft more pronounced each minute. When he arrived in nuclear control, he was winded from his sprint.

Immediately he started the reactor restart procedure as he had before, except this time without the luxury of having power from the diesel. For the next twenty minutes he sweated as he brought back the reactor systems, in the back of his mind worrying about the torpedoes that had been circling *Le Vigilant* like so many sharks. Perhaps the shock wave of the nuclear detonation had damaged them, or the time without detecting a target had made them run out of fuel.

Concentrate, he commanded himself as he almost made a mistake paralleling a turbine on the electrical bus. That could have made the steam turbine jump out of its casing. Finally the reactor was again self-sustaining.

"Open the throttles and give me thirty RPM," he ordered Bishr. As he hurried forward he keyed his radio to talk to Fayyad Raboud, the man on the ship control panel. "Fayyad, I've got four knots speed on. Take control of ship's motion and depth. Ascend to a depth of two hundred meters, and make sure we are steering course west."

Raboud answered immediately. Tagreb rushed forward, the sweat of the previous hour making his coveralls completely soaked, the cool of the renewed air-conditioning systems making him suddenly cold. He stopped in his stateroom, dropped the soaked coveralls to the deck and pulled on a dry pair, then continued to the control room. He stepped to the ballast control panel and restarted the hovering computer. The system booted up and began its self-checks, which would take a minute or so. Tagreb left and ran to sonar, where he restarted the sonar computers and reinitialized the system. It would take a few more minutes for sonar to provide any useful data. He returned to control and started the firecontrol computers, then went back to the navigation room and checked on the SINS computers. During the complete loss of ship's power, the number one unit had gotten worse, but the number two unit had switched to its battery backup system and seemed to be functioning normally. Tagreb brought up the interface computer and instructed it to keep the failing SINS system out of the averaging circuit. The next missile would be launched from the own-ship's position of SINS unit two alone, but that should be perfect to get a hit on Paris.

That done, Tagreb returned to control. The hovering computer was nominal.

"Ring up all stop," he instructed Fayyad. On his radio he commanded Bishr, "Shut the throttles, answer all stop." As the ship coasted to a halt, he checked the depth. They were cruising again at two hundred meters. When the ship's speed decayed to zero, Tagreb reengaged the hovering computer. *It worked,* he thought. He dialed in an ascent rate of one meter per second and then dialed in the stopping depth at thirty meters— missile firing depth.

As the ship rose slowly Tagreb went into sonar and checked the displays. They had lost a considerable amount of data. He frowned at the display. There was a bright noise trail on the entire northeast sector. Could the sonar hydrophones have been damaged? He looked at it more closely—no, the sector's noise signature was changing with time. That was the result of the nuclear detonation, which had caused a "blue out," a billion bubbles in the seawater from the explosion, making sonar reception impossible for much of the compass azimuth.

"Scan for torpedoes. Check every transient out there," Tagreb instructed Jaul Karim and Asad Javadi. "And keep checking the frequency processor output. I want to know if there is an intruder submarine out there."

"Yes, Mr. Tagreb," they both answered.

Tagreb glared at the displays. One good thing about all this—the nuclear miss at least had killed the torpedoes that were after them, and perhaps even knocked the offending Maritime Patrol aircraft out of the sky. They were alone in the sea. He nodded and left, pausing in control to check the hovering system. The ship was rock steady at thirty meters, the deck perfectly level. He checked the navigation room, and was happy to see that SINS unit two was working perfectly. None of the troubles of the first missile launch would affect this one, he thought. He took the ladderway back down to the middle level and into the missile control center. Inside the MCC, Zouabri paced impatiently.

"We'll continue with the launch now," Tagreb said, sitting at the console zero seat and bringing up the guidance computer display for Missile 02.

"Wait," Zouabri said, his voice dangerous.

"Yes," Tagreb said, turning to face his leader.

"The men who launched these torpedoes, the airplane that attacked us. Was it French?"

Tagreb shook his head. "I don't think so." The noise of the torpedo sonars was unique to the American designs, he thought, remembering the exhaustive training he'd had in the Russian Northern Fleet. "American."

"What missile is targeted to Washington?"

"Sixteen," Tagreb said. "And fifteen was targeted for New York."

"We'll launch those two first."

Tagreb lifted an eyebrow. "Are you sure?"

Zouabri nodded. "The only thing worse than our infidel enemy is an infidel trying to stop us from smiting our enemy. Launch your missiles starting with fifteen and sixteen, then proceed to missile two."

"Yes, Issam," Tagreb said.

"Tell me again the targets of the multiple warheads," Zouabri said.

Tagreb selected missile sixteen. "Sixteen is set for Washington, with warhead one targeted at the White House, two for the Capitol building, three for the Old Executive Office Building, four for CIA Headquarters in McLean, five for the Supreme Court building, and six for the Pentagon."

"And New York?"

"Missile fifteen—warhead one is for Freedom Tower

in Wall Street, two for Central Park, three the Empire State Building, four for JFK Airport, five for LaGuardia Airport, and six for Crown Heights in Brooklyn, the home of the Jews."

"This time you won't miss?"

"This time our shots will be perfect," Tagreb promised.

"Good, let the shooting begin."

Commander Peter Vornado tried to open his eyes, but his face was stuck to the cold deck, his eye glued shut. He tried to open the other, but it was wet with something. He raised his hand to his eyes, a flash of pain shooting up his arm. Either he'd broken something or he'd sustained a bad bruise or laceration. He tried again, this time more slowly, finding his face and wiping away the goop that was sticking his eyes shut. He tried to sit up, his head spinning slowly. He stared stupidly at a view he could barely understand. He was on the deck of a dimly lit room. The deck was stained with dark liquid. He put his fingers in it. It was lukewarm, but warmer than the deck, which meant it was blood. His head spun, and he felt sicker than he had felt since the *Stolen Arrows* run. What was it that had hit him? He knew he was in the control room of his submarine, and that they had been pursuing the French ballistic missile submarine, but other than that, he had lost his memory of what had happened before being dashed to the deck.

He looked around in the darkness for another conscious soul. Only Henry the Bull del Toro showed signs of life.

"XO," Vornado croaked in a raspy voice. "What happened?"

"Whoa, Captain," del Toro said, his gentle voice odd coming out of his massive body. "You've got yourself a nasty head wound; you're bleeding everywhere."

"I think I'm okay," Vornado said, wiping his forehead and looking at the room. "What in God's name did this to us? Did we get hit with a torpedo?"

"I don't know, sir. I remember going to firing point procedures."

Vornado remembered suddenly. The French ballistic submarine was out there. He tried to stand, the dizziness making him weave. "Lights are off, XO. Something hit us hard. Shock must have tripped all the breakers."

Del Toro looked up, as if scanning the surface. "Wouldn't surprise me if it was some kind of nuke."

Vornado nodded. "But the Triomphant-class doesn't have antisubmarine nukes."

"I know, but they've got ICBMs. Maybe the missile they launched didn't get the right target. Maybe it fell down on the launching point."

Vornado looked at del Toro, a smirk coming to his face. "You think he may have missed?"

"Fuck, yeah," the XO said. "Nothing else has the force to hammer us like that except a torpedo. And if it had been one of Le Vigilant's fish, we would have heard it. And we'd be on the bottom of the ocean now. It was his nuke, Captain. He tried to shoot at Paris and his aim was off. Or maybe he targeted it at us, you know, missile goes straight up, then back down, zero-altitude burst, one way to kill us."

"I guess," Vornado said. "Maybe, but that would be the last tactic I'd use against another submarine. The entire world knows where he is now."

"If he still exists. That thing could have hit him as hard as us. For all we know, he's already dead and gone."

"That would be a blessing."

"Damn straight." Del Toro stretched gingerly. "I'll get the battery breaker myself."

"Anyone else awake in here except us?" Vornado reached into the overhead to turn on a battle lantern. When the lamp clicked on he pulled it down and shone it on the unconscious control room crew. They must have taken one hell of a shock by the looks of the piled-up bodies.

Del Toro shook his head. "We're it."

"Go." Vornado found a coiled 7MC microphone. The internal communications circuits were fitted with battery backup systems, as it would be a bad day when they couldn't talk to each other. "Maneuvering, Captain." There was no answer. "Maneuvering, Control, answer up." Still nothing. It was worse than he thought. He turned his head to see the ship control panel. The Bourdon tube backup pressure gage showed them drifting at 600 feet, but they were sinking, and the deck had inclined downward. Vornado stepped over groggy bodies to get to the ballast control panel. He selected the hovering system and blew high-pressure air into depth control tank number two, the system automatically shutting the vent valves and opening the seawater valves to let out the water. The ship was a few tons lighter after a few seconds. Now they were drifting up. He looked over at the chief of the watch, who blinked. Vornado slapped the man's cheeks.

"Chief, come back to earth here," Vornado said.

The men began slowly to wake up, the sound of groans filling the room.

The lights suddenly clicked on just as the 7MC speakers blared out the voice of Engineer Mike Logan. *"Control, Maneuvering, reactor scram, all breakers tripped."*

Vornado lunged for the 7MC. "Maneuvering, Captain, commence fast recovery using emergency startup rates!"

Logan's voice crackled on his transmission—the shock must have damaged the circuit. *"—already started."*

That was close enough to an acknowledgment. The fans in the overhead suddenly restarted as the nonvital buses came back to life. The firecontrol screens lit up for a moment, then went back out. The firecontrol technician of the watch reinitialized the systems and nursed them back. Vornado limped to the door to sonar and found the sonar screens back on. Chief Simansky stood with caked blood on his face, a crack in the glass of the central panel.

"You okay?"

"I'll live, Captain," he said emotionlessly. "I wish I could say the same for the Q-5."

"Why, what's the matter?"

Simansky looked at Vornado like a surgeon standing over a flatlining patient. "It's not good, Captain, every self-check is failing. I'm laying to the sonar equipment space to get on it."

Vornado wanted to curse, but backed away so the chief could get by. In frustration, he found the 7MC microphone. "Maneuvering, Captain, Engineer, JA." He dropped the mike and picked up the JA phone handset.

"Engineer," Logan's distorted voice came over the phone.

"What's the status of reactor startup?"

"Sir, we have—" the sound of the reactor siren suddenly blared in Vornado's ears. "Shit. Sir, reactor scram. What? *Oh Jesus, fire in the aft compartment!*"

A burst of adrenaline shot through Vornado's veins as he dropped the phone and lunged for the 1MC microphone. He clicked it and his voice boomed throughout the ship. "Fire in the aft compartment, fire in the aft compartment, casualty assistance team, lay aft! All hands, don EABs!" He dropped the mike and shouted to the chief of the watch. "Chief, sound the general alarm and rebroadcast the announcement!" Vornado reached into the overhead, to a cubbyhole containing emergency air breathing masks. He pulled one out and put his face into it, and plugged the regulator hose into a manifold. Only then did he pull out the other masks and start strapping them onto the men. The fans shut down as del Toro ran into the room looking like an enormous insect in his mask and air hose.

"I'm going aft, Captain," he said.

"Report as soon as you can," Vornado said. "Chief of the Watch, blow depth control to sea and bring the ship to one five zero feet!"

"Blow depth control and come to one five zero, aye, sir," Petty Officer First Class Swillerton replied formally.

Vornado concentrated on his breathing. Acting frightened would panic the crew. He took his breaths slowly and evenly as he waited for the crew aft to fight the fire.

A figure materialized next to Vornado, the battlestations officer of the deck, Lieutenant Nate Hanscomb, an athletically built man of medium height with an air of confidence no matter the situation. His breathing seemed louder than normal with the mask.

"Good to have you back, OOD," Vornado said, wondering if his cool act would hold up to Hanscomb's scrutiny. The younger man was adept at cutting through facades, but up till now he'd never been able to read Vornado.

"Sorry, Captain. What happened?"

"XO thinks the boomer's own nuke fell back on top of him. All we can hope is the boomer is in as bad shape as we are, because short of a miracle we won't be landing any punches on his jaw for a while. We've got a fire in the engineroom. XO laid aft to see to it."

"I've got the picture, Captain."

"Get the communicator to code a message into a SLOT buoy," Vornado ordered. "Give our position and our assessment of what went down with *Le Vigilant*, and report that we have a severe casualty."

"I'll have it coded, Captain," Hanscomb said, "but if it was a nuke detonating topside, the electromagnetic pulse will make radio communication impossible. EMP's a bitch."

He was right, Vornado thought. Still, it was worth a try.

"Send it anyway," Vornado said. He frowned as smoke began to fill the room, a small bit of haze at first, then thicker. "OOD, we need to prepare to emergency ventilate." The smoke came billowing in then, the black, noxious gases making the room immediately thirty degrees hotter. What the hell was holding up del Toro's report?

"Maneuvering, Captain, status of the fire!" he shouted into the 7MC.

He got the most chilling answer of all—silence.

Commander Burke Dillinger glared at the sonar repeater panel. The news was not good. There was a nuclear-detonation-induced sonar blue out from bearing 060 all the way to 085, and in between there was nothing detectable by the Q-5 sonar system. It was all loud white noise, hundreds of billions of bubbles popping and flowing and gurgling, and the bubbles would be rising for hours, perhaps even days, and during that time nothing between the blue out and the *Hampton* would be audible. Even narrowband processing would be useless, despite its talent for picking the baby's voice out of the roar of the crowd. As bad as it was, it was even worse because of the position of the missile launch. At the point that *Le Vigilant* had launched, Dillinger had done an immediate range maneuver, driving the ship fast to the right of the bearing line to the launch, then left, the computer calculating range based on the bearing drift and *Hampton*'s speed across the line of sight, the distance calculated all the easier because the noise from the launch had zero speed. And the detonation that had happened fifteen minutes later that caused the blue out was on the other side of the missile launch point. Which meant *Le Vigilant* was between *Hampton* and the blue out. And so was the USS *Texas*. Somewhere to the northeast, in that shroud of sonar noise, were both ships; one he had to kill, a second he had to spare.

Dillinger felt the maddening tingle up his spine again, but consciously ignored it as he ordered the ship back on a flank-speed run due east toward the missile launch point. It no longer mattered if the French ballistic missile submarine heard their approach—they were out of time. Odds were, if the boomer had missed with his initial weapon shot, he was right then fixing whatever problem had caused the miss. The next missile to leave the maw of his launch tubes would be dead on. And Dillinger had to fill his hull with Mark 48 ADCAPs before that nightmare became reality.

Dillinger turned to Lieutenant Eddie Scottson, the battlestations officer of the deck. "OOD, you got the launch plotted on the chart?" Dillinger knew the answer; he'd watched the quartermaster transfer the position from the firecontrol system, but he wanted to get the OOD away from the crowd.

"Yes, Captain," Scottson answered, nodding his large head.

"Show me. XO? A moment please?"

Steve Flood walked from his spot in front of the attack center consoles to the port aft corner of the room at the navigation plotting table. Dillinger leaned over the chart, imagining what the sea would look like from high above, as if the scale of the chart below his eye were instead the Earth's surface viewed from orbit. Where was *Texas*? And where was the target?

"Yes, Captain?" Flood said, looking up at Dillinger with his light brown eyes. For just an instant Dillinger remembered the Barents run in the moments before he had fired at the enemy. Hadn't he leaned over a chart table in a control room identical to this one? And hadn't Steve Flood been there then, but as officer of the deck instead of as his firecontrol coordinator? And right next to Flood had been Natalie D'Assault, his executive officer and advisor. He remembered the way she had been then, the way she stood, the way she wore her coveralls, the way she looked wearing the single-headphone wireless headset, her hair shimmering in the light of the control room. In that battle, he had stood side by side with her, fighting the vicious enemy, the two of them bonded closer than any two human beings other than mother and child. And, the thought came to Dillinger, where was she now, right now? The answer seemed to invade his mind as if from outside: *She was here, she stood right there at the chart table with Flood and Scottson, as if leaning over it to decide on strategy.* Dillinger shook his head, as if willing the strange feeling to leave him.

"What did you say?" he asked Flood.

"I said, the position of *Le Vigilant* is inside a circle drawn around the missile launch point. We know he was there at time zero." Flood had grabbed a compass and the quartermaster's calculator, then inscribed a circle an inch in diameter around the launch point. "That's the five-knot circle, the radius equal to the distance traveled by a five-knot target over the twenty minutes since the launch." He widened the compass and drew a larger circle. "Ten knots." He widened the compass again and drew the fifteen- and twenty-knot curves, then put down the maximum speed of the French submarine. That circle almost touched the position of the *Hampton*. Dillinger nodded. "The trouble is, Skipper, that from where we are, the blue out is interfering with our ability to see the bastard." Flood pulled the drafting arm over and drew a straight line from the lit own-ship's position dot out to bearing 060, then another one to bearing 085. "This sector of the sea, from where we are, is invisible due to the blue out. But look what happens if we change course to east-southeast, say one one zero. If we go this way," Flood said, drawing another bearing line from the lit position along bearing 110, "we'll move to the south part of where the maximum-speed circle is now, and by the time we get there, at time fourteen twenty Zulu time, we'll intersect the southern part of the ten-knot circle." Flood calculated frantically again. "At this point here, Captain, anything that was going less than ten knots will be *north* of us while the blue out will be northeast. If we drive out on course one one zero, then slow here in twenty minutes, we'll drive the target *and* the *Texas* out of the blue-out bearing. Not only that, we'll have bearing separation between the two ships. We can fire on *Le Vigilant* without putting torpedoes on the *Texas*."

Dillinger looked down at Flood's chart. Flood would make a goddamned good captain, he thought, wondering how much credit he himself could take for training him.

"What do you think, OOD?" Dillinger asked Scottson. He had already made up his mind, but it was important he not overlook something. In a situation like this, the OOD was supposed to act as counterpoint to the XO's reasoning, as a final check that they didn't do anything stupid. Scottson made a good pessimist, Dillinger thought, but he and Flood got along well, which would make it more difficult for the younger officer to play devil's advocate.

Scottson frowned at the chart. "It's conservative, Captain. Odds are this guy isn't blasting out of there at high speed. If anything, he's using the blue out as cover. Fuck, if it were me, I'd drive right into the blue out. You'd never find me in all those bubbles. But even if he's headed there at fifteen knots, we'll still have bearing separation between the blue out and *Le Vigilant* to hear him. If he goes twenty knots, though, he'll reach the blue-out zone and we'll miss him."

Dillinger nodded. "OOD, change course to one one zero. Maintain flank, and watch the chronometer. Make sure you slow at fourteen twenty."

"Aye, Captain," Scottson acknowledged. "Helm, right one degree rudder, steady course one one zero."

"Sonar, Captain, supervisor to control," Dillinger called to Senior Chief Tom Albanese. In no time Albanese stepped up to the plot table, his wiry body and flaming red hair somehow reassuring to Dillinger during a time when he could desperately use reassurance.

"Gentlemen," Albanese said to the senior officers.

Dillinger knew Albanese, despite his athletic frame, was a smoker, and occasionally smoked in the sonar room during the midwatch, which was expressly forbidden, but condoned by the officers of the deck who had been trained by the genius of a sonar operator. Dillinger looked at him and snapped his fingers three times. Albanese smiled and produced a cigarette and a lighter. Dillinger lit the cigarette and took a puff. He almost never smoked, but somehow in a situation like this, standing next to Albanese, it made him feel better.

"Go ahead," he said to Albanese. The sonarman lit his own cigarette and offered one to Scottson and Flood. Scottson shook his head but Flood accepted the smoke.

"Senior Chief," Dillinger said, jabbing his cigarette at the chart's ten-knot circle, "we're here, the blue out is here, and *Le Vigilant* is somewhere in this circle. We're going to slow to eight knots here, at time fourteen twenty, and peek north into this circle. I expect to snap up *Le Vigilant* almost immediately. If we don't, I'm going to drive us northwest, toward the missile launch site, and see if we get him there. It's possible he hasn't left the area, crazy as that sounds."

Albanese nodded and glanced at his watch. He stubbed out his cigarette on the bottom of his boot. "We slow in ten minutes? I'd better get back to sonar, Captain."

"Good luck, Senior," Dillinger said, clapping the sonarman's shoulder, then discarding his cigarette butt. His heart pounded as he waited for the ship to reach the point at which he'd commanded Scottson to slow down. He told himself it was the nicotine and not fear.

Peter Vornado sweated under his emergency breathing air mask. The lights were on, but the control room was as dark as midnight from the thick, noxious smoke. The rule was to get the fire put out first, and only then ventilate the ship, but the smoke was starting to seep inside their masks. Already two of the men in the room who wore beards, and hence had poor air mask seals, had collapsed to the deck from smoke inhalation, and odds were right now they were dying. There had been no word from aft since the fire broke out. As the fire raged unchecked in the aft compartment, soon every man there would soon be dead, and with no one to combat the fire, every system aft would malfunction, one after the other, and when the hydraulic plant failed, they would no longer be able to operate the hovering system to stay shallow. And soon the entire electric plant would be gone.

As if listening to Vornado's thoughts, the lights—barely perceptible in the smoke-filled room—went out, as did all the systems that had been operative. The ship was drifting now, submerged and helpless. There was nothing they could do except bubble the ballast tanks from the emergency blow system, since the air that operated the valves came from the same air banks that would lighten the ship. Vornado could surface and open the hatches, and if he absolutely had to, abandon ship, but that would expose the crew to being torpedoed by the damned French submarine. And as long as he had torpedoes, he wouldn't surrender to the casualty. They might be dying, but there remained a mission to do. He coughed under his mask, thinking he must be inhaling smoke, because that last thought was absurd. Two hundred feet beneath the waves, in a smoke-filled ship engulfed in flames, with not a single electrical circuit energized, they had minutes, not hours, before death came for them.

Vornado's options were rapidly shrinking.

"Missile fifteen," Youssef Tagreb announced. He sat in the chair after having sprinted up the steps to the upper level to check on the inertial navigation system one last time, but unit 2, the phase B SINS, was functioning perfectly, and it was the one fed into Missile 15's targeting computer. Tagreb checked the targeting one last time. The warheads all had their specific instructions, and with the reactor operating and the air conditioning going full blast, the electronics would perform as designed. He scanned through the error message screen one final time, just to make sure all was nominal. He smiled. Perfect.

Well, not exactly perfect. The sonar system was having trouble reinitializing the narrowband processors after the explosion, but it was healthy enough to detect the gigantic blue out so close to them that they were shrouded from any incoming torpedo sonars. No invading submarine would find them now, assuming the infidel had survived the nuclear detonation, which was perhaps the best thing about the miss. Tagreb would never have thought of using the ICBMs to defeat an attacking naval force, but that is essentially what had happened. There was no one out there—the airplane that had been impolite enough to launch the torpedoes at them was gone, the torpedoes had shut down, the infidel submarine was either paralyzed or on the bottom, and the Western world did nothing except tremble and wait for the vengeance of Allah.

Tagreb shot a quick smile at Zouabri, who nodded confidently. Tagreb vented and flooded the muzzle door of Missile 15, and when the indication flashed that pressure was equalized, he hit the variable function key OPEN MISSILE DOOR. With a quiet hydraulic noise far aft, the upper door to tube fifteen opened slowly, then came to rest with the protective membrane exposed to the seawater. Above the submarine, the sun had come out of the clouds, and the waves and bright light interacted to make a shimmering net of bright highlights to move across the turtleback of the ship.

One more button, and the missile would be away. It would be good luck to check the targeting and navigation systems one last time, Tagreb thought.

"This is the captain, I have the conn," Dillinger announced in a loud, angry voice, his hands clasping into fists. "Helm, all stop, mark speed ten knots! Sonar, Captain, slowing at the planned point-of-intercept! Attention in the firecontrol party. We're slowing now to a search speed of eight knots, slower than I'd like to do target motion analysis, but we're going to have to keep our speed down to minimize own-ship's noise and strain to hear any emissions from the target. My intentions are to maintain course one one zero while sonar does a full-spectrum search. If we detect the target, I will come around to the west—turning toward the target—to get maximum speed across the line of sight and nail down a firing solution. Gentlemen, I do *not* intend to waste a single second. The instant we have a curve, I want to maneuver. I will power us through the turn and steady up on course west, and I want an immediate leg-two curve and a call of firing solution. Remember, people, perfection is the enemy of good enough, and good enough accomplishes the mission. Everyone fucking got that? Let's take this son of a bitch down before he gets off another goddamned missile. Carry on."

Dillinger glared at the sonar repeater screen as if he could intimidate it to produce the sounds of the target.

"Sir, speed ten knots!" the helmsman called.

"Very well," Dillinger said. "All ahead two-thirds. Sonar, Captain, steadying on speed eight knots. Report all sonar contacts!"

"Captain, Sonar, aye," Albanese said over the circuit. *"Stand by."*

Dillinger counted to ten impatiently. Just as he was about to open his mouth and scream at Albanese, the circuit clicked.

"Conn, Sonar, sonar holds two contacts; Sierra One bearing zero zero eight, believe possible submerged warship, no turn count, and multiple transients coming from the target. Second sonar contact, Sierra Two bearing zero zero nine, this target indeterminate, definitely not a surface ship, also no turn count, multiple transients, and . . ."

"Captain, data incoming from sonar, we're getting a curve on both," Flood reported.

"Very well, Coordinator. Sonar, Captain," Dillinger said through clenched teeth, "are you *sure* you don't just have a single contact?" Two contacts with no screws turning, both found with transient noises? It was one submarine, Dillinger thought. Albanese was wrong this time.

"Captain, Sonar, we hold two definite contacts, both close, inside twenty thousand yards, excellent signal-to-noise ratio, and we have deflection/elevation differences to the targets—they're at different depths. Also, Sierra One is operating rotating machinery. Sierra Two is not."

"Sonar, Captain," Dillinger called, "is it possible Sierra Two is a failed decoy?"

Dillinger could almost see Albanese shaking his head. *"Captain, Sonar, no, believe Sierra Two to be the USS Texas and we believe there is some kind of casualty going on, high levels of white noise from Sierra Two. He could be flooding."*

Dillinger glanced at Scottson. Jesus. "Coordinator, designate Sierra One as Master One."

"Coordinator, aye. Captain, we have a curve," Flood said. "Recommend maneuver."

"Helm, all ahead full, left ten degrees rudder, steady course west."

"Ahead full, aye, left ten degrees rudder, aye, engineroom answers all ahead full, my rudder is left ten degrees, steady course west, aye."

Dillinger glanced at the speed indicator. He'd best slow down or he'd lose the target. "Helm, all ahead standard."

"Ahead standard, aye, engineroom answers ahead standard, passing course north, sir."

Dillinger clenched his jaw as he waited. He stepped over to Lionel Tonelle's weapon control panel and checked the torpedo status.

"Steady course west, sir," the helmsman reported.

"Helm, all ahead one-third. Coordinator, get a curve. Sonar, Captain, steady on leg two."

"Sonar, aye. Conn, Sonar, we have a transient from Master One. Sounds like . . . a missile door coming open."

"Oh fuck," Dillinger muttered to himself. "Snapshot tube one!" he shouted. He couldn't afford to waste any more time. He had to send out a torpedo *now* or else suffer that *Le Vigilant* would launch another missile.

"But, Captain," Flood said, his eyes wide, "we'll have both contacts in the torpedo search cone!"

"We have Master One shallow and the *Texas* deep," Dillinger said. "Weps, torpedo presets, floor setting two hundred feet! Set the unit for immediate enable, medium-to-medium, passive snake mode, down the bearing line!"

"Aye, Captain," Tonelle reported. "Settings input."

"Set," Mikey Selles, the position two operator called.

"Stand by," Tonelle said.

"Shoot!" Dillinger ordered.

"Fire," Tonelle said, pulling the torpedo trigger.

The deck jumped as the torpedo was launched.

"Conn, Sonar, own-ship's unit, normal launch!"

"Snapshot tube two," Dillinger ordered, and within fifteen seconds a second torpedo was launched, bound for the combined bearing to both submarines, one about to launch a nuclear missile, the other a friendly submarine commanded by Dillinger's best friend.

Five minutes before—at least Vornado thought it was five minutes, as there were no clocks and every minute in the hellish emergency had become an hour—he had sent Lieutenant Commander Henry del Toro aft to see what the status was. None of the sound-powered phone systems worked, so he had been unable to make a report, but Vornado hoped that del Toro would find a way to get to the aft compartment without the fire blasting into the reactor compartment. He felt someone jostling him, then a muffled, distorted, shouted voice.

"Skipper, it's me!"

"XO," Vornado said. "What's the status?"

"It's bad, Captain. I got to the hatch to the reactor compartment shielded tunnel. I'm sorry, sir, but the flames were blasting against the hatch; it's like someone was holding a blow torch to the hatch window." The executive officer huffed, trying to catch his breath. "I think . . . sir, I think the engineering crew are all dead. And we're next. We've got to abandon ship, sir. It's over. For us, the battle's over."

Vornado took a breath. Could this situation possibly get any worse, he wondered.

The sound of a torpedo screw came in through the thick metal of the hull, then a second one.

Obviously, he thought, it could get worse.

And with that thought the room began to tilt and he became immediately dizzy. Something was terribly wrong, Vornado thought. Somehow the noxious poison of the smoke must have gotten under his mask, or it had contaminated the breathing air system.

It was his last conscious thought before he hit the deck.

25

"Conn, Sonar, the bearings and deflection-elevations to Master One and the Texas have merged," Senior Chief Tom Albanese said, his voice trembling slightly. *"We have zero bearing separation."*

Steve Flood looked up at Dillinger, who stood with his arms crossed on the conn. "Captain, that's it, we have to shut the torpedoes down. We'll hit the *Texas*. They're already in trouble, Skipper; they may not be able to run."

Dillinger stared at the sonar screen. Albanese was right. It was miserably fucked up, and all he needed to do was drive the ship further west to drive the bearings to the two ships—one friend, one foe—apart enough to allow a hit on the target without killing the *Texas* and, with it, his lifelong friend.

"Conn, Sonar, transients from the bearing to Master One."

Dillinger shook his head—Master One, *Le Vigilant,* was about to launch another ICBM, and this one surely wouldn't miss. The torpedoes were already on the way. He couldn't just shut them down now. Odds were, Master One was the closer contact.

"Conn, Sonar, loud transients from the bearing to Master One, but believe these are from *Texas.* Conn, we believe the closer contact is the *Texas.*"

Flood's eyes were huge. "Skipper, *Texas* is between us and *Le Vigilant.* The torpedoes will hit *Texas,* sir, we *have* to shut down the torpedoes! Sir—"

Flood's mouth froze open, the syllable dying in his throat.

The noise of the air handlers stopped.

The whine of the 400-cycle electricals ceased.

The room became whisper-quiet. Dillinger continued to breathe, but as he turned and scanned the room, not a soul moved. One of the plotters at the navigator's manual plot table—the backup to the firccontrol computers—had dropped his pencil. It hung motionless in the air.

Dillinger stared at the firecontrol computers, the bearings to *Le Vigilant* and *Texas* identical. He looked at the weapon control console, the torpedoes frozen in their headlong dash toward the target, but likely to simply hit Vornado and the *Texas* unless he shut them down.

Which meant the battle couldn't be won. If he shut down the weapons, *Le Vigilant* would get her missile launched and tens of millions of Frenchmen would die. If he let the torpedoes continue, they would stupidly vector in on the *Texas* and kill his fellow Americans and his Annapolis roommate, who was the man who had saved his life in the Barents. His life and Natalie's.

Natalie.

He felt her suddenly. When he had stood in the control room of the USS *Tucson* in the Barents Sea and prepared to fire on the enemy submarine, she had stood just to his right, her left shoulder almost touching him, her body sometimes brushing his. In the time-warped control room of the USS *Hampton*, he felt her spirit in the exact same place. He turned his head, at first seeing merely empty space, but as he watched, he could make out the edges of her, and then she stood next to him, as real as any of the people in the room. She wore the coveralls she had worn that day during battlestations in the Barents, her hair on her shoulders, as shiny as it had been that Arctic morning, her sleeves rolled up the same way. The only difference was that she seemed to glow, as if her body were made of light, yet she was as solid as he was. If there were any doubt at all that she were truly there, it was eliminated when he realized he could smell her, he could breathe in her scent and it was *her*. His Natalie. She looked up at him, her expression both knowing and empathetic.

Hello, Burke, she said, her voice as silky and smooth as it always had been, yet her lips not moving.

"Hello, my love," he said, also without using his voice, his thoughts alone speaking to her. "Somehow I knew you would be here." He said it without thinking, and as the shiver again moved up his spine to the hair at the back of his head, he realized it was true. He knew she would come. It was why he had felt as if he were rolling on rails of destiny rather than his usual adrift feeling. When she appeared, he had felt no surprise.

I wanted to come to you one last time, Burke.

"I know, honey," he said. He suddenly felt moisture rising in his eyes. "Are you okay, dearest? Wherever you are? I've worried about you so much. I just want to know that you're all right."

I'm fine, Burke. She smiled, the same beautiful, dazzling smile he'd seen on her face the first day he saw her, the smile that made him fall in love with her. *I'm allowed to see little Burke until he's older. He smiles and coos when I'm in the room, you know.*

Dillinger thought about what she'd said and nodded. Of course she'd be with the baby, he thought, the strangeness of the moment somehow receding, a feeling that this was completely normal filling him.

"You said not to hesitate at the moment of decision," he thought. "You made it sound like I would have a choice between sacrificing Peter and fulfilling the mission, but I can't win. All I can do is try to save my friend. The battle is lost."

Natalie frowned for an instant, as if trying to find a way to tell him the answer. Finally her face brightened. *It was Christmas Eve, wasn't it?* she said. *By the Vornado family's Christmas tree? Rachel wore a red gown and she missed.* She smiled again. *The temper on that one. Peter wasn't able to tame it, but I think you will. Good-bye, my dearest.*

"What are you talking about, Natalie?"

But she was gone. In an instant, a blink of the eye, she was there one second and gone the next, and it happened so fast that he doubted for a moment that he'd ever seen her at all, but the beautiful scent of her lingered for just a moment, and he still felt her spirit. For that short time, she was still with him even though he couldn't see her. But then even that faded away, and Commander Burke Dillinger stood sadly alone in the control room of the USS *Hampton*, surrounded by a frozen crew with time at a standstill.

Which left him an eternity to ponder what Natalie had said.

It was Christmas Eve, by the Vornado family Christmas tree, and Rachel Phelps had worn a red gown. It had been a month since Vornado and Dillinger had met her, and Dillinger hadn't quite given up competing with Vornado for her affection. That night he had had too much to drink, and had been teasing Rachel all night about how beautiful she was and how he still wanted her—which he would never have done sober, and certainly never in front of Peter—and at one point he chased her from the kitchen to the den while reaching out to try to pinch her behind. He realized too late that Rachel no longer thought it was funny, and she had spun around with a full glass of eggnog, red-hot fury on her face, and she tossed the contents of the glass at Dillinger. Perhaps he had been expecting it. Or maybe it was the swiftness he'd developed in Brigade Boxing, which had worked for him even when he was drunk. For whatever reason, in a split second he ducked, and the egg nog sailed over his head, not a single drop hitting him, but the liquid splashed right into Peter Vornado, who had been chasing Dillinger to get him to leave Rachel alone, the egg nog soaking his face. As he stood there, the three of them began laughing hysterically, the friendship between all of them an unbreakable bond ever since.

Or at least until the Barents operation, he thought.

And what had Natalie said next, that Vornado had been helpless in the face of Rachel's famous temper, but that Dillinger would tame her? What in God's name could that mean? And why on earth did he sit here suspended between the ticks of the clock wondering about Rachel? And if this were truly real rather than a deranged mental flash from the stress of the moment, why would Natalie have picked that crazy Christmas Eve story to tell him in this moment of death?

Dillinger blinked. Of course, he thought. On Christmas Eve, he had ducked.

He spun toward the conn's command station and lunged for a red microphone hanging in the overhead. And time suddenly restarted, as if his sudden action made the clock tick again.

"Sonar, Captain, line up the UQC and patch it to the conn ASAP!" he shouted into his boom mike. *"Hurry!"*

"Line up UQC, Sonar, aye, UQC is line up and patched in!"

UQC was the acronym for the underwater communications suite, also called the underwater telephone, an unsophisticated idea from the early days of submarining. The UQC microphone could be tied into the active sonar sphere of the BQQ-5E and used to transmit a human voice. It was a troublesome, temperamental system. Most of the time the human voice was too indistinct to be transmitted across miles of ocean, and instead of communication it simply sounded like a voice shouting in a tin barrel. But there were sound conditions that occasionally came up in which the human voice sounded as clear as the voice of God, which was what Dillinger hoped for.

He clicked the microphone button. *"Texas, Texas, Texas,"* he said clearly into the mike, his voice deep and commanding. "Go . . . deep! I say again, *Texas, Texas, Texas*, go deep!" He beckoned Scottson. "Keep it up," he commanded, handing the younger officer the microphone.

Scottson stepped up and kept talking into the mike: "USS *Texas*, USS *Texas*, go deep, I say again, USS *Texas*, go deep!"

Scottson's voice could be heard through the hull, the echo of it off the ocean bottom coming in through the speakers, making each word sound out in duplicate, his voice deep and ghostly and godlike as it reverberated through the sea.

"*Texas, Texas, Texas,* go deep!"

Dillinger hurried to the weapons control console. "Attention in the firecontrol party," he shouted over the voice of Scottson, "cut the wires in tubes one and two and shut outer doors. Weps, make weapons in tubes three and four ready in all respects. Floor setting two hundred feet, immediate enable, medium-to-medium passive snake."

Scottson kept transmitting on UQC while Weapons Officer Lionel Tonelle lined up the next two torpedoes. Finally Tonelle was ready. "Tubes three and four ready in all respects, Captain!"

"Firing point procedures, Master One, tubes three and four, tube three first," Dillinger ordered.

"Ship ready," Scottson said between UQC calls.

"Weapon ready," Tonelle said.

"Solution ready," Flood said, both his eyebrows raised.

"Shoot on generated bearing," Dillinger said.

"Set!" Selles reported.

"Stand by," from Tonelle.

"Shoot!" Dillinger barked.

"*Fire!*" Tonelle said as he pulled the trigger! For the third time the deck jumped as the torpedo was launched.

Dillinger launched the torpedo in tube four, then reloaded tubes one and two. Soon there were six torpedoes on the way to *Le Vigilant*. Or the *Texas*, if Peter Vornado failed to hear and heed the UQC call.

When the sound of the first explosion reached the *Hampton*, the crew sat silently and attempted to understand what had happened. Had they hit the *Texas* or *Le Vigilant*?

"USS *Texas*, USS *Texas*, go deep, I say again, USS *Texas*, go deep!"

"Eddie," Dillinger said softly to Scottson, "you can stop transmitting now."

Scottson put the UQC microphone back up into the overhead, his face drained of color.

Youssef Tagreb felt poised on the edge of history. Finally the soldiers of Allah were about to land a telling blow on the cheeks of the infidels. He selected the LAUNCH AUTOSEQUENCE fixed function key for Missile 15 and pressed it. The software message SIMULTANEOUS INPUT INTERLOCK SATISFIED came up on the screen. The missile countdown began, the numbers rolling backward on the screen.

"5" flashed up, then "4" then "3."

Tagreb smiled. In two seconds, the beginning of the end would start for the city of New York, USA.

The first-fired Mark 48 ADCAP torpedo launched by the submarine USS *Hampton* sailed through the sea with its presets lined up for an attack on a ballistic missile submarine. Rather than pinging with active sonar, it strained to listen quietly with its passive sonar as it ran at medium speed toward the location where its onboard guidance computer insisted the target would be. The torpedo would never recognize the term "target-rich environment," but the two targets directly in front of it presented opportunities and problems. The torpedo compared them for signal strength, then maneuvered slightly left toward the louder of the two.

As it sailed closer to the target, it felt the magnetic lines of force concentrating as the iron of the hull affected the surrounding seawater, until the torpedo was half a torpedo length from the target. The torpedo was fully armed, and the proximity sensor's closing relay completed the circuit to the detonation devices, and the high explosive blew up in an instantaneous conflagration. The fireball and pressure wave smashed into the two-inch HY-130 steel of the target submarine and blew it inward. Where before there had been a three-deck-tall missile compartment, suddenly there was a gigantic hole and water smashing into the insides of the vessel. The explosion force roared into missile tube four and blew up the solid rocket fuel, which detonated in the tube, turning the heavy metal of the tube into a fragmentation grenade that blew apart missile tubes six, two and three. Those three tubes disintegrated, their solid rocket fuel exploding and causing a sympathetic detonation of the neighboring tubes. In a few hundred milliseconds, what had been an intact nuclear submarine became like a string of firecrackers, one explosion setting off the next. Two seconds after the first torpedo hit, the missile compartment of what had been the submarine *Le Vigilant* had become one oblong fireball, the solid rocket fuel detonations setting off the high explosives in half of the TN-71 nuclear warheads and scattering the nuclear material into the sea.

As missiles ten and eleven were busy exploding, the second Mark 48 ADCAP torpedo hit the hull further forward, low on the curvature of metal, and the explosion ripping into the hull blew up three ECAN torpedoes, their fuel first igniting, then their warheads, and as the first ECAN torpedo warhead exploded, eight more detonated in sympathy. The torpedo room was directly under the missile control center, where Issam Zouabri and Youssef Tagreb were busy monitoring the flight of Missile 15, but as the computer reeled off the numeral "0" the room blew apart and upward, the hammer of a pressure pulse rocketing both Zouabri and Tagreb's bodies into the curvature of the hull above them, their blood vaporizing in the heat, their bones fragmenting into splinters, their brain matter cooking to black dust in less than a tenth of a second. Tagreb's last conscious thought was satisfaction at the successful launching of the missile bound for New York City. He was not even aware that he had died, so sudden were the explosions.

On the third level of the forward compartment, in the huge frozen stores locker, the bodies of the French crewmen of the submarine lay in their dark mausoleum. When the torpedoes exploded on the fourth level, the explosions spared the walls of the frozen stores locker, except to make a small rupture hole in one corner.

Far aft, missile tube number fifteen had been pressurized when the torpedo hit. As the explosions roared through the missile compartment, the missile began to move from the impulse of the gas generator's steam pressure. Missiles 11 and 12 came apart in dazzling blasts and ripped into tubes thirteen and fourteen as Missile 15 was halfway out the tube, its upper half enveloped in its steam bubble as it rose toward the surface. The blast had the effect of jarring the missile sideways violently at twice the acceleration of gravity as it was almost two-thirds of the way out of the tube, and as the pressure front reached tube fifteen, only the bottom nozzle of the missile was still in the tube so that the explosive force tore open a mostly empty tube. Empty but for the pressure of the steam that was ejecting the torpedo, which lost some of its energy to the missile compartment instead of pushing upward on the missile.

But though the tube ruptured as the missile left the hull of the ship, the steam bubble had enough power to rise with Missile 15 as it broached the surface, because the gas generator had been designed to have the power to push a missile through thin polar ice. With no ice, the diminished steam pressure was still adequate to lift the missile from the water. The rocket had been shaken hard by the violence of the ship's disintegration below, but remained whole. For a long moment the missile froze in the sky just above the water, the zero-gee contact closing. As the solid rocket motor began its ignition sequence, the ocean seemed to rip open beneath the missile as the explosions reached the surface. Vapor and steam and fragments of the nuclear submarine blew upward out of the water as the flames from the missile's nozzle roared downward.

Below the surface, the missile compartment, ravaged by the explosive force of so much energy released in seconds, separated from the forward compartment, and the submarine plunged for the bottom in three parts; the largely intact aft compartment and reactor compartment, the fragmented metal of the former missile compartment, and the forward compartment, its bottom half blown open by the violence of the torpedo detonations. The aft compartment smashed into the rocky bottom first, then the forward compartment, and finally the steel shreds of the missile compartment rained down on the hull fragments. In the wreckage of the forward compartment, the frozen stores locker; even after the explosions, the passage through crush depth and the impact with the rocks of the Atlantic bottom, remained largely intact, the bodies of the proud French crew of *Le Vigilant* finally at peace. The corpse of *Capitaine de Frégate* Jean-Paul Gardes lay high on the frozen pile of dead men, and as the wreckage settled with a final lurch, his body turned slightly so that he faced the direction of Brest, France, his left hand floating so that it came to rest over the bullet holes where his heart had been.

Far above the grave of the submarine, in the foamy waters tortured by the blast of the explosion and further up, to the churning surface, the rocket body of Missile 15 hung in space, its exhaust gases roaring out at supersonic speed, the water and vapor from the catastrophe below it blowing upward past it. The force of the rocket exhaust took hold of the heavy missile and lifted it away from the boiling sea, slowly at first, then more rapidly. The missile reached Mach 1 at an altitude of 4,000 meters above the ocean and continued in its flight upward.

The sky darkened and the earth became curved. The stars came out above and the missile arced over in its trajectory. The first stage flamed out. Explosive bolts detonated and the stage fell behind as the second-stage engine ignited, and the missile continued in its mission, turning slightly to the west. Finally exhausted, the second stage fell away and the third stage kicked in, lifting the missile in its suborbital path, traveling more west than up as the third stage's thrust finally died. The third stage detached, the main bus of the M45 weapon carrying the six warheads now at apogee above the Atlantic. The splendor of the morning spread out below the missile, the magnificence of the North American eastern seaboard underneath it, a glowing, verdant jewel.

"Oh, for God's sake," Senior Chief Tom Albanese said as he threw his headset to the deck. He vaulted out of the sonar room and into the control room.

"Captain, we have multiple explosions on the bearing to Master One—sympathetic detonations from either torpedoes or submarine-launched ballistic missiles but—"

"So why the long face?" Dillinger said, thinking that Albanese was about to pronounce the USS *Texas* a battle casualty.

"Sir, we have a ballistic missile launch. We were too fucking late."

Dillinger didn't hesitate. "Helm, all ahead standard, Diving Officer, make your depth six five feet, steep angle. Sonar, Radio, coming to periscope depth! Communicator, this is a communications emergency, prepare an Oprep Three Pinnacle to the Pentagon and the White House."

Selles jumped out of his position two console seat. "Aye, Captain."

Flood looked over, shaking his head. "The EMP from the first missile will probably keep us from communicating, Captain."

"Maybe so, XO, but we have to try." Dillinger clenched his jaw, knowing he needed to concentrate on informing Washington that again they had failed to stop a missile launch, but now that the target was gone, all he wanted to know was—did the *Texas* die?

*   *   *

The main bus of Missile 15 opened as it descended toward the Earth's atmosphere and the six reentry vehicles separated one at a time. Small thrusters carried each warhead gently away from the others, though they were only a few miles apart as they fell. Reentry vehicle 01 was targeted for New York City's Freedom Tower, built near the grave of the World Trade Center, its spire pointing proudly skyward as if in defiance of all terrorists, its windmills lazily rotating in the breeze off the Atlantic. Below, in the financial district, hundreds of thousands of U.S. citizens went about their business in the midmorning hour, oblivious to the six death machines reentering Earth's atmosphere at hypersonic speed far above them.

The sharply pointed nose of reentry vehicle 01 sped downward in its curved arc toward Manhattan, the ionization of reentry building up, the heat immense as the warhead zoomed through the thickening air molecules. Finally the firestorm in front of it from the supersonic shock wave died down and it could again see the beauty of the coastline far below. Long Island spread out in a long pointing arm to the right, the green forests of New Jersey and Connecticut surrounding Manhattan Island. As the reentry vehicle fell, the other vehicles were barely visible dots on either side of it as they fell toward their destinies. Lower Manhattan grew steadily closer, the streets visible now.

The altimeter indicated a height of a thousand meters. The warhead clicked over and armed itself, the heavy metal safety plate opening passages between the low explosive and the high explosive. The TN-71 warhead continued to fall, plummeting toward Earth, the buildings beneath it now discernible in considerable detail.

Freedom Tower could be made out, its twisting sides elegant and shining in the morning sun. The skyscraper grew closer and closer until each blade of the windmill could be seen as it spun to generate the skyscraper's electrical power.

The warhead's detonation, carefully programmed by

the former terrorist Youssef Tagreb, would commence when it was thirty meters above the high spire of Freedom Tower. The nuclear explosion would be ripping its way out of the warhead casing as the tip of the warhead drew even with the antenna of the spire, and before the warhead would fall another fifty feet, the fireball would emerge from it and, within seconds, all of Lower Manhattan would be leveled in the titanic blast.

Thirty meters, the altimeter read. The low-explosive charges detonated, and the flame front propagated through the safety plate's passages to the high explosives of the conically shaped uranium masses.

"Message transmitted, HDR antenna coming down," the radioman chief announced over the control room overhead speakers.

"Very well, Radio," Dillinger said. "Sonar, Captain, do you have any tonals at all on the former bearing of the *Texas?*"

"Conn, Sonar, no."

"Any breakup noises?"

"Conn, Sonar, no."

Dillinger sighed. He wasn't sure whether to stay at periscope depth so he could determine if the Pentagon Op Center had gotten his message or to go deep and search for the wreckage of the *Texas*. That *Le Vigilant* was gone was obvious. Sonar data had correlated the launching of the missile to the torpedo hits. Dillinger had tried to see if any of the six torpedoes he'd launched had detonated elsewhere, but from what he could see, all of them had either hit *Le Vigilant*, or they had been destroyed when the French ballistic missile submarine went up like a powder keg.

The other reason he had to stay at periscope depth was to see where the ballistic missile had gone. Had it made it to its target, Paris, or one of the other French cities?

The nuclear warhead's low-explosive charges detonated, the hot gases roaring down the passages of the safety plate, all except for one. The sixth low explosive's electrical detonation cap had become unwired by the force of the sideways acceleration the unit had taken as it left the missile tube, and the warhead's safety interlocks kicked in. As it realized that it had only five low-explosive charges instead of six, it slammed shut the safety plate, but not in time to keep one of the high-explosive charges from detonating. The explosive charge blew open the weapon casing and cut it in half, scattering some of the uranium on the building's roof. The lower half of the warhead bounced off the roof edge and smashed forty-seven windows on its way down to sidewalk level, where it smashed into the top of a garbage truck and badly dented it. The warhead's upper half smashed a large air-conditioning unit completely flat.

The other five TN-71 warheads fell exactly on their targets. The one bound for the Empire State Building never detonated but put a twenty-foot-deep crater in the sidewalk in front of the building. The one targeted for Central Park only lit off one low-explosive charge and its safety plate latched shut before the high explosive detonated. It landed in a canopy of high trees and came to rest in a tangled mess of branches near the boathouse. The LaGuardia Airport warhead smashed into the long-term parking garage and scattered radioactive uranium over half an acre. The warhead bound for JFK Airport never armed itself or lit off the low-explosive charges, and fell with a huge splash in the shallows of Jamaica Bay. The Brooklyn-targeted warhead also never armed itself, and when it fell to earth it hit the roof of a six-story apartment building on Nostrand Avenue and blew down the elevator shaft to the basement.

The total damage of the six nuclear warheads that came down on American soil was numbered in the millions of dollars, mostly for the radioactive cleanup, and the usual union jurisdictional issues of exactly what emergency response unit handled undetonated nuclear bombs. The Mayor of New York exchanged harsh words with the President of the United States over the issue, which the media filled the airwaves with for many weeks after the incident.

"Skipper," Scottson said from the periscope. "I've got an aircraft in sight, looks like a P-3. Also, distant on the horizon, two destroyers. Okay, the P-3 sees us, sir. Hopefully he knows we're friendly."

"Let's see if we can talk to him," Dillinger said. All he needed was to be torpedoed by an airplane after having sunk *Le Vigilant*.

"We've got more company, Skipper," Scottson said.

"Conn, Sonar, multiple sonar contacts, surface ships, warships."

"Belay your report, Sonar," Dillinger said. "We have them visually."

"Conn, Sonar, aye."

"I've got a chopper, no, multiple choppers headed our way, Captain."

Where was the cavalry when he'd needed them, Dillinger thought. Figured, the skimmer pukes and airdales would swoop in and claim the kill, or worse, drop ordnance on the *Hampton*.

"Conn, Radio, UHF secure voice is patched into the conn. Our callsign is 'Bravo Kilo Delta.' The nearest task force callsign is "Uniform Victor,' and the 'all NATO units' callsign is 'November Tango.' "

"Conn, aye. Chief of the Watch, raise the HDR mast." Dillinger picked up the UHF radio mike and keyed it. "Uniform Victor, this is Bravo Kilo Delta. November Tango, this is Bravo Kilo Delta, over."

The UHF radio sputtered with static, but then a man's voice with a Boston accent boomed into the control room. *"Bravo Kilo Delta, roger, this is Echo Whisky of Uniform Victor, over."*

"Radio, Captain, who the hell am I talking to?" Dillinger called to the overhead.

"ASW helicopter from the USS Nimitz."

"Roger, Echo Whisky, this is Bravo Kilo Delta, stand by, over." Dillinger found Selles, who brought over the message Dillinger had wanted transmitted, in code, telling the Pentagon and the neighboring task forces that *Hampton* had taken down *Le Vigilant*, that the rogue boomer had gotten off a missile, and that the *Texas* was missing. He began reading the coded message into the UHF system, but was cut off a few words in.

"Break break break, Bravo Kilo Delta, this is Echo Whisky, Uniform Victor copied your previous Oprep Three Pinnacle transmission. From Uniform Victor, message reply reads, bravo zulu, bravo zulu. Good job, Commander."

Dillinger blinked, unsure of what to say.

"Roger Echo Whiskey," he finally uttered, realizing that the day's "victory" had been recognized as his.

"Communicator," he yelled at Selles, "Callsign for the *Texas*?"

"Charlie Papa Victor," Selles said.

"Echo Whiskey, we need to initiate a search for Charlie Papa Victor."

"Roger, Delta, that search is presently underway. We have new tasking for you by satellite transmission. Meanwhile, commanding officer is requested to transfer immediately to Uniform Victor."

"Captain," Selles said, "message received on the HDR, marked 'personal for commanding officer.' "

Dillinger read the message. It simply told him to surface, turn the ship over to his XO for the transit back to Norfolk, and be taken by helicopter back to the aircraft carrier *Nimitz*. He pursed his lips. This was beginning to sound like another supersonic aircraft ride back to the East Coast.

But there was one last thing—what happened to the missile?

On the submarine *Hampton*'s deck, Commander Burke Dillinger stood as Steve Flood connected his harness to the hovering helicopter's hoist.

"Take care of my boat!" Dillinger shouted in the blast of the chopper's rotors.

"Aye, aye, Skipper," Flood said. "Be sure to write!"

The hoist lifted his feet off the deck, and for a long moment Dillinger hung in space, his graceful, sleek black submarine beneath him, the helicopter overhead. He looked out over the ocean in the direction of the last known position of the *Texas*. Poor Peter, he thought. Natalie had called it all along. *He saved your life. You can't save his.* All she had been able to do was allow Dillinger to connect with his torpedoes. She'd been right. Vornado had been sacrificed to the mission. Dillinger shook his head. All he could hope for was that Peter Vornado was in as happy a place as Natalie. The bottom of the sea was a cold and lonely place, and he didn't want his old friend to be there.

The chopper crew hauled him into the aircraft, and they turned to the north and throttled up. A half hour later the gigantic form of the aircraft carrier *Nimitz* came into view. The helicopter settled onto the deck. There was a small reception party, with the ship's senior staff and the embarked battlegroup commander standing, waiting. The commander, a three-star admiral, came to attention when Dillinger stepped onto the deck of the *Nimitz*. He called the group to hand salute Dillinger even before Dillinger could salute the senior officer first. The admiral broke into a huge grin and shook Dillinger's hand.

"Bravo Zulu, Burke, good job! Excellent work!"

"Um, thank you, Admiral," Dillinger said. "Am I here to brief you?"

The admiral smiled. "Oh, no, son, see that F-14 over there? You've got time to go to the bathroom and get a sandwich. At nineteen hundred hours you're having dinner with the President of the United States. He wants to hear all about this."

"What happened with the missile?" Dillinger asked. "Did it hit Paris?"

"Paris? Hell, no, Commander, it hit New York."

Dillinger stopped dead, his mouth open.

"It's okay, Burke, one of your torpedoes fixed it good.

None of its MIRVs detonated. They just made big holes in the ground. That and politicians' soundbites. Come on, you're keeping the president waiting."

Dillinger nodded, but instead of reveling in the glory, all he could think about was Peter Vornado. And Rachel. God, who was going to give the news to Rachel? Once the supersonic fighter jet took off and headed west, Dillinger shut his eyes, barely realizing how tired he was. He fell into a deep sleep, and when he woke up, one of the runways of Andrews Air Force Base was underneath him. He glanced at his watch, knowing he should be enthusiastic to meet the president, but all he wanted was a long night of sleep without worrying about the fate of the world.

And he wanted to talk to Rachel Vornado and the kids and somehow offer them consolation.

BOOK 5:

▼

Death Do Us Part

EPILOGUE

Vice-amiral D'escadre Thibaut D'Aubigne walked slowly into the hospital room. For a long time he stood there as he watched Danielle Gardes breathing. She was still on a respirator and lingering on the edge of death in her coma. Standing next to the admiral were Danielle's four-year-old daughter Margaux and her five-year-old son Marc. Danielle's sister held the baby, one-year-old Renée. Danielle's respirator hissed and clicked, but other than that, there were no sounds in the room.

D'Aubigne walked up to the figure in the bed. Danielle once had such a pretty face, he thought. He turned his thoughts to his old friend, Jean-Paul Gardes, and he opened the velvet box holding the gleaming *Croix de Guerre*, withdrew the medal and pinned it to Danielle's pillow. Normally the wife of the honored would simply be given the medal, but somehow just laying the box on the side table made no sense. D'Aubigne stood there for a long time, then leaned over and kissed Danielle's face and stroked her hair. He looked over at her children, the thought coming to him that their capture as hostages could have caused five thousand megatons to rain down on Paris and resulted in the entire country spending this very day dying. And all the security measures had gone to the physical security of the submarine—no one had even thought about guarding the crew and their families. The children were becoming restless, D'Aubigne realized. He turned to them, sank down on one knee and smiled at them.

"Your father was very brave," he said to them. "He fought very hard at sea to protect the Republic. That's

why I came here to give your mother the medal that
your father earned. He was a great man." He looked
from one child to the next, but they just seemed sad.
He hugged each of the older ones, then touched the
baby's face. As he walked out of the room he realized
he felt ten years older. Perhaps that was fitting, as the
minute the government hearings ended, he would turn
over his position to a younger man, and who was to
say that the *Force Océanique Stratégique* would even
exist in a year? A force that had been built to protect
the Republic, but had ended up almost ending it, all on
his watch.

He sighed. Regardless of what happened to him personally, it seemed such a harsh punishment. It was bad
enough to lose the entire crew of *Le Vigilant*, but now
he had to live to see all of France's strategic submarines
scrapped. Maybe, he thought, maybe it was time. Maybe
the world had changed. True, brutes like the terrorists
who had taken the crew's families hostage and tortured
them still walked the earth, but when he looked at a
global map, no longer did entire nations seem gripped
by evil. Perhaps the era of the strategic submarine had
ended years before, but they simply hadn't realized it
yet.

He left the hospital and climbed into his staff car.
From the window of Danielle's room, the admiral's car
could be seen making the turn onto the main highway
before driving out of sight. There on the bed, Danielle
Gardes' eyelids fluttered. Over the next eight hours, she
slowly rose toward consciousness. Two days later the
room came into a hazy kind of focus. One of the first
things she saw as she regained her senses was the *Croix
de Guerre* pinned to her pillow, and immediately she
began to cry, for she knew that had Jean-Paul lived, they
would have pinned it nowhere but his chest.

The black limousine had taken Dillinger from the White
House to the Old Executive Office Building, where he
repeated the briefing he'd given the president to the sen-

ators and congressmen in the secure conference room. At the end of his presentation, a Navy captain, an aide to the Chief of Naval Operations, took him aside. He smiled at Dillinger as if there were good news. Not that Dillinger could imagine any good news at this point.

"Yes, Captain?"

"Commander, there's a phone call for you on the secure line. Please come with me." The captain walked Dillinger to an empty conference room. He pressed a button and handed the phone to Dillinger, then left him alone.

"Commander Dillinger," he said formally on the phone.

"Hey, B.K.," the solemn voice of Smokin' Joe Kraft said. "How you doing up there? Your pinky in the air while you brief the VIPs?"

"I guess you could say that, Commodore," Dillinger said, his voice flat. He himself couldn't say whether it were fatigue or depression that was making him so down. Everyone he talked to acted as if his mission were the highest success, but he knew the one thing he'd wanted had been denied him.

"Well, there's someone here who wants to talk to you," Kraft said.

"Okay, sir. Put him on." Dillinger realized he had no curiosity about the caller. He sat down in the chair, feeling like he was ninety years old.

"B.K., you slacker, Smokin' Joe said he told you to get your head outta your ass, but instead you go and shoot torpedoes at the wrong damned submarine."

Dillinger shot to his feet. "*Peter?* Vornado, what the hell are *you* doing alive? Strike that, that didn't come out right. Where were you? We thought you and the *Texas* were dead. We couldn't hear anything."

"I know, B.K. Sometimes I think we were dead. There was a fire in the aft compartment." Vornado's voice became somber. "We lost the entire engineering crew and a couple dozen of the forward watchstanders from the fire. We got carbon monoxide in the breathing air system, knocked most of us out for a while. We should have died, but somehow the ship floated to the surface. A chopper saw the tip of the sonar sphere poking above the waves, and a destroyer heaved to and sent down divers to bubble the ballast tanks from the outside. They worked fast. They hauled us out and medevaced everyone they could, and treated the rest at the scene." Vornado coughed. "But I think I still have black lung from the fire."

Dillinger sank back down in the conference table seat. "I can't believe it. You're alive, you're actually alive."

Vornado laughed. "Get back down here. I think you at least owe me a barbecue for stealing my glory. That was my kill."

"Just one question for you, Peter. Did you hear my UQC call to go deep?"

Vornado was quiet for a moment. "What are you talking about, B.K.?"

That was odd. If Natalie had really been there in that moment, why would she tell him to get Vornado to duck out of the way if he wouldn't hear it? Could it be that it hadn't been about saving Vornado, but about giving Dillinger the confidence to shoot? Perhaps if she had told him that Vornado wasn't in danger, he wouldn't have believed her, so she had concocted the ruse about getting the *Texas* to go deep.

Or the more likely explanation—Natalie had never come to him in that moment of decision. It had just been his own brain trying to think his way through the problem, his subconscious mind flashing a movie of Natalie on the background of the ship's control room. That had to be it.

He felt a momentary sadness at the thought that she hadn't really been there. And she had said those words about that being the last time she would come to him.

"B.K.? Are you there?"

"Sorry, Peter, just thinking."

"Listen, there's another surprise waiting for you here. Rachel went to work on it."

"Are you and Rachel back together?" Dillinger asked. He felt a flutter in his heart at the mention of her name, but he knew he had no right to think of her as anything but Vornado's wife.

"B.K., brace yourself, my friend. Rachel and I are done. We've both filed the papers. In a month our marriage will be over officially."

"I'm sorry, Peter."

"Don't be. We're figuring out how to be friends."

"Then I'm glad for you, I guess."

"Get down here, B.K."

Dillinger hung up, a smile coming to his lips as he packed his briefcase.

"I can't wait for you to see it," Rachel Vornado said, her voice shaking with excitement. A hundred steps behind him, Peter Vornado waited in his car while Rachel walked Dillinger up the grassy hill toward Natalie's grave. He held Burke in his arms, the baby fast asleep. He looked down at the boy's face, his features all from his mother. He'd be a handsome youth, Dillinger thought. He was so busy staring at the baby that he didn't see Rachel's surprise.

When he looked up he caught his breath. There at Natalie's grave was a tall stone covered with a blue cloth.

"Usually this takes two years," Rachel said, "But Smokin' Joe and I put some serious heat on the stonemason. Are you ready?"

Dillinger nodded. Rachel pulled the cloth off, and there in front of him was a life-size statue of Natalie D'Assault Dillinger. She wore submarine coveralls and at-sea combat boots, her sleeves rolled up the way they had been the morning of the battle in the Barents, her hair lying straight on her shoulders as it had that morning. There was an expression on her face, that battlesta-

tions face, of toughness, a fighting spirit that was so
Natalie D'Assault. But he could read tenderness there
as well. She was beautiful. The statue was beautiful. And
when he looked at it, he noticed the strangest thing. He
stood exactly the same distance from it that he had from
Natalie's spirit when she had come to him—or when he
thought she had come to him—in that moment of decision on the deck of the *Hampton*. So much so that in
later years he would wonder if he remembered her in
the control room that way because he was just remembering the pose of her statue.

"I love it, Rachel. It's her. It's Natalie. It's like she's
here. Thank you. Thank you so much."

"You're welcome, Burke," Rachel said.

He stared at her. She'd rarely called him anything but
B.K. since the first day they met. The wind blew her
dark hair off her forehead. Her brown eyes looked into
his, and in the light of the late afternoon he could see
those bewitching flecks of green in them.

"Would you do me a favor?" he asked her.

Her eyes became liquid as she looked at him. "Anything, Burke," she whispered.

"Would you take the baby for me? I want to be here
for a while. I just want to look at her."

Rachel's eyes grew wet. "Of course. Come here, baby
Burke," she said softly to the infant as Dillinger handed
him over. He stirred in her arms, then snuggled to her
breast. She walked by him, paused, and put her hand on
his shoulder. He reached up and touched her hand, feeling the spark from her skin as he did. He clamped his
eyes shut, trying to ignore the feeling.

When Rachel was gone, he stood there for a long time
staring at the statue. The shadow from it grew long on
the grass as the sun began to set.

Finally, as the afternoon grew cold, Dillinger decided
to leave. Before he did, he stepped close to the statue
and touched her shoulder.

"Natalie, dearest, thank you," he whispered.

He looked at her, wondering if he would hear her voice in the wind, but there was nothing.

He was alone at her grave.

The stone of the statue was cold on his fingertips.

He ran his hand down the arm of the statue, reluctant to let go, but finally he turned away and walked slowly back down the hill to his truck.

ACKNOWLEDGMENTS

Vertical Dive was written during one of the most difficult periods of my life. Without my friends and partners, it would not have happened.

I want to thank editor Doug Grad at Penguin for his insight and vision for this book, and my agent Jake Elwell for making the deal, and to both for their patience as I tried to write while putting the pieces back together.

Foremost in my thanks are my dear friends and partners Christopher Barnas, George Christatos, Patti DiMercurio, Arnie Katz, Paul Reed, Jonathan Rowe and Dan Shultz.

Special thanks to my webmaster and friend, the creative genius Bill Parker of Parker Information Resources, a specialist in author and literary-agent websites, who set up and maintains the incomparable ussDevilfish.com website as well as Dale Browns' Megafortress.com site and the sites of many other renowned authors. His own website is Parkerinfo.com and he can be reached at bparker@parkerinfo.com.

A gigantic debt of gratitude goes out to Tim Sharp, the president of the Michael DiMercurio Fan Club and my chief of staff for email matters. Tim has taken care of grooming the incoming emails and covering for my absences from email while finishing this novel.

I want to thank Matt, Marla and Meghan DiMercurio for their kindness, devotion, enthusiastic, unconditional love and understanding beyond their years.

My grateful thanks go to Patti DiMercurio, my former wife and former soulmate, who even after the marriage ended remained my best friend and kept life in perspective.

Special thanks to the woman I realized too late was the great love of my life, for simply having existed and for being in my life at the crucial moment, and for showing me more meaning than anyone else could. I also want to apologize to her for the pain, heartbreak and drama. In the next life, I'll find you and make it right.

Finally, deepest thanks to all my friends for their consolation in my darkest hours until dawn—which I was certain had forsaken me—finally returned.

THIS MARINE UNIT IS FIGHTING A
VERY DIFFERENT KIND OF COLD WAR...

DEEP CURRENT

by
Benjamin E. Miller

A marine unit, accompanied by a science
team, is deployed to investigate an iceberg
larger than Manhattan that poses a threat
of incalculable scope as it flows against
the current, leaving a path of destruction
in its wake.
And it's heading—*aiming*—for Hawaii.

Their mission: land on the floe, itself, and
do whatever it takes to disable the threat.

0-451-41129-3

S825